Any Given Moment

Any Given Moment

Laura Van Wormer

Crown Publishers, Inc.
New York

MP

Copyright © 1995 by Laura Van Wormer

Published by Crown Publishers, Inc., 201 East 50th Street, New York, New York 10022. Member of the Crown Publishing Group.

Random House, Inc. New York, Toronto, London, Sydney, Auckland

CROWN is a trademark of Crown Publishers, Inc.

Manufactured in the U.S.A.

Design by Mercedes Everett

Library of Congress Cataloging-in-Publication Data

Van Wormer, Laura
Any given moment : a novel / Laura Van Wormer.—1st ed.
p. cm.
1. Consolidation and merger of corporations—California—Los Angeles—Fiction. 2. Authors, American—California—Los Angeles—Fiction. 3. Literary agents—California—Los Angeles—Fiction. 4. Friendship—California—Los Angeles—Fiction. 5. Los Angeles (Calif.)—Fiction. I. Title.
PS3572.A42285A59 1994
813'.54—dc20 94-25533
CIP

ISBN 0-517-59214-2

10 9 8 7 6 5 4 3 2 1

First Edition

For Nancy Levin

You must remember, dear,
at any given moment your whole life could change.
Dorothy Dunstable Hillings

Prologue

Everyone in the boardroom was nervous. After serving as chairman of International Communications Artists for twenty-seven years, Ben Rothstein was being forcibly retired. What happened next would be up to Ben; he could come down and face them, or he could simply leave the building.

After fifteen tense minutes, all heads swiveled at the sound of the door.

Ben Rothstein walked in smiling. (*He's killed Creighton,* one board member thought.) Rothstein was a powerful and attractive-looking man with a thick head of iron gray hair, but he was anything but handsome. His face looked as though it had been hit with a baseball bat more than a few times back in the Bronx of his childhood, and it probably had been.

Granted, some from his old New York neighborhood had traveled through highly suspect channels to reach top positions in Hollywood, but not Ben Rothstein. Although he *looked* like someone who might be tied to the Mafia, he was, in fact, one of the most ethical men in business. And the distinguished reputation of the ICA empire—the global leader in entertainment representation—was synonymous with his name.

It was he who had first seen the advantage of packaging entire projects, not only representing actors, but screenwriters and directors, and later producers, composers, singers, and choreographers, too. ICA was then in a powerful position to suggest combinations of talents, properties, and production executives to the studios and networks. It was a highly successful strategy that worked well for ICA's clients, and also for ICA, which could then build hefty agency fees directly into the production's budget. William Morris and ICM and other entertainment agencies caught on quickly, but they had high overheads to maintain from running elaborate literary divisions in New York City. ICA, always the renegade, had steered clear of that kind of expense, preferring instead to form ties with a few premiere literary agencies.

ICA's most famous alliance was with Hillings & Hillings, a distinguished New York literary agency run by Henry and Dorothy Hillings. In 1955 they first collaborated with ICA to sell the movie rights to the 1950 Pulitzer Prize–winning novel, *A Dark Garden.* Since that time ICA and Hillings & Hillings had collaborated on so many projects and had made so much money for so many authors, that to benefit from their alliance was to be considered a member of "the royal family."

Last year the Hillingses and Ben Rothstein had decided to formalize their alliance with a gradual merger of the Hillings & Hillings agency into the ICA empire, a process which would not be completed until the day the Hillingses decided to retire.

Walking into the boardroom behind Ben Rothstein this morning in Los Angeles was the man who would replace him, young Creighton Berns, most recently president of ICA. The well-heeled son of a Toluca Lake dentist, Berns had earned a combined undergraduate degree in film and business administration from UCLA and an MBA from Wharton. He had achieved immediate success in network television programming, and then had jumped to movies, where he made unparalleled profits as the youngest studio head of Metropolis Pictures ever. He was just thirty-five.

The board had decided that Creighton Berns was the future of Hollywood. The cost, however, would be Ben Rothstein. After much secret deliberation, they had agreed to retire Ben and offer to set him up as an independent producer.

It had all sounded good a month ago, but now that it was actually happening most of the board members felt vaguely ill. No matter how golden the handshake they gave Ben, they were still essentially firing the man who had made the company everything it was.

(Had *Vanity Fair* not published the last ICA corporate Christmas card and suggested that its message and graphics were better suited to a retirement home, things might have been different.)

"Gentlemen, good morning," Ben said as he rounded the table to take his place at the head. His comportment was the same as it had been at every board meeting for the last twenty-seven years. He was wearing an impeccably cut gray suit, white shirt, red bow tie, and black loafers. His face was tan from the golf he loved, and his body fit from the personal trainer he always said he was going to strangle if and when he could get fit enough to do it.

Instead of sitting at his place, Ben stood, leaning forward over the table. "It is a very generous settlement I have been offered, and I am grateful to you. I am also excited about trying my hand at some entertainment projects for ICA. I have nothing else to say, gentlemen, except thank you—for a hell of a career, for a very nice life, and for asking me to step down while I still have a lot of my life left to live."

After one dazed moment, the board began to applaud.

"And may I officially welcome the new chairman of ICA," Ben said, straightening up. "Gentlemen, Mr. Creighton Berns."

The board applauded again as Creighton made his way to the head of the table. Ben, with a slight bow, slipped away to the side and graciously left the room.

Only after the door had closed behind him did board members realize that Ben had managed to avoid the symbol of closure—a handshake with his successor.

As he had done almost every weekday morning since 1947, Henry Hillings held the door of 101 Fifth Avenue open for his wife. They were always the first people in the office. They liked an hour to themselves to sip coffee and read through the final mail delivery from the night before. It was also the most convenient time to make overseas calls.

"I hate to admit it, Henry," Dorothy Hillings said, "but it makes me feel old. He's only sixty-two."

Dorothy had turned seventy in April; Henry was seventy-six.

"I know, darling," Henry sighed, pushing the elevator button. "It's the end of an era." The elevator doors opened.

"It just won't be as much fun anymore," she said, stepping inside. "Half of the excitement was doing business with old friends like Ben." The doors closed and the elevator started its ascent. She looked at her husband. "And I hate to say it, but do you realize that most of our contemporaries in the business are either retired or dead?"

"Doe," he said, giving his wife a sideways look.

"Well, it seems so unfair. One would think one received a little extra credit for being a decent person, wouldn't you think?"

Henry smiled. "But we have been given extra credit, Doe. We've been given the opportunity to ease out of the agency, now, while we're still healthy enough to enjoy ourselves."

"Enjoy ourselves doing what? Running off to Bora Bora to visit Ben and poor Ruth, or wherever in Sam Hill he took her? We started the agency, I hasten to remind you, dear, because we couldn't stand doing what everybody else was doing—and everybody else is retiring, and frankly I hate it."

"Maybe it's time we tried a little harder to be like other people," her husband said. "We are getting older." The elevator was easing to a stop.

"Nonsense, Henry, you're twice the—"

As the elevator doors opened, Dorothy's mouth fell open. The two stood there staring, speechless, until the elevator doors tried to close. Henry found the button to control the door at the same time that Dorothy found her voice.

"What in God's name!" she said, stepping out.

There were padlocks and No Trespassing signs all over the doors of their offices. "Henry, what is going on!"

Henry dropped his briefcase, took his glasses out of his pocket, and read the notice on the door. "This is ridiculous," he said after a moment. "This must be some kind of a joke—or a very serious mistake. This is a sheriff's notice of repossession."

"Henry—" Dorothy said in a strangled voice.

He turned to find her leaning against the wall, hand to her chest. Her bag lay at her feet. "I can't breathe," she managed to get out.

He held her, murmuring that everything was going to be

all right. Slowly he eased his wife down along the wall to a sitting position on the floor, falling heavily to his knees in the process.

She was having a heart attack. Dorothy was having a heart attack.

One

~ 1 ~

She could remember the day she decided to be smart instead of shy.

It had been the first day of fifth grade, and Elizabeth had known she absolutely could not stand being shy anymore, couldn't stand blushing, feeling awkward, being unable to say anything. She had always been a brain, but up until then she had never considered using her intellect as a shield, one that often seemed to intimidate people in a very gratifying way. Looking back, Elizabeth realized what a gift it had been for that dreadfully shy girl to be given the ability to hide whenever she was scared—but to be able to do it right out in the open. All she had to do was revert to her "smart self," she who could merrily prattle intelligent instant analyses like an interesting third-person narrator who wasn't even really there. Like a walking book, someone once said, and Elizabeth had smiled, pleased.

Like all of today's gifts, however, this persona of brain extraordinaire became one of tomorrow's problems. As Elizabeth grew older, cultivating her smartness and downplaying her emerging good looks, her life began to take on a certain unreality. More and more she felt like she *was* a third-person narrator to her own life, and that she was only occasionally an actual participant in it, and that when she was, she would more than likely mess things up.

As a matter of fact, Elizabeth's life as a brain had become so extraordinary (on darker days, Elizabeth would say weird), that today, at thirty-three, she had to wonder if it was even possible at this point to achieve the sense of belonging she had always craved— the sense of belonging for which she had become a brain in the first place—so that she could at least participate on some level in the world.

She was either the youngest emotional has-been, she thought, or the world's oldest adolescent. In the meantime, she got to move through the world as a celebrated professor of history.

But she was lonely. Almost as lonely as she had been on the first day of fifth grade.

Young Mr. A. W. Babcock, self-important junior clerk of the British Library, was shaking his head as he came back to the desk of gorgeous mahogany. "There are no such letters in our archives," he announced.

"But I know they're here," Elizabeth insisted, opening her briefcase. "This is the receipt you gave to the family."

"Receipt *I* gave the family?" Mr. A. W. Babcock loftily asked. He looked at the document. "This receipt is from 1924. I was not even born until 1960."

Elizabeth laughed politely, thinking, *You might get away with bullying the public, but you're not going to get away with it with me.* But she didn't say it. No big surprise there. In the face of adversity, Elizabeth always automatically moved into her fallback position, that of the surprisingly likable and accessible young professor whom anyone would be pleased to know. While she was indeed a wonderful teacher, and was very glad of it—outside of reading and writing, teaching was the joy of her life—Elizabeth wished she could be a little less eternally pleasant and start demonstrating a lot more backbone in dealing with everyday life. But no. Professor Robinson was a wimp at heart. Always had been. She had never been able to complain about poor food in a restaurant; she had never been able to return anything to a store; she had never pushed her way into anywhere or anything.

No, what Elizabeth did was to go to extraordinary lengths to charm and cajole and befriend complete and utter strangers so that she might tactfully ask for whatever it was she wanted or needed. While other women had gotten married and had children, Elizabeth had spent her life becoming best friends with people like taxi drivers so they would slow down and enjoy the ride and not kill her in a horrible accident. So while Elizabeth would probably never be able to tell a cashier outright that he had overcharged her, she would always probably know a little something about, say, Pakistani politics.

Elizabeth had been made a full professor by age twenty-nine on the merits of her academic scholarship, but it was her charismatic charm and accessibility in a world of posturing, politics, and jealousy—in other words, academe—that had made her a star. And too, of course, it hadn't hurt that Elizabeth had turned her dissertation on an obscure eighteenth-century duchess into a best-selling biography, *The Duchess of Desire*, which had been made into a hit movie starring Faye Dunaway. The academy loved nothing more than to counter the saying, "Those who can't, teach," by offering as proof professors like Elizabeth, who clearly *could* choose other professions but chose to continue teaching—and make a small fortune on the side to boot!

Elizabeth's smile broadened as she leaned closer to Mr. A. W. Babcock of the British Library. "I've checked very carefully," she told him in her I-may-be-a-professor-but-I'm-still-a-woman-lost-without-a-man voice, "and there is no evidence the letters were ever moved." What a coward she was.

"Not to the British Museum?" he asked, looking into her eyes.

"Not to the British Museum," she said earnestly.

"Not to the Theatre Museum?" he said, looking at her hair.

"Not to the Theatre Museum," she said, practically batting her eyes. *Some feminist, Elizabeth Robinson!*

"Not to"—the librarian paused, swallowing, thinking, eyes briefly landing on Elizabeth's mouth and then quickly darting away, a blush starting down his neck—"the Victoria and Albert?"

"No, I'm afraid not," she murmured.

"Well, then, if this is true," he said, looking at the document again, "we have a box of letters somewhere that has been missing since 1924." He made a sound in his throat. "I'll need you to register, Professor, before I can write up a search request." He pushed a form across the counter to her. "If the letters are here, they'll be in the rare manuscripts division." He paused for a moment. "You know, they're right about you. You *do* look like Katharine Hepburn."

"Thank you," she said, as she handed him her passport and

faculty card and began scribbling information on the form. Her face was burning in embarrassment. Regardless of any vows taken in fifth grade, Elizabeth still had trouble accepting compliments about the looks she always pretended not to rely on, but often felt she had to.

And it was true, she did look like Katharine Hepburn, though her eyes were green instead of blue, and her hair various shades of brown instead of red. This past year, when the BBC had hired Elizabeth to Americanize a history series and be its host for American PBS audiences, one of the London tabloids had called her the "Katharine Hepburn of Academe. A Real Yank Media Star at Oxford." They had run a BBC publicity still of Elizabeth, a faculty photo of her in her somber black teaching robes, and a candid of her in a bathing suit at the indoor university pool, which they had obtained God only knew how.

"You wrote the Duchess of Schellingford biography, didn't you?" Mr. A. W. Babcock said, looking up from her passport.

"Yes," Elizabeth said, thinking how posturing as an intellectual added at least fifty years to anyone's age, certainly to young Mr. A. W. Babcock's here. She wondered what had scared him so badly in adolescence that he had to hide, too.

"And now you're working on the Countess of Derby?" He was reading upside down from her form.

"Yes, but you would know her better as Miss Farren, Elizabeth Farren, the comedienne of the Drury Lane."

"What are her dates?"

"Seventeen fifty-nine to 1829."

"Ah, the time of Mrs. Siddons perhaps?" he asked.

"They were friends," Elizabeth told him, in a voice that promised they could be friends too if only he'd get on with it and find her those letters.

He cleared his throat, put her faculty card down on the counter, and met her eyes again. "You're teaching at Oxford."

"Just one course, at Balliol."

"An American teaching British history at Oxford," he murmured, shaking his head in world-weary disbelief.

She shrugged, smiling, as if to say she couldn't help any of it: her American citizenship, her B.A. from Princeton, her Ph.D. from

Columbia, her teaching posts, her best-seller, her decision in fifth grade to be smart instead of shy.

"There's a curator in rare manuscripts who's a Hepburn fanatic," Mr. Babcock said. "Maybe he can do something for you."

"What an insipid little twit you are, Babcock," a voice said.

Startled, Elizabeth turned to see a rather peculiar-looking man limping over.

"Professor Robinson," young Mr. A. W. Babcock said, Adam's apple rising and falling in nervousness, "this is Mr. Thorp of rare manuscripts."

"How do you do, sir?" Elizabeth said respectfully.

"Professor, ha!" he snorted. "You're not old enough to change the twit's nappies. Katharine Hepburn of academe, indeed. Ha! Phooey! Come along."

No one ever claimed that rare manuscript curators were any more normal than academics, and so Mr. Thorp and Elizabeth got along just fine, particularly after she went to see the Katharine Hepburn pictures he kept in his tiny office. By late afternoon, Elizabeth had donned a blue cloth surgical gown and mask, and latex surgical gloves, and was happily sorting through undated letters from the late eighteenth century in the document rehabilitation room. The technician assigned to her was very good; they had already found two letters written by people who had known Miss Farren well.

At four o'clock they called it a day since the technician needed to pick up her child at day care by half past. Elizabeth needed a fresh start and fresh eyes anyway. She had been up until three the night before reading student papers, and she had learned over the years—the hard way—that examining documents with a tired mind and body only prompted unholy errors that could take months to catch.

Elizabeth flagged a cab and headed across the city to pick up the latest episode of the TV series for PBS. As she always did when arriving at Broadcasting House, she thought of her first visit here, in early 1988, when she had arrived just in time to see two medics carrying out a victim of Legionnaires' disease. Elizabeth never failed to remember what she had thought while watching the stretcher being loaded onto the ambulance: how strange it was to be in the middle of an event she knew someone like herself would be trying to research two hundred years later. It always made her feel like leaving a note.

"Professor Robinson," the BBC security guard said, greeting her.

"Hello, John," she said, signing in. "How are you?"

"Cannot complain, no I can't."

"Good, I'm glad," she said, putting the pen down.

"School's out, is it?" he asked her.

"After a paper or two, I'm a free woman."

"I only wish it were true," he said, pouting.

"Now John," Elizabeth gently scolded, walking briskly toward the elevators.

"Well, well, if it isn't the one and only and highly memorable Elizabeth Robinson, Ph.D."

She had almost walked into Bill Staugher from PBS in New York.

"Hello, Bill," Elizabeth said, holding out her hand. "On a buying trip?"

"Maybe, maybe not." Bill squeezed her hand and kissed her cheek.

"Did you see the new episode?" she asked him. "It really is quite wonderful, even if I do say so myself."

"King George the Third?"

"Yes," she said, eyes sparkling.

"I've got it here," he said, patting his briefcase.

"I hope you like it as much as I do."

"I'm sure we will." And then his expression turned to one of concern. "So," he said, lowering his voice, "what do you think about the news from New York?"

"Well," Elizabeth said, making a face, "they say they can't fund another program on the same period, but I told them, for heaven's sake, it *is* the American Revolution, after all, one would hate to think *that's* the only part of the series PBS wants to skimp on—the part most relevant to their audience—"

Bill cut her off and took Elizabeth by the arm to pull her aside. "I meant about ICA and the Hillingses."

Dorothy and Henry Hillings represented not only Elizabeth's

books, but also her TV and film rights through ICA. It was they who had instigated her BBC deal.

"Are you referring to the merger with ICA?" Elizabeth asked. "Because Dorothy wrote to me a while ago and said it was a good thing."

"So you haven't heard."

"Heard what?"

"That ICA impounded the offices of Hillings & Hillings and caused Dorothy to have a heart attack."

Elizabeth blinked, trying to take this in. "Is she," she finally managed to say, "alive?"

"Yes, she is. She's at Lenox Hill Hospital. And the doctors say she'll be okay—but I'm not sure if she and Henry will ever be fine again, if you know what I mean. The whole thing is really quite a mess."

"Any given moment," Elizabeth murmured.

"Excuse me?" Bill said.

She looked at him, eyes starting to fill. "That's what Dorothy always says, 'At any given moment your whole life could change.' "

There was a flicker of a smile from Bill. "So you'll make the most of every day?"

"No," she said, blinking rapidly, "so I won't give up." Elizabeth looked around. "Excuse me, but I must find a telephone."

～ 2 ～

"I love you, darling," Henry Hillings murmured, kissing his wife softly on the forehead. But she was already asleep.

Although more than fifty years had passed, it seemed to Henry that Dorothy looked very much the same as she had that first afternoon at the tea dance at Grovesnor House during the war.

He had been able to tell right off that she was new to London, because she had been wearing her Canadian Red Cross uniform instead of her "glad rags," the civilian clothes the other women changed into the minute they were granted leave. He could also tell she was new because she had been talking to Potty Harper when he had first seen her, and everyone knew that although Potty came to tea dances to find a "good girl," he'd do his damnedest to make her a "bad girl" by nightfall, and, failing that, might simply attack her in a doorway if he'd had enough to drink. But then, a war was on and they had all been so starved for passionate attachment, that when granted leave, the soldiers flocked to London to blow their pay on the best women they could find. And why not? Who would outlive this war?

Henry was different from the others. He was in U.S. Army Intelligence and his country was not yet at war. The British, the Canadians, the Australians had already seen many of their comrades slaughtered. Even Potty Harper, it would turn out, would not see his next tea dance.

That night a group of them had gone to dinner, and Henry could not seem to keep his eyes off of Dorothy, although she did her best to ignore him. They were just getting their food when the sirens started. Though startled, they obediently filed out of the restaurant—carrying their plates and glasses—following the maître d' to the underground station near Marble Arch. There they nestled against one another on the cold, damp cement platform, trying to eat in the dark but not succeeding well at all, as they listened, trembling and cringing, as the bombs continued to fall. Henry finally fell asleep and awakened to find the old man next to him asleep on his shoulder. When Henry's eyes adjusted to the faint glow from the dim emergency lighting, he saw that Dorothy, sitting on the other side of the old man, was dozing against his shoulder. Remembering Doe then, Henry thought, she had looked almost exactly as she did now in this hospital room.

Noble. Strong. Exquisite.

Irresistible.

Indeed, she had been that. And still was.

Henry smiled to himself when he remembered asking her, as they had been leaving the underground, if he had, in some way, offended her.

"Not you in particular, sir," she had said, "but your country. It is beyond our comprehension why America has not joined us against—"

Henry had taken her by the arm to face him. "But I *am* here," he said. And then he had kissed her. And she had kissed him back, and he had felt as though his life had finally begun.

"Let me know if there is any change," Henry murmured to the private nurse he had hired to stay through the night.

"You'll be at home?" she whispered.

"Yes, and don't hesitate to call." After one more look at Doe, he left.

"Excuse me, Mr. Hillings?" an aide said at the nurses' station. "A Joshua Lafayette is here to see you. He's in the waiting room."

"Ah, yes, thank you," Henry said, continuing down the hall.

In the green room with its stubbornly uncomfortable furniture, a tall young black man in a dark suit was sitting on a couch with a bulging briefcase open in his lap. Joshua Lafayette was a bright and ambitious attorney whom Henry and Dorothy had met at Lincoln Center when he was still at Fordham Law School. A chance conversation about the ownership of a runaway dog turned into an interesting conversation over a drink at the Saloon across the street. A year later, the result was a job with the distinguished communications law firm that handled Hillings & Hillings. Josh had come to handle so much work for the Hillingses over the years, that Henry wanted him to run the agency after their retirement.

When Joshua saw Henry he shoved the briefcase aside and jumped up. "How is she?"

"She'll be all right, thank you, Josh," Henry said quietly, taking his handkerchief out, dabbing at his nose, and smoothly depositing it back into his pocket. "So—what did they say?"

Joshua shifted his weight and looked straight at Henry. "They say there was no mistake. The order to impound the offices came straight from the top, from Creighton Berns in Los Angeles."

Color started appearing in Henry's face.

"I told my contact," Joshua continued, "that I found it very difficult to believe that the new ICA chairman, on his first day of work, decided to impound the offices of Hillings & Hillings without a word of discussion with the Hillingses. She said she couldn't believe it either, but that's what it looked like. Everybody's been fired, Henry. Compensation packages were hand delivered to their homes. I don't know what's going on, but I do know there's not a single person at ICA who knows anything about your agency or how it works."

After a moment, Henry said, "He sent flowers, you know."

Josh looked a bit startled. "I'm sorry, what?"

"Creighton Berns sent flowers to my wife. He impounded our offices, fired our employees, won't take my phone calls, but he did, mind you, send flowers to my wife after he caused her to have a heart attack." His eyes narrowed. "I'll have his head, I swear to God I will."

"Do we file?" Josh asked.

"Not yet. We take him to court now and he'll drag it out for years and try to bankrupt us in the process. In the meantime our clients will get jilted on representation, and he'll try to ruin our name by claiming that we were the ones who tied up everything and everybody in court. No," he murmured, shaking his head, "I know the kind of creature this Creighton Berns is. But what I've *got* to know is what he's after. Even a reptile like Berns wouldn't risk compromising his reputation, and the reputation of ICA—not unless he was after something big. Something very big." His eyes shifted to Josh. "We've got to find out what it is."

"How do we do that?"

Henry's face cleared and he smiled. "Don't look so glum, my young friend." He touched Josh's arm. "Doe's going to be fine and"—he dropped his voice—"I'll get this son of a bitch, you wait and see."

"But how, Henry?"

"Don't you worry about that."

"I have to worry about it! You're my client and Creighton Berns is one of the most powerful men in communications right now."

"Yes, he is, and you have a long life and career to think about, and I don't want you involved in this any longer."

"Forget it, Henry. You can't get rid of me."

He studied Josh's face for a long moment. "Your firm's not going to like it."

"My firm doesn't have to know anything until you're ready to sue. And God knows, Henry, it's not as if ICA's going to hire me."

They stared at one another intently. "So you're in," Henry said with the beginnings of a smile.

Josh nodded.

"It's going to mean a lot of work on our behalf. I have to take care of Doe, and I don't want her knowing anything about what's going on. Understand?"

Josh nodded again, clamping a hand on Henry's shoulder.

"And no one on the outside is to ever know that I had any prior knowledge of what is about to happen," Henry added.

Josh looked at him. "What is about to happen?"

"Well"—Henry smiled—"you'll just have to wait and see."

~ *3* ~

Seventy-three-year-old Millicent Parks put the list down, took a sip of her tea, and said, "So what is it, exactly, you wish me to do?"

"I want you to send this letter to every client represented by Hillings & Hillings," Henry said, passing her a legal pad. "You can skip Elizabeth Robinson, because I've heard from her—she's already on her way here from England. The letter explains what happened, how it happened, and that you want to organize a committee to talk to ICA about the way they're handling the transition of your representation."

"Fine," Millicent said, passing Henry a plate of cucumber sandwiches. They were in the living room of her suite at the Plaza. Millicent was wearing her hair the same way she had for forty-five years, still piled high on her head, only it was white now.

He took a sandwich and swallowed it absently, as though it had been his first thought of food for quite some time. "And then you'll ask them to attend a meeting in New York. Here is the date, time, and place."

"Sheridan Square? Why Sheridan Square?"

"It's just a place where the meeting can be held that isn't connected to me."

"Oh," Millicent said, nodding and scanning the list. "Very clever, Hill."

Long before she had hit the best-seller list in 1950 with her first novel, Millicent Parks had merely been the severely spoiled wife of Henry's roommate at Yale. Later, after her husband, Tommy, was killed in the war, Henry and Dorothy made an effort to keep in touch with her. When Millicent was at a loss about what to do with herself—she had no children and a good deal of money—Henry encouraged her to finish the novel of high society she had started years before at Vassar.

Time went by and the drafts of the novel continued to improve under the editing of the Hillingses. Four years later, *A Dark Garden* was finished and Henry, using his father's law firm as the operating base, negotiated a publishing contract for Millicent. *A Dark Garden* was published in 1950 and sold like crazy. Hill and Dottie, as Millicent had always called them, had then formally founded the literary agency, and the Hillingses had been looking after her interests ever since—which was a good thing, since Millicent's charming rogue of a second husband very nearly took her to the cleaners.

For over forty years—through seven books, a third husband, the adoption of a daughter, widowhood yet again—the Hillingses had never steered Millicent wrong with their advice. And now that poor old Hucky was dead and her daughter had moved to Moscow (of all the ungodly places), Hill and Dottie were just about the only people in this world who could lure Millicent away from Bridgehampton, Long Island, where Millicent had a palatial Victorian home on six acres.

Frankly, after reading in a popular gossip column that "Millicent Parks, aging grand dame of the purple prose set, bestowed her presence upon the gathering in a manner befitting the Queen of Hearts," Millicent decided the world could go to hell in a hand basket for all she cared, and that if anyone really wanted to see her, they could damn well come to her from now on.

In this case, however, her duty was clear. The Hillingses had been cruelly treated and the "new" ICA had to answer for their actions. To impound the offices of two of the most distinguished literary representatives in the world? What on earth kind of world was this? But Millicent knew that today's world was indeed quite different from the one she had grown up in. She wasn't even sure exactly how one fought the vermin of the world today, a world that was so distorted and obscured by the media. How could anyone know who the enemy was until it was too late? Saddam Hussein,

Creighton Berns—what difference was there between their goals and their manipulation of the media?

Of course Creighton Berns wasn't a murderer (at least not yet, although he nearly had become one with Dorothy's heart attack), but there was no earthly reason why some ridiculous little upstart should get away with humiliating three of the finest people in the history of American entertainment—Ben Rothstein and Henry and Dorothy Hillings—and overthrowing their institutions in the process. No, it had to be dealt with, Millicent knew, fire with fire; this would be a battle for public opinion.

"What's the matter?" Henry asked her.

"Oh, nothing," Millicent said, "nothing but a few ruminations, Hill. Here, let me pour you some more tea."

"I've checked off the names of the clients on the list who'll want to help," Henry said. "My idea, Millicent, is to mount a public relations campaign against Creighton Berns, a client protest."

Millicent put the teapot down and let her eyes run over the list. She was pleased that Hill had come to the same conclusion, that the only place to wage war was on the public relations field, but her spirit sagged when she noted how many of the names on the list were not checked off. Most of these names belonged to best-selling writers and celebrities at the top of their game, clients who no doubt correctly perceived that opposing ICA might pose a threat to their career. Young hooligan or not, Creighton Berns was now in charge of one of the most powerful talent agencies in the world.

The thirty or so names that were checked off did little to boost Millicent's spirits. They were almost all once-famous Hillings & Hillings writers who had long since retired from the best-seller lists. Millicent knew almost all of them personally, and had known them for years.

Who is Patty Kleczak? Millicent wondered, seeing a name checked that she didn't recognize at all.

Elizabeth Robinson she knew. Millicent had met her years ago at a party in Sag Harbor. Elizabeth had been staying with Hill and Dottie in Water Mill. She had written a best-seller about an English duchess, and then there had been a movie. Now Elizabeth

Robinson was on TV, on PBS—Millicent had seen the show—so at least she was *somebody*, and that would help their cause.

Millicent pushed another sandwich on Hill. He looked dreadfully thin. For herself she skipped the sandwiches and went straight to the iced tea cakes she so adored the Plaza for.

Toward the end of the client list were two names checked off that Millicent thought could lead to something. One was Montgomery Grant Smith, the ultraconservative right-wing radio talk-show host. He was a rather obese young fellow, half-intellectual and half-adolescent, who hosted a radio show out of Chicago that had exploded in popularity in recent years. Millicent had actually met him; after "Big Mont" said at a *Chicago Tribune* book and author luncheon a few years ago that President Carter was really Eleanor Roosevelt back from the dead without lipstick, she had tripped him on the podium with her pocketbook.

However, as much of a jackass as Millicent considered Montgomery Grant Smith to be, there were millions of people who listened to him, and his book, *Visions for America*, had been on the best-seller list for two straight years now. In other words, a big mass-media right-winger like Montgomery Grant Smith could give a Hollywood-type like Creighton Berns a very bad time.

The other promising name was the last one on the list, last perhaps because Georgiana Hamilton-Ayres technically had not been represented by the Hillingses since she was eight years old. The Hillingses had also represented the memoirs of her mother, Lilliana Bartlett, a movie star Millicent had always loved. Today, Georgiana Hamilton-Ayres was a brilliant young actress in her own right, and few people remembered the book she had written and published as a child, *Bunny on the Run*, which had made news at the time because of the author's age and the fame of her mother.

Georgiana's mother, Lilliana, had, in fact, starred in the movie adaptation of Millicent's first novel, *A Dark Garden*. She had also been married four or five times and was an alumna of just about every sanatorium in the country, but if poor Lilliana was completely crazy and pathetic now, she had once been an utterly brilliant and gorgeous actress. In 1960 she had made a movie in Scotland, where she met and subsequently married eccentric old Lord Hamilton-Ayres. In less than two years, however, she was back in Hollywood, back into pills and alcohol and increasingly wild situations, only this time with a nanny and little baby in tow.

At one point, Millicent could remember, Lilliana had gotten so bad that Dottie and Hill had to take the child in.

At any rate, Georgiana Hamilton-Ayres had grown up to be a much better actress than her mother, and apparently without the pitfalls of her mother's excesses. At thirty-two she had already been nominated for two Academy Awards, and had become something of an international sex symbol. In short, Georgiana was great box office. And Georgiana was an ICA client whose concerns they would surely pay heed to.

"So what do you think?" Henry asked.

Millicent sighed, sipped her tea, and returned her cup to its saucer. "My dear Hill, with the exception of Georgiana Hamilton-Ayres, Montgomery Grant Smith, and to a much lesser degree Elizabeth Robinson, I don't think ICA will care what the people checked off on this list think."

"To a certain extent, you're right, Millicent," Henry said, "but to the world, they're still household names, and from a public relations point of view, they can still pull in the press."

"Perhaps," Millicent said doubtfully. She really did not want her friend to get his hopes up about this.

"The key," Henry said, "is that Doe and I remain completely unconnected to what the clients do. No one can know I ever had anything to do with this. Millicent, this is *your* idea, the clients banding together for a protest."

"Yes, of course, not to worry," she said, reaching over to pat his hand comfortingly. "But one thing you must tell me, Hill, is what, in heaven's name, is a Patty Kleecker-zak?"

"*Klee-zak*, it's pronounced *Klee-zak*," Henry said. "She's one of Doe's most promising romance suspense writers. As a matter of fact, we were going to ask you for a quote."

"Oh," Millicent said, frowning slightly. There was nothing worse than being asked to endorse yet another writer who would probably dwindle her own sales, but she would trust her friends' judgment. If they thought this Patty Klee-clacker-knacker woman deserved a quote from her, then at least she could read the book. "It's a first novel?"

"Yes," Henry said, "but she's been working on it for, oh, I don't know, about eleven years, I think."

"Eleven years," Millicent repeated. "I see, a regular Egyptian pyramid of romance suspense."

Henry looked at her. "Millicent."

"I'll be very nice, I promise," she told him, thinking, well, she'd try anyway.

~ 4 ~

No one who saw her that afternoon was likely to recognize Patty Jamison Kleczak as the next Phyllis Whitney. Dressed in blue jeans, a man's striped cotton shirt—the long sleeves rolled up over her elbows—and a Boston Red Sox hat, which was yanked down over her eyes, Patty was yelling at the umpire.

Her son Kevin was at the plate, squinting into the sun, his jaw locked in determination. It was the ninth inning and his team was trailing by one run: he had two strikes, no balls, and there were no runners on base—and two outs.

His team—the Dodgers—was undefeated. The regular coach, Ted Kleczak, Patty's husband and Kevin's father, was on the road with the Stanton High School Tigers at the championships in Omaha, where their elder son, Jimmy, was playing second base.

The pitch.

Kevin's bat hit the ball with a resounding crack as he fouled off what would have been the third strike.

"That's good, Kev, that's good, Kev, you know what to do!" Patty called to her son, clapping her hands. "Come on, straighten it out." Having been married to a gym teacher for eighteen years, she knew what to say.

Kevin adjusted his helmet and stepped into the batter's box again.

"Wake up, you guys," Patty growled to the team on the bench. "Let's have a little support here."

"Come on, Kev!" the boys started yelling. "You can do it!" "Big hit coming, big hit!"

Patty watched as her youngest child brought his bat back and crouched, trying to anticipate the pitch. He was the best of her three kids, which was a terrible observation for a mother to make, but nonetheless true. She never had to worry about Kevin; he was good-looking but didn't know it; athletic and a good sport; he liked girls in a shy but admiring way, and otherwise enjoyed getting A's in school just to see if he could do it. It was almost a full-time job *not* to smother this baby with affection and love, particularly since he was an anomaly—an affectionate thirteen-year-old.

Was she, in return, a good mother? She hoped so, but some days she had to wonder.

Her desire to be a writer had grown into a real passion for writing. Her mood swings almost always occurred when she felt used or taken for granted by her family while every other part of her was screaming to be upstairs in the attic with Jimmy's old Radio Shack computer and her little fan, working on her novel.

Working on her novel. After eleven years, it was finally finished. Only this morning a woman from International Communications Agency had called from California to ask for a fresh copy of the manuscript.

California. What would her life be like if someone in Hollywood wanted to make her story into a movie? She couldn't even think about it without shaking.

She'd never forget telling Ted that Mrs. Hillings had said her novel was ready to submit to publishing houses. He had been standing in front of the TV, playing with the remote control, and he had frozen before swiveling around on the balls of his feet, like a wide-eyed Bela Lugosi on a revolving pedestal. "You're kidding," he had said.

She shook her head, beaming. The poor guy didn't know what to do. He had seen that manuscript go in and out of the house probably a hundred times over the past eleven years and now it was ready to sell. What had been called—alternately in anger and in jest—"your endless fucking book" was finally going to be submitted for publication by one of the country's finest literary agencies.

"Now, honey, let's not get too excited," he had said softly, taking her face in his hands, "not until we see what happens."

"I know what's going to happen," she told him confidently, sliding her arms around his waist and resting the side of her face against his chest. "And I'm going to like being a published writer just fine."

"I hope so, baby, for your sake," he had murmured, not for the first time.

The pitch.

Crack went Kevin's bat.

Necks craned as Patty held her breath.

"Foul ball!" the umpire yelled, crouched over the line, as the left fielder chased down the ball.

Still two strikes. No balls. Nobody on base. Behind by one run. If anyone could pull this off under this kind of pressure, Patty knew it would be Kevin. He had always had a cool head. When he was ten he had thought to pick up the end of his brother's finger and bring it inside the house after Jimmy had cut it off while using the electric shears. He had even prompted his shocked mother to pack it in ice. Today, it was back on the end of his brother's left index finger.

The pitch.

There was a muffled *thud*.

"Ooooooo," said all the boys.

The ball lay at Kevin's feet. He had dropped his bat and was clutching his shoulder.

"Kevin!" Patty cried, running over. "Oh, sweetheart, are you all right?" she asked, touching the hand that was holding his shoulder.

"It's *okay*, Mom," he said out of the side of his mouth, keeping his eye on the ump.

"Batter takes a base!" the ump announced.

The team applauded as Kevin trotted off to first base. When he reached it, he took off his helmet and made a humble bow to the bench.

Patty smiled. Their three children were so different. If that had been Jimmy, he would never have looked at the bench. He would have focused solely on the game, face ablaze, embarrassed to be the center of attention. And if it were their middle child, Mary Ellen—oh well, Mary Ellen refused to play any sport.

Mary Ellen had been transformed into a rather horrible child recently, a child who deeply resented everything her mother said or did, which, of course, made her difficult adolescence an experience shared by her entire family.

Before the game tonight, when Patty had asked Mary Ellen to set the table and turn on the oven at 6 P.M. she was told that she was an evil, wicked woman who couldn't possibly be Mary Ellen's real mother. Looking at her watch now, Patty couldn't help but wonder if the daughter of the evil, wicked woman had turned on the oven. Whether they ate dinner tonight or not depended on it, not that Mary Ellen would care. Lately she had steadfastly refused to eat most of Patty's nutritious meals, wishing instead to live on cookies and chocolate and potato chips so she could wail and scream and pout and sob over her weight and skin.

"Why didn't you give me your thighs?" Mary Ellen would demand. "Why did I get Daddy's awful legs? And why do you have such nice hair and I have such stringy hair?"

As for Mary Ellen's complexion, on that subject she was very clear. "Look at what you've done to me, Mother!" she would say, glaring, pointing to the acne on her chin. "You disfigured me."

Kevin had raised the team's hopes to a fevered pitch by getting to first base, only to be the one to dramatically dash them when Cokey Drasso, up next, hit a legitimate single and Kevin, pressing his luck, tried for third. After a lousy slide, he was tagged out almost a foot away from the base.

So they lost the game and Kevin was crushed, as Patty knew he would be, until his father the coach came home that night and explained to him why it was all right to make a mistake. Kevin refused a ride from Patty, asking to walk home so he could think over the game. She said fine and stopped at the bank cash machine a few blocks away to deposit some money into their account, hoping to cover the check she had written the day before for her new dress before it bounced. She thought of this purchase as her new author dress.

Why was it there always seemed to be money somewhere for everyone in the family but herself? Her friend Alice had first pointed this out to her and it was true, but ever since Alice started going to therapy she had become a pain. Everything Patty did suddenly had subtle but important implications, instead of reflecting exactly what she was: a tired mother and housewife who did free-lance typing and longed for the writing career she had postponed for years.

*   *   *

She had been a daddy's girl. Daddy had been given four daughters in a row before Patty; she was his last chance for a son. When things didn't work out, her father decided to teach Patty everything he had been waiting to teach a son. So when Patty Jamison graduated from St. Mary's, she was a lovely, accomplished young woman who could change a tire in under five minutes, mow a lawn, build a tree house, throw a perfect spiral, and balance a checkbook.

It was as if she had been raised to marry Ted. He was a gym teacher and an aspiring coach, and he had been looking for a different sort of woman, someone who was interested in what he did and could keep up with all he did. He wanted a woman who could play ball, who loved the femininity of being a woman, who also wanted to be pals with an out-and-out jock, and who wanted a passionate sexual attachment. He found her in Patty.

She had fallen in love with him very early on. And what attracted her wasn't only how handsome he was, or what all-star qualities he had, but the way he related to her, and to *all* women. Ted had grown up the only son in a family with three girls, and he had become one of those wonderful men who loved women as his friends.

Patty had been a sophomore at Rosemont College in Philadelphia when she met Ted. He had been one year out of Holy Cross and was teaching in Bala-Cynwyd. They dated for a few months and then went away for a weekend together in Cape May, where they had sex for the first time. It was wonderful.

He was a tender and strong and terrific lover. And best yet, he was in love with her.

They had used condoms and done very well with them until the wee hours of the morning on Sunday, when they had sort of forgotten.

It had been wonderful to awaken then, feeling Ted's arms around her, his body curved behind hers, and realize, in an instant, that he was awake and trying not to wake her, although he had an erection straining against her. Ted was so in control about everything, that to feel his need and desire thrilled her and excited her enormously. And so she had reached down and taken his hand, brought it up to her mouth, kissed it, and then moved it down to hold her breast, still lying away from him.

They didn't say anything. He massaged her breast and kissed her neck and his erection brushed lightly against her buttocks.

She pulled her leg forward, instinctively, not really understanding what she was doing, but doing it all the same because it seemed lovely and right and Ted murmured something and she moaned softly, and then he had slowly tried to find his way in from behind.

It surprised and delighted Patty and she wasn't sure why—because she was wondering, does it work this way? and she was pretty sure Ted was wondering the same thing, for he was being very cautious, which made it all the more wonderful—and then the next thing she knew, he was inside her from behind, holding her with his left arm above, his mouth in her neck, and right arm holding her below, hand down over the front of her, pulling him toward her, rubbing her in the most marvelous way.

It was the first real orgasm she had ever had and after that, sex was never the same. Sex was Ted. Love was Ted. Ted was a miracle of emotion and now of physical exquisiteness, too, which she had never felt before.

Her father had said Ted was just a gym teacher, not some sort of a god.

But he had been. To her.

Their elder son, James Edward, had been conceived on that lovely morning in Cape May. A great deal of confusion and pain and torment ensued when Patty didn't get her period and finally went to the Planned Parenthood clinic to get a pregnancy test.

When it came back positive, Ted immediately offered to marry her, and she knew he meant it. The problem wasn't him, or that they didn't love each other. For Patty the question was whether she was prepared to give up her schooling and freedom for immediate marriage and motherhood.

At twenty, Patty became a wife and mother. While she didn't regret her decision, she came to resent the fact she could not get a job that paid more than it would cost her for daycare. So until Jimmy was old enough to go to school, work was out of the question. By the time the Kleczaks moved to Stanton, New Jersey the following year, where Ted got a job as the assistant football coach at Stanton High, Patty decided she might as well go ahead and have two more children while she was at it. A year later she gave birth to

Mary Ellen and scarcely a year and a half after that Kevin was born.

Sweet little Kevin. He was thirteen now and she was thirty-seven; where had the time gone.

Sometimes Patty would feel like an alien from a lost world after chatting in the supermarket checkout line with a forty-year-old investment banker who was on her first maternity leave.

And yet, despite the bankers and analysts and sales directors who thrived in residential Stanton, Patty was very happy with her gym teacher. They could use more money—always—but they had been blessed. Very blessed.

And every once in a while—and almost always around Jimmy's birthday—she and Ted made love the way they had in Cape May. And it was still great.

"Mom, you got a Federal Express letter," Mary Ellen said, never turning her face from the TV.

"Thanks, sweetie." Patty appreciated the instant alert, but hated finding her daughter in front of the TV. This was not a good sign and she dreaded her next question. "Did you start dinner?"

Mary Ellen turned, screwed up her face, and said, "Yes, I started dinner." She rolled her eyes. "God, if I hadn't, I'd probably be thrown into prison."

Kevin walked through the front door, straight across the living room, and up the stairs.

Patty watched him and then turned to Mary Ellen. "Homework?"

"Done," Mary Ellen said triumphantly, moving closer to the TV.

Patty walked over and touched the top of her daughter's head.

Mary Ellen gave an exaggerated sigh and looked up. "What now?"

"Kev lost today, they won't be in the playoffs." She winced a little. "I'm afraid he caused the last out and he's feeling pretty rotten."

Patty could tell Mary Ellen was torn between the TV show and her brother. "Oh, okay," she sighed, turning off the TV, "I'll go up and talk to him."

Patty smiled. Mary Ellen had a lot of faults, but not loving her younger brother was not one of them. "Thanks, sweetie, you're the best," Patty said, giving her a pat on the rear and heading for the kitchen. "Where's the letter?"

"Kitchen table," Mary Ellen called.

"Millicent Parks?" Patty murmured, ripping open the cardboard envelope. "What could this be?"

~ 5 ~

"Oh, he's got a good thing going," the president's wife said when asked her opinion of Montgomery Grant Smith and his repeated attacks on her husband. "Not to write him off, but when a person's making the kind of money he is, they can hardly afford to change their mind about anything. And when a person never changes his mind, it's usually a pretty good indication that he's stopped thinking."

"Screw you, madam," Monty said quietly, sitting in his easy chair at home in Evanston, Illinois, watching CNN.

"To be perfectly honest," the first lady continued in response to another question, "I'm not sure Montgomery Grant Smith has political relevance anymore. His views are expressed solely for commercial profit. If he really wanted to see this country change for the better, he'd be a public servant. He's not. My husband is."

His phone rang and he picked it up. "Are you watching this?" Mike, his producer, asked.

"Yeah. And they just let her go on and on, you notice? I can always tell when there's a feminist producer."

"I'm taping it," Mike said. "Let's use it tomorrow. And we can add those jokes we've got."

"Not the personal stuff," Monty said. "I don't want to make cracks about her body."

"But those are the best!"

Monty, who had trouble with his weight, hated personal attacks on anyone's physical appearance. "No," he said. "I'll do a riff on the first couple's pillow talk at night. It'll be great. Tell engineering to key up her voice to make it sound more shrill."

"Gotcha," he said. "Gotta go."

Most nights Monty was still pretty excited when his name came up on TV. Back when no one would give him the time of day, the Hillingses had sold his book of essays for five hundred dollars to an academic press and landed him a job as a substitute on a radio talk show, and he had been blown away. But the Hillingses had believed in Monty. He had the courage and convictions to think for himself, they said. And they felt he could teach a lot of other people to do the same through talk radio.

They had been right and they had been wrong. Right in that people had wanted to hear him, but not for the reason the Hillingses had thought. The sixties and seventies were over and people—at least Monty's audience—were sick of change. In fact, the majority of the people who would become Monty's listeners were almost obsessed with shutting the system *down* to preserve it the way they had been taught it was supposed to work, i.e., to their advantage. The last thing they wanted was someone on the radio who would let people think for themselves—they wanted unity against what they saw as the encroaching enemy.

And so, Monty filled the bill. He was nearly six feet four, had thinning blond hair, blue eyes, and was Christian. His mother had stayed at home to raise her children while his father had gone out in the world to support his family. Montgomery Grant Smith, these people decided, was the leader of the revolution they had been waiting for. He was someone who understood their fears, he was someone who spoke to the far Right. The fears of his audience had at one time actually been listed in a confidential ratings research report Monty's radio network swore didn't exist:

Greatest Fears of MGS's Audience
1. White Christians becoming a minority.
2. White male Christians losing economic seniority.
3. White Christians losing economic seniority.
4. White Christians marrying out of faith and/or race.
    a. Birth control and abortion
    b. Homosexuality
    c. Feminism
5. White Christians losing ability to segregate.

At thirty-seven, Montgomery Grant Smith was considered the hero of the ultraconservatives, despite the fact that he had been divorced, had no children, and had no time to do anything but prepare for his show. In short, the reality was that his life had so very little in it outside of the show it could hardly be considered a life at all, conservative or otherwise.

He was a Floridian who lived in Evanston, Illinois, the lively suburb of Chicago where Big Mont—as he was known—broadcast what was said to be the most popular radio talk show in America. He was young for this kind of success, but even Monty would occasionally admit, in private, that it was the lefty kooks and perverts like Howard Stern who had ridden his right-wing show up in the ratings through backlash.

"But how left wing can Howard Stern be," one caller from New York had asked Monty on the air recently, "when he's the father of three children and is faithful to the one and only wife he's ever had?"

"Sir," Big Mont had said, "New York Jews are not known for conservative views, period."

"And how 'bout failed leftist playwrights from Florida who can't get a date?" the caller responded.

Even Big Mont could be surprised occasionally by what a caller said. And in this case, the caller's claim was true. As a youth, he had written an idealistic play about a new government conquering all ills, but how did this wacko know about that? And about his dating woes? It was that goddamn *People* article again, the one that quoted a well-known feminist as saying, "No self-respecting woman could bear to be in the same room with him, much less imagine a romantic involvement."

"Sir," Big Mont said quietly, "I did not fail as a playwright. The one play I wrote as a misguided youth was a great success—of course, in a city like Miami, what do you expect?—and then I came to my senses. As for getting a date, I beg to disagree. Many fine, beautiful women enjoy my companionship."

The part Big Mont failed to mention was that almost all of his ex-lovers in recent years had been married—and usually to one of his wealthy conservative supporters. He was also far too polite to explain that his nickname came not from his height and weight, but from the gossip the wives exchanged at political rallies and fund-raisers. Standing by a lily pond in South Carolina during a five-hundred-dollar-a-seat dinner for Strom Thurmond one woman was heard to say, "Honey, a battering ram's more like it. I was sore for a week." Her comment was followed by gales of laughter.

Either the male supporters of Montgomery Grant Smith had never heard of his battering ram, or they were simply content with mistresses of their own, but Monty's decision to stop carousing among married women last year was his own. He knew he couldn't preach family values and run the risk of getting caught.

Once he stopped sneaking affairs with the women who came to him, he had no affairs at all, so he worked and ate and gained weight.

He knew he could get a date if he wanted one. Plenty of them. The *People* article was not true. He just didn't have time.

"Hello, America," Monty said jovially on Monday, pushing aside a plate of glazed donuts. "This is your leader speaking, the illustrious Montgomery Grant Smith, who, many say, is the last hope of the free world." A deep, gentle laugh rolled over the airwaves while he adjusted his headset. "I will not agree with that statement, nor will I disagree absolutely." The show was off to a good start.

During the news, Mike brought him a Federal Express packet marked Personal and Confidential. Monty opened it and found a letter from Millicent Parks.

Ben Rothstein at ICA had negotiated Monty's first radio contract, and although he had warned Monty against going into partnership with The Right Way, Inc.—Hollywood liberals could be such a pain—Ben had been an honorable old guy, and had done very well for Monty. Evidently, however, the sharks out there had finally gotten him.

But the point of this letter, Millicent wrote, was to inform Hillings & Hillings's clients that Creighton Berns, the new head of ICA, had literally torn the agency out of the Hillingses' hands, physically locked the couple out of their own offices, and caused Dorothy Hillings to suffer a heart attack, for which she was still being hospitalized.

Would Mr. Smith come to New York for a meeting to lend his support to an effort to reinstate the agency to the Hillingses?

Monty thought about the request for the rest of the show. And then, during the last news break, he buzzed his producer. "Mike, tell Stazza I want to do the show from New York three weeks from today."

When Monty's weight had crept up to nearly three hundred pounds six months ago, he had given in finally and gone to a therapist, who had immediately and urgently suggested that Monty break out of his work isolation and do something for someone else. "Like what?" he had asked. "Anything that involves other people and *their* needs, not just your own." Although Monty had never gone back, the sense of urgency in the therapist's voice had stayed with him. And reading the letter again, he knew, deep down, that this trip would be a good thing for him to do. After all, without the Hillingses, God only knew where he would be today. Selling insurance in Orlando?

"New York," Monty confirmed to his producer, glancing up at the clock. "The whole week, Monday through Friday." He put his headset on, nodded to the engineer, and said into the microphone, "Okay, folks, you're back with the mighty me, in this, the last precious half hour of wisdom, guidance, and intellectual euphoria, from yours truly, Montgomery Grant Smith, known to millions as Big Mont—and Golden Boy to my mama." He glanced at the monitor. "And now we're going straight to the phones and take a call from Glen in—Glen in Glendale—yes, ladies and gentlemen, Glen in Glendale, California." Click. "Hey, Glen, don't you think you should consider moving? Or Paul in St. Paul?" Pause, chuckle, voice dropping to its lowest register. "Or Hannaloooo in Honalooolu?"

"I tell ya, Monty," the caller said, "if your words were manure, I could fertilize the world with it."

"Ah!" Monty cried, pounding the console. "A democrat! I knew it! I knew one day one of you would call!"

~ 6 ~

Georgiana Hamilton-Ayres was waiting for the light to change on Santa Monica Boulevard when a pest-control company van slammed into the back of her car. Her head was thrown back against the headrest and then into the steering wheel. It was a sickening sound.

There is no airbag on a '78 Jaguar convertible.

The next thing she heard was the horn of the van behind her blaring in her ear. Dazed, she looked down in her lap and saw her sunglasses neatly snapped in two amidst the torrent of blood that was streaming out of her nose.

A frightened teenage boy with a gold tooth was looking at her. "Don't move, lady," he said. "You're hurt. Don't move. Help's on the way."

There was a woman peering around his shoulder, and then a man in a dark blue suit. Soon there were a lot of people. Then sirens. Georgiana simply sat there clutching the steering wheel, her eyes closed. She couldn't bear to see all the blood and know that it was hers. And too, an earlier look in the rearview mirror had told her that the man who had hit her had gone through his windshield and was not a pretty sight either.

When she opened her eyes again, there was a policewoman in the passenger seat beside her. "You'll be fine," the woman said, "the ambulance is here." And then Georgiana heard someone say, from far, far away, "It's Georgiana Hamilton-Ayres, the actress."

"Jesus," another voice said, "of all the people to hit. God, look at her face."

Well, Georgiana thought before passing out, if they can still recognize me, it can't be too bad.

When she awakened in the emergency room of Cedars-Sinai, the first thing she became aware of was the strange and ghastly sensation of her tongue sliding through a small, wet, bumpy place on the left side of her mouth, instead of stopping at the back of her tooth. Georgiana cried out when she realized what this meant. Her mouth ached, her face throbbed, her forehead felt like it was going to explode, and her jaw seemed to be rusted shut.

She was covered by the movie's insurance, her agent from ICA explained to her in a businesslike manner as she lay there, hooked up to an IV, getting stitches from an intern.

"The delays and cost of replacing you in the movie will be covered in full by insurance—including your salary for the film. We're very lucky."

"Ah shee," Georgiana said, which meant "I see," the best elocution she could manage while getting the inside of her mouth stitched.

"By the way, Creighton Berns is very upset and says to tell you he is praying for your recovery."

Georgiana's nose was broken in two places. All of her teeth were fine except for the jagged remains of her front left eyetooth. She was suffering from a mild concussion, a cracked jaw, and a broken cheekbone. Other than that, she was just fine.

She was taken to a private room in the plastic surgery wing.

Georgiana thought she was dreaming. Alexandra Waring, the DBS anchorwoman, was standing next to her bed looking concerned. Georgiana blinked, trying to focus.

"Hi," the dream said softly. "I was in town and I heard about the accident—I snuck in to see how you're doing."

Georgiana tried to speak, but her mouth was wired shut. Her head was swimming and though she wasn't in pain, exactly, she thought she could feel her head throbbing.

"Don't even try," Alexandra whispered, touching her arm. "Look, I'm going to leave the name and number of a good friend of mine on your bedside table. Kim works for DBS here in Los Angeles and she can get you anything you need, or do anything you need done. I've asked her to check in twice a day with you." Alexandra put the paper on the table and turned back to Georgiana. "She's doing this for me, so please let her do it. Okay?"

Alexandra smiled and Georgiana felt her eyes filling with tears. To distract her guest, she pointed to Alexandra's beaded evening dress. "Oh, it's the anniversary of our affiliate. That's why I was here. I was going to give you a call anyway. I wanted to see you again."

Georgiana must have drifted back to sleep, because she remembered nothing after that, and she had been awake for hours the next day before she realized that it really might have happened, that Alexandra Waring might have actually been there the night before. The nurse went to check and returned, saying, "She was here, all right! Signed autographs for the night shift."

Georgiana and Alexandra Waring, the fiercely bright, more than slightly enigmatic workaholic star of DBS News, had met in New York at a party given by Jessica Wright, a talk show hostess Georgiana knew. They had hit it off immediately, something Georgiana frankly did not often do with journalists. Waring had the most extraordinary blue-gray eyes and a slow, dazzling smile—a trifle shy perhaps?—that made Georgiana feel both well liked and worthwhile.

Usually the hair on the back of her neck went up when she met a journalist at a party, basically because they were always working, and while Alexandra was no exception (asking smart questions, listening closely, responding perfectly to what was being said—in short, being charming while sniffing out possible story leads), the contrast between the woman and the anchorwoman on the nightly news was, well, endearing. There was a vulnerability about Alexandra Waring when she was not on camera, an accessibility, that Georgiana liked. She liked it even more when she saw this trait disappear when Alexandra talked to other people.

"I don't usually trust journalists," Georgiana said to her at the party, after witnessing this on-again, off-again vulnerability, "but for some reason I want to trust you."

"Well, thank you," she had said, smiling, sipping her Perrier. "I'm not usually terribly trusting of actresses, I must confess—especially gifted ones—but I feel the same way about you."

Georgiana had felt her face grow warm.

It was hard being a public figure. As time rolled on and you were approached in so many different ways for so many different things, you simply had to form protective layers—translucent veils that could be lifted one by one as you got to know someone well, someone who could be trusted. Georgiana was always oblivious to the process until she witnessed it in someone else. And that night, she knew, intuitively, Alexandra Waring, for some reason, had made an effort to let Georgiana get close to her, and so she had responded in kind.

The anchorwoman was probably lonely. They all were.

They said good-bye as Georgiana hurried off to catch a 10:30 flight to L.A., and Alexandra promised to give her a call soon.

Two days later, when her housekeeper announced that Ms. Waring was on the phone, Georgiana had been delighted.

"I hope you don't think it's odd that I'm calling you," Alexandra said. "It's just that I don't have many friends outside of work, and you seem to understand a great deal about the kind of life I have to lead."

Typical Alexandra sentence. Straightforward on one level and cryptic on another.

"Of course not, I'm glad you did," Georgiana said. In the background, she could hear the noise of the DBS newsroom, which confused her until Alexandra explained that she had been working for thirty-two straight hours and was waiting for a bulletin and had decided to make a short call to the outside world to see if it was still there.

No one seemed to know very much about Alexandra beyond the fact that she was the most pleasant and charismatic of the TV news stars, a feat no doubt accomplished at the expense of a personal life. She wasn't married, but she had been engaged to a longtime beau, a TV producer, and people said Alexandra had never gotten over the breakup. Apparently her fiancé had wanted a wife instead of someone who was launching a national TV news network; he had married his secretary.

Alexandra called Georgiana again about a week later just to say hello. When they hung up, Georgiana called Jessica Wright.

"She's my best friend and probably saved my life—what more do you want to know?" Jessica said.

"I suppose I wanted to know who she is, what she's really like," Georgiana said, suddenly feeling foolish.

"Gee, that's a tough one," Jessica joked. "Maybe you should just ask her."

What Georgiana really wanted to know was whether the ambiguity she sensed in the air was a product of her imagination or not. She didn't trust Jessica with that one, however, and so she changed the subject.

*   *   *

After three days of lying around in the hospital, Georgiana begged her doctor to get to work on her nose. She didn't care about the pain.

While waiting to be wheeled into the operating room, Georgiana ran into two people she knew, who were, like herself, lying horizontally on gurneys in the hallway. One, who was out cold, was an actress she had worked with in a Joe Papp "Shakespeare in the Park" production in New York three summers before. The other person was a television director with whom she had once worked. Like Georgiana, he was on a divine preop combination of Demerol, Valium, and morphine shots, so the two of them sat up and gaily chatted away, laughing and gossiping as if they were at a cocktail party.

"I'm having my eyes done and Carmen's getting her boobs lifted," he said, nodding in the unconscious actress's direction. Leaning forward, he added, "She needs it. And you, darling, it's really good you're getting everything done now, because you look like shit. I'm sorry, but you do. I was so shocked when I realized that was *you*." Suddenly Georgiana decided she wasn't having such a good time anymore and laid back down, feeling very sorry for herself because she was one of the few actresses who had actually been born with a beautiful nose. After years of working so hard to care for her body, at thirty-two she had to go under the knife because some stupid pest-control truck with a demonic plastic ant on its roof had been speeding.

Her housekeeper, Cachi, arrived late the following afternoon with her mail and a week's worth of newspapers. When Georgiana read that the driver of the van that had hit her was in a coma, she felt badly and started to count her blessings.

Kim from DBS News arrived in the early evening to see how she was doing, and Georgiana wanted to crawl under the bed. She knew how awful she must look, with a big X of adhesive tape accenting the black, blue, green, and yellow bruises. Her nose was in a cast, her neck in a brace, and her mouth in a retainer. Georgiana had been receiving an awful lot of flowers and Kim suggested that they could be distributed throughout the hospital. Georgiana quickly agreed, grateful for Kim's help, but happy to see her leave because she couldn't stand people seeing her this way!

The phone rang all day, which was maddening since Georgiana

couldn't say anything with all the wire they had put in her mouth. She'd pick up the phone and listen and people would say, "Hello? Hello?" and then hang up. One person got it, though.

"Georgiana? It's Alexandra calling," the voice said. "I know you can't talk, but if you just tap the receiver on the bed I'll know it's you I'm talking to."

Georgiana smiled and hit the phone against the metal side bar and brought the receiver to her ear.

Alexandra was laughing. "Well that was an Oscar-winning slam if I ever heard one. Bette Davis would have loved it!"

Georgiana started to laugh but, oh God, it hurt!

Alexandra called her every day. Sometimes twice. And as soon as she got the wires removed and the swelling began to go down, Georgiana started talking back.

Millicent Parks's letter was waiting for Georgiana when she got home. Its contents disturbed her deeply. ICA without Ben Rothstein was bad enough, but the thought of ICA hurting the Hillingses made Georgiana wild. She would have to do something, but what?

The next morning she stood in front of the mirror and took a hard look at what she had come to call the Architectural Revitalization Program. She was beginning to resemble herself. She no longer had those charming black and purple rings around her eyes, and the whites of her eyes were almost clear now. Her hairdresser had already come over to rehabilitate her long, light brown hair which was streaked with blond, and that was looking okay. Her nose was still badly swollen, but it was beginning to look human, and her mouth, while still very puffy, felt almost okay. Since she had pale, fine skin, every nick and stitch and bruise looked far worse than it was.

Georgiana was said to be every bit the Scottish beauty that Lady Harriet Hamilton-Ayres, her paternal grandmother, had been, but it was clear to Georgiana that most of her curves in life had come from her mother, the former Miss Lauren Rosenblatt of Brooklyn, better known as Lilliana Bartlett. Her mother's marriage to her father had been the second of four, and she could not remember her parents ever being together, so brief was their cohabitation.

Georgiana had read an unauthorized biography of her mother

not long ago that her mother would kill her if she knew about. But how else was Georgiana supposed to know anything, since her mother was forever being committed and her father rarely spoke of anything but how Corn Laws had destroyed Great Britain? The biography reported that Lilliana had married Lord Hamilton-Ayres to have a child, and that she had used the eighteen months with him in his ancestral home outside Inverness as a kind of self-imposed detoxification center to produce a healthy baby. Lord Hamilton-Ayres, for his part, had married the wealthy actress to get the ancestral estate out of hock.

Georgiana had only been nine months old when her mother bolted for Hollywood, taking her with her. At the time Lord Hamilton-Ayres hadn't a clue that his wife had no intention of coming back. And when he learned the truth, the famous custody battle ensued, a mighty clash familiar to anyone who read the papers in 1962. As for Georgiana, all she had ever known for sure was that whenever her mother got hold of alcohol or tranquilizers, she turned into someone else and went crazy; and her father, although very distinguished looking and socially active, was not, in truth, very bright. In fact, Georgiana found him rather thick. ("It's the inbreeding," her mother would say. "They're like a bunch of royal hillbillies up there in Scotland.")

Georgiana's fondest memories of childhood were the two years she had spent living with the Hillingses in Gramercy Park while her mother had been bouncing in and out of rehabilitation in Michigan. The alternative would have been for the courts to ship the young girl off to Scotland, where, in turn, her father would have shipped her off to boarding school in England. And so, secretly, Georgiana had lived with the Hillingses and attended the Dalton School.

She had been twelve. Her fourth day there she had gotten her first period. It was awful, how scared she had been, not because she didn't know what it was, but how—if possible—was she to ask for help? For someone to explain what it was she was supposed to do. She had wadded up Kleenex in her underpants and returned to the dinner table where Mrs. Hillings instantly asked if something was wrong. Georgiana had shaken her head, staring at her plate. Mr. Hillings asked if she would like to go for a walk after dinner and Georgiana had said no, she was sorry, she couldn't, and then she looked up and saw the concern in his eyes and it made her burst into tears. Her parents never looked at her that way and she knew, intuitively, that maybe they should sometimes—and she apologized, before running from the table to her new room.

She was still crying when Mrs. Hillings came in. For a while she refused to tell her what was wrong, but then, finally, she said she wanted to go for a walk but she couldn't.

"Darling heart, do you have your period?" Mrs. Hillings asked.

Georgiana was so surprised that she stopped crying. The way Mrs. Hillings said it made it sound like a great achievement. She sat up, wiped her eyes with the back of her hand, and nodded.

Mrs. Hillings handed her a tissue and told her she would be right back. When she returned with a sanitary belt and a box of Kotex napkins, a quick painless lesson ensued. "Contrary to rumor, this is quite simple. You'll do it without thinking in no time, my dear, I promise you." And then Mrs. Hillings had sent her off for a quick shower and a solo effort. "When you're ready, I'll tell Henry you've changed your mind about a walk. If you don't mind, I'd like to come too. I'm feeling a little off myself."

After that, Georgiana found herself able to tell Mrs. Hillings anything. And there had been a lot to tell.

She sighed, still looking in the mirror, gingerly touching her nose. Numb. Exactly. Like what all the rest of her life would become if she did not focus on what was important.

Georgiana had always wanted to have an opportunity to repay a little bit of the kindness and love Mrs. Hillings had so freely extended to her over the years. This ICA business was her first chance.

And so she would go to New York for that meeting. In the meantime, she'd call Dorothy to see how she was. And, if she didn't look too awful, while she was in New York she'd try to see Alexandra.

~ 7 ~

"Ya gotta pay your bills, man," the guy in his driveway said.

This was unbelievable. Unbelievable. David made more than a million dollars a year and these assholes said they were taking his car. "Wait a minute, wait a minute," David said, pacing the front yard with his portable phone pressed to his ear, dressed only in boxer shorts. "He'll be on in a second."

But his business manager's secretary came back on the line again, sounding scared now. "I'm terribly sorry, Mr. Aussenhoff, but Mr. Trent isn't here. I thought he was, but I was mistaken."

"Ya gonna give me the keys, or do I have to tow it?" the guy asked him. At the end of the driveway was a tow truck and standing outside of it were two of the biggest thugs David had ever seen. This whole thing had to be a joke.

"Just get the receipts for the car," David yelled into the phone at the secretary. "I've got these assholes over here trying to repossess my car!"

"Assholes," the guy said to his companions, "the gentleman called us assholes. And he doesn't even pay his bills." He gave David the finger and turned to his companions. "Take it. He doesn't know his head from his ass."

"Wait!" David said. Into the phone, "Get the friggin' receipt for the Lamborghini, will you?"

"I'm not sure there is one," the secretary finally admitted.

"Fuck!" David said, hurling the telephone over the fence into his neighbor's yard and whirling around. "All right!" he yelled. "Take the goddamn car. But when I get the receipt for it, I'm gonna haul your asses into court!"

"Let the man have his moment of self-righteous indignation," the guy explained to his men as they hitched the towline hook onto the rear axle. "This is yet another sad story of Hollywood."

Even the damn repo man in this town sounded like an actor! David stormed up the stairs of his house and went inside.

"What's the matter, honey bunny?" Susie asked him, wandering out of the bedroom with his robe on. She looked out the front window. "Why are they taking the car? Is it broken?" Susie was an actress. Susie was built. They each understood their relationship perfectly and its relation to the new movie David was producing.

"Honey bunny's business manager is a stupid fucking shithead!" David explained, going to the bedroom. "And I'm going to pound his mangy little head in." He began tearing clothes out of the closet and yanking them on. Brooks Brothers blue-striped cotton shirt, khaki pants, cowboy boots.

The doorbell rang.

"Now what?" David muttered, going to the front door.

"David Aussenhoff?" the Federal Express man asked.

David grunted and reached for the pen and clipboard. "Thanks," he said, handing the guy a couple of bucks and closing the door.

"God, now what?" David asked, tearing open the cardboard envelope. He read the letter quickly, frowned, dropped his hand to his side, and looked to the ceiling.

"What is it, Davey?"

Davey. Only his worst enemies called him Davey. Or women he didn't know well who wished to feign intimacy. He liked honey bunny better. He sighed, walked over to the couch, and plunked down next to her. "I gotta read this again," he said. He looked at her. Kissed her briefly on the mouth. "Not a very nice good morning for you, is it?"

"I've had worse," Susie said. She looked out the window. "They repossess your car?"

"That's what they said."

"You broke?" she asked him.

"Not that I know of."

"I got a little money," Susie said. "About three thousand. If it'll help—"

His heart hurt at this. Susie meant it. When it came to being broke and desperate, like most actors, she identified. But unlike almost anyone he knew, Susie instinctively offered to help. And suddenly Susie became real to David. A charming girl, actually.

She reminded David of someone he had once loved. Someone he had made a terrible mistake with.

But then, this letter reminded him of a lot of mistakes he had made in the past. Back when he really did something, wanted something, still had a life ahead of him to live.

His novel had been called *Darkness Visible*. The Hillingses had suggested a new name, *The Young Man*. Whether it had been the Hillingses' editorial suggestions or their clout or the new title, what another literary agent had been unable to sell became a fifty-thousand-dollar project in the Hillingses' hands. There had been a *Publishers Weekly* article about the sale:

NYU undergraduate wrote novel about being single and confused in New York. Got an agent. Couldn't sell manuscript.
Was sitting, depressed, in Washington Square, debating
whether to finish school or kill himself. A couple sat down on
the same bench. Woman caught his eye and smiled. "Regardless
of what they tell you, young man, this too shall pass," she said.
Turned out they were Dorothy and Henry Hillings, the famous
agents. They would like to read his manuscript. The rest is
history. Book big best-seller for the fall, sold to the movies for
six figures by Ben Rothstein himself, chairman of International
Communications Artists.

What the article—and all the other off-the-book-page stories
about this best-selling twenty-one-year-old first novelist—did not
write about were the painful scenes that were to come between the
author and his agents.

"You aren't listening to me, David," Henry Hillings had said,
sitting behind the beautiful mahogany desk in his office at 101 Fifth
Avenue. Dorothy had been there, sitting in a chair next to David's,
as if she were part of his defense against what her husband had to
say. "What I said," Henry continued, "is that I worry about what
living that life-style in Los Angeles might do to you—as a novelist—at this point in your life. I do not doubt, not for a minute, that
you can write a good screenplay from your book."

"Look, you're my agent," David said, "you should want me to
go—it means a lot more money for you."

"Oh, David," Dorothy sighed, looking upset, "if our only wish
was to make money, dear, we would be very different people than
the ones who sat down next to you on that park bench. We care
about our clients and what's best for them."

"It's your temperament, David," Henry said. "In two years—a
year, maybe—the story would be different, but all of this is so new,
we can only caution you against diving in all the way."

"So you'd want me to lose this opportunity just to finish goddamn school," David said.

"We would like to see you get your college degree, yes," Dorothy said.

"I can work on my degree out there." David leaned back in his chair, waiting for them to respond.

The Hillingses looked at one another and then back at David. "You're twenty-one years old," Dorothy began, "a very talented, handsome, nice young man."

"You'll be given a swanky apartment, a sleek car, and a tremendous amount of money," Henry continued. "You'll be let loose in an environment where you will be seen as only one thing"—he paused for emphasis—"a person to be taken advantage of." David looked puzzled. "Taken advantage of by the studio, by women, by men, too," Henry added, "if that's—"

"God, no way!" David said indignantly.

"You'll be offered drugs," Dorothy said. "Better drugs than what we know you are already experimenting with now. In short, David, dear, every conceivable temptation will be yours."

"And you don't think I can handle it," David said angrily. "Well, look, I hate to shock you folks, but this doesn't sound bad to me."

"Of course not," Henry said, "because you're not yet accustomed to being a talented writer of note. If you were, you would understand how tenuous your position is—and in certain circumstances, how tenuous your hold on your talent might be."

"And what are you going to do if I take it? If I go?" David was pacing around the office by now, hands jammed into his trouser pockets.

"We'll simply be here if you need us. And I'll pray for you, dear," Dorothy said evenly. She was serious, he knew, which made the whole scene seem even more ludicrous to him.

He had gone to L.A. anyway, of course. And, as the Hillingses had foreseen, he had been thrown every temptation in the book. And, as he had hoped, he had sampled every one—many, many times. He was never able to write a second novel, so he concentrated on screenplays for four years. Eventually, he lost the ability to write *anything* very good. And so he became a producer. David became one of "them." If nothing else, it was a lot easier to make big money doing this than by being a writer.

As he reread Millicent Parks's letter, he realized it had been twenty years almost to the day since his first novel had been published. His only novel. The only thing in this world that genuinely belonged to him.

"Wow, Davey," Susie said, reading the letter he handed to her. "Mr. Rothstein was forced out of ICA by Creighton Berns? I thought he retired."

"That's what the announcement said," David sighed, sitting down. He liked Ben Rothstein a lot and had always appreciated his advice over the years. He did not feel the same way about Creighton Berns. The only time David had produced a film for him at Metropolis Pictures, it had been a horrendous experience. Berns not only played hard, he played greedy. But he was that kind of a kid. Yeah, kid. At thirty-five, he was still a kid. He made David feel ancient.

And now Creighton Berns was chairman of ICA. David's agency; the agency that was packaging his next film.

Millicent Parks's letter wanted to know if David would come to New York for a meeting to help the Hillingses.

Why didn't she just ask him outright to commit professional suicide and confirm for the Hillingses that twenty years ago they had been right and he had been wrong?

"But you can't go to this meeting!" Susie gasped, reading ahead. She looked up, panicked. "Don't they know what would happen to you and the movie if you did?"

"Don't worry about it," David said, taking the letter from her. "I'm not going and they know it."

She blinked. "Then why did they ask you, Davey?"

~ 8 ~

"You wanted to see me, sir?" Joseph Colum asked, standing inside the office in a pale gray Armani suit.

The top-floor offices of ICA were finished. The impressionist paintings had been replaced with abstract, the antiques with stainless-steel-and-leather designer furniture. The chairman was sitting behind his huge new desk, which had nothing on it but a phone console, a gold Mont Blanc pen, and a yellow legal pad.

"Close the door," Creighton directed.

His assistant pushed the heavy teak door shut with a soft click and walked over to Berns. He did not sit. He was not invited to.

"Joseph, I need to keep tabs on the Hillingses—who they see, who they're talking to. I need daily reports," Creighton said, looking up at him.

"Through me?"

"No, directly to me."

"I understand."

"That's it then," Creighton said. "Let me know how you plan to set this up."

His assistant nodded and left the office.

Creighton sat there for a moment, thinking, and then leaned forward to pick up the phone and punch in a number. "It's Creighton Berns, is she there?" A pause. "Hello yourself. Have you found anything?" Pause, listen. "Keep looking." Pause. "Okay, babe, let me know—soonest." He hung up the phone and then shook his head, as if to clear his thoughts. He sniffed once sharply, cleared his throat, and pressed the intercom button.

"Okay, Mary, I'm all yours," he said to his secretary, signaling that he was now ready to begin dealing with the ten million details that made up his new job.

∼ *9* ∼

Not for the first time did Elizabeth fly into JFK with mixed feelings. It would be good to be home, but even after all this time it was always a little confusing to remember that "home" was two separate households, her father in Greenwich, Connecticut, her mother in Rowayton, each with different spouses and different combinations of children.

Her parents' marriage had been one of those in the 1950s meant to be picture perfect. Elizabeth's mother had graduated from Wellesley and her father had graduated from Wesleyan. Her father started a banking career and married his college sweetheart. Donelly was born and then Elizabeth, and before too many years went by, Sarah, whose birth coincided with the Robinsons' big new house in North Stamford.

The family had the makings of a wonderful life: they were all healthy, they had money in the bank, a summer cottage on the Cape, and a devoted golden retriever named Trapper McGee. Just after Elizabeth turned twelve, her father and mother announced they were getting divorced. It had nothing to do with the children, they said; the marriage was simply not working—and had never really worked.

In other words, their father was in love with another woman.

He moved to New York immediately, and a year later married a young loan specialist who had once worked for him at the bank. Trapper McGee got hit by a car and died. About a year after that, Elizabeth's mother announced she was marrying the neighbor down the street, Stephen Castlehart, a man with three young children whose wife had left him to pursue a music career in Vienna. The Castleharts agreed a fresh start was in order and a new house was bought in Rowayton. Elizabeth, feeling nothing if not baffled by her parents' behavior, went off to boarding school.

As it turned out, Elizabeth's parents married well the second time around. At least, they had each married people who brought out their better sides. Elizabeth's father had undergone the most startling changes, but her mother had blossomed, too. Most significantly, she laughed a great deal because she was very often quite happy in her new life.

As a matter of fact, there had been only two times Elizabeth could remember her mother crying in this second marriage: one, when her own mother had passed away, and two, when Elizabeth had fallen, sobbing, into her mother's arms because her fiancé had run out on her and their wedding was off. "What made me think I was capable of being loved?" Elizabeth had sobbed.

"Mrs. Hillings had a heart attack," Elizabeth told her stepfather, "but she's going to be all right. It was brought on, though, by some smarmy corporate machinations by a West Coast firm and we—some of the clients—are meeting to see if there's anything we can do to help straighten things out."

"She's been very good to you," Stephen said, as if to remind himself how or why an outsider could be responsible for his step-daughter's return to the States when almost everything else had failed.

"She sure has," Elizabeth sighed, looking out the window of the navy blue Lincoln Stephen had driven to JFK. They were getting comfortable with each other again on the drive to Rowayton. Stephen was a very nice man but Elizabeth had spent maybe five minutes alone with him in twenty years.

"We were surprised when you called. Your mother and I thought you were too busy to get away, what with the TV series and your new book."

"I'm going to try to do some work while I'm here," she explained.

He smiled. "I didn't think you would leave your countess in England."

When she had been writing her thesis and then the biography from it, the family had teased Elizabeth that she couldn't go anywhere without "the duchess." And it was true, she couldn't. To move at the time would have involved the transportation of unbelievable amounts of printed material.

"I'm only bringing part of the countess over," she said, smiling. "Just enough to feel as though she's here." A 210-pound, fireproof, waterproof, pickproof steamer trunk was on its way to the Hillingses' apartment in New York by airfreight from Oxford. It cost a fortune and contained only a fraction of Elizabeth's research materials, but she wanted to be able to work on the book when she had time.

"So you're going to stay a while," Stephen said hopefully.

"We'll see how things go," she said.

"Then you can spend a week or two with us at the Cape this summer. Don and Sarah and their families will be there."

"That would be great," Elizabeth said diplomatically. Over half the conversations she had with her family involved pinning her down about when she would next see them.

"So the book is going well?" he asked, turning off the highway and onto a tree-lined secondary road.

"I think so," Elizabeth said.

After a few moments, he asked, "How *are* you, Elizabeth? Your mother worries about you."

"I'm fine, Stephen," she said quietly. "I really am."

"Are you seeing anyone?" he asked her.

"A veritable battalion of men."

"No, I'm serious," he said, glancing over.

"So am I. Any eligible man who I think won't give Mother a stroke, I'll date at least once."

"Maybe you shouldn't try so hard, Elizabeth. Just let it happen, you know?" He glanced over.

"I know," she said, looking straight ahead. She felt so disoriented when she came home. Maybe because it wasn't really home. Or maybe because she had felt so disoriented growing up here. Growing up, period. But then, she still wasn't sure she had done that, either.

She felt exhausted already.

"Good heavens," Elizabeth's mother said, "Millicent Parks! Is she still *alive? A Dark Garden* was published a hundred years ago!"

"Not quite, Beverly." Stephen laughed.

They were sitting in the den of the house in Rowayton. Pictures of all the children and grandchildren were scattered about. Through the windows and sliding glass doors, the jade green lawn sloped down to Long Island Sound. Elizabeth was trying to explain what she was going to be doing in New York, why she had come back from England, but the Castleharts were obviously still puzzled as to why Elizabeth would show up for the Hillingses, after years of bypassing all other requests for her to visit *them*.

"But darling, they're old, they *should* be retired," her mother said. "It sounds to me like the last thing Mrs. Hillings needs is more work. Maybe this is a blessing in disguise."

Her mother, Elizabeth knew, was jealous of Dorothy Hillings. Before the agent had appeared in her daughter's life, in her mother's mind Elizabeth had been an aspiring college professor; one who would teach, get married, have children, and live a nice conventional life. After Mrs. Hillings it was notoriety, best-seller lists, talk shows, movie stars, money, and, of course, that no-good man who had nearly destroyed her daughter's life. And who had introduced them? The Hillingses! And then Hollywood! Good God, Elizabeth abandoning Columbia and turning down a teaching position at Yale to live in Hollywood and teach at UCLA! Who could *not* have seen the disaster that was to come?

"At the very least, Mother, the Hillingses should have the right to oversee the transfer of their clients' representation."

"But won't your involvement hurt you with your new agent? With ICA?" Stephen asked.

"It shouldn't." She tried to sound more certain than she actually felt.

"I think you may be a bit naive," he told her.

Her mother sighed. "Elizabeth has always been naive."

"In any event," Elizabeth continued, "I met Millicent Parks a few years ago—"

"That must have been before you moved to England," her mother said. Elizabeth added the unspoken words she knew her mother was thinking, which were, "unless something has happened to you we don't know about, because you have utterly ceased to function socially since you came home brokenhearted from California."

"Uh, yes," Elizabeth said, "it was before. At any rate, she's organized a meeting in New York—"

"How old is Millicent Parks now?" Stephen asked. Now that he was retired and getting on in years, he was obsessed with how old people were and their state of health.

Elizabeth realized that her mother and stepfather's interest in the Hillingses' problems was severely flagging now. "In her early seventies, I think." She smiled and added, "But she doesn't look anything like you do. But then, few people look as well as you two always do, no matter what age they are."

Her mother beamed. Even after everything that had happened, Elizabeth was still her good girl.

∼ *10* ∼

It took Creighton Berns at least five minutes to get across the room at Le Dome. He was the new powerhouse in town, and everyone was eager to have a word with him—or, better yet, a project. David, in fact, had been shocked to be asked to lunch; he was not considered a big player, not at all. And so the fact that Creighton felt free to arrive twenty minutes late and then take his time, shaking hands, patting backs, accepting the glory that was now his as chairman of ICA, did not surprise him.

"You've got the green light on your project," Creighton told him in a loud voice as he finally approached the table. "I thought you'd like to know right off."

Clearly it was a statement meant to be heard. And it was.

David stood up and held out his hand. "Creighton, how are you?" They shook hands and when they were seated, David said, "That's great news, thank you."

"It's a terrific package for the firm. Serial killers are very big. We should be thanking you."

They ordered mineral waters and grilled chicken salads and started going over the package, the roster of ICA clients who could potentially be involved with the movie.

"Did you know Dorothy Hillings had a heart attack a couple of weeks ago?" Creighton said out of the blue.

"Yes, I heard." David took a sip of his sparkling water. "I sent her some flowers."

"I did, too," Creighton said, taking a bite of salad and chewing slowly. "So what do you think about the merger?"

Merger? David thought. Was he kidding? Is that what he still called it? Terrorist takeover of Hillings & Hillings was more like it.

"It doesn't really affect me," David said. "The Hillingses represented the novel that I wrote years ago, but ICA's been my agent ever since."

"Right," Creighton said. They ate in silence for a while. "I've heard something about a meeting in New York next week. Do you know anything about it?"

"I might have heard something," David said, hoping his tone was as casual as he was trying to make it sound.

"You going?"

David looked at him sharply, surprised that he'd ask. "No."

Creighton's eyebrows went up. "Not even if it could be helpful to me?"

The little fuck wanted him to be his spy. And David knew better than to think the green light would stay green on his movie if he didn't do as Creighton wanted. David swallowed the food he was chewing and wiped his mouth with his napkin. "I really don't want to do it," he said.

"But you will if I ask you to," Creighton told him.

After a moment, David nodded.

"Good," Creighton said, picking up his fork. "Because I'm asking you to."

~ *11* ~

"No, baby, why would you want to?" Ted asked her, tipping back in the kitchen chair in the precise manner she had begged him not to for the last eighteen years.

Patty Kleczak was cleaning up after dinner and, for the tenth time, they were discussing the letter Millicent Parks had sent about the meeting in New York.

"I want to see what they have to say," she replied, wiping the countertop with a sponge. "Mrs. Hillings worked on my book for eleven years, honey! I can't just let these people in California take it away from her after all that. I need to at least find out what's going on."

"But she *sold* the agency to them, didn't she?" Ted asked, reaching for the jar of Oreos.

"Yes and no. I mean, in the letter the Hillingses sent me before the merger, they said they'd continue to be my agents. But now, suddenly, ICA just *tells* me the Hillingses are no longer with the agency and I'm supposed to send them the manuscript and forget all about Mrs. Hillings. I mean, honey, if it was all fair and square, why do they have to ask *me* for a copy of the manuscript? Why don't they already have it from Hillings & Hillings?"

"Maybe they want to make sure they have the most recent copy," her husband suggested. "It's not as if there haven't been a hundred versions."

"But the letter from Millicent Parks; I can't just ignore that. What if there has been some sort of foul play? At least I should find out."

Ted looked uncomfortable. He always did when he suddenly

suspected that his view of a situation might not be completely allied with the rules of good sportsmanship.

"Honey, look," he finally said, "you're completely new to this. You've been working for eleven years on that book, and there's no reason to risk your success now. Mrs. Hillings told you that she thought she could get in the neighborhood of a hundred and fifty thousand for it. But now an agent at ICA represents you, who says she thinks she can get you the same money. Since the Hillingses sold ICA the right to sell the book, let ICA go ahead and sell it. Let's get your money, *then* you can go and find out what's going on."

It made Patty smile the way Ted bandied about that sum of money now. Three months ago he had been incredulous, and then frightened by it.

"What do you mean, a hundred fifty thousand?" he had said, his face turning blotchy.

"Well, it's not going to be paid out all at once," Patty had explained, trying not to explode with pride. Eleven years of writing, eleven years of her family resenting those few hours every other day when she refused to answer their pleas (which always began the second they suspected she was on her way upstairs to write), eleven years of writing on blind faith, eleven years of revisions—laboriously following Mrs. Hillings's advice—and then that fateful day when Dorothy Hillings telephoned and said, "My dear? I've called to congratulate you. The book is finished and is ready to be sold. It will be published to great acclaim, too, I believe. And, if I'm not mistaken, tremendous sales will follow. You're an extremely talented writer and storyteller and I am very proud to be representing you."

Only that very morning Patty had been wondering what it would be like to have enough money to buy all new underwear. Underwear she *liked*, not the kind that lasted ten million washes, which of course was the kind she was always forced to buy. She was so tired of being sensible.

After the call, Patty had persuaded Ted to go into New York City with her so that they could have lunch with Mrs. Hillings, and Ted could learn a bit about how the book publishing business worked. While the trip did nothing to assuage Ted's fears about New York, his fear about the sum of money vanished, because it had been put into a perspective that couldn't fail to reassure him.

"My dear Mr. Kleczak," Mrs. Hillings had said, "let us take the sum of one hundred and fifty thousand dollars. This will probably be paid out in installments of, say, fifty thousand on the signing of the contract, twenty-five thousand on the delivery of a complete and satisfactory manuscript—which I think your wife has most adeptly produced, although her editor may ask for further revisions—twenty-five thousand on the hardcover publication of the novel, which would be about one year later, and then fifty thousand on the publication of the paperback edition, which would be slightly less than two years after the contract is signed, I'm sure.

"And you must remember," she continued in her soft, earnest voice, speaking directly to Ted, "that Hillings & Hillings receives fifteen percent of *all* earnings on the book. And so, right there, the advance I have predicted I can get for your wife will be reduced to one hundred and twenty-seven thousand, five hundred dollars.

"And so, Mr. Kleczak, when you consider that it took Patricia eleven years to write the novel and that she will have to wait one year for it to be published in hardcover, and then another year for the paperback, that adds up to an investment of thirteen years." She paused, smiling sympathetically. "And that, I'm afraid, works out to be only around ninety-eight hundred dollars a year in income—well below the poverty level in this country." Pause. "And so I am ever so grateful to you, Mr. Kleczak, for not only supporting your family very well over the years, but for enabling your wife to develop her craft. I know she is delighted to be in a position to make a significant financial contribution to her family after all of your support."

Ted had beamed. Suddenly Patty's new career was a family achievement, a perspective he desperately needed since everything about his wife seemed to be changing after eighteen years.

And so Ted was comfortable enough now to bandy about the probable sum of her advance like it was the norm, and the kids had learned that adults were always responsive to them when they made a casual reference to *their mom the writer.* "Mom's agent's

ICA," Patty had overheard Kevin explain to the meter reader recently.

"Ted," Patty said, coming over to the kitchen table to sit next to him and unconsciously pulling his chair back down to all fours with a solid thump, "there would be no book if it hadn't been for Mrs. Hillings. I would have given up years ago." She kissed his cheek. "Honey, the letter said ICA had acted unfairly, without conscience. The other clients are asking for my help. How can I say no?"

"The other clients are established and have a lot of money." Ted's voice had begun to weaken. "And I think Mrs. Hillings would be the first person to tell you to stay out of this." He brightened, a new idea coming to him. "If she needed your help, wouldn't *she* have asked you?"

"No," Patty said.

He looked uncomfortable again.

"I hear what you're saying, honey, but I just don't know," Patty murmured, resting her hand on his thigh and dropping her forehead down on his shoulder.

"You don't want to get hurt, baby," Ted said, rubbing her back. "You haven't done anything to anyone—and you deserve your day in the sun."

Patty raised her head. "Then why do I feel so awful?"

"Oh, baby, you were raised to feel guilty," he said, yawning and giving her a hug. She noticed, for the first time, how bloodshot his eyes were, how hard he was trying to stay awake, even though he was dead on his feet. He had taught all day and traveled to and from a track meet twenty miles away. Patty loved him, she really loved him.

"I want to go see her, Ted. At least I could do that. She's been in the hospital for over two weeks."

He frowned, yawned again, and then nodded. "Okay. Why don't you go see her, if it'll make you feel better."

And so the Kleczaks went upstairs to bed and fell asleep quickly, with only one of them knowing that Patty had made up her mind to go to the meeting of the clients after visiting Mrs. Hillings in the hospital. Conveniently, Ted had never asked when the meeting was going to be.

"Hello," Elizabeth said softly, standing by Dorothy's bedside.

Mrs. Hillings, looking thin and pale against the pillows of her hospital bed, was wearing a beautiful blue silk dressing gown which matched the blue of her eyes exactly. "Hello, Elizabeth dear," she said, smiling and pushing her hand across the bedcovers toward her.

"Oh, Dorothy," Elizabeth murmured, feeling close to tears. She leaned over and kissed her.

"Sit and tell me how you are," Dorothy directed, patting the bed.

Elizabeth did as she was told. She was fine, home on a holiday to see her family. She had heard the news of Dorothy's illness and had wanted to see her. Henry had very kindly offered her the guest room at their apartment.

"And how is our friend the countess?"

"Oh, she's wonderful. She's arriving on Monday." One of the things she had always loved about Dorothy was how she spoke of the subjects of Elizabeth's work as if they were her dearest friends. Of course, by the time Elizabeth finished writing a book, they were.

"Is she arriving by ship, perhaps?" Dorothy inquired.

"By air," Elizabeth admitted, laughing, "in a roomy steamer trunk. She always prefers speed to comfort."

The room was choked with flowers and Elizabeth was glad she had brought a Sony Walkman and an audio tape of Trollope's *Barchester Towers* for Dorothy instead.

Elizabeth left when a woman arrived to be interviewed for the position of Mrs. Hillings's household aide after Dorothy's release. Elizabeth thought this was rushing things a bit, but she was glad to see her agent was so optimistic.

The Hillingses' apartment often took people's breath away. It was located on the east side of Gramercy Park, an old and elegant square which lies between Twentieth and Twenty-first streets, and Park Avenue South and Third Avenue. In the nineteenth century a bright real-estate developer had offered prospective buyers a novel idea: a regal square whose residents would *own* the green, tree-shaded park in the middle of it. When each new owner closed on his home, he would receive a set of golden keys to the park. Well over a century later, the eight-foot iron fence still surrounds the park, and after many unsuccessful attempts by business groups to raze the park so Lexington Avenue could continue its commercial assault all the way downtown, Gramercy Park remains largely the way it always has been—beautiful and quiet, the keys to the park still in the possession of residents.

After the British had overthrown the Dutch colony of New Amsterdam in 1664, they changed the city's name to New York and tried to erase the city's cultural and hereditary ties to Holland by refashioning the names of the geographical areas. The origin of the distinguished Gramercy Park name is in actuality quite humble. The Dutch had named the area *Krom Moerasje*, "little crooked swamp," which the English later changed to Crommashie Hill. In 1831, when the developer wished to drain the marsh and create an urban paradise, he wisely changed the name to Gramercy Park, thus imbuing the area with entirely mythical ties to England, unless you counted the exquisitely modeled buildings' resemblance to the best squares in London.

Sometimes being a historian could be a bit of a pain, Elizabeth decided, walking to the Hillingses' building. While other people could simply enjoy the beauty of the square, Elizabeth had to imagine what a mess the park must have been in 1863, when federal troops had to camp there during the Draft Riots.

She entered the Hillingses' building, number 34, one of the two original apartment buildings on the square. While the other houses which dominated the square were of English design, Richard M. Hunt had created his own version of French Empire for number 34. It was a gorgeous, soaring old building with an enormous octagonal turret and an octagonal courtyard in the middle. The bay windows and panels of foliated details were original. So was the Tiffany glass dome in the entryway.

The doorman greeted Elizabeth and the elevator man took her up to the Hillingses' apartment. Their home took up an entire floor. It was a charming but decidedly unusual place since it, like the building, was octagonal in shape. Elizabeth stepped out of the elevator into a foyer which was actually in the middle of the apartment. To the left was the living room, which overlooked the park. Through an open archway stood a formal dining room, which also overlooked the park. A swinging door led into the kitchen, which looked inside to the courtyard and which, in turn, had a door back out to the foyer.

Leaving the foyer again, but taking a right led to a study and a powder room, and across the hall, a guest room and bath looking inside to the courtyard. Farther down the hall (which angled off to the right) there was another very small bedroom across the hall, and then, finally, the hallway ended at the entrance to the Hillingses' suite: a bedroom, which looked out to the East River and was linked to the inside by a dressing room and then a bathroom that looked down on the courtyard.

Despite the building's French design, the Hillingses' taste in furniture ran to English, no doubt due to Mrs. Hillings's English-Canadian ancestry. The living room's treasures included an eighteenth-century secretary Elizabeth would have given her right arm to own. The rest of the furniture was mostly Empire: dark mahogany sofas, settees, and chairs upholstered in rich, faded orange and red. The paintings were mostly by imitators of Turner and other landscape artists. The Persian rugs in the living room and dining room were gorgeous. They had come from Dorothy's grandmother's house in Westmount, Montreal, and, before that, *her* grandmother's grandmother's house in Manchester Square, London.

What really made the apartment was the obvious time and effort that had gone into the lighting design. At the turn of a few dials, what could have easily been a dark and museumlike atmosphere could be illuminated to varying degrees, from a hushed, romantic retreat to a bright and far more contemporary looking house.

Today, however, there were few lights on at all. Elizabeth found Henry and Millicent Parks in the dining room with papers strewn around them and a strong afternoon sun streaming in. Henry looked exhausted and thin, but Elizabeth was struck by Millicent's fine color and stalwart presence. Obviously it was she who was helping to keep Henry going.

After Elizabeth was settled at the table with a cup of tea—which the Hillingses' housekeeper, Sasha, poured for her—the three set to business.

"Okay now, let's see," Henry said, lifting his refilled cup, reading glasses perched on the end of his nose. He swallowed and continued. "The noteworthy attendees who've responded are—by the way, Elizabeth, this absolutely cannot reach Dorothy's ears. The doctor said no stress—none—at least until the angioplasty is done." He sighed, dropping his head in his hand. "I'm beginning to wish I hadn't started any of this."

"We're not backing out now, Hill," Millicent said. When her friend didn't answer, she looked to Elizabeth. "Talk to him. He thinks you're very bright."

Elizabeth reached over to give his arm a squeeze. "I think, Henry—no, I *know*—we're all going to feel much better when we find out why ICA has acted the way it has. Your part is nearly over; it's time for us—your friends—to find out for you. And to straighten it all out."

Henry took off his glasses, pinched the bridge of his nose, and said, "What kind of lawyer gets his own company taken from him, Elizabeth? Doe kept asking me if I was sure we should do this deal with ICA. She wondered where we'd be if something happened to Ben." He sighed, rubbing his eyes. "I should have listened."

"You had only been doing business with ICA for thirty-eight years, Hill!" Millicent said. "How were you to know that nearly four decades of loyalty and honor could be erased overnight?"

"Where is Ben now?" Elizabeth asked. "Is he coming?"

"We haven't the slightest idea where he is," Millicent sniffed.

"I know where he is," Henry said to her.

"In Bora Bora!" Millicent cried.

"I know how to find him if I need him," Henry said.

"Well I should think you'd consider needing him now!" Millicent said.

"Does he know about Dorothy's heart attack? Or what happened to Hillings & Hillings?" Elizabeth asked Henry.

"No," he said. He looked at Millicent. "Leave him out of it, Millicent, I'm warning you. His position is too tenuous to involve him either."

"Well," Elizabeth said, a bit at a loss still about what exactly it was they were to get involved in, "who is coming to this meeting?"

"Montgomery Grant Smith is definitely coming," Millicent said.

"Really?" Henry said, eyes brightening. "Monty is? That's wonderful."

"I'm sorry, but I'm afraid I don't know who Montgomery Grant Smith is," Elizabeth said, taking a biscuit from a plate in the center of the table.

"He's a right-wing buffoon who has overthrown American radio in your absence," Millicent explained.

Elizabeth was squinting, looking at Henry. "Didn't he write a play or something once?"

"Good memory," Henry said. "But that was a long time ago. Monty's a political commentator now—"

"David Brinkley would have a stroke if he heard you say that," Millicent said.

"He has an enormously successful daily talk show, national," Henry continued. "He does wonderful satire in political sound bites and he can talk a blue streak to prove just about any point he wants to make. And while his focus is political, there is also an unmistakable entertainment value to his work."

"In other words," Millicent confided to Elizabeth, "he's a complete jackass."

"Whose book, *Visions for America*," Henry added, "has been on the best-seller list for two solid years."

Millicent laughed. "Are you implying that I'm jealous?"

Clearly, Elizabeth thought, she was.

"I do not want you insulting him," Henry told his friend. "He's a very busy man and he must have gone to a great deal of trouble to rearrange his schedule to come."

"Whatever," Millicent said, looking at the list again. "Now, who else do we have coming? We've got Elizabeth here—La Profesora, I like to think of you as, I hope you don't mind. I once wrote a novel where the heroine was a professor in Mexico."

"*The Teacher*," Elizabeth said. "I enjoyed it very much."

Millicent positively beamed. "Oh, did Dorothy send it to you?"

"No, I bought it," Elizabeth said. "Though, I must admit, Dorothy did tell me about it."

Millicent cocked an eyebrow. "Well isn't it wonderfully kind of you, Elizabeth. Thank you." She looked at the list again, a touch of pink in her cheeks.

Henry turned to Elizabeth and winked. He had guessed right. If there was anyone who could get along with Millicent, it would be Elizabeth.

"Oh, Hill," Millicent suddenly said. "I heard from that young lady in New Jersey this morning. But I didn't know what to tell her, because you said you'd had second thoughts about whether or not she should participate."

"Mrs. Kleczak?" Henry said.

Millicent nodded. "And she says she'll be at the meeting come hell or high water." Pause. "Well, that's not exactly what she said, but that's what she *sounded* like."

"I'm sorry," Elizabeth said, "she is . . . ?"

"A very talented young housewife who has written a first-rate romantic suspense novel," Henry said. "Doe was just getting ready to sell the book when . . . everything happened. ICA has already made a move to sell it."

"Uh-oh," Elizabeth said. "In that case, Mrs. Kleczak may either be extremely loyal or extremely foolhardy. I can't imagine her involvement would go over well with ICA." When she saw how concerned Henry looked, she hastily added, "So I'll make sure to keep an eye out for her, Henry. I'll look after her, I promise."

He gave her a grateful look, which made Elizabeth wince inside. He looked so old and beaten!

"Oh, heavens, how could I forget?" Millicent said, looking at the list. "The crazy Cubans are coming."

"We don't have any Cuban clients," Henry said.

"Of course you do," Millicent said. "Louise and Jordan Wells."

"The screenwriters?" Elizabeth asked. "I thought they were from Puerto Rico."

"They are," Henry sighed, rolling his eyes. "It's just that Millicent still hasn't forgiven him for spilling tomato juice on her white rug twenty years ago."

"He never properly apologized," Millicent said, defending herself.

"Perhaps if you hadn't called him Ricky Ricardo, he would have," Henry said.

"All I know," Millicent said, shrugging, "is the first time I met him his name was Jorge Ricardo or something and he wrote novels, and the next time he was Jordan, of Jordan and Louise Wells, Hollywood TV writers, and he was spilling tomato juice on my new carpet."

Henry looked even more exhausted than before.

Millicent returned to her list, smiling happily. "This will make you feel better, Hill—Georgiana Hamilton-Ayres is coming."

"But ICA is Georgiana's agent," Henry fretted. "She shouldn't get involved in this."

"Why not? She's a big client of theirs," Millicent said.

"Well, there are—well," Henry said, "other considerations."

"Like what?" Millicent asked. "The mother?"

"Lilliana Bartlett?" Elizabeth said. "Is she a client of yours?"

"We represented her autobiography years ago," Henry explained. "That's how we became close family friends. Georgiana lived with us for a couple of years while her mother was, well, not up to taking care of her."

"What on earth could ICA do to poor Lily that she hasn't already done to herself?" Millicent wanted to know.

"It is not about Lily and I'd prefer to let the whole subject pass," Henry said carefully, which immediately made Elizabeth wonder what he was holding back about Georgiana Hamilton-Ayres.

"Let's see," Millicent said, looking at the list, "I think that's it for the big guns. The rest of the people coming have names the press will recognize, but don't have any clout—financially, I mean—with ICA."

Elizabeth cleared her throat. "I suspect Montgomery Grant Smith might well be our strongest asset. People expect writers and artists and actors and academics to protest the abuses of big business, but they're not accustomed to hearing conservatives object to it. And so if we could persuade Mr. Smith to be our official spokesperson . . ." She let her voice trail suggestively.

Millicent looked at Henry. "My, but she *is* a bright girl." She turned to Elizabeth. "It's lovely that we have so very much in common."

Elizabeth smiled. "Yes, it is," she said graciously.

~ *13* ~

Elizabeth and Millicent were in perfect agreement; 101 Fifth Avenue was a grand old office building. In the beginning, back in 1947, after Henry decided he hated being a tax lawyer and Dorothy said she needed more to do than sit at home crying because the twins never stopped crying, the Hillingses had leased a tiny office on the second floor.

"I loved it then," Millicent said, "because for six months I was their only client." She laughed. "I wish you could have been there, Elizabeth. Hill sat behind a small desk, all dressed up. Dorothy sat in a chair next to him in her Sunday best—and the twins sat behind them in their playpen screaming bloody murder. What a lovely agency!"

It was a particularly funny image for Elizabeth because the only Hillings & Hillings establishment she had ever known was the elegant penthouse offices that took up the entire eleventh floor. She laughed, enjoying Millicent's memory.

Suddenly Millicent looked at her watch. "We had better go over this once more."

Elizabeth nodded quickly. "I go up to the eleventh floor," she began.

"See if you can tell who's in charge up there," Millicent said. "Tell them you've been out of the country for a long time and you stopped by to surprise the Hillingses and let them know you are back for a nice, *long* stay."

"And whom do you suppose I'm going to find up there?" she asked, looking up at the offices.

"That's what we need you to find out, my girl."

Elizabeth nodded. "All right then, I best be on my way. Where will you be?"

"The Book Friends Café. It's just around the corner on Eighteenth and they have lovely tea."

"Hello," she said, holding her hand out to the man standing in the doorway of the offices. "I'm Elizabeth Robinson, a client of

Hillings & Hillings, and I'm afraid I'm a bit confused as to who you are, exactly."

"James Stanley Johnson," the young man said, shaking her hand. He was in an expensively cut pin-striped suit, but his jacket was off, his silk tie was loose, his collar unbuttoned, and the expensive white linen sleeves of his shirt were rolled up over his wrists to show a Rolex watch. He was balding, wore wire-rim glasses, tasseled loafers, and was looking very hot, tired, and harassed. Certainly he was a contrast to the Hillings & Hillings staff Elizabeth had always known, the energetic young people at various apprenticeship levels who were always dashing about with friendly efficiency.

Elizabeth waited a moment and then asked with a nice smile, "And what do you do here, James Stanley Johnson?"

"Uh," he said, standing there, clearly uncertain as to what to say.

"May I come in?" Elizabeth asked him.

"Uh," he said again.

"Miz Ballicutt wants to see you," a gruff male voice said.

James Stanley Johnson, using his body to shield the view from Elizabeth, said over his shoulder, "I'll be there in a minute."

Elizabeth took the opportunity to push the door open and walk into what used to be the gracious reception area of Hillings & Hillings. Today it looked like the set of "Romper Room" gone mad. Books were pulled down from the shelves and boxes and papers were everywhere. The man who had spoken to James Stanley Johnson wore dirty gray overalls and looked more like a garage mechanic than an office worker.

"You can't go in there," James Stanley Johnson said as Elizabeth started toward the hall.

"Of course I can," she said, walking on, "the Hillingses won't mind." She hurried down the hall, inwardly flinching at what she saw on the way to the Hillingses' connecting offices: file cabinets had been flung open; desk drawers were pulled onto the floor; files, papers, and computer disks were everywhere. Given that the Hillingses had always been sticklers for neatness and organization, it was a rather horrifying sight.

Elizabeth turned the corner and charged into Mrs. Hillings's

Laura Van Wormer

office, nearly colliding with a woman standing in the middle of the room. She was a very tall redhead, dressed in a sleek dark suit, who whirled around to glare at Elizabeth. But only for a moment, because she recognized her and a smile quickly replaced the frown. "You're Elizabeth Robinson, aren't you?" she said, holding out her hand. "I am an enormous fan of your work."

"I'm sorry, I missed your name," Elizabeth said, not yet shaking hands.

"Marion Ballicutt," the woman said, "legal counsel to International Communications Artists—and so, I am, in effect, your legal counsel as well."

"Oh, on the television series," Elizabeth said, taking her hand, "I'm very pleased to meet you."

"And that's my associate, James Johnson," she gestured to the distressed-looking man standing in the doorway behind Elizabeth.

"We've met," Elizabeth said, walking across the office, looking around. "If you don't mind my asking, what on earth are you people doing? The Hillingses will have a stroke when they see this mess."

"We're trying to spare Mrs. Hillings any more stress," Marion said smoothly. "That's why we're consolidating files while she's not here."

How easy the words come, Elizabeth thought. But then, Marion Ballicutt was a lawyer.

"And what do you do, James?" Elizabeth suddenly asked, turning to face him. "Are you also an attorney?"

He looked first at Marion and then Elizabeth. "I'm ICA's senior accountant," he said quietly.

"Ah," Elizabeth said, perching on the edge of the windowsill, "doing the books." She looked down at Fifth Avenue and then asked, "And where's everybody else? Henry and Dorothy and Sally and Reb and Blakey and Sid and Jessie?" Only then did she turn around.

Marion was trying to figure out where Elizabeth's questions were heading. "With the merger," she said carefully, "these offices will no longer be necessary."

Elizabeth frowned and crossed her arms over her chest. "Look," she said, "I hate to be a bother, but since I am a best-selling writer for Hillings & Hillings, you'll have to excuse me if I seem a trifle

68 ~

annoyed. I've been overseas for quite some time, and as far as I knew, when I stopped in today I was stopping in to see my longtime agent and friend Dorothy Hillings, and instead I find a lawyer and an accountant tearing her office apart and talking about a merger."

James looked at Marion. Marion gazed steadily at Elizabeth. "You mean you haven't heard about the merger?"

"Merger with whom?"

"ICA," James said.

"I don't know what the devil you're talking about," Elizabeth lied. "ICA represented us on the movie deal, I know, and my television program, but this . . ." She wrinkled her forehead. "Should I call Ben Rothstein and talk to him?"

Marion continued to gaze steadily at Elizabeth, meeting her eye. "Mr. Rothstein has retired," she said evenly, "as have the Hillingses. How long have you been away, exactly?"

"Long enough, clearly." Elizabeth was looking around again, trying to figure out what was really going on here.

"But all of the Hillingses' clients were sent letters about the merger," Marion said. "Someone had to have signed for yours."

"Well, I don't know about that," Elizabeth said, lying again. "But I do know that I am finishing a new book and I would certainly appreciate knowing what in God's name is going on around here."

"Yes, of course," Marion said.

Elizabeth gestured to a chair. "So perhaps you would be so kind, Marion, as to explain the situation to me. Because if you are, indeed, the legal counsel for ICA, and ICA has taken over Hillings & Hillings, you should be looking after my interests—isn't that right? And so I would appreciate a full and immediate accounting of what, exactly, is going on."

"Of course," she said, not missing a beat, "let me give you my card." She pulled one out of her blazer pocket and handed it to Elizabeth. "You should call my office for an appointment, I'm afraid, because I'm due in court within the hour. Otherwise I would be delighted to talk with you now. What bad luck."

Right, Elizabeth thought, taking her card.

Marion Ballicutt and James Stanley Johnson stood there, waiting for her to get up. She didn't. "So why don't *you* talk to me instead, James?" Elizabeth suggested.

"No," Marion Ballicutt said, "we're leaving now. James has to get back to ICA."

"Oh, I see." After a moment, Elizabeth smiled and added, "Well, then, I'll just wait so I can walk out with you, because I certainly don't have anyplace I need to be."

Elizabeth tore into the Book Friends Café and spotted Millicent at a table near the back. With her was a very big man—a little older than herself, perhaps—who was shoveling bites of apple pie and vanilla ice cream into his mouth as she arrived.

"Elizabeth!" Millicent said, looking relieved. "This is Montgomery Grant Smith, the radio talk-show host whom I told you about. I called Hill after we parted and Mr. Smith was there, so I told him he might as well come over." Judging from the expression on Millicent's face, clearly she believed this to have been a mistake.

Montgomery Grant Smith carefully put his fork down, patted his mouth with his napkin, and hauled himself out of the creaking wooden chair. He was at least six feet three and big.

"Hello," Elizabeth said, shaking his hand, "it's very nice to meet you."

"Probably the first and last time any academic ever said that to me," Smith said, shaking her hand. "Please," he said, gesturing to an empty chair. Elizabeth thanked him and sat down. "May I order you something?" he asked, sitting next to her.

"Tea, please, Earl Grey," she said. "But may I have a sip of your water in the meantime?"

"It's all yours," he said, sliding it over to her. "So what's going on up there?"

Elizabeth swallowed and put the glass down. "There was a lawyer named Marion Ballicutt who says she's legal counsel for ICA, and an ICA accountant named James Stanley Johnson—"

"Quite a day for the pompous," Millicent said. "He sounds like a relative of yours, Montgomery Grant Smith."

Montgomery Grant Smith ignored Millicent, took out a pen and index card from his inside jacket pocket, and scribbled down the names Elizabeth had mentioned.

"It looks like they're going through the files," Elizabeth continued. "There's some sort of a workman up there with them. I haven't a clue who he is, but he's a rather mean looking fellow in dirty overalls, the sort one sees at a rundown gas station."

"Were they packing files, or just looking through them?" Smith asked her, shoveling the last of his sweets in his mouth and dropping his fork.

"I'm not sure, but the place is a mess. I think they've left for the day now. When I made it clear that I was going to stay as long as they did, they all suddenly had appointments, so I waited to go out with them."

Montgomery Grant Smith considered this a moment and suddenly heaved himself up from his chair. "I'll see you ladies tomorrow," he said, placing a ten-dollar bill on the table. "There's somebody I've got to talk to about this."

"I hope your day is as pleasant as you are," Millicent told him.

Montgomery Grant Smith looked at her. "Likewise, ma'am, I'm sure." Then he looked under the table, muttering, "Good, no pocketbook this time." To Elizabeth, he bowed, "Ladies," and then he hurried outside where they watched him flag a cab.

"What was that about a pocketbook?" Elizabeth asked.

"I cannot possibly imagine," Millicent said haughtily, catching the waiter's eye. "Waiter, bring this young lady a pot of Earl Grey tea, hot, and a scone, please."

~ *14* ~

It seemed to Henry Hillings that he had just laid down for a nap when the phone rang. Disoriented, he fumbled, first to find the telephone and then to pick it up. "Hello?"

"Darling, you're exhausted, I knew it."

"Doe?" he said.

"Hi, dear," she said brightly. "I thought I should call you and tell you that I have definitely taken a turn for the better and the doctor quite agrees. I feel much, much better."

"That's wonderful," he said.

"Elizabeth's been here all afternoon and evening."

Evening? Henry looked at the clock. Good God, he *had* fallen asleep. It was nearly six.

"We went for a walk around the hospital and it was simply marvelous, just to get a breath of fresh air—"

"But, Doe, you mustn't overdo—"

"Well that's just the point, darling, I did overdo and I'm calling to tell you that I'm going to go to bed very early and so you must not come tonight."

The thought of staying in tonight and having dinner and a quiet glass of wine and then going to bed sounded too good to be true. Lord, he was tired. And so he did not protest as he told his wife he loved her, and that she should call him anytime if she wanted to talk, and that he would see her in the morning.

"Oh, and, darling?" she said. "That woman Bernadette came again and Elizabeth liked her, too, so I told her she had the job."

"Oh, that's great, Doe," Henry said. "But let's not rush things."

"I'm not rushing things," Dorothy said, "I just want to get out of here as soon as I can."

"I'm not worried about getting you out, darling," Henry assured his wife. "I just want to make sure there's someone to help me tie you down when you decide to rebuild the house or something while you're supposedly waiting to get your strength back." They both laughed and said good night.

Almost as soon as Henry hung up, the phone rang again. This time it was Joshua Lafayette. "Henry," Josh said in his firm young lawyer's voice, "I've got good news and bad news."

"Did Monty find you?" Henry asked him.

"That's the good news. He was not only here, but he's hired a private investigator to watch your offices. Evidently Elizabeth Robinson was up there today—"

"Yes, I know all about that," Henry said. "What is the bad news?"

"Montgomery Grant Smith absolutely refuses to work with Millicent Parks. He came barreling in here today insisting that Millicent is a doddering old lefty and that somebody has to take charge before she wrecks everything. On top of everything else, he claims she tripped him with her pocketbook on some podium in Chicago a few years ago." Pause. "He fell into someone's lunch?"

"And who does Monty think should take charge of the clients' meeting?" Henry asked, already knowing the answer.

"Montgomery Grant Smith, of course," Josh said. "And I don't mind telling you, Henry, I'm not sure even I can put up with that kind of arrogance."

"Monty's?" Henry asked.

"Montgomery Grant Smith's *and* Millicent Parks's," Josh said. "Henry, you have to do something. I see disaster written all over those two."

"Elizabeth? Is that you?" Henry called later that night when he heard the front door close.

"Yes," she called. And in a moment, she appeared in the study doorway, smiling. "She really is on the mend, Henry. It's a wonderful sight to behold. I think she'll sail through this angioplasty procedure."

"Let us hope so," he sighed, smiling.

"But now she's worried about you," Elizabeth added. "And I must admit, I am a bit concerned myself about the strain you've been under."

"I am too, Elizabeth, and that's why I wish to speak to you. Sit down, please."

Some three hours later, Elizabeth was on the telephone, leaving a message on Montgomery Grant Smith's hotel voice mail.

"Hello, Montgomery, this is Elizabeth Robinson calling," she said. "If you get in before, say, midnight, would you please call me at the Hillingses'?" She repeated one of the Gramercy Park apartment's three phone numbers and hung up. Crossing her arms over her chest, she turned to look at Henry. "You understand that I am a teacher by nature, not a general?" she asked him.

"Oh, of course, Elizabeth," Henry said, straightening the pile of papers he had gone over with her.

"And that I don't know half of these people, even by reputation?"

"I understand that."

"And that the legal parts of things—"

"Joshua will handle," Henry said. "You call him whenever you need him. He'll be there every step of the way."

"And Montgomery—"

"You will use him, but keep him in check. I'm sure you can manage it, Elizabeth, I have every confidence. Millicent, too."

"Henry," she said, looking at him.

"Yes?" He looked old. And so very tired.

Elizabeth went over and wrapped her arms around him. "I love you," she said. "But you must swear to me that you will absent yourself entirely from all this and get some rest. You cannot go on like this."

"You have my word," he said. He hesitated and then kissed her cheek and squeezed her hand. "Thank you, Elizabeth, from the bottom of my heart. With you around, I know I need not worry."

Elizabeth could only hope to God he was right. Functioning in the everyday world was certainly not her strong point.

~ 15 ~

It had been a most unsatisfactory day for Monty, full of unpleasant surprises. The first was how terrible Henry Hillings looked. When Monty saw him at the Gramercy Park apartment his immediate thought had been, He's going to die if he keeps this up. Henry's cheeks were hollow, he had violet bags under his eyes, and his pallor seemed nearly as gray as his hair. And so right then and there Monty realized he had no choice but to straighten this mess out for the Hillingses, which meant staying in New York for as long as it took.

Millicent Parks was the second unpleasant surprise. He had restrained himself from murdering her three years ago when she tripped him on the podium at that book and author luncheon and sent him crashing down onto Susan Isaacs' lunch, but he wasn't so sure he could restrain himself now. So if he was to straighten out this Hillings & Hillings/ICA mess, the first thing he needed to do was send that Parks woman back to wherever she had come from.

As for the professor woman, Elizabeth Robinson, he wasn't sure what to make of her. She certainly looked more like Katharine

Hepburn than any kind of historian Monty had ever met. His hopes for her ability to work with him, however, were not high; she was good-looking, an academic, a writer, and rich, and so he did not have to ask what her politics would likely be.

And so Monty had abandoned any hopes of there being anyone else who could handle this situation adequately, and so he had gone to see the private investigators his lawyers had recommended, and he had set them to work to keep an eye on the Hillings & Hillings offices.

Monty had literally had to run across midtown after that—nearly killing himself with the effort, huffing and puffing—because traffic was gridlocked. People who saw him and recognized him kept yelling, "Hey Big Mont! How are ya? Kudos from Connecticut!" and the like. He had made it to the network studio with only about two minutes before he had to go on the air at noon.

And nothing was ready for him. This was supposed to be the network's headquarters, the best-equipped studios in the country, yet everybody was futzing around as if he were putting on a Punch-and-Judy show or something. Monty's faxes weren't there; the computer link home to Chicago wasn't set up; his notes for the day and his newspaper clippings were nowhere to be found; and after literally begging for black coffee, the young assistant brought him some kind of weirdo herbal tea.

When the show was over at three he charged out of there, announcing, "If this network cannot learn how to put on the most popular radio talk show in America by Monday, perhaps another network will have to!" He hailed a cab and went to see Josh Lafayette, the Hillingses' lawyer. The meeting was very productive and Monty didn't leave Lafayette's office until well after six. Exhausted, Monty took a cab uptown to the Regency Hotel where he was staying.

He was crossing the lobby, cursing the fact that his feet hurt in his fifteen-hundred-dollar alligator loafers, when he glanced over at a woman and did a double take, jerking his head back so hard he nearly pulled a muscle in his neck.

Her face looked a bit swollen on one side, but Monty had no doubt that it was Georgiana Hamilton-Ayres. Blond, about five foot five, with large blue eyes, she was what Monty would have called an intelligent beauty. In other words, she was very pretty, with a smashing body and a confident detachment from anything that could be construed as bimbo glamour. He had seen all of her movies and he had always wanted to meet her.

On the other hand, Monty prided himself on being able to spot a feminist a mile off, and he was sure she and he would never see eye to eye. Still, the man in him was excited, and he had the best entrée in the world. He was pretty certain she was here to attend the meeting about the Hillingses tomorrow, too. So maybe everything that had happened today had been for a reason. This reason.

"Excuse me, Ms. Hamilton-Ayres," Monty said, walking over to her.

"Yes?" Her expression was pleasant, but guarded.

"Allow me to introduce myself. I'm Montgomery Grant Smith," he said.

"Yes?" Georgiana Hamilton-Ayres said again.

"I know why you're in town." He looked around and then took her arm to move her away from the people who might overhear them, but as soon as he touched her, she threw his hand off and stepped back, slightly alarmed.

"I'm sorry," she said, "but I don't believe I know you." She was looking around for assistance when the concierge noticed her distress and began to walk toward them.

"I'm here to support the Hillingses," Monty quickly whispered.

She looked up at him and blinked those big blue eyes. "Who *are* you?" she asked him.

"I told you!" he whispered, embarrassed and annoyed. "Montgomery Grant Smith! Only the most popular radio talk-show host in America!"

She looked at him a moment longer and then her eyes widened in recognition. "Oh, Lord, you're that bloody right-wing fanatic." Miss Hamilton-Ayres turned to tell the concierge she did not need him after all. "I'm sorry," she said, returning to Monty, smiling, "I didn't really mean that you're a fanatic. Although, you know, it *is* rather fanatical, that act you do."

Monty sucked in his stomach and threw out his chest. "Madam, what do you take me for?" he said in his deepest, darkest radio voice, though he actually didn't mind what she had said, since most professional women said it to him all the time anyway.

"I won't be taking you for anything, Mr. Smith, I assure you," she said. "It was nice to meet you, and I guess I'll see you tomorrow. If you'll excuse me now, I must check in."

The manager who had been waiting for her told the desk clerk, "Please see that Ms. Hamilton-Ayres gets comfortably settled in the blue suite."

"Will you have a drink with me?" Monty asked, following her.

"I'm sorry," Georgiana said, signing the register, "but I already have plans for this evening."

"You have a message, Ms. Hamilton-Ayres," the clerk said, handing her an envelope. She opened it, obviously disappointed by the contents. "Damn," she murmured.

"Is everything all right?" Monty asked. "Is there anything I can do?"

"Hmmm?" she said, glancing over at him. "No—no thank you, everything's fine."

"Maybe there's been a change in your plans and you can have a drink with me after all? I can fill you in on everything that's been going on. I saw Henry today, and Millicent Parks, and Elizabeth Robinson, and the lawyers, and a private eye. I'd say I have a pretty good overview."

"Well, why not?" she said, more to herself than to him. "My plans seem to be on a plane to the Middle East anyway."

"Really?" he said. "You mean you'll have a drink with me?"

"Here at the hotel, though, all right?" she said.

"Great!"

She smiled. "Let me freshen up, and I'll be right down."

Just how Georgiana had managed to get herself into this situation, she had no idea. Montgomery Grant Smith was one of those men so utterly awful that she found something oddly attractive about him. He was almost a cartoon version of masculinity. Everything was too much. He had nice hair and a nice face, but he needed to lose at least twenty pounds, if not thirty. He had enormous hands, talked too loudly, and was surely the biggest, most pompous ass she had ever met.

He was also one of the most insecure men she had ever met and she had little doubt that he was a mama's boy.

They had a drink. And then, foolishly, she had another. She was drinking martinis as if to show Montgomery Grant Smith that she was capable of handling herself. Although she also felt she needed this surge of alcohol to blot out her disappointment that Alexandra Waring was off tracking some Arab terrorist instead of having dinner with her as they had planned. After the second martini, Georgiana wondered how she would feel if Alexandra were killed this weekend, and she decided that she would feel bad but probably not as bad as she did right now, having to sit here listening to Montgomery Grant Smith.

He talked about his life. His family's farm in central Florida. His father's career as a sales director, and his death due to lightning on the golf course. Monty had put himself through school, but had dropped out his junior year. He moved with his mother to Atlanta and got a job as a radio copywriter. The Hillingses met him through a mutual friend and read his self-published political journal. Henry encouraged him to write and got him a column where Monty became a young conservative voice. Through that job he was offered a national radio spot and got married. He had been a big hit ever since. But the marriage had lasted only a year. She got what she wanted: a lot of money. She had never wanted him and he was not sure why he had fallen into her trap.

By the time he had gotten to this part of the story, Georgiana's interest had picked up.

"I suppose," he said sadly, "that it was the case of the fat kid being presented with a beautiful woman any man would die for. I couldn't believe she loved me, and I shouldn't have. She was in love with security, that's what she was in love with, and as soon as she knew she could get good money from a divorce, she was out of there." He winced as he looked at Georgiana. "If you can believe it, I thought I *deserved* her, a gorgeous woman like that." He shook his head and sat back in his chair. "That's it, that's my life story."

They were supposed to be talking about the Hillingses, not about trophy wives, but Georgiana felt touched by what he had shared with her. Deeply insecure men were taken advantage of by women like that all the time, but rarely had Georgiana heard of one who had learned anything from it, or had broken through the self-deception that a remarkably beautiful woman had been drawn to them for any reason other than the security they offered.

They were now on their third drink and getting potted, but Georgiana had begun to enjoy herself. For one thing, she found the looks they were getting as a couple in the Regency bar very amusing. Although she hadn't recognized Montgomery Grant Smith, clearly a lot of other people did. ("Hi, Big Mont," the new waiter who came on duty said, "kudos from New Jersey.") Montgomery told her—about five times—that this attention was due to his raging best-seller, *Visions for America*, which to Georgiana sounded something like a watered-down version of *Mein Kampf*.

"The Hillingses represented your book?" There was doubt in her voice, even she could hear it.

"Yes, why not?" he said in his deep, beautifully modulated voice.

"Oh, I don't know," Georgiana said politely.

"Their job is publishing, not censorship," he told her. "They're smart, decent people who may vote incorrectly once in a while, but who are still the best Americans I know. Besides," he added, leaning forward, "my book is better than *Mickey Monster Moose* or whatever the hell that book was you wrote when you were a kid."

Georgiana laughed. "It was called *Bunny on the Run* and I wrote it when I was *eight* years old. I would hope your book is better than mine. Oh, never mind, that was a very long, long time ago."

Monty knew she was getting drunk. He knew he should push her to eat something, but he didn't want to stop what felt like a roll. In the beginning, being seen with Georgiana Hamilton-Ayres was kick enough, but then she had begun to like him, or at least he had begun to interest her, and he liked that. A challenge.

Besides, she was a very beautiful woman and he liked sitting there, drinking with her, fantasizing about what it would be like to go to bed with her. He did worry that he might somehow hurt her; she was so fragile looking and her face still looked tender from the accident she told him about. He wondered if he could manage not to touch her there. The one thing he did not worry about, sitting there fantasizing about her, was hurting her with his dick, because he knew from experience that with insecure women, like all actresses were, the bigger the better and they wanted it all.

"So why are you here?" Montgomery Grant Smith asked, moving into the chair next to her. "You haven't had anything to do with Hillings & Hillings since you were eight."

Georgiana nodded, sipping the wine she had unwisely chosen to continue drinking after the martinis. She was getting smashed and it felt good. It had been a long time. She wished, however, that she would stop noticing the enormous erection America's most popular radio talk-show host was sporting next to her. It was most distracting.

"Um," she said, trying to remember the question. "Oh, yes, my relationship with the Hillingses. They've been wonderful to me, you have no idea."

"How so?" he asked, letting his arm rest lightly against hers.

"At one point in my life, I lived with them. For two years. They took me in because my mother was having a lot of problems and my father was in Scotland. I suppose in some ways they view me as a child of theirs," she said. "Neither of their own children has ever been interested in anything to do with the arts."

He nodded and smiled. "I'd adopt you," he told her.

For some bizarre reason, this sounded sexy to Georgiana. Or maybe it was because she realized that Montgomery was smashed, too. Vulnerable. She used to love that in men in the old days; the bigger the better; the more prone to vulnerability, the greater the turn-on in rendering them helpless with desire.

He reminded her a bit of Duane, her ex-husband. She had disliked Duane at first, too, and then, for a period of time, had come to find seducing him enormously erotic. Soon enough, however, the dislike heartily outweighed the sex. Oh, what a wonderful relationship that had turned out to be, a marriage of pretense and playacting, making everyone happy but themselves. Duane had begun drinking and snorting coke in earnest, and she had turned an innocent friendship into a torrid affair.

It was ghastly to think back to those days. Yes, she had been young—twenty-three, twenty-four, twenty-five—but still, there wasn't much excuse. And yet, in those days, living so despicably (she thought now, cringing at the memory), her approval rating from friends, family, and publicists had never been higher.

"Excuse me, Montgomery, but I need to visit the ladies' room." She smiled to herself as he stood, holding a napkin in front of his crotch.

The ladies' room attendant was looking at her oddly.

Well, of course she was, Georgiana was bombed. Georgiana Hamilton-Ayres was tottering around loaded in the attendant's immaculate domain and the woman was probably worried that she'd get sick or something. How was she to know that Georgiana didn't do that sort of thing? "I had an accident," she said, talking to the attendant in the mirror, pointing to her cheek. "A pest-control truck hit me."

"Oh no," the attendant said. "Today?"

"No, some weeks ago. I had to have surgery. He broke my cheek." She pointed this out. "He smashed my nose." She pointed again. "He broke my tooth." She pointed once more. "Do you know who Alexandra Waring is?"

The attendant nodded. "The anchor lady. I've seen her here."

"Really? What do you think of her?"

"I think she is a great role model for young women."

Georgiana didn't like that response, but she wasn't sure why. "You have a daughter?"

"Yes," she said. "Fourteen. She would like to be a TV news journalist."

"I see," Georgiana said. "Do you know who I am?"

The attendant smiled and nodded. "Miss Hamilton-Ayres."

"I'm not a good role model," she said.

"Oh, yes, of course you are." Lowering her voice, the attendant added, "I would ask you for your autograph for my daughter, but we're not supposed to."

"Then I guess I'll just have to give it to you," Georgiana said, thinking how loaded she must be to be having this conversation. She also was aware of the effect bringing up Alexandra's name was having on her, while, at the same time, she was experiencing a very strange and strong desire to seduce Montgomery Grant Smith.

Was a man's erection like the applause of an audience? If it was, then America's most popular radio talk-show host was giving her a standing ovation.

Oh, she was drunk all right. She had to be.

He was waiting for her outside the ladies' room. "Are you all right?"

"I'm fine," she said, "I was chatting with the attendant." She smiled and slung her arm through his. "Well, where to?"

He turned to her, clasping his hand over hers. "I'm not clear what our relationship is."

She burst out laughing, falling against him. He staggered, but caught them both. She knew they were a sight, but who cared? This was fun.

"Do you want to come up to my suite?" he whispered. "For something to eat or drink—or something?"

"For something," she said, giving him a look that she was pretty sure would send him to heaven. And if that were not enough to get the message across, she made a slow and rather elaborate process of moistening her lips with her tongue.

They went up to his suite and he held open the door for her. "I'd like to shower, would you mind?" she asked matter-of-factly, turning around. "I've been traveling all day."

He gestured to the bedroom. "There are clean towels in the bathroom."

"Thank you," she said, walking in and making herself at home.

"Uh," he called from the living room, "what do you want me to do?"

She peeked around the door. "Get very, very excited," she said.

"No, I meant," he stammered, "do you want something to drink? To eat? Room service?"

She put her hand on her hip. "Why would I want anything to eat when I have you to eat, Montgomery Grant Smith?" she said, and closed the door.

The water felt wonderful, but it also had the distinct effect of bringing her to her senses.

What are you doing? she asked herself, toweling her hair dry in front of the mirror. The terry cloth robe she found felt heavenly.

"I am demonstrating my womanhood," she told her reflection, and then she laughed, feeling a delicious anticipation between her legs. Were they hereditary? These drunken urges?

She expected to see him in the bedroom, waiting, but he wasn't. He was sitting obediently in the living room, still fully dressed, legs crossed to conceal his crotch, waiting, she supposed, for instructions.

"We have to talk," she said, walking across the room and sliding down next to him on the couch. "What I said before about eating you."

His face was bright red. She was dying to look down, but she didn't. Instead she kissed him lightly on the mouth and said, "I'm afraid I don't know you and I can't afford to risk trusting you—no offense, but I have no way of knowing what you've been up to for the past ten years."

He was startled and blinked several times. "Me? I—you mean, you think I might have AIDS or something? ME?"

"You could have anything," she said, "and I told you not to take it personally. So now," she added, "I have to ask you—do you have any condoms? If you don't, we'll have to rely on things that don't involve my mouth or my . . . well, you know."

He swallowed. "Like what?"

She shrugged. "You could come between my breasts, maybe," and she took his hand and slid it inside her robe to hold her right breast. He responded with a groan, closing his eyes.

She looked down. She was right. A standing ovation. He was cocksure because he was cock-sure and it was exciting. This was like being a teenager again.

"How long has it been?" she murmured, kissing his ear.

"Not as long as you think," he said, massaging her breast.

She reached down and rubbed the tremendous bulge in his pants, measuring, and then sighing, feeling herself responding in a way that was about as subtle as the opening of a garage door. "I really think I want us to find a condom," she whispered.

"I really think so, too," he said. "And I've got some."

"Good boy, don't move, tell me where," she said.

She followed his instructions and came back to the living room, holding one. She stood in front of him and said, "Pull down your pants, please."

He looked at her a moment. And then, swallowing, eyes on her, undid his belt and unzipped his pants. "Do you want me to stand up?" he asked her, voice faint.

She shook her head. "Just pull them down to your knees."

He swallowed again and arched his back, sliding his trousers down to his knees, and sat back down again, meeting her eyes.

"Pull down your underpants, Montgomery Grant Smith," she told him, meeting his eyes still.

He arched again and pulled them down to his knees.

Then she looked. He was huge. And purple. And aching. A divine pillar of swollen desire, the whole sagging a little to the side against his abdomen from the weight of it.

She slid off her robe, let him look, pulled his knees apart, and kneeled in front of him. "Hold it," she instructed him, and as he held it, she was turned on completely. Before placing the condom on him—he was moist already, he was so excited—she kissed the side of his hand. She put it on and, with both hands, gently but firmly rolled the condom down over him. It was a tight fit and she felt sorry for him, murmuring, "You're huge, Montgomery, you need to find someone to make them especially for you."

He said nothing, but swallowed. She climbed up and stood on her knees over his lap, felt down to find his hand, still holding himself, and eased herself down on him. The condom wasn't the only tight fit. She eased herself down slightly and then up, and then down, slowly, to take him in, and still, with how wet she was and with the lubrication, it was not easy. If he were only thick, it would be one thing, but he was so long that coming down on him felt dangerously like impaling herself.

She was making sounds, she couldn't help it, and he made none; he was sitting rock still, his hands clamped to her hips but applying no pressure. She looked down at him; his eyes were closed, his mouth frozen in an agonized grin. "Montgomery," she said. His eyes opened. She pressed her breast into his face. He took the nipple into his mouth and sucked. Almost immediately he pulled down on her violently, startling her as well as hurting her, and she said, "Easy," but she realized what was happening and what was happening was that he was jamming her down on him because he was ejaculating already. And so she let herself go and started in on him for herself, and he was fortunately big enough so that she had time to have a luxurious orgasm around his melting erection, which actually made it even more marvelous, because she could move better around him. She shuddered, her back arching, and the phone rang. She groaned, collapsing on him, letting her head fall forward to rest on his shoulder. The phone rang and rang. Finally it went silent. In a few moments, the red message light started to flash.

Two

~ 16 ~

The Saturday morning meeting of Hillings & Hillings clients was to be held in the offices of an independent film distributor in Greenwich Village. Elizabeth arrived early, along with the caterers, who were setting up a large buffet brunch in the reception area of the offices. The caterers looked to her as their employer, which at first threw her. What did she know about catered affairs except that she usually had to have a glass of wine to even get in the door of one?

"Montgomery Grant Smith, at your service, Professor Robinson," he suddenly said, bowing, seeming to appear out of nowhere. He was dressed in preppy attire: khaki pants, a blue-striped shirt, blue blazer, and red-white-and-blue tie. He even had a little American flag on his lapel. "I apologize for not returning your calls last night, but I was, er, socializing until very late."

Elizabeth thought he seemed inordinately pleased with himself this morning. But then again, from what she knew of him, it could be that he was inordinately pleased with himself every morning.

"Henry tells me that you are to be the grand pooh-bah of today's affair," Montgomery said, eyeing a tray of food as it went by. "And I am delighted to be your designated assistant."

There was definitely something loose in his head, Elizabeth decided, but she simply smiled and nodded and thanked him for coming.

"Kudos from the Upper East Side!" one of the caterers said to Montgomery on his way by.

Montgomery beamed and looked at Elizabeth. "You begin to realize the awesome power of radio." He looked down the hall.

"Young sir, would you happen to have some cool water about?"

"Sure, Big Mont!"

"Big Mont?" Elizabeth said.

"That's me," he grinned.

"Hey, Big Mont!" the caterer yelled. "Catch!" The radio talk-show host was tossed a small plastic bottle of Poland Spring water, which he caught with his right hand in an easy sidearm snag.

Looking doubly pleased now, Monty unscrewed the cap and asked, "So where's Madam Battle-ax?" He scanned the room behind Elizabeth as though he might find Millicent Parks hiding in there.

"Millicent will be along a little bit later," Elizabeth said. As she was leaving the apartment, Sasha, the Hillingses' daytime housekeeper, reported that Mrs. Parks had called to say she had to do something for Mr. Hillings this morning and would be delayed.

"Is she staying at Henry's?" Montgomery asked, proceeding to drink thirstily from the bottle.

"No, she's at the Plaza."

He nodded, considering this, swallowed, and then lowered the bottle. "So what's the deal when Dorothy gets out?"

"If the angioplasty goes well, she and Henry will go directly to the house in Water Mill."

"And then am *I* going to be allowed to stay at the apartment, too?" Montgomery asked, smirking a little.

"I have no idea," Elizabeth said, distracted by the jumble of papers in her hands.

"Naw, I was only kidding. Besides, I've got a great setup at the Regency."

"I'm so glad," Elizabeth said, and truly, she meant it. She finally got her papers in order and handed Monty the annotated list of who was expected at the meeting this morning, and they went over it, hoping that between them they'd be able recognize most of the authors. It was the least they could do after the Hillingses' clients had made the effort to come.

"Hello, Mrs. Tomlinson," Elizabeth said, when the first elevator of visitors arrived, "I'm Elizabeth Robinson and this is Montgomery Grant Smith—"

"What's your Christian name?" Mrs. Tomlinson shouted with great fanfare.

"Isn't this the lady who played Miss Habersham in *Great Expectations?*" Montgomery whispered in Elizabeth's ear.

Elizabeth poked him in the stomach.

Becky Tomlinson had been on Bess Truman's protocol staff and had written an etiquette book in 1957, which had become a classic and was still in print. At just over ninety, Becky had become something of a classic herself.

"My name is Elizabeth," she said again in a loud voice, stepping forward to offer Mrs. Tomlinson her hand, "and this is Montgomery."

"Well you look marvelous, my dear, younger than springtime," the old woman said, shaking hands, "though I wouldn't have recognized you in a thousand years. Wonderful what these doctors can do, although I did always think you were quite beautiful the way you were." She turned to her companion, a small, quiet woman dressed in navy blue and sensible shoes. "Look alive, Marta," Mrs. Tomlinson said, "I want you to meet Elizabeth Montgomery—wonderful actress."

"Oh, geez," Montgomery said, turning to stifle a laugh.

"No, Mrs. Tomlinson, I'm sorry, I was mumbling," Elizabeth said quickly, bending near to the lady's ear. "My name is Elizabeth Robinson, I am a historian, a teacher, a friend of the Hillingses. And this is the radio host Montgomery Grant Smith. We're running the meeting this morning."

"Oh," Mrs. Tomlinson said brightly, "well that's all right, then. I couldn't imagine why you wanted to look this way."

This time Montgomery didn't hide his laughter.

The elevator came up again and everyone seemed to be arriving within moments:

First in line was Dick Stone, a hard-boiled detective novel writer who had not had a best-seller in years—but whose style, he told Elizabeth and Montgomery, was about to swing back into vogue.

("It better swing soon," Montgomery said under his breath. "He needs a pacemaker in his brain." "Stop!" Elizabeth shot out of the side of her mouth in her best scolding-teacher voice.)

The appearance of Gerald Traubner, a newspaper columnist, was a complete surprise, since he had not responded to Millicent's letter. Even though he could not walk without two canes, he was still writing a good deal and Montgomery recognized him immediately. ("Well, well, well, if it isn't the last of the great Trotskyites," he muttered.)

Patricia Kleczak, the New Jersey housewife turned romance/suspense writer, was the next to be greeted. Patty, as she asked to be called, was warm and friendly, and Elizabeth liked her immediately. She was in her late thirties, and, they could plainly see, nervous about being at this meeting.

Alice Mae Hollison, a best-selling historical novelist from Charleston, whom Elizabeth knew fairly well, was behind Patty. Alice Mae, who was at least seventy-four, turned out to be one of Montgomery's biggest fans. "Kudos from South Carolina, Big Mont," she said when she was introduced.

"A lady of obvious good taste and breeding," Montgomery told Elizabeth as Alice Mae moved inside.

Elizabeth could only look at him. Was he for real?

Clarky Birkstein, or the Dog Lady, as she was known to the millions of people who had bought her training books and videos, arrived with a little something called Pookiesnips peeking out of the top of her handbag.

Warren Krebor, a sci-fi writer, arrived with Sidney Meltner, a mystery writer, both of whose ages were exceeded only by the number of paperback originals they had written over the years.

Jordan (he who spilled tomato juice on Millicent's white carpet) and Louise Wells, the television writers, arrived with Georgiana Hamilton-Ayres. The Hillingses had launched the Wellses as novelists years earlier under their given names, Jorges and Luisa Mantos. The Wellses, now in their late fifties, were hip to the nth degree, decked out in designer clothes and jewelry and arguing over the last time they had seen Georgiana. Louise said it was at a Reading is Fundamental fund-raiser at Dodger Stadium and Jordan said it was at Spago.

After the Wellses went through—still arguing—Georgiana introduced herself to Elizabeth, shook her hand, and said how wonderful she thought it was that Elizabeth was doing this.

"Well, we think it's quite wonderful that you're here," Elizabeth confessed. "And this is Montgomery Grant Smith," she said, turning to him and instantly realizing that something strange was going on. He was staring at the actress with a very silly smile.

"We've met," Georgiana said. "Hello, Monty." She didn't shake his hand, but looked past them and said, "Oh, is there food? Wonderful. If you'll excuse me, I'm starved," and quickly moved on.

Watching her go, his face fell.

"Are you all right?" Elizabeth asked gently. He was looking positively ill.

"Why shouldn't I be?" he asked with a withering glare. "I'm going to get something to eat."

Golly, no mood swings here, Elizabeth thought, turning back to the door.

Lucy Boyle, a sixty-six-year-old playwright, arrived dressed in a white work shirt, white jeans, and big heavy boots. For a moment, Elizabeth had mistaken her for a man.

Lucy looked Elizabeth over from head to toe and said, "Are you married?" When Elizabeth said no the playwright asked, "Why not?" Elizabeth said, "I'm probably too smart," and the playwright laughed a very hearty laugh (which made Elizabeth think, for some reason, of cowboys huddled around a campfire), and then Lucy slid her hand around Elizabeth's waist and gave her a squeeze before going on her way.

Sissy Connors, a retired helpful hints lady, was the next person through the door. She gave Elizabeth an autographed special edition of *Sissy's 101 Best Hints for the Home*, which the First Mercantile Bank of Cincinnati was giving to new customers.

Claire Spender Holland, a "novelist of manners," made an impressive entrance, given that she was nearly seventy and living in Ireland (to avoid some sort of taxes in her native England, Elizabeth knew).

Anthony Marcell followed Claire in. A wonderful writer and courtly gentleman (whom Elizabeth had met twice before in earlier years), Anthony had recently undergone his own crisis when an opportunistic young man had filed a rather tacky palimony suit against him, which, of course, had hit all the papers.

John Gabriel Menez, the screenwriter of the 1956 hit movie *Lost*

Land, looked very dapper in a white dinner jacket, black tie, and a jet black toupee that was only slightly askew. It became quickly apparent to Elizabeth that he was either crazy or was, as he said, actually dating Hedy Lamarr.

When Montgomery returned with a plate of chocolate eclairs, all traces of his former good humor had vanished. "The only one missing from this bunch is Queen Victoria," he grumbled, picking up an eclair and biting into it.

"You say one more word about these good people," Elizabeth said, "and I will mash that plate in your face."

He paused long enough to say, "That's a death threat, if ever I heard one," and resumed eating.

"What is the matter with you? Or should I say, what is going on between you and Georgiana Hamilton-Ayres?"

His face brightened immediately and he put the half-eaten eclair back on the plate. "You can tell?"

No, impossible, Elizabeth quickly thought to herself. *Him? And her? Absolutely impossible! Impossible!*

"Elizabeth?" a voice behind her said.

Her body stiffened. She did not have to look to know who it was, and all at once the bits and pieces of a hundred memories hit her. Even after all this time, Elizabeth felt scared and weak. Heart pounding, she turned around.

"David," she heard herself say. "How wonderful of you to come. We hadn't expected you."

David Aussenhoff, the dashing Hollywood wunderkind who had once swooned over her, stood too close to be easily dismissed. Of course Elizabeth had never heard of him when she had first fallen in love with him, because she never read the newspapers in whose gossip columns David's name was often mentioned. No, all she had known was that a six-foot, dark haired, extremely handsome and charming—though rather uneducated—man had decided to win her.

When David realized that she was not going to touch him—not even for a handshake—he turned to Montgomery. "I'm David Aussenhoff," he said.

"Montgomery Grant Smith," Monty said vaguely, looking from Elizabeth to David and then back to Elizabeth as he wiped his hand quickly on his napkin and transferred the plate and napkin to his left hand in order to shake David's hand.

"David's a movie producer who wrote a novel that the Hillingses represented," Elizabeth explained.

"You look as wonderful as ever," David said to her.

"Who are you again?" Montgomery asked, looking from David's face to the list he had pulled out of his blazer pocket.

"Oh, Georgiana's here," David said, spotting the actress in the next room.

Montgomery looked surprised. "You know her?"

"Sure," David said. "We did a movie together."

Elizabeth winced. Of course David knew her. He had probably slept with her, too, like he had slept with every other attractive woman he could get his hands on.

David looked at her. "We'll talk later, okay?"

Numb and shaking inside, Elizabeth nodded. He smiled and murmured, "Good," before moving inside. They heard him say, "Georgiana!" before she said, "David! What a surprise!"

"Now who the hell is *he?*" Montgomery said, frowning.

"My ex-fiancé," Elizabeth said without thinking.

Montgomery looked at her. *"Him?"*

She nodded.

"And *you?"*

Elizabeth flinched. Even Monty could see how unlikely it was that someone like her could have held on to David.

"Oh Professor," he said, shaking his head, "you can do better than that. *Much* better."

She looked at him, taken aback. He thought she was too good for David? Buffoon or not, she realized Montgomery Grant Smith might be her best crutch to get through this day. *David* was here. Good God.

"We should start, don't you think?" Montgomery said, looking at his watch. "I've got to go into the studio this afternoon to get my show straightened out for the week."

"Sure," Elizabeth said, trying to pull herself together. "Let's get started. Just let me visit the ladies' room first, all right?"

"Good idea," Montgomery said, "I'll stop at the men's room." They walked down the back hall together. "If it makes you feel any better," he said, stopping in front of the ladies' room, "I've got kind of a secret relationship, too."

She looked at him.

"I'm in love," he told her. "And I think you know with who."

"With whom," Elizabeth said, going into the ladies' room. She closed the door behind her, went into the nearest stall, and was quickly, quietly sick.

David was here. She couldn't believe it.

~ 17 ~

Elizabeth explained to the assembled group of Hillings & Hillings clients that Millicent Parks would be along soon, and that she hoped they would bear with her as she tried to bring them up to date on the matters concerning the merger of Hillings & Hillings with International Communications Artists.

"The facts are these," she began, leaving her notes on the lectern and starting to pace, just as she did in her classroom. "Hillings & Hillings entered into a merger agreement with ICA under the auspices of Ben Rothstein, who had been, at that time, chairman of ICA for twenty-seven years. The agreement was to provide a smooth transition of representation for the Hillings & Hillings clients over a period of approximately two years, during which time the Hillingses were to school some of ICA's agents in the finer points of literary representation."

She cleared her throat, more out of sympathy than anything else. It was dusty in the screening room and almost all of the older people were coughing slightly and dabbing at runny noses.

"What was meant as a plan that would allow the Hillingses to gradually retire," Elizabeth continued, "was completely abandoned when ICA ousted Ben Rothstein and replaced him with Creighton Berns. Soon after, ICA took possession of the Hillings & Hillings offices, literally padlocking them and denying access to all employees—employees who were subsequently fired. ICA then proceeded to contact Hillings & Hillings clients directly, claiming that the Hillingses had decided to retire immediately and that ICA would henceforth be representing them."

"No one notified me," Warren Krebor said, a comment echoed by most of those present.

Elizabeth paused; she could not tell them that ICA had no interest in representing them.

"Because of the nature of their core business," Montgomery volunteered, suddenly moving through the room to stand next to Elizabeth in the front, "we believe their first inclination was to contact those clients who had the greatest ties to show business."

"But they could get me a TV series," Warren Krebor said, "like Ray Bradbury got. I could do that. I'd *like* that."

"Yes, well, at any rate," Elizabeth said, trying to get back to the point, but just then a high and mighty voice from the doorway at the back of the room interrupted her.

"We are not here to talk about *your* career, Warren, but Elizabeth is simply too kind to tell you that."

Everyone turned as Millicent Parks entered the room and took a seat near the back.

"You may proceed, Elizabeth," she told her.

After a moment, Elizabeth nodded. "Yes, well, thank you, Millicent."

"Wait, before we go any further," Jordan Wells said, raising his hand, "I'd like to say something."

"Yes, Mr. Wells?" Elizabeth said.

"Like everybody else here, Louise and I owe a great deal to the Hillingses. As I understand it, the purpose of this meeting is to come up with a way to force ICA to honor the agreement the Hillingses negotiated with Ben Rothstein."

"That is correct," Elizabeth said. She looked around the room. "Is everybody clear on that? The reason we're here is to think of a way to force ICA into making amends for their actions. Which included provoking Dorothy into a near-fatal heart attack, I might add."

There were murmurs of agreement. Elizabeth nodded to Jordan. "Go on."

"Well, all I wanted to say is, unlike most of you, almost all of our work *is* represented by ICA now. In fact, we're working on a TV miniseries which, quite frankly, we'd hate to see killed by our participation here."

Elizabeth nodded and then looked to David Aussenhoff. "David, you're a producer. Don't you have a movie being packaged by ICA?"

Jordan Wells sat down as David reluctantly stood up. "Yeah, I do," he said, running a hand through his thick, dark hair.

"And you know Creighton Berns, don't you?" Elizabeth asked.

"Yes," David said, standing there.

"Yeah, so?" Montgomery asked after a moment. "What are we waiting for, Aussenhoff, the new edition of *Who's Who?* Tell us what he's like."

David paused before saying, "He's very, very tough and I think Mr. Wells's concern is valid."

"I know Creighton Berns," Georgiana Hamilton-Ayres volunteered, standing up.

"What do you think of him, Georgiana?" Montgomery asked, his voice softening to nearly a whisper.

Elizabeth looked at him. He had it bad all right.

"Creighton Berns can be quite charming," Georgiana said, "but that's when he's getting what he wants. I've heard a lot of negative things about those times he doesn't."

"Like what?" Montgomery softly asked his lady love.

"Blackmail," she said dramatically. "And he takes revenge on those who cross him." She looked at David. "We once saw him destroy a director we both worked with at Metropolis." She looked around the room. "Is everyone aware that Creighton Berns used to be president of Metropolis Pictures?"

"Destroyed a director how?" Elizabeth asked, looking to David.

"Um," David said, "he undermined a big project."

"And the director hasn't worked since," Georgiana said. Then she frowned, and added, "And didn't something happen to Ginny Stokes, David?"

"Yes," David said reluctantly.

"Who's that?" Montgomery asked.

"A producer we both knew."

"What happened to her?" Elizabeth asked.

"She got blackballed by Creighton, and then, well, she ended up killing herself," David said quietly.

There was an outbreak of murmuring.

"Good Lord, I had no idea," Georgiana Hamilton-Ayres said. "I didn't know she was—"

David cleared his throat and addressed Elizabeth. "Listen, if I may make a suggestion, anyone who currently has an active project with ICA is better off not going up against Creighton Berns."

"Then why are you here?" Elizabeth asked him.

He hesitated. "Because I care."

Elizabeth was thrown by his answer and could only stand there, looking at him.

Montgomery picked up the reins. "And you, Georgiana? Why are you here?"

"I have no burning desire to wage war with Creighton Berns, I must admit, but I am more than willing to talk to him, one on one, about this situation."

"ICA handled the dramatic rights to some of my books," Alice Mae Hollison said. "Do you mean to say that my attendance at this meeting might in some way threaten my dealings with them?"

"I don't know," Elizabeth said truthfully.

"Did they contact you to tell you that the Hillingses had retired and that ICA was taking over representation of your work?" Montgomery asked her.

"No," she said.

"Then I don't think your involvement will affect your relationship with ICA," Montgomery told her.

Gerald Traubner was waving his hand. "I'm still not absolutely clear on something—did Henry and Dorothy sell the agency to ICA or not?"

"Yes, they did," Elizabeth answered.

"And what do Henry and Dorothy want now?" Traubner asked.

"They want Dottie to get well, you damn fool," Millicent said impatiently, twitching in her seat.

"And the Hillingses want to oversee the transition of their clients' representation—as was originally agreed upon," Elizabeth added. This was perhaps the most difficult class she had ever led.

"I wish Ben Rothstein was still at ICA," Alice Mae Hollison sighed. "I've always trusted him."

"Forget it. Ben is out," David said with a firmness that made everyone look at him. "It's final. He has no support on the board. He's gone."

"This is appalling!" Becky Tomlinson suddenly announced. "We have to rid ourselves of this bad fellow at ICA immediately!"

"What we need is a major media event that will embarrass the agency," Sissy Connors said.

"Publicity," Lucy Boyle agreed. "We must mount public opinion against him."

"Exactly!" Millicent yelled from her seat. "Bravo, gals, you've got it! We need a demonstration in front of ICA!"

There were excited murmurs of agreement about the idea.

Jordan stood up. "As I said before, Louise and I would love to help, but for us to publicly demonstrate against ICA—"

Georgiana stood up. "I'm afraid I couldn't participate in something like a public demonstration either. But, as I said, behind the scenes, I am willing to do whatever I can to help."

"Look," Montgomery said, "it's clear that I'm the only major celebrity here who's in a position to do anything publicly without getting hurt. I've got fifteen million listeners and I own my own show."

"But not your television show," David said.

There was an uncomfortable silence.

"And how, pray tell, do you know about that?" Montgomery said slowly.

"Think, Montgomery. Simon Grey, your producer."

Montgomery frowned and, after a moment, shook his head. "I don't get it."

"His outfit is an affiliate of ICA," David said. "That means ICA has a piece of your TV show if they want—if they let you keep it, that is."

"How the hell do you know this?" Montgomery demanded.

"It's a small industry," David said.

"But you don't work in my industry!" Montgomery thundered.

"Look," David said, "I don't want to argue with you—I'm just trying to warn you. ICA's into *everything*—somehow, someway—and if you go up against them publicly, they're going to hurt you."

Montgomery turned to Elizabeth. "Sounds to me like your friend's got a whole lot more than just a movie thrown in with ICA."

"That's enough, Montgomery," Elizabeth said sharply.

"I have a suggestion," David said. "Can we have a show of hands of everyone in this room who currently has a project with ICA?"

"Good idea," Elizabeth said. "Okay, current projects with ICA, please raise your hands."

Hands went up: Jordan and Louise Wells, David Aussenhoff, Georgiana Hamilton-Ayres, Patty Kleczak, and Elizabeth. "What is your connection with them, Patty?" Elizabeth asked.

"They want to send out my novel on submission," she explained. "They keep calling me from Los Angeles. They want a fresh copy of the manuscript—which I haven't sent yet."

Elizabeth nodded. "And let's see, Jordan and Louise, you have a miniseries script. And Georgiana—?"

"They handle everything for me," she said firmly.

"As for me," Elizabeth said, "through the Hillingses they represent my BBC and PBS contracts." She looked at Monty. "And they might have an in on your TV show."

"Not anymore they won't. Not after this breach of confidentiality." He pounded his fist into his cupped hand, making a loud smacking sound that made the older people sitting in the front look nervous.

"Elizabeth?" David said. "I think perhaps we should break up into two groups."

"Who the hell put you in charge, anyway?" Montgomery snapped.

Ignoring him, David continued, "I think those of us with active projects with ICA need to have a discussion. Meanwhile, the other group can go ahead and discuss a demonstration." He looked around before focusing on Millicent. "Perhaps Ms. Parks would chair the group planning to demonstrate."

"Very well," Millicent said, rising to her feet and walking up to the podium.

Elizabeth was not pleased. In a matter of minutes David had taken over the meeting, segregated the group, and was telling everyone what to do. He had not changed.

Montgomery didn't look pleased either, but he said, "There's a conference room we can use next door." Montgomery, Georgiana, Elizabeth, David, Jordan, Louise, and Patty Kleczak got up quietly and filed out.

When the door closed behind them, Sissy Connors said, "If I didn't know better, I would say that we have just been the victims of discrimination. The average age in this room just rose by thirty years."

The writers looked around at each other and nodded, murmuring, but then Millicent began to laugh. "But don't you understand? If we play our cards right, we can get the young people to do all the work, we'll get a tremendous amount of free publicity, and the Hillingses will get sweet revenge."

There was a moment of silence.

"That's right," Dick Stone finally said, smiling. "I didn't even think of that. This is a publicity stunt that'll benefit all of us."

"I would prefer to keep our motives a bit more pure, if you don't mind," Claire Spender Holland said. "I owe a good deal of my success to Dorothy and Henry Hillings."

"And you're going to help them," Dick said. "But admit it, Claire, it wouldn't be a bad thing to be in the papers again, would it? Been a long time."

Claire Spender Holland looked at him as if he were the scum of the earth. But she, like everyone else in the room, had vivid memories of their celebrated days as best-selling writers, when no one would leave them alone.

Millicent called the meeting to order.

No, no doubt about it. It had been a long time.

~ *18* ~

David caught Elizabeth's arm outside the screening room. "I swear I didn't know you'd be here," he whispered.

"I was told you weren't coming," she whispered back.

"I changed my mind at the last minute."

She stared at him, as though looking for something specific in his face, then lowered her eyes without saying anything.

"I've got to talk to you," he murmured. "There was a good reason why I—"

The look she gave him then stopped him dead.

"Elizabeth, listen," he pleaded after a moment, "I want to explain to you what happened."

She sighed, shaking her head, looking down the hall. "It is so like you to think this is an appropriate time." She pulled her arm free and walked to the conference room.

"Elizabeth!" he whispered.

She whirled around. "Later!" she whispered back. "Let's do what we're here to do!"

Oh, God, it was all so familiar: David appearing out of nowhere at an important meeting no one could count on his attending, his decision to slip in an explanation of why he had run out on her three years ago in the middle of it. And it was just like her, wasn't it, to scold him like a schoolmarm?

In the conference room Elizabeth found Jordan and Louise arguing in hushed tones; Montgomery and Georgiana whispering furiously back and forth; and poor Patty Kleczak sitting by herself, trying to remain cheerful and confident in a world of writers, Elizabeth was sure, that she had to be finding utterly bizarre. Elizabeth made a point of sitting next to Patty and establishing them as a pair. David could do whatever he wanted.

"Damn it, Monty, I said no!" Georgiana Hamilton-Ayres suddenly lashed out. She realized everyone was looking and so she got up, murmured something about needing a drink of water, and slipped out the door.

After a pregnant silence, David said, "I didn't want to hurt anyone's feelings next door, but they don't have anything to lose going up against ICA."

"And we lose our integrity if we don't," Montgomery said sharply.

David looked at him. "Then I sure as hell hope you have a plan, *Big Mont*."

"As it happens, I do indeed," Montgomery said.

Georgiana returned to the room and, after hesitating a moment, took the seat next to Montgomery again. This seemed to perk him up a little.

"By Tuesday," Montgomery said, "I will have a court order to impound the offices of Hillings & Hillings. I intend on delivering it myself, and any of you who wish to accompany me, may."

No one spoke or looked at anyone else.

"I must say," Elizabeth finally said, "I am in awe of you. How did you manage to do that?"

"I know the right kind of people," Montgomery told her, staring coldly at David. "Good, decent people. People who honor confidentiality, a man's word, hard work for an honest dollar."

"Oh, brother," Louise Wells groaned. "Save it for the radio, okay? We can't turn you off here."

Montgomery looked at her.

"Go ahead, Montgomery," Elizabeth said.

"I've also got people watching the offices who have orders to see that anything leaving the premises gets back inside," Montgomery added.

"That sounds good," Patty Kleczak said.

Encouraged by her receptiveness, Montgomery focused on Patty, lapsing into his radio voice again. "As soon as I became aware of the urgency of this matter, I immediately engaged the services of the finest private investigation firm in the city to assist me in clearing this entire situation up."

"Great," Louise said, elbowing Jordan. "Since Mr. Smith here is taking care of everything, we can all go home." As if on cue, the couple stood up to leave.

Elizabeth looked alarmed. "Please," was all she managed to say, and the couple sat back down. She then turned to Montgomery. "Let's tone it down a bit, all right?"

There was a timid knock on the door.

"Yes?" Elizabeth called.

The door opened and a young man's face appeared. "I'm sorry to interrupt, but Alexandra Waring from DBS News is calling from Iraq for Ms. Hamilton-Ayres."

"Oh, thank you, I'll be right there," Georgiana said, springing out of her chair.

"A major press contact! That's great, Georgiana," Montgomery said appreciatively.

Georgiana hesitated, her smile faltering a little, "Yes, I guess so. I'll be back," she promised, leaving the room.

When the door closed, Monty turned to the group. "So, who wants to go with me Tuesday morning to serve the warrant at One-Oh-One Fifth?"

"I'll go," Elizabeth volunteered, imagining all kinds of dreadful things that might happen if she didn't keep an eye on the talk-show host.

"Good!" Montgomery said, looking around the table. When his eyes landed on Georgiana's chair, he shook his head and said, "Georgiana's going to talk to Creighton Berns privately," but when his eyes got to David, he smiled. "What about you, tough guy? Mr. Hollywood Inside Information?"

"You know he shouldn't go," Elizabeth said. "And so he's not, and that's that."

Both Montgomery and David looked at her, surprised.

"We're not going," Louise said.

"Maybe she's not," Jordan said, "but I want to be there."

"No way, baby," Louise said.

"Jordan, I appreciate the gesture, but I don't see any reason why you should have to come on Tuesday," Elizabeth said.

"I could bring a video camera and take pictures," Jordan insisted.

"Great idea," Montgomery said, sitting up straighter as though he were already on camera.

"No!" Louise thundered.

Everybody looked at her.

"If I may say so, Mr. Wells," Montgomery said then, "I think you may be of better use to us on the West Coast. Perhaps you would be willing to talk to Creighton Berns privately, like Georgiana is planning to do."

"If you need support, I might be able to come back into the city on Tuesday morning," Patty Kleczak offered.

"No, absolutely not," Elizabeth answered. "Mrs. Hillings would have another heart attack if she even knew you were here." She thought a moment. "No, I think it's settled—Montgomery and I will go. I was at the offices yesterday, playing dumb, pretending to be shocked that the Hillingses weren't there. Returning with Montgomery and the warrant will seem like a knee-jerk reaction on my part. As for the rest of you, I agree with Montgomery; I think you should return to the West Coast and talk to Creighton Berns one-on-one."

With their meeting concluded, they trooped back into the screening room.

"We're planning a press conference for a week from Monday," Millicent announced as they filed back in. "Everybody here has agreed to stay on so they can participate."

"Monday is an excellent day for a publicity event," Becky Tomlinson announced. "Newspaper readership is always high on Tuesdays."

"We've got enough star power in this group to hit the front page of every paper in the country," Millicent said with conviction.

"President Truman once held a news conference on a Friday," Becky Tomlinson continued, to no one in particular. "I don't think anyone in the world even knew about it. Very few people are interested in the news on Saturdays."

"We'll use all of our press connections to get your protest covered," Montgomery promised the group. "As a matter of fact, Georgiana's on the phone right this minute with Alexandra Waring of DBS News!"

There was an outbreak of applause. The meeting was a success. They were a success. The Hillings & Hillings clients were going to be able to do something for Dorothy and Henry, two people who had done so much for all of them.

Elizabeth could only hope that she herself wouldn't have a heart attack before all of this was over.

~ 19 ~

On Sunday afternoon, the day after the clients' meeting, Henry Hillings asked Elizabeth where Millicent Parks was. They were standing in the corner of Dorothy's hospital room, keeping to themselves while Dorothy talked to a visitor of hers.

"Do you want the truth or the company line?" Elizabeth whispered.

"The truth, please."

Elizabeth winced. "She's in an absolute snit at the Plaza. She says it's either Montgomery Grant Smith or her, we have to choose, there's no room for both."

"Josh says there's no room for either one," Henry sighed.

"From my view," Elizabeth said, "we must have Montgomery Grant Smith on the front lines."

"But what do I do about Millicent?" Henry murmured. "I'm the one who asked her to start all of this in the first place."

"You could tell Millicent that you're at wit's end about how to get Dorothy out to Water Mill without her hearing about any of this," Elizabeth suggested. "You could ask her what to do, tell her you don't know how to keep Dorothy under control out in Water Mill so she'll recover."

Henry smiled. "That's not a bad idea." His smile widened. "No, that's really rather good, Elizabeth. I'll try it." He turned to look at his wife, sitting up in bed, talking with David Aussenhoff sitting in a bedside chair beside her. "And how is *that* going?" he asked Elizabeth.

"I went numb about an hour after I first saw him," she said, "and that seems to be working."

"If you want, I'll speak to him."

"No, Henry," Elizabeth said, giving his hand a squeeze. "It's better we see each other, put it behind us."

He looked doubtful but didn't say anything. Elizabeth felt more than doubtful, but didn't say anything either.

"David, dear, how long will you be in New York this trip?" Dorothy asked.

"Not long," David said. "But I wanted to make sure to see you."

Dorothy smiled and her eyes traveled across the room to Elizabeth, as if to ask a silent question.

"It was purely accidental, our running into each other," David said. "Then, um, we decided maybe it was time we talked. I have a lot to explain to her. About what happened. There was a lot more that went on than anyone knew. I'd like to explain it to you, too, but it's very personal, and I'm afraid I'm having a hard enough time trying to explain it to Elizabeth."

Dorothy looked at him. "And we will not raise the past in order to play upon the present, will we, David." It was not a question.

He looked at her for a long moment. "I didn't know she was here, honestly, I didn't."

"Be genuine, David, or leave her alone."

He leaned forward, dropping his voice. "I wouldn't hurt her again for anything, I swear."

She held his eyes as he straightened up. "I will hold you to that."

David swallowed, nodding.

"Henry," Dorothy said after Elizabeth and David had gone, "would you be so kind as to tell me what in Sam Hill is going on?"

"What?" Henry said. "Why, nothing."

"Nothing," she repeated, drumming her fingers on the bed covers, the diamond of her engagement ring sparkling. "Elizabeth suddenly appears with David Aussenhoff and you say nothing is going on."

"Apparently they ran into each other yesterday," Henry said, picking up the *New York Times* and pretending to peruse the front page.

"*Where*, Henry? Where did they see each other?"

"I'm not sure," he said, eyes still on the papers.

"Did you tell everyone I'm dying?"

"What?" he said, finally meeting her eyes. "Good heavens, Doe, what is the matter with you?"

"Well then, why are they all here? Millicent never leaves Bridgehampton. Elizabeth hasn't left England in two years. David, who wouldn't dare show his face before, is now suddenly running into people on street corners. Georgiana appears last night out of the blue. Flowers arrive with a note from Jordan and Louise saying they're in town and hope to see me soon. Monty's show is suddenly being broadcast from Penn Plaza. Don't try to deny it—I heard it with my own ears on Friday on that Walkman Elizabeth gave me."

"These are all people who find themselves in New York on occasion. This is the cultural capital of the Western Hemisphere, Doe."

Dorothy pursed her lips and, after a moment of silence, said, "And why can't I go home first before we go to the country?"

"Because all of your things are already out in Water Mill," he said. "Elizabeth and Sasha packed everything, the medical transport is all arranged, and Bernadette, the aide we hired, is coming with us. Besides," he added, "Elizabeth is staying at the apartment and you need complete quiet, the doctor said so." He went back to reading the newspaper.

"I don't like this a bit, Henry!" Dorothy said, irritated.

"Don't like what, darling?" he asked.

"Being treated like a child. Playing the role of father is most unbecoming in a husband, Henry, if I may say so." She resettled herself against the pillows of her hospital bed. "I know you're up to something, Henry Alfred Hillings," she added, "and as soon as I have that angioplasty procedure, I'm going to find out what."

Henry smiled. For the first time he knew for sure his Doe was really going to get better.

~ 20 ~

"I'm sorry, Mr. Smith," the clerk at the front desk of the Regency said, "I have no idea when she'll be back."

"Has she picked up her messages?"

"I'm sorry, but we are not allowed to tell you that, sir. And I think you would appreciate the same kind of discretion."

"Yeah," Montgomery sighed, leaning against the desk. A beautiful spring Sunday in New York and he couldn't find anyone to spend it with. Well, there were lots of people, actually, but he wanted Georgiana. He thought they could eat at Tavern on the Green, then walk through Central Park, maybe watch the skaters, and later go to Lincoln Center for a matinee, or to the Plaza for tea. But he couldn't even find her to ask her.

Depressed, he went back upstairs to do what he always did on the infrequent Sundays he was not on the road doing speaking engagements: watch the political shows and major sporting events, and sift through the *New York Times*, the *Washington Post*, the *Chicago Sun-Times*, and the *Times* of London.

*   *   *

"I really appreciate this, Buzz," Georgiana told her mother's old friend, wiping her face with a towel. She was glistening with perspiration after working out in the gym in Buzz's loft.

"The masseur is here, lovey," Buzz said. "You can shower in there and then throw yourself down on the table. His name's Dom and he's great."

Buzz had been a very successful choreographer who had helped Georgiana convincingly stumble through a jazz film years ago. Decades before, he had done the same for her mother. Like many of Lilliana Bartlett's oldest friends, Buzz had transferred his affection to her daughter, if for no other reason than because he could reasonably count on Georgiana's staying alive until the next day.

A panicky call to Buzz the night before had gotten Georgiana an invitation to hide out in his Tribeca loft all day Sunday. It meant a workout, a massage, and a nap—all without having to worry about Montgomery Grant Smith stalking her.

"Thank you so much, Buzz," she said, kissing him on the cheek as she left.

"And thank you, darling girl, for being you. You're gorgeous and wonderful and I want you to be happy. God knows, it would do my heart good to know that one of you found what you were looking for in this life."

Buzz was referring to her mother, she knew. And Georgiana thought to herself that drinking was something that absolutely had to go in her own life. If she had had any doubts, Friday night with Montgomery Grant Smith should have clinched it.

Monty called two names in his address book, planning to see if one of the women would like to go out with him, but he hung up before he finished dialing. He simply wasn't in the mood for anyone but Georgiana.

He knew his behavior was stupid, but he couldn't help wanting to pursue her. Georgiana was so bright and beautiful and talented and funny and sexy.

Not to mention the fact that his track record with women was abysmal.

So why did he think he could do better with Georgiana

Hamilton-Ayres, of all people? he asked himself. Why did he think this could be the one?

Because Georgiana was different, for starters. Unlike the Hollywood pack, she brought class and breeding to her profession and this appealed to Monty enormously. In fact, Georgiana made hanging out with the movie jet set seem like a fun thing to do. It wasn't that he didn't have the confidence to do something like that on his own—he had become friends with President Bush on his own—it was just that with Georgiana by his side, it would be fun. And with her on his arm, he could really be a part of it.

On his own, they all hated him out there, of course. On the Left Coast.

And he supposed if he dared show his face he would become the brunt of a lot of jokes, just because he didn't have a build like Arnold Schwarzenegger (although Monty had nothing against Arnold, and heartily approved of his political views). But Georgiana Hamilton-Ayres found Monty sexually attractive, he knew that for a fact!

Suddenly he was no longer the smart and funny fat kid who would have done anything short of murder to get out of gym class and avoid the showers! He had been the class clown, forever grateful to Sarah Skyler for not laughing at him when he asked her to the senior prom. Though she had accepted and carried out her part as if she had enjoyed it, he had made a joke out of the whole affair, dressing up like Oliver Hardy, with a bowler, spats, and mustache. It had been too scary to play it straight. And dancing—oh, God—he had not danced since Miss Mott's ballroom lessons in sixth grade. Still, though, Sarah had made him get out on the dance floor, and he had done okay and no one had laughed at him. That was the night he had thought he might be able to win a lady love for himself after all.

Sarah had let him kiss her good night, but he had only the courage to peck her on the lips.

In college, all of that changed. With the help of beer and fraternity life, he learned how to get laid. "You don't have to fuck her face, Mont, get with it" had been the advice he had taken. And when he realized that he had something most of the guys in the house envied—namely, a big dick—he had the courage to try and do something about the rest of his body, too.

One of the guys in the frat house, a junior named Luke, had also been fat as a kid. In between bouts of throwing up Purple Pisser Elixir (the frat's specialty cocktail) one night in the bushes, he told Monty the story of his life. Since Monty had looked after Luke that night, Luke felt as though he owed him, and so one day he invited Monty up to his room to see his weights. Luke showed him a few simple exercises and Monty kind of liked it, and he stuck with it, working out every night that semester and, by the end of it, seeing an incredible difference in his body. Girls did, too.

The only problem was that one night, at the end of the semester, Monty was lying on his back doing bench presses when Luke came in drinking a glass of Purple Pisser Elixir. Monty had barely gotten the barbell back up onto the rack when he sighed in a way that Luke clearly misinterpreted. Setting his drink aside, he came over, unzipped his pants, and pushed his fully erect penis in Monty's face. "Come on, suck it, boy, you know you want it," Luke insisted. Monty screamed and fell sideways off the bench before scrambling out of the room, never to so much as look at Luke again.

Monty had never told anyone about the incident. He was honorable that way. After all, Luke had shown him what he could look like if he wanted.

"Well, you have to admit it, when Alexandra Waring breaks a dinner date, she does it with great flair and style," Jessica Wright, the DBS talk-show hostess, said over the phone.

Georgiana laughed. "What on earth was she doing in Iraq?"

"Oh, interviewing guerrillas in the hills or something."

"I don't think there are hills in Iraq, Jessica."

"Well, whatever. Anyway, Alexandra Eyes asked me to tell you she's on her way home."

"Hi, Mom, it's Monty," he said, stretched out on his bed, watching the Weather Channel with the sound off.

"Hello, Montgomery, how are you?" she asked distractedly.

"I'm just fine. Is that company I hear?"

"Yes. Mr. and Mrs. Woolster from next door are here."

"Oh, well, I won't keep you then."

"Call me tomorrow night," she suggested. "Oh, wait, that's not very good, I've got the girls coming for bridge."

"I'll just call you later in the week," he promised.

He smiled as he hung up, thinking how his mother's social life had changed for the better since he had bought her that condo. And, too, it seemed to give her standing as a single woman a boost to have a celebrity as a son. Couples usually liked to socialize with other couples, but everyone, it seemed, enjoyed counting Mrs. Smith as a very good friend now.

He called room service and ordered a porterhouse steak, medium rare, a baked potato with sour cream and butter, a salad, a bottle of red wine, and two pieces of chocolate cake. He hoped it would arrive before "60 Minutes" started. He liked to have his food all set up before a show began.

∼ *21* ∼

It was strange to be with David again.

After visiting Mrs. Hillings, they left Lenox Hill Hospital and walked west, crossing Park Avenue and Madison Avenue, and then heading north on Fifth Avenue toward the old Stanhope Hotel. David wanted to have dinner there.

As they passed the beautiful town houses and apartment buildings facing Central Park on Fifth, Elizabeth thought of the house in Laurel Canyon where she and David had lived together in California. And, for some reason, she thought about how one of them had always been coming down with something and was forever giving it to the other.

They had kissed a lot.

Affection had been one of David's greatest charms—how often he had wanted to kiss her, hold her, touch her—but this was not something Elizabeth wished to think about right now. Frankly, she couldn't. Not and keep going.

The Stanhope was not an accidental suggestion on David's part and Elizabeth hadn't had the presence of mind to veto it. Six years before, after the publication party for a Hillings & Hillings client where they first met, they had come here for a quiet drink. At the time Elizabeth had been rather flattered and amazed and astounded by David's attentions; she had never been approached by a playboy before. ("But you're so beautiful," David had said that night, "you must have guys coming on to you all the time.")

The Stanhope, as regal and elegant as ever now, had suffered one horrendous financial crisis after another in recent decades. It was still valiantly carrying on, exuding the quiet, old-world charm Elizabeth so loved. The only thing that had changed was the old men's saloon in the front, which years ago had been converted into a tiny but exquisite tea room. Dorothy Hillings was the only person Elizabeth knew who could obtain a reservation there.

A reservation in the spacious restaurant was more obtainable, and they were shown to a lovely table immediately. Over a glass of wine they talked about New York and London and Elizabeth's research; they had not even looked at the menus yet when David reached across the table to take Elizabeth's hand.

The numbness inside Elizabeth vanished and was replaced by fear. Real fear. Touching David again felt like deliberately choosing a descent into madness.

She excused herself and went to the ladies' room. She smiled at the attendant, went into a water closet, and, behind the full-length door, slid to her knees, afraid she might be sick. She wasn't, though. And when the nausea had passed and the perspiration on her forehead had cooled, she closed her eyes, trying to force her mind onto one of the many meditations Dr. Hettington had taught her.

In therapy it had come as a shock to Elizabeth to discover how extremely undisciplined her mind actually was, how it was apt to go sailing off in whatever emotionally alarming direction it cared to with little or no resistance from her.

Dr. Hettington had told her that learning to harness her emotions, to not let them run off unchecked, would do a lot toward getting her stabilized. Life would hand her enough unchecked madness to deal with; she did not have to create any more on her own.

Not any more. Not even if she felt it creeping up on her, like now, that awful sensation at the back of her neck. *I just can't deal with this*, she thought. *I just want to get out of here! It's going to happen all over again.*

She could see Dr. Hettington's gentle face. And so she knew what she should do. She needed to talk herself down. She needed to recognize the knee-jerk reaction of old feelings, that today was not three years ago or even last week. That she was all right, really she was, and there was nothing to fear.

The meditation she chose worked. She repeated it in her mind, over and over again: *I am completely safe because I am here with me, I am taking care of me.* Slowly she felt the fear and shaking leave her. For good measure, she said a quick prayer, the same one she had said about seven times that morning at the Fifth Avenue Presbyterian Church, asking to be protected from all the hurt she associated with David.

Washing her hands at the sink and smiling at the attendant again, Elizabeth wondered how many of the Stanhope's elegant patrons had to kneel by the toilet to meditate and pray in order to get through their dinners.

"Are you all right?" David asked, standing when she returned to the table.

"I was nervous," she confessed, sitting down.

"So am I," he said.

"Tell me about everything you've been working on," she said then, knowing that David would quickly lose himself in the subject.

After he told her about two movie projects that he was working on, Elizabeth was tempted to interrupt him and say, "I hate you, you know. It makes me jealous and angry to hear how happy and productive you've been without me." But she didn't and he prattled on, making her feel as though she hadn't meant anything to him at all. Ever.

Elizabeth, she told herself, *the only way to feel better is to stop the abuse in your head the moment you become aware of it.* Amazing how old habits came back the moment people from her past reappeared. Instantly, she began setting herself up; creating stories in her head about why other people had acted the way they had, making assumptions about what they felt, and then acting on that information as if it were absolutely real.

"I guess I should just come out with it," David said suddenly, startling her back to the present.

"Maybe not quite yet," Elizabeth said, eyes on the waiter who was coming to take their order. "David," she said, "I'm afraid I'm not really hungry. Not at all, as a matter of fact."

He looked at her. "Neither am I."

They ended up making apologies, paying the bill with a handsome tip, and leaving the restaurant quickly.

"It was kind of heavy-duty being back there, wasn't it?" David asked.

She didn't say anything.

"Do you want to sit over there?" he asked, pointing across the street to the benches in front of the Metropolitan Museum of Art. "I really need to get this off my chest."

Elizabeth felt her stomach seizing up again, so she tried to remember all the reasons why she should hate this man, why her body need not be paralyzed by his presence, and most of all, why she should kill the hope she felt that he might still love her. She was a mess inside. But hadn't she always been?

I am completely safe because I am here with me, I am taking care of me.

Elizabeth had already accepted a teaching post at Columbia, her alma mater, when she had met and fallen in love with David. When it had come to wanting to share her life with him, however, it meant going back on her word to the university.

"UCLA?" the department chairman had said, eyes wide with disbelief. He had frowned then and asked, "Why, Elizabeth?"

"I've fallen in love," she confessed.

"And Greg got a job out there?"

Greg was the man Elizabeth had dated all the way through graduate school. He was an older and very successful magazine editor, who had happily escorted her to all the Columbia functions over the years, so everyone knew him.

"No," she said, "Greg will be staying in New York."

After a long silence, the department chairman said, "I hope you know what you're doing, Elizabeth. It's not wise to abandon a post you have formally accepted."

She was still horrified to remember what she had said at the time. "But I've never had anyone really love me before!"

The chairman had murmured, "Be very careful, Elizabeth, and keep in close touch. We'll miss you terribly." And then, as if offering formal forgiveness, he had held out his arms and she had rushed into them. They had been through a lot over the years. She was his star student. Leaving Columbia had been like moving away from her childhood home in North Stamford all over again.

And for what? Elizabeth thought now—with another warning flip-flop in her stomach—as they sat down on a bench near the museum.

"Oh, God, not again," David said, making Elizabeth look up. Walking toward them, in the shadows of the trees, was a homeless man who had approached them earlier on the way to the Stanhope. David had given him a dollar, an act which Elizabeth had suspected had only been for her benefit.

"Donation for a suit for a Merrill Lynch interview?" the homeless man asked David. In that instant, the man recognized them from before. "As you can see, madam," he said to Elizabeth, "I have made enormous progress since the last time I saw you."

"Oh, God," Elizabeth said, laughing, "you sound just like Montgomery Grant Smith."

"A compliment, madam," the man said, mimicking Montgomery fairly well. "We the homeless are committed to listening to Mr. Smith as the consummate act of self-hatred."

Elizabeth searched in her bag, carefully scrunched up a twenty-dollar bill so David couldn't see how much it was, and handed it to the man. "Good luck to you," she said.

"God bless you, ma'am." He had the sense to back off before looking to see what she had given him. When he did, he saluted her.

"All he'll do is spend it on drink and drugs," David said, shifting his weight.

"He might get something to eat."

David sighed. "I never remembered New York being like Calcutta."

"It wasn't before the Reagan and Bush years," Elizabeth said.

"Oh, don't be an ass, Elizabeth. What are you voting as these days, socialist?"

"As you may recall," Elizabeth said crossly, "*I* was originally a registered Republican, not you. And if we ever get a normal Republican party, I might be again."

"Some things never change," David sighed, looking at the sky overhead.

"Basic human kindness never should, regardless of politics."

"We're fighting," he told her.

"Of course we're fighting!" she said. "I can't believe you still think that somebody else is going to fix the problems—"

"Elizabeth—enough!"

"No, not enough!" she exploded, jumping to her feet. "I put up with the most unbelievable garbage from you. You'd happily turn every American city into Calcutta if you thought it meant getting a new sports car. What I can't believe is that I just sat there, listening to you rationalizing the economics of your greed!"

"Oh, you didn't just sit there and listen, believe me," David said, angrily crossing his arms over his chest and looking down Fifth Avenue. "Some great citizen you turned out to be," he added. "You bailed out to a foreign country, that's how much you cared about solving this country's problems."

"You arrogant, self-centered son of a bitch, I hate you!" she cried, turning on her heel and hurrying down Fifth Avenue. She was sobbing and she didn't care that people saw; she only wanted to get away from him. After four blocks she slowed down, took some Kleenex out of her bag, wiped her eyes, and blew her nose.

"Better?" David said from behind her.

She turned around and slapped him across the face. She had never hit anyone in her life, and his look of shock and amazement made her think that she might be losing her mind.

"Elizabeth," he murmured, trying to hold her.

"Don't touch me!" she said, pulling away, sobbing.

They stood there a while, her sobbing, him holding her, people walking by with their dogs and children.

"Elizabeth, this is crazy, we've got to go somewhere and talk."

She wiped her eyes and blew her nose. "I wish to God you had never come." When he didn't say anything, she looked up.

And then she saw that he was crying, too.

~ 22 ~

"Is that you, Elizabeth?" Henry called down the hall.

"Yes," she said, slipping off her coat and hanging it in the front hall closet. "David's here, too," she added.

They walked down the hall. "I was just going to bed," Henry said, appearing in his robe, slippers, and striped pajamas. "There is a lot of good food in the kitchen—I hope you kids will help yourselves."

Elizabeth kissed him good night and David and Henry shook hands. Elizabeth and David went into the kitchen and poured themselves some juice, found some oatmeal cookies, and went into the study.

Elizabeth had spent many evenings in this apartment over the years, sometimes at a cocktail or dinner party in honor of one of Dorothy and Henry's clients, but most often it was to slip off her shoes and curl up in one of the big leather chairs in this den and sip tea and gossip with Dorothy about nothing. Elizabeth felt tired and glad to be home, where, within moments, she could simply tell David to leave and she would be alone. She slipped off her shoes and curled into one of the leather chairs, yawning.

"I need to sit near you," David said. "Please, Elizabeth."

Without a word she moved to the couch, tucking her legs under her and turning to face him.

After hesitating a moment, he took hold of the hand that she had rested on the back of the couch. He held it in both of his hands and sighed, looking at her. "What happened was . . . ," he began.

She waited.

He averted his gaze and swallowed. "What happened to me . . . ," he tried again.

"You went on location for six weeks," she said, "and when you came home you wouldn't touch me, you wouldn't talk to me, and you left after three days."

He sighed, but said nothing.

"That was three weeks before our wedding," she added.

"It seems so stupid, now, but at the time—" He looked at her, squeezing her hand. "At the time, Bets—"

She stiffened, withdrawing her hand.

"Sorry," he murmured. "Oh, my God, I'm so sorry."

Neither was looking at the other. She didn't know what he was thinking about, but she was remembering how he had come to call her Bets. He had said that the whole world knew her as Elizabeth, but only he would know her as Bets. It all seemed so ludicrous now.

"I always assumed it was another woman."

"Not the way you think." He looked at her, took a breath, and added, "But I did cheat on you."

She let out a cynical laugh. "You would have to be an idiot to think this comes as news to me."

"Do you remember the night? I swore to you that I hadn't? And wouldn't ever?"

"Of course I do," she said. "The Mexican operator kept breaking in on the line to say you had an emergency call from some woman—probably the one you were sleeping with!"

"I got the clap." He looked at her. "And I got herpes. When I got home to L.A. it had broken out everywhere—especially my crotch."

Elizabeth sighed, rubbing her eyes.

"So when I slammed the door that time," he said quickly, "when I was in the bathroom—I wasn't rejecting you. Oh, God, Bets, I just couldn't tell you what I had done after I had sworn to you so many times that I hadn't."

"So you did nothing?" Elizabeth said, slamming her hand down on the couch beside her. "You just left?"

He stood and began to pace. "When I finally got my act together, you'd taken off, and then it just seemed like—well, like I didn't deserve you. Never had."

She looked at him, tears streaming down her face. "I don't buy it, David. I don't buy it for one minute! Why make up a ridiculous story now? Why even bother? What the hell could you possibly want from me now?"

"It's the truth," he said quietly. "I felt like I had the fucking plague."

"You didn't want to get married! That's what the problem was!"

Instead of protesting, he sank back down on the sofa and covered his eyes with his hand as he rubbed his forehead. "I didn't want to get married," he admitted, lowering his hand. "Not even to you."

In the silence that suddenly filled the room, they could hear the tick of the brass clock on the mantelpiece.

"Finally," she sighed, sniffling and wiping tears off her face with the back of her hand. "Well, thanks for telling me, even if you are three years too late."

David got up and walked over to the mahogany cabinet near the windows. On top sat a silver tray holding a crystal decanter and six small brandy glasses. He poured an inch of the amber liquid into two of them and gave one to Elizabeth. She noticed the tears in his eyes and handed him a tissue.

"Do you still have it?" she asked him.

He nodded, sitting down and rolling his glass between his palms. "The clap they could cure, but not the herpes." He blew his nose. "It goes in remission and then it comes back—stress sometimes brings it on. And that's when you're infectious."

"You should have told me, David," she said.

"I couldn't. Not then. We were getting married in three weeks, for chrissakes. Somehow it all just started to snowball the second I came through the door. You were so happy to see me. You were in that silk thing I loved. And you wanted to make love and I had to push you away. You were upset, and you thought . . . but I couldn't—hell, I just had to get out of there, I couldn't stand it. I was going to come back that night, but I didn't. The next day I . . ." He sighed, rubbing his eyes. "I don't have any excuse, Bets." He dropped his hand and looked at her. "But I was in love with you. You know I was."

Elizabeth's mind had safely detoured into the matter of his health and this last part did not fully register. It would later, she knew, when she was alone and she replayed this conversation in her head. For right now, it was best to take the detached course. That way none of this seemed quite real, not the past, not the present. "Are you seeing anyone now?" she asked him.

"Yes," he said.

Well, of course, he was. When had he ever been alone? When would women ever find him not attractive? When would women like her stop thinking they were different, that they could be the one he'd fall in love with and settle down with? Good old irresistible David.

"And does she know about the herpes?"

He paused, then shook his head.

"Shouldn't you tell her?"

"It's in remission," he said. "I will, I—"

"David, you must tell her. How else will you know who really cares for you, if you don't?"

He raised his head and looked at her. "I love you," he said.

Her breath was gone, her body froze. "I love you, too," she said.

They sat there, unmoving, as the clock chimed twelve times.

"But you should leave now," she murmured.

"I know," he said. He put his glass down, got up, and walked to the door. "I do love you, Elizabeth." And he left.

~ 23 ~

"What do you think you're doing?" Georgiana demanded when Montgomery Grant Smith jumped into her cab late Monday afternoon and slammed the door shut behind him.

"Go, driver, wherever she told you," he said. Instantly the car took off.

"Wait, driver," Georgiana said. They lurched forward as the car stopped.

"Go!" Montgomery yelled. "Go!" They began to move again.

"Stop!" Georgiana screamed.

The driver shouted something foreign into the rearview mirror and shook his fist as he applied the brakes.

"He's on my side," Monty told her.

"Oh, all right," Georgiana said. "Go on, the West End Broadcasting Center, Sixty-seventh and West End Avenue." She turned to glare at Montgomery. "What has gotten into you?"

"I'm crazy about you," Montgomery said, trying to kiss her.

"What the devil do you think you're doing?" Georgiana said, pushing him away.

"What's the matter? What's wrong?"

"What's wrong? What's *wrong?* What is wrong with *you?* You've been stalking me all weekend and now you jump into my taxicab and attack me!"

"I wouldn't call that an attack. I just want to spend some time with you." He took her hand in his.

"Would you please stop it!" she said, wrestling her hand away.

"Okay, fine!" he said, moving over toward his window.

They drove along for a minute or two in silence. Georgiana glanced over. He wasn't pouting, exactly, but she could see that his feelings were hurt.

"Look, Montgomery."

"Monty," he said.

"Look, Monty."

"No, you look," he said suddenly, "we had a wonderful night Friday night. It was obviously no big deal for you, but it was a big deal for me. There. Okay? Satisfied? Now you know. And now that you know that, you should know that I don't see anything wrong with my wanting to know you better, and to perhaps court you properly. So if you're insulted, I'm sorry. I'm offering the greatest compliment I have to offer."

Georgiana was silent, trying to think of what to say and how to say it. "I feel as though you're trying to cage me," she finally said. "And I don't react well when people try to touch me—without my permission."

"I know," he said. "I'm sorry. No one should touch you without your permission. I apologize."

"About Friday night," she added.

He held his breath.

"I made a mistake. For both of us. I had too much to drink . . ."

"I hate that excuse," he said.

She looked at him, but let the comment pass. "Had I known it would mean anything more to you than it did to me, I would not have done it. I guess I thought that with your fame and success, you were simply as lonely as I was."

"I am," he told her. "And I'm looking for a partner."

"And I'm not," she said, looking down at her lap.

"I think you lie like a rug, lady, but I accept your attempt to make peace." He cleared his throat, looking out the window. "So, where are we going, DBS?" he asked, as if they had been planning to go there together all along.

She looked at him.

"You're a very beautiful woman, have I told you that?"

"For a moment," she said, "I thought you were going to be rational."

"I am, I am," he assured her. He shrugged. "So why are we going to DBS?"

"*I* am visiting Jessica Wright," she said, "and then having a bite to eat with Alexandra Waring. *You* are going back to the hotel."

"But I know Jessica, the Terror of Tucson," he said.

Georgiana had to smile. It was Jessica's nickname from the old days, when her talk show had originated out of Tucson, Arizona.

"She used to be a real hot ticket, I hear, but I didn't know her *that* well."

"She also used to drink too much," Georgiana said. "But not anymore, not for years. Seems to me, Monty, you know a lot of women who shouldn't drink."

"What about blow?"

She looked at him.

"Cocaine," he clarified.

"And what would you know about cocaine?"

He shrugged, smiling.

"You right-wingers, I tell you," Georgiana sighed.

"So Jessica doesn't do blow and she doesn't drink anymore," he said. "Interesting."

"So you'll have to think of another way to entertain her, won't you?"

"Ms. Hamilton-Ayres?" Montgomery said, after staring at her for a moment.

"Yes?"

"Go fuck yourself, ma'am," he said.

"Thank you, I will, Mr. Smith," she said.

At the gates to West End they had another argument over how Georgiana did not want to be responsible for helping a radical right-wing media star infiltrate DBS.

"I don't know what to tell you, Ms. Hamilton-Ayres," the security guard said, hanging up the telephone. "Ms. Wright said Mr. Smith is more than welcome, and Ms. Wright is in Ms. Waring's office right now, so short of holding him here for thirty seconds and making him walk in by himself, I'm not sure what to do except let him go in with you the way he wants to."

"I don't believe this," Georgiana said, pressing the bridge of her nose.

"Thank you, kind sir," Monty said to the guard.

"This is unbelievable," Georgiana told him, dropping her hand. "Don't you have anything better to do?"

"Than talking to DBS about press coverage on the ICA protest? No way, this is a killer idea, and I must commend you on it."

Oh, right. She had forgotten about that. Monty thought she was seeing Alexandra about press coverage.

They walked into the lobby of the DBS complex where a security guard stopped them at a second checkpoint. They were issued badges with their names, the time, the date, and the code number of who they were visiting.

"Ms. Hamilton-Ayres, Mr. Smith?" yet another security guard said to them, this time a woman. "I'll take you to Darenbrook Three."

Aboveground the West End Broadcasting Center consisted of three three-story office buildings that were built in a U-shape around a park, facing west toward the Hudson River. Hidden below street level were the labyrinths of electronics that were at the heart of Darenbrook Communications—the newspapers, the magazines, the broadcast network, and the electronic reference companies. The lowest level was the DBS television studio facility, including the DBS newsroom.

The guard was taking them to Darenbrook III, the office building for the DBS Television Network. Although scarcely five years old, DBS had made use of satellite technology to link independent TV stations around the country into a part-time network. As everyone knew, Alexandra Waring and Jessica Wright were two people responsible for much of the network's success. America's first anchorwoman with her own national evening news broadcast would be thirty-five this year, and America's only national prime-time TV talk-show hostess was only thirty-three.

After walking through miles of corridors and riding two different elevators, they were led down the hall toward the voice of the famous talk-show hostess. "The mountain comes to Mohammed! Montgomery Grant Smith comes to DBS!" Jessica Wright called as they came into view.

Heads peered out of offices on either side of the corridor and scattered applause broke out, to which Monty responded by bowing gracefully. "Greetings, O left-wing liberals of the media!" he said.

"You are the dopiest son of a bitch I know," Jessica told him, striding into the middle of the hallway in a miniskirt and ornate cowboy boots, "but I like you anyway," and she gave him a hug and kiss on the cheek.

"Georgiana," she said, reaching to give her a hug and a kiss, too, "seeing you with this guy is like tripping over Betty Crocker at a sit-in."

They all laughed.

"Boy, do you look great," Jessica said, holding Georgiana's arms and studying her face carefully.

Georgiana smiled. She had forgotten about her face and that she was not quite healed. Amazing how a lunatic like Monty could take her mind off things.

"You look marvelous, Jessica," she told her. Jessica Wright's feminine attributes—long, wild auburn hair, dazzling green eyes, and a bustline that had provoked more comments than Jessica's show—made her wildly attractive to men, but her boundless energy and humor and compassion made her irresistible to women as well. In short, she was a network executive's dream of a TV talk-show hostess.

"Mr. Smith," a low, charming voice came from an office doorway, "how utterly remarkable it is to see you in our hallowed halls."

It would have been difficult to find a more striking contrast to Jessica Wright than Alexandra Waring. Tall, thin, and elegant, Alexandra was the epitome of conservative good looks and good taste. She was in a simple navy blue dress, pearls, silver earrings and bracelet. Her shoulder-length almost black hair was swept back off her face as if by magic, and the blue of her dress made her eyes startling intense.

As Alexandra shook hands with Monty, she complimented him

on his constant reminders to his listeners that he was not a journalist and therefore never had to be fair to anyone or any issue. Characteristically, she said it in such a way that Monty felt flattered and laughed loudest.

"Why don't we all go to my office?" Alexandra suggested. "Jessica, will you show Monty the way?"

Jessica nodded and took Monty's arm. "Since I let you in, I'm responsible for you." After the two had walked off together, Alexandra turned to Georgiana and smiled. "It's so wonderful to see you," she said softly, touching Georgiana's face where there were still traces of a bruise. She dropped her hand quickly, but the smile lasted.

Monty evidently decided he should run the meeting, informing them that he and Georgiana were here to ask for media coverage for the ICA demonstration. Georgiana gave Jessica and Alexandra full marks for their patience, as Monty launched into a recap of everything that had happened to Hillings & Hillings to date. Jessica, who was represented by ICA, asked a lot of questions, but Alexandra merely listened and took a few notes.

"So what do you say?" Monty asked as he finished explaining everything. "Will you send a camera crew to cover the protest a week from today, next Monday? We need national coverage *bad*."

"At this point," Alexandra said, "all I can promise is that we'll look into it. If the story warrants it, we'll be there. I'm sorry, but that's the best I can do right now."

"The story'll warrant it," Monty promised her. "If we weren't in the right, I wouldn't be getting a court order."

"When is that order being served?" Alexandra said, eyes sparking with interest.

"I'm getting it tonight and I'm serving it tomorrow," he said.

"*You're* serving it?" Alexandra said, sitting up a little straighter.

"Yep."

She sat back in her chair. "Let me get this straight. Montgomery Grant Smith is going to personally serve a court order for International Communications Artists to vacate the premises of Hillings & Hillings."

"You can bank on it," he grinned, sensing her excitement.

"It's a deal; you've got a camera crew, my friend. We'll be there tomorrow. And I'll make sure we're at the demonstration next week." She was up in a shot and opening the office door. "Ralph? Ask Kate to come up from the newsroom, will you please? And see if you can get Will on the phone."

"Mr. Right-wing Radio busts the chops of Creighton Berns," Jessica was saying. "I like it. I wish I hadn't sent him a congratulatory note when he got promoted."

"Do you have a blue suit?" Georgiana asked Monty.

"Blazer," he said. "The one I wore on Saturday."

"Right, wear that," Georgiana told him.

"Why?"

"Listen to the lady," Jessica said. "On camera the jacket you're wearing will make you look like the entire state of Utah."

"My field producer's coming up from the newsroom," Alexandra said, sitting down again. "I'd like you to go over a few details with her, okay, Monty?"

"Hey, that's great," Monty said, sitting up straighter and straightening his tie as if he were on camera already. "I really appreciate this." He looked over at Georgiana. "What's the matter?"

"What?" Georgiana said, startled. "Nothing." And she offered him her best smile, the one that was designed to reveal everything except what she was really feeling.

~ 24 ~

"Track down Aussenhoff in New York," Creighton Berns said to the person on the other end of his car phone, as his Mercedes drifted from one lane to another on Sunset Boulevard, "and tell him if he doesn't return my call within an hour, his movie's history!" He slammed the phone down and it bounced out of the cradle.

Marion Ballicutt picked it up and put it back in the cradle.

"There's something going on I don't like," Creighton muttered, suddenly veering across Sunset onto a road by Hamburger Hamlet, causing traffic to honk and swerve in all directions.

"It's okay, Creighton, they're swinging in the dark," Marion assured him, holding on to her armrest.

"I want those Hillings & Hillings offices cleaned out," he said, driving up the street. "I want you to fly back to New York tonight and see to it yourself." He turned left into a driveway, pushed a button, and the gate to the garage swung open; he drove inside, cut the engine, and the door closed behind them. As they got out of the car, the door to the house opened and a young houseboy said, "Mr. Berns, shall I be leaving now?"

"Thanks," he told him, walking in. Marion Ballicutt followed behind, high heels clicking. Creighton went straight to the master bedroom, where he took off his jacket, threw it on a chair, and loosened his tie. Marion closed the door behind her and walked over to the closet, where she began systematically taking off her clothes and hanging them up. Down to a black brassiere and panties, she slipped off her wedding and engagement rings, put them in her blazer pocket, and walked over to Creighton, who was sitting at the vanity table doing a line of coke.

He dropped the solid gold straw and reached for her. "I want to fuck you bad," he growled, stroking his face against her lace-covered breasts.

She laughed, messing up his hair. "Let's get to it then," she said, pulling him out of his chair. "We've only got an hour."

~ *25* ~

With the nine o'clock newscast approaching at the West End Broadcast Center, Alexandra and Georgiana only had time for a quick supper in the cafeteria, over the course of which they were interrupted four times—by an executive news producer, a senior producer, the weatherman, and a guest expert on terrorist psychology. Just as Alexandra was finally managing to finish her soup and salad, a stunning blonde in her late forties came dashing into the cafeteria waiving a videocassette.

"Brilliant, brilliant!" the woman cried, making her way to them as Kyle McFarland, DBS's executive producer, trailed in behind her. At first Georgiana thought she knew the woman; she possessed the fading classic beauty of a celebrity. But her suit was definitely that of a chic businesswoman, although her hair looked as though it were simply thrown up on the back of her head the way hip women had worn theirs in the early seventies.

"Glad you like the piece," Alexandra said, putting her fork down.

"There's just one problem: I don't think anyone is going to understand it," the woman finished, handing the tape to Kyle. "You guys are going to have to fit in a recap of the history of religious wars in Iraq somewhere."

"Oh, fine," Alexandra sighed, "let's just make the piece three hours long while we're at it."

"We can do it," Kyle told her, "and it won't be that much longer."

"But I wanted to use it tonight," Alexandra said.

"I would wait and use it on Thursday," the blonde suggested. "Make it a three-parter. Let's start with an intro tomorrow, the recap on Wednesday, and save the best for Thursday. If you do, I'll get the gang started on network promos tonight."

Alexandra was looking at the woman with open amazement. "That's a fabulous idea," she said, smiling.

"Thank you," the woman said, smiling back.

"Georgiana," Alexandra said, "this is Cassy Cochran, president of DBS."

"I'm a great fan of yours, Ms. Hamilton-Ayres," Cassy said.

"Georgiana, please."

"Georgiana," she said, transferring the videocassette to her left hand (where, Georgiana noticed, there was an elegant rock of an engagement ring and no less than three bands—*very married*, she supposed it meant), and shook hands with Georgiana across the table. "Are you being interviewed, or—"

"No, no, I came to see where Jessica and Alexandra work."

"I hope you'll stay for the newscast," Cassy said. "It's a lot of fun to watch."

"Fun?" Alexandra said. "Watching twenty people running into each other, screaming louder and louder, until the red light comes on and I go into self-imposed hypnosis while everyone behind the camera keeps running into each other, only now screaming in mime?"

"Georgiana," Cassy said, ignoring Alexandra, "I would love it if you would stay and watch the show with me. I'll give you the whole tour and it *is* fun—I only ask that you give me an autograph for my son, Henry, who is completely and totally in love with you."

"Done," Georgiana said, smiling. She looked at Alexandra. "As long as you don't mind."

"To the contrary," Alexandra said, beaming, "I'd love it if you'd stay."

And so while Alexandra and Kyle went charging off to the newsroom, Cassy Cochran gave Georgiana a tour of the entire news facility, from editing to engineering, satellite room to video shader. "I'm very proud of what we've accomplished," she explained.

Cassy, it turned out, was married to Jackson Darenbrook, CEO of the print side of the Darenbrook Communications empire. She had originally joined DBS News as Alexandra's executive producer, but from what Georgiana could read between the lines, it seemed Cassy had wound up in charge of launching not only the DBS news show, but the entire DBS network itself. In the process she and Darenbrook had fallen in love, and so he had stepped over to the other side of the empire, and his brother-in-law, Langley W. Petersen, took over as CEO of the broadcast and electronic research divisions.

After five years, DBS was doing very well, offering thirty hours of programming to their affiliates each week.

As the newscast drew closer, they trailed Alexandra through the news catacombs, observing her as she watched video segments, read over copy, and visited with each of the on-air reporters to go over their copy. Finally, she sat down and pounded out copy that she would read over the air in less than an hour. After keying her final draft into the computer—which Kyle and the segment producers were standing by to read on their terminals—Alexandra went into wardrobe where a lady named Cleo did her makeup and hair. She then took her place at the desk on the set, reading through a copy of her script from beginning to end.

Sound levels. Tests. Segment transitions. Alexandra looked up from her script or stopped her discussions with on- and off-air talent to comply with requests coming into the studio from the director in the control room.

Long accustomed to retakes and sometimes entire days of preparation to shoot a single scene, live television scared Georgiana to death. The entire process was full of the tension and controlled panic she had been trying all her life to avoid, yet these people worked here, day after day, under the most stressful conditions imaginable. It was they who were held accountable for producing the most on-target, error-free, and intellectually exacting performance of all.

Sitting in the control room with Cassy, watching as the newscast began—the set aglow in the hushed, eerie cavern of the darkened studio—Georgiana wondered how Alexandra could do this five days a week, month after month, year after year. After all, the woman had just gotten off a plane from Iraq this afternoon.

No wonder she seemed so much older.

After a quick post-newscast wrap meeting, Alexandra offered to drop Georgiana at the Regency on her way home. They climbed into Alexandra's limo and tried to make small talk, but they were both a little shy now. The foundation of their friendship had been forged over the phone, not in limousine jump seats.

"Could we go to your apartment for a bit?"

Alexandra hesitated. "Aren't you tired?"

"Yes," Georgiana said, "but I'm also so glad to see you."

Alexandra looked at Georgiana, smiled, and slid open the glass partition to tell the driver to go directly to Central Park West.

Alexandra's apartment overlooked Central Park. The living room was traditional, with a gorgeous down-filled sofa, some pretty wing chairs, pastel drapes, and several landscape paintings. The big, lovely—though windowless—kitchen looked as though it belonged in some huge old country farmhouse. There was a large guest room with striped wallpaper and twin beds separated by a Martha Washington table. Alexandra's bedroom also overlooked the park. A king-sized bed with a handmade quilt on it was against one wall, while a couch and chair formed a sitting area by the window.

The most telling room, however, was Alexandra's office: a towering mess of videocassettes, computer terminals, VCRs, TV screens, magazines, reference books, and torn-apart newspapers. "My life," Alexandra said, gesturing to the entire apartment. "Vast neatness confining a small area of rampant turmoil and disorder."

Georgiana liked that. And she suspected it might apply to Alexandra herself.

Alexandra poured them each a glass of sparkling water and they went into the living room. Georgiana chose the couch and Alexandra slipped off her shoes and curled up in a chair, demurely tucking her legs under her.

"I liked Cassy a lot," Georgiana said.

"She's great," Alexandra agreed, sipping.

"But for the life of me," Georgiana said, "I do not understand how you can do what you do for a living without being addicted to tranquilizers."

Alexandra laughed. "It takes years of practice and a rare form of mental illness, I think."

She was lovely, Georgiana thought. So warm and lovely, but capable, too. This was a woman who could handle anything.

"You know how much I'm attracted to you, don't you?" Georgiana heard herself say.

Alexandra jerked forward, trying not to spill water in her lap.

Georgiana smiled weakly. "Sorry."

"No, that's all right," Alexandra said quickly, straightening up, smoothing her dress, doing a good job of avoiding Georgiana's eyes.

"How do you feel about that?" Georgiana said.

"I, well, um, I'm obviously drawn to you, too, and . . . well, friends are like that. Aren't they?"

"I'm sexually attracted to you," Georgiana said quietly.

"I know that you were married," Alexandra said, looking down at her drink, as if she were carrying on another conversation with someone else. After a long pause she said, "You've made your attraction pretty clear in our phone conversations."

"You never acknowledged it."

Alexandra looked up. "No, I didn't."

"Talk to me. Tell me what you feel," Georgiana said.

Alexandra got up and walked over to the window. "I can't do this, Georgiana."

"Of course you can. If you want to. And I think you want to."

Alexandra's head fell forward and stayed there for a long few minutes. When she finally turned around, glass still in hand, she said, "I have over two hundred people whose jobs depend on me. So does it really matter what I want?"

"You can't hide behind your work forever," Georgiana said, setting her glass down on the coffee table. She was gaining confidence now. She had not been mistaken. "Because I think you know," she added, sitting back, extending her arms along the back of the couch, "that if you shut yourself down, it's only a matter of time before you use up all the emotional energy you have in reserve."

Alexandra was looking at Georgiana's chest, but didn't realize it. When she did, her eyes darted away, and she looked as though she were about to bolt from the room.

"Come over here and sit down," Georgiana said, raising an arm. "We need to sort this out."

Alexandra did not move.

"Are you seeing anyone?" Georgiana asked.

"I see different people," Alexandra told her.

"Are you sleeping with anyone?"

Alexandra shook her head.

Somehow Georgiana knew this was not the time to tell Alexandra that she had just had sex two nights ago with the King of Right-wing Radio.

"Alexandra," she asked softly, "have you ever made love to a woman?"

Alexandra let out a slow breath. "Georgiana, I'm sorry. It was wrong of me to bring you here."

"I asked you to bring me here."

"In fact," Alexandra said quickly, "I think all of this is a mistake . . ."

She stopped because Georgiana had gotten up and was walking over to her.

Georgiana put her hands on Alexandra's shoulders and looked her straight in the eye. "You're happy with the way things are in your life, Alexandra? You're not thrilled and terrified that you might have finally met someone? Someone who's played the same game you have, but to lengths you can't even imagine?"

Alexandra's eyes were searching hers. "It's no match—no game.

It's real life, Georgiana." And then, completely catching Georgiana by surprise, she kissed her.

There was nothing shy about the arms that pulled Georgiana to her; there was nothing inexperienced about the mouth that was kissing her. If Alexandra wanted to show she knew more than Georgiana thought she did, she had succeeded.

When Alexandra pulled back to look at her, Georgiana knew she had just lost whatever control she had thought she had over the situation.

"We need to think about this," Alexandra told her.

A few moments later, Georgiana was heading downstairs, wondering what on earth had just happened to her.

~ *26* ~

The telephone was ringing as Georgiana unlocked the door of her hotel room and she hurried to answer it.

"Where have you been?" Montgomery Grant Smith demanded. "I've been worried sick about you! The security people said you left DBS hours ago! I thought someone had kidnapped you!"

"I was in the newsroom and the studio," Georgiana said, cursing herself for answering the phone. "I stayed on to watch the newscast."

"It's nearly two o'clock in the morning!" he said.

"I stayed to talk for a while afterward," she said.

"Jesus, Georgiana, do you know what can happen to a woman in this city? Get in a cab and they'll take you to some godforsaken lot and—"

"This has got to stop, Monty."

"What has to?" He sounded startled.

"Your watching my every move."

"So shoot me, I was worried, okay?" he said. She didn't say anything, so he added, "I care about you, Georgiana."

"I appreciate that, Monty, but it's quite unnecessary and inappropriate for you to worry about my comings and goings. Besides, I'm home safe and sound now, and I'm going to bed."

"You don't want to have a quick nightcap, do you?"

She was tempted to throw the phone across the room, but instead she said, "No, no thank you, Monty. I don't. And you have a big day tomorrow and so you better get some sleep."

"Will I see you tomorrow?"

"I don't know, Monty," she said crossly. And then she softened. "Look, probably. And good luck tomorrow with the court order. I want to hear how it goes, okay?"

"Okay."

"Good night," she said.

"Good night, Georgiana."

"Oh, pooh!" she said, slamming the phone down. Almost immediately it rang again. She picked it up. "Now what?" she wanted to know.

"I only wish I knew," Alexandra said with a laugh.

~ 27 ~

At nine forty-five on Tuesday morning, Elizabeth Robinson, Montgomery Grant Smith, and David Aussenhoff were standing next to a cart selling coffee on the southwest corner of Fifth Avenue and Eighteenth Street, each alternately looking up at the carved-stone facades above the windows of 101 Fifth across the street and then looking north up the avenue. Monty's private investigation firm had already reported that Marion Ballicutt and James Stanley Johnson and some workers had been in the Hillings & Hillings offices yesterday, tearing the place apart, and were back in there again this morning.

Despite the seriousness of their mission this morning, they were all in pretty good cheer. Dorothy Hillings had come through her angioplasty procedure the day before with flying colors, and the doctors were talking of releasing her tomorrow.

"Where is he?" Elizabeth said nervously, looking up and down Fifth Avenue. She was referring to Joshua Lafayette, the Hillingses' attorney, who was to bring the court order and deputies from the city sheriff's office.

"Relax, he'll be here," Monty said. "What I want to know is, where's the camera crew Alexandra Waring promised?"

As if someone had heard him, an unmarked van pulled up to the corner of Eighteenth Street and honked. "Mr. Smith?" a young man called.

"Here!" Monty said, holding his hand up.

"Alexandra says, 'Kudos from DBS,' " the man said. "We'll park and come back." The van surged ahead as the light changed.

"I can't believe you got DBS News," David said, sipping the cup of coffee he had gotten from the vendor. He wouldn't be going up to the offices with them; he was there, he said, simply to support Elizabeth.

"That's Georgiana's doing," Monty said. "Alexandra Waring loved the idea of us repossessing the offices after ICA repossessed them from Hillings & Hillings." He paused. "I don't know why, but she seems to have trouble believing what a terrific guy I am."

"Perhaps you tell people that too often, Montgomery," Elizabeth suggested, as a cab pulled over on the other side of the street and Josh jumped out and waved, waiting for traffic to clear so he could cross.

"Where are the cops?" Monty demanded when Josh reached them.

"Al Sharpton's got some protest going on in Brooklyn and everybody's been pulled to emergency duty," the lawyer said, balancing his briefcase on one knee to open it.

"Damn it," Monty said. "We've got the cameras, we need cops."

"I'll get you cops," David said. "When you guys go up, I'll call the police and tell them there's a robbery in progress."

"Here's the warrant," Josh said, handing a sheaf of papers to Monty. "I'd like to go up with you, but Henry says for me to stay away."

"And well you should," Elizabeth said. "Scoot, the newspeople are coming."

"Good luck!" Josh said, walking down the sidewalk and instantly blending in with the crowds of people hurrying to their offices.

"All right, now," Monty said, looking at his watch, "let's get this straight. The professor and I are going up and you're going to call the police—"

"Uh-oh," Elizabeth said, looking over Monty's shoulder.

Millicent Parks and Louise and Jordan Wells were coming toward them, and Jordan was carrying a video camera. "I have decided to help you!" Millicent sang out. "Well," Millicent said to Monty, stopping at his side, "here I am, back-up troops in tow."

Monty looked at her. "You must know how much I've missed you."

"How foolish you must be to miss someone who so dislikes you, Mr. Smith," the older lady returned. "But we—that is, most of America—already know what a fool you are."

"I'm going to strangle her," Monty promised under his breath to Elizabeth.

"Millicent, Monty, please," Elizabeth said.

"Louise, I know how to *do* this," Jordan said, jerking the camera away from his wife's hands.

"Mr. Smith?" the DBS man said, appearing with a young woman carrying a video cam on her shoulder. "I'm Will Rafferty and this is Deb Goldberg. Our orders are to just follow behind you and film, so you can go on and do what you need to do and we'll try and stay out of the way."

"We're glad you're here, thanks for coming," Monty said congenially, tie blowing in the wind.

"I guess I don't need my camera then," Jordan said.

"They don't need us period, Jordan," Louise said. "I told you."

"Control these people," Montgomery told Elizabeth.

"Okay, let's calm down, everyone," Elizabeth said. "If you want to come up, fine, that's your decision, but we are not to say or do anything until after Montgomery serves the warrant."

"We've got to move," Monty said, checking his watch. "I've got a show to do after this."

"I'll go make my call," David said, looking at his watch. "I'll give you five minutes, okay?"

"Make it four," Montgomery said. "Okay, let's go."

Elizabeth caught the sleeve of his jacket and pulled him back as a taxi narrowly missed him.

"Good luck, Bets," David said, giving Elizabeth a kiss on the cheek.

The light changed and they made their way across with the DBS news crew following closely behind.

"Didn't I tell you they were going to need us?" Elizabeth heard Jordan asking his wife.

"Need us?" Louise wailed. "Did you see their faces?"

"Why doesn't she just leave him alone?" Monty growled to Elizabeth. "I can't stand couples who bicker and fight."

Their first hurdle was the security man in the lobby of 101 Fifth Avenue, who had quickly surmised that this was not a group of regular workers entering the building. Elizabeth talked them through, though, explaining they were part of a surprise birthday party for Marion Ballicutt upstairs, and that he shouldn't wreck the surprise by calling up there ahead of them.

"You'll have to sign in," the guard said.

And so Elizabeth Robinson, best-selling historian, dutifully signed them all in as Elizabeth Farren, Lord Derby, Charles James Fox, Sarah and William Siddons, and the Drury Lane Theatre press corps, hoping against hope the guard was not overly familiar with eighteenth-century British history.

The building elevators were not large, and so it was with a bit of pressure that they managed to pack themselves and all of their equipment in. The DBS camera started to roll.

It was a long and heavy haul up to the eleventh floor and the creaking elevator was causing all of them mild anxiety.

"Wait!" Elizabeth suddenly cried, pushing the 10 button.

"What are you doing?" Millicent asked.

"They have to buzz us into the offices," Elizabeth said as the elevator stopped. "When they see all of us and these cameras, there's no way they're going to let us in." The doors opened and Elizabeth stepped out, holding the doors back. "I think Monty should go up and get in first, or I should, and then we'll let you people in."

"She's right," Monty said quickly, "everybody out."

"Oh, dear, this *is* getting rather complicated," Millicent said.

"So how do we know when to come up?" Jordan asked.

As the crowd got out the elevator doors were shaking and banging, trying to close after being held open so long. People on the tenth floor were peering at them out of the reception window. The DBS camera was still rolling and every time it swung in somebody's direction, they instinctively stopped frowning and touched at their hair.

"Look, I'm going up," Monty said. "Elizabeth, I think you should come with me. You guys, come up in about two minutes, okay?"

They agreed and Monty and Elizabeth got back in the elevator and continued up to the eleventh floor, where Monty pushed the buzzer for Hillings & Hillings. They both smiled very nicely when James Stanley Johnson looked through the glass door. He did not smile back. He did not buzz them in either. Instead, he turned around and dashed out of the waiting room.

"Damn," Montgomery said. "He's not going to let us in."

"Is there another way in, I wonder?" Elizabeth said.

"Freight elevator?" he asked her.

They turned around to find that their elevator was gone. They pushed the button about nineteen times and it did not come up. "The stairs, Monty," she said, pointing.

They opened the staircase door and a bell went off, but it stopped when the door closed behind them. They went down to the tenth floor and tripped another alarm, which soon went off again, but the only people standing there were the office workers. "Where are the people who were here?" Monty demanded.

"They're in there," they said, pointing to the elevator. "It's not moving, they're stuck."

"Wait!" cried a worker, his ear against the elevator door. "It's moving, I think."

"Upstairs?" Elizabeth asked Monty.

They ran back up the stairs to the eleventh floor. No one was there. No one would answer the buzzer to the offices. They looked at each other and ran back down to ten, setting off alarms wherever they went. "Is there a freight elevator?" Monty gasped to one of the women. She nodded. "Can we cut through?" he begged. "We have to get up to the eleventh floor."

She hesitated until someone said, "It's Montgomery Grant Smith, the radio guy, help him," and that seemed to give her permission because she quickly led them through the maze of the accounting offices to a fireproof back door. She slid the bolt across and opened it, revealing a hallway, bathrooms, another staircase, and the freight elevator.

They pushed the elevator button and pushed it and pushed it.

Elizabeth whipped around to Monty, who was very red in the face. She prayed he wouldn't have a heart attack. "Stairs?"

He nodded, heaving himself in that direction, and they went tearing up the stairs, throwing open the door on the eleventh floor, and literally careened into Marion Ballicutt and James Stanley Johnson, who were standing by as two workmen pushed out a trolley of boxes through the back door of Hillings & Hillings.

"In the name of the Supreme Court of the state of New York, I hereby impound these boxes and all property belonging to the offices of Hillings & Hillings at One Hundred One Fifth Avenue!" Monty said, flinging the papers at James Stanley Johnson.

"*No*, to her," Elizabeth said, snatching them back from the accountant and thrusting the papers into the hands of the lawyer.

"What the hell is this?" one of the workmen said under his breath.

The other workmen said something in another language.

"You two," Monty bellowed at them, "get out of here—before it's too late."

They looked at each other but didn't move, hands still on the trolley.

"Take these boxes downstairs as I instructed," Marion Ballicutt told them.

"Bullshit you do!" Monty said. He was a mess, sweaty, nearly purple in the face, shirttail completely out of his pants.

"Montgomery Grant Smith, I believe," Marion Ballicutt said. "And Professor Robinson," she said, nodding to Elizabeth. "I must inform you that we are no longer on Hillings & Hillings property, and that you have no right to impede us, or the removal of these boxes from the premises."

"Lady, if you think you're moving these boxes out, think again," Monty said, pushing the trolley back toward the doorway of the offices.

"I'm warning you, Mr. Smith!" she said, as the two workmen stood their ground, hefting their shoulders against the trolley to squarely oppose Monty's efforts. Monty gave a grunt and a heave and pushed the trolley back about six inches. The workmen countered, but Monty, gritting his teeth and jamming against the trolley like a linebacker, grunted, "No way, you fuckers, no way," Marion

Ballicutt yelled, "Help them, James!" and then there was a horrendous crashing sound from inside the Hillings & Hillings offices, and all of them just stood there a moment stunned, trying to figure out what the noise had been, and then they heard men shouting and squawks of walkie-talkies and suddenly the door of the offices came crashing open, smashing against the wall, and New York's Finest were standing there, guns drawn, crying, "Halt! Don't move!" and after the first initial shock wave passed over her, Elizabeth had to smile, because over the shoulders of the police was the DBS News camera getting the scene.

Everyone started talking at once and the talk turned to furious shouting and the police, doubting just about everything everyone was saying, made them all leave the premises. They proceeded to seal the offices with padlocks and chains and alarming yellow banners that announced it as a crime scene. Marion Ballicutt, the workmen, and James Stanley Johnson were taken downstairs in one elevator by the police, while Monty, Elizabeth, and the DBS news crew were taken in another. As Monty and Elizabeth were escorted across the sidewalk to a waiting police car, they spotted Millicent, Louise, and Jordan in the crowd that had gathered behind a police blockade.

"Call Josh," Elizabeth shouted over the noise. "Tell him the police impounded the office—they didn't get any files out, but we can't get at them either."

"Call this number and page this guy," Monty said, stretching to hand Jordan a card. "Tell him to call Josh Lafayette—the number's on the back—tell him to call immediately for instructions."

"Wait, where are you going?" Jordan said.

"The cops are going to drop me at the studio," he said. "I go on the air in twenty minutes!"

"What about Elizabeth?" Millicent called.

"Elizabeth is the sacrificial lamb," Elizabeth answered as she was led away by the police. "Thanks a lot, Mr. Smith!"

"The show must go on!" Monty called back, hopping into a squad car that immediately sped away, lights flashing.

Elizabeth gave Millicent and the Jordans a sad little wave of farewell before a police officer directed her toward one of the patrol cars.

"She's going to jail?" Louise said to Millicent in disbelief.

"That buffoon has done it," Millicent muttered, leaving Louise and Jordan behind and walking toward the car where Elizabeth was sitting in the backseat.

The Jordans watched as Millicent pushed the policeman aside and climbed into the car next to Elizabeth. "I am also a felon," she announced.

Creighton Berns's telephone at his home in Pacific Palisades rang while he was shaving. Karen, his wife, was still in bed and rolled over to answer it.

"It's Marion," she called.

Creighton picked up the phone in the bathroom. "Got it, honey," and waited for her to hang up.

"Hello?" Karen heard her husband say. There was a pause and then, *"What the fuck are you talking about! They can't get those back!"*

For all the power and prestige of Creighton's new position at ICA, Karen was beginning to wonder if her husband was going to be able to handle it. Running the studio had been bad enough—at the office night after night; headaches, nosebleeds, and complete exhaustion when he did get home—but this ICA position . . . She had to wonder if there was a reason why thirty-five-year-olds hadn't been given jobs like this before. Creighton was a mess, and he'd only been in the job a few weeks.

"No! *No!*" her husband was yelling in the bathroom. "Marion, listen to me—*we have to have them.*" Pause. "Got it? Now, you do whatever you have to do, but *see that they do not get their hands on those files. Do you understand me?*"

"Mommy?" little Jeffy asked from the door.

"It's okay," Karen told him. "Daddy's just upset. Go find Nanny Antonia and tell her to give you breakfast."

～ *28* ～

Joshua Lafayette arrived at the police precinct just as two ICA lawyers did. The police begged him to get Millicent Parks out of the precinct. After much discussion, Millicent finally acquiesced and allowed a handsome young detective to drive her back to the Plaza. Josh then went to the police chief's office with the ICA lawyers and Elizabeth sat down next to James Stanley Johnson on a bench in the hallway.

"You must admit, James," Elizabeth finally said to him, turning and crossing her legs in his direction, "it was rather strange of ICA to impound the offices of people they had been doing business with for twenty-seven years for absolutely no reason."

He looked at her but said nothing.

"I know you're just doing your job, but what I mean to say is, well, perhaps you should be looking for another job. You seem to be a bright and talented and very nice person. Wouldn't it make more sense to be in a job where people could afford to like you?"

He continued to look at her with a blank, impassive face.

She sighed, staring at a poster on the opposite wall. "Life is short. But then," she added, looking over at him, "I made a good deal of money on my first book, so I guess it's easy for me to be on my high horse about ethics."

"Yes, it is," James Stanley Johnson told her.

She nodded to herself, as if she had learned what she wanted to know. She sat back against the bench and crossed her legs the other way.

About a half hour later, Josh and the other lawyers emerged. "Okay, we can go," he told Elizabeth, holding his hand out to her.

"Good-bye, Sergeant," Elizabeth called. "Thank you for the tea."

"Our pleasure, ma'am. But stay out of trouble, now!"

"If I don't," Elizabeth said, laughing, "I'll make sure to bring Millicent with me."

As soon as they were out of earshot of the ICA crew, Josh murmured, "The files are tied up for at least a month. No one—and I mean *no one*—can get at them, including us." He opened the front door of the precinct for Elizabeth.

"Professor Robinson," a male reporter said, hurrying over with a microphone extended. Behind him was a camera and parked curbside was a WST news van with a microphone antenna on top. "Is it true that you were arrested for trespassing?"

"How can a client be arrested for trespassing in her own agent's offices?" Elizabeth said.

"But you were attempting to steal files," the reporter said.

Elizabeth looked at him. "I most certainly was not."

"Oh," the reporter said, looking frantically at his notes.

Elizabeth answered a few more questions and then Josh nodded that it was enough.

"How do they know about it?" she asked, getting into a cab with him.

"WST is the DBS affiliate in New York," he explained. "I spoke to one of the reporters on my way into the station house. Apparently DBS is all over this story—big time."

Elizabeth smiled.

"Did you see it?" Alexandra asked Georgiana over the telephone.

"Yes, it was wonderful!" Georgiana declared. The local news had run the story and footage about the "incident" at Hillings & Hillings on their noontime broadcast, starring crazy Montgomery Grant Smith as the fire-breathing hero battling evil in the hallway, and Elizabeth as some sort of intellectual damsel in distress. It was very dramatic and very funny. Marion Ballicutt was seen giving a quote: "All we are able to tell you at this time is that the offices and what is in them belong to ICA and we have no idea what prompted this bizarre incident."

"Thank you so much for sending the crew over," Georgiana said.

"To tell you the truth," Alexandra said, "I don't have any idea what's going on at ICA either, so I'm afraid our story tonight will be limited to the shock value of the film we've already let WST show." She chuckled. "Montgomery Grant Smith shouting and wrestling with people does have a certain news cachet, I suppose."

"It's great," Georgiana said, "and I'll tell everybody to watch tonight." They were quiet for a moment. "I don't suppose we could have dinner or something after?"

"I'd like to, but—"

"But what?" Georgiana asked, heart pounding. She had been up most of the night and had been riding an emotional roller coaster all day. Suddenly, she felt dangerously like a fool.

"I'm sorry, Georgiana," Alexandra said, "but I can't see you again so soon."

"I asked you to have dinner, not to get married," Georgiana said in her best Lord-Hamilton-Ayres's-daughter-is-annoyed voice.

"Tomorrow I have to do the newscast from Maine," Alexandra said, ignoring the comment. "It's the opening of fishing season."

"Ah, we mustn't miss that," Georgiana said. "From terrorists to trout, I understand completely."

"Don't be angry," Alexandra said gently.

"What should I be?"

"You could try being patient." Pause. "Please."

She was right. Georgiana took a breath. "Patient I can be," she said, her voice softening considerably. "Listen, the people here want me to meet with Creighton Berns anyway, so I think I'll book a flight home to Los Angeles and get that out of the way."

"When will you be coming back?" Alexandra asked her.

Georgiana smiled. It was the right question to ask.

"Henry, what on earth are you talking about?" Dorothy asked, staring at her husband in amazement.

"I must have your opinion on this movie," he insisted, putting the videocassette in the VCR he had brought to her hospital room. "I need your advice."

"Can't it wait until after the news?" she said.

Outside and down the hall, Millicent Parks was at the nurses' station, whispering, "The TV must be out of commission until we get Mrs. Hillings away from here tomorrow."

"Why?" the nurse whispered back.

"There's something being featured on the news that might very well impede her recovery."

"We can't protect our patients from life," the nurse said.

"This one you can—at least until tomorrow. Otherwise," she added, narrowing her eyes, "I'll know whom to blame."

The nurse blinked twice and said, "But the TV man isn't here this time of night!"

"Then tell the TV man we'll pay the damages," Millicent said, walking away.

"Damages?" the nurse asked.

Henry and Millicent turned on the bogus video project and waited until Dorothy finally excused herself to use the bathroom. As soon as the door closed behind her, Millicent yanked the cable wire out of the back of the hospital TV. When Dorothy came back out, she found the two of them muttering. "What is it?" she asked.

"Darn thing just came apart," Henry said, scratching his head. "Dottie, I'm afraid without the TV, we can't watch the rest of the video."

"Well, I must confess," she said, sitting down on the edge of her bed, "I'm not heartbroken. It was rather a bore, I thought, if that is at all helpful to you, Henry, darling."

"It is," he said, making sure the TV would not work.

"Perhaps it's just as well we can't watch it," Millicent added, trying to look disappointed, "since we have such a big day to-morrow."

"How they expect one to sleep when they wake you every hour of the night is beyond my comprehension," Dorothy said. "Millicent darling, may we please say good night to each other so I may climb back into this bed with some illusion of being able to handle the task gracefully."

"Ah, Dottie, you're your old self," Millicent said, giving her a kiss.

"Probably better, if the truth be known," she said. She touched Millicent's arm. "You are coming back to the country, aren't you? I'll die of boredom without you."

"Yes, of course, Dottie," Millicent said. "I'm going back with you tomorrow."

"You've been so wonderful to support Henry through all this," Dorothy said, looking sleepy now. "You are the dearest of dears."

"Yes, I know," Millicent said, beaming.

"I wasn't planning to say anything about it on the air," Monty explained to Elizabeth that night, following her down the Hill-ingses' hallway, "but after I heard WST was running a story on it, it seemed perfectly natural for me to explain my side of the altercation to my audience."

"No harm done," Elizabeth said. "In fact, the publicist we hired for the demonstration says it's great, now she won't be able to keep the press away from the protest next week. But better yet, Montgomery, as soon as Henry heard that ICA was trying to cart out boxes of files, he realized there must be something in the files that's not on the computer and that ICA is trying to find—which means whatever it is, it must be an old file, one older than at least 1978."

"What kind of file?" Monty asked.

"That's what we need to figure out," Elizabeth said. They had reached the doorway of the study and Elizabeth held Monty back. Josh Lafayette was in there, on the telephone, holding up one finger to signal he'd be off in a minute.

When Josh hung up, it was clear he was upset. "Well, now we know how ICA will react to today's negative publicity." He frowned. "They've filed a fifty-million-dollar suit against the Hillingses for breach of contract."

"ICA's suing *them?*" Monty exclaimed. "The Hillingses didn't do anything—the *courts* issued the repossession order!"

"Well, that's just the point," Josh explained. "ICA's not out to win. It's just a warning shot to demonstrate that, from here on in, they're prepared to drag the Hillingses into court on the slightest provocation."

"But the courts would dismiss a suit like that, wouldn't they?" Elizabeth asked.

"ICA could drag things out for years before they do. The idea is to force the Hillingses to show up in court again and again, and keep getting it postponed. And if that suit doesn't go well, they'll sue them about something else. The idea is to threaten the Hillingses with one lawsuit after another until they either kill them or bankrupt them with legal fees."

"But Henry's a lawyer," Monty said.

"And he's almost seventy-seven years old," Josh said quietly.

"Well then let's sue them!" Monty said.

"Well," Josh sighed, "we'll see." His eyes shifted to Elizabeth. "One bright note, though," he added, smiling a little, "I've got your plan all set up, Elizabeth. She starts tomorrow."

"Fabulous!" Elizabeth said. She turned to Monty. "Remember how much Patty Kleczak wanted to help us?"

"Patty? You mean the housewife from New Jersey?" Monty said.

"The romance–suspense novelist," Elizabeth said, correcting him. "Well, Patty's been working on and off for years as a temporary secretary. And so Josh has arranged some short-time employment for her."

Monty frowned, confused. "Yeah, so?"

"So Patty's going to be a temp," Elizabeth told him, "at ICA."

∼ *29* ∼

"Oh, must I?" Dorothy Hillings asked her doctor on Wednesday morning.

"I'm afraid so, Mrs. Hillings," he said. "It's hospital policy."

Her left eyebrow twitched in agitation as she looked at the wheelchair. She was standing, holding her husband's arm, dressed to the nines in a blue suit, gray silk blouse, three strands of pearls, and matching pearl earrings. She was also wearing a blue hat, which was rather jauntily pinned to the side.

"Well," she sighed, "if I must." And she walked over and sat down in the wheelchair, laying her pocketbook in her lap.

Bernadette, the aide Dorothy had engaged to look after her affairs, was dressed in street clothes. She went around to take the wheelchair, but the attendant explained that he had to do all discharges.

At the front entrance of the hospital on Seventy-seventh Street, Dorothy signed out and was taken to a gleaming black limousine. Millicent was standing beside it, talking to the driver. "Good grief, Henry," Dorothy said loudly, "anyone would think we had just gotten married."

Everyone laughed. Dorothy got out of the wheelchair and walked over to the car. She and Millicent climbed in, with Henry bringing up the rear. Bernadette climbed into the front seat with the driver. They were off to the Hamptons.

*   *   *

"Yes, of course," Elizabeth said, smiling, holding the portable telephone to her ear in the Hillingses' living room, as five pairs of eyes watched her, "Henry, yes, I've got it. Give her my love and tell her I'll see her soon. . . . Okay, great. . . . Yes, good-bye." She turned the phone off and announced, "Well, they're on their way. Henry was calling from the Long Island Expressway."

"And that battle-ax went with them, I hope," Monty said.

"Yes, Millicent is with them," Elizabeth confirmed, sitting back down on the couch next to Monty. She picked up her pad and pen. "Okay, so where were we?"

"Louise and I are going home to L.A. tomorrow," Jordan said. "And we're going to call our press contacts and ask them to cover the demonstration next week."

Elizabeth nodded, then looked at Georgiana Hamilton-Ayres.

"I'm booked on a flight to Los Angeles tonight, and I've already requested a meeting with Creighton tomorrow."

"But you can't leave now," Montgomery said quickly, looking upset.

Georgiana looked at him. "I thought you wanted me to talk to Creighton."

"But I don't want you to go," Montgomery blurted out.

"We *do* want you to meet with Creighton," Elizabeth said, trying to cover for the vulnerable talk-show host. "But do we want her to do it before or after the demonstration?" she asked, looking to Monty.

He wasn't listening. He was just looking at Georgiana with round, pleading eyes.

"I think you should see him as soon as possible," David said to Georgiana. "Tell him you were in New York and heard about the uproar and want to know what's going on. That would be perfectly natural."

"What do you think, Georgiana?" Elizabeth said.

"Oh, I'll do it," she said quickly. "And I'll be tactful—but to the point. And then I guess I'll call you, Elizabeth? Here? To report in?"

"You can call me," Montgomery said.

Everyone looked uncomfortable. Finally Georgiana said, "Where? In Chicago?"

"No, here, in New York," he said, sounding almost hostile. "At the Regency. I'll be here through next week, or as long as it takes to get this situation settled."

"You will be?" Elizabeth asked him. "I didn't know that."

Still looking at Georgiana, Monty said, "Now you do."

"Yes, well," Elizabeth said brightly, trying to move things along, "that would be enormously helpful, Montgomery. Thank you."

People murmured their approval; Elizabeth shouldn't be left to handle everything by herself. Elizabeth looked to David next.

"I'm afraid I need to go home tonight, too," David said.

Elizabeth tried to cover her surprise. "I thought you were going home tomorrow."

"It would be better if I went back tonight," he told her.

"There's room on the flight I just booked," Georgiana said.

"What are you flying?"

"American."

"Okay, I'll call," David said, getting up to take the portable phone into the kitchen.

"Wait, David," Elizabeth said. He turned around. "Are you going to call Creighton Berns when you get back?"

"I'm going to see him first thing," he said. "We had a meeting scheduled anyway."

"Yeah, I bet you did," Monty muttered under his breath.

"Okay," Elizabeth said, making a note for herself. "Well, that's it then. You all know what you're supposed to do."

"Elizabeth," David said in a low voice.

He was standing in the doorway of her room, the Hillingses' guest room, and his tone made her feel weak. More than anything, she wanted to slide her arms around his waist and press her head against his chest and hold on to him until she could sort her feelings out.

"I will be back to see you as soon as I can," he said.

She swallowed, not knowing what to say.

"I always loved you," he said. "I never stopped."

Elizabeth closed her eyes. It astounded her how fresh the pain was, how ready to return. She was scared of having it come back again. She would not get through it a second time, that much she knew.

"Oh, Bets, no," he said, coming over to her. She let him take her into his arms and hold her. She let him press her head against his chest and stroke her back. "I love you."

She had waited years to hear those words again. But instead of happiness, she felt her body starting to shake. He felt it, too, and held her tighter.

She was really scared now, but she couldn't help herself.

He reached down and pulled her face up and kissed her softly. Their mouths parted, her eyes still closed, and then he kissed her again, this time deeply, longingly.

Someone gruffly cleared his voice, and it startled them both, forcing them to break off their kiss, but David would not let her go. They turned their heads to see Montgomery in the doorway, looking acutely embarrassed.

"Sorry," he said, "but someone's on the phone for you, David. A woman named Susie. She says it's important."

"Oh," David said. He looked at Elizabeth and let his arms drop. "It's someone from the movie, I need to take it," and he left the room.

Elizabeth went into the bathroom for a tissue, wiped her eyes, blew her nose, and came back out, startled to see that Montgomery was now standing in her bedroom.

"It's none of my business, I know."

Elizabeth gave him a look that usually stopped any student dead in his tracks, but Montgomery Grant Smith, of course, was no student.

"But I've got to say it. Be careful, Professor. I'm sorry, but . . . I know the type."

"I need to put it to rest," she said, "one way or the other."

Montgomery nodded. And then he said, "Listen, while we're on the subject, could I ask your advice about something?"

Elizabeth hesitated and then nodded. "Sure." She gestured to a chair.

"The telephone is there," the housekeeper said to David, pointing to the phone lying on the breakfast table in the kitchen. "Ms. Hamilton-Ayres is using the other line in the study, I'm sorry."

"It's fine, thank you," David said, picking up the phone. "Hello?"

"Hi, Davey!" Susie said. "Is it true? You're coming home to-night?"

"Yeah, but I won't be getting in much before midnight."

"Oh, I'll wait up," she said happily. "I've really missed you."

He didn't say anything.

"And I've got a big surprise for you," she said.

"You didn't have to do that," he said uncomfortably.

"Should I just tell you? Oh, I can't wait—honey bunny, I got your car back!"

"What?" he said, a smile spreading across his face. "How?"

"I went right down to your money manager's office and I told him he was going to be history if he didn't straighten this out before you came home. And he did! The car came back this afternoon. It's outside in the driveway."

"Wow, thank you. Really—thanks a lot."

"And I got the phone back from next door," she continued gaily. "But I had to take it to Mr. Fix-It because you hit one of the neighbor's sprinkler heads with it. I took the sprinkler head, too, since your neighbor said it wasn't working right. Anyway, every-thing's all fixed and you're coming home!"

"Oh, she is," Georgiana was saying on the telephone behind closed doors in the study. "Just tell her I called and that I'll call her again when I get home." She frowned and then smiled. "No, of course, I'll hold."

A full minute went by.

"Hi!" Alexandra said, snapping onto the line. "I'm afraid I've only got about forty-five seconds. What time do you leave?"

"Six."

"Well, why don't you give me a call when you get in? Just so I know you got home okay?"

Georgiana swallowed. "Absolutely."

"Great. I've gotta dash."

There was a soft knock on the study door. "Me, too," Georgi-ana said. She hung up and went over to open the door. Monty was standing there, looking like a forlorn puppy.

"May I come in for a minute?" he said.

She shrugged, backing away slightly. He closed the door behind him, turning to face her. "Georgiana, you've got to tell me. What did I do that was so terribly wrong?"

"Oh, Monty!" she said, tired, walking over to a chair and throwing herself down in it. "Must we?"

"But I still don't understand. You still haven't told me why you're running away from me."

"I'm not running away from anyone," she said to the ceiling. She looked at him. "I don't know what else I can say to you except what I have already. Had I known you would take one evening and turn it into a minefield of rejection for yourself, I never would have slept with you."

"One *evening!*" he said. "What kind of woman *are* you?"

She looked at him. "Obviously a lonely one, Monty, one who certainly should have known better than to get drunk with you."

"But how could I *not* want something more with you, Georgiana?" he said softly, swiftly, moving near, stretching his hand out to her. "I think you are the most beautiful and talented woman in the world, and you shared your bed with me—"

"Bed?" she said. "We used the couch—and for about five minutes before I passed out, I might add."

"But I think I love you."

"Love me?" she gasped. "You don't even know me!" She couldn't help it. He was going too far. She shook her head, as if to get the words out of her ears. "Monty, I'm simply not available. That's it, end of story."

He winced and sighed, dropping down in a heap on the couch. She looked over at him. "I'm sorry."

"Don't you think I know how sorry you are to have ever met me?" he said in a depressed voice. "Don't you think I know you never would have slept with me if you hadn't been drunk?"

This took Georgiana by surprise. She might have suspected that he had a streak of self-hatred, but she didn't expect him to show it. The poor guy really was upset. "Wait a minute, Monty, you're turning this into some pivotal moment of your life when it isn't one. Believe me, you're just lonely and isolated and I just happened to be there. You may be disappointed that things can't go any farther, but soon you'll meet the right person and you'll be relieved that nothing more happened between us."

"I may be a nerd in your book, but that doesn't mean I can't have a relationship with a woman as beautiful and talented and bright as you are," he growled.

"Exactly," Georgiana said quickly, wondering if he had heard a word she'd said. "And that's why you need to look for—"

"But you're lonely, too! You admitted it, Georgiana! You're as lonely as I am. And I know for a fact that you're as isolated in your personal life as I am."

She hesitated. "But not for the reasons you think."

"I don't think," he said, standing up, "I *know* you're different from other women, Georgiana! And I know you need someone who can take your mood changes."

"Monty," she sighed.

"Someone who understands the creative swings, the need to be in the spotlight, and the need to be safely alone, protected, cared for—"

"Monty, you don't get it!" she said sharply.

"Then explain it to me," he demanded.

"I do not want to pursue a relationship with you!" she said. "I'm sorry, but that's the honest to God truth."

"But—"

"And you have to ask yourself why you want to pursue a relationship with someone you know is not available."

"But you slept with me," he said weakly.

"I did not *sleep* with you!" she cried. "We *fucked*, Monty, and then I passed out, for God's sake! Go to any bar and find any woman who's drinking too much, and you can have the same experience as often as you want!" She was losing patience fast. "I'm sorry to leave things this way, but you leave me no choice." She stood to go. "Now, are you going to shake hands and say good-bye and be civil about this, or not?"

He hauled himself up. He was a very large man. Silently he held out his hand to her.

She took it.

And then he tried to take her in his arms and Georgiana screamed. He released her immediately and simply stared at her, breathing heavily.

There was a knock on the door. "Is everything all right in there?" Elizabeth asked.

Monty flung open the door so hard it crashed against the bookcase. "Great advice, Professor," he said. "Thanks a lot!" And he stormed past her down the hall. In a moment they heard the front door slam.

"Bets?" a voice called.

"It's all right, David," Elizabeth said. "I'll be there in a minute." She turned to Georgiana.

"*Your* advice," Georgiana said accusingly. "I echo the man's sentiments—thanks a whole hell of a lot, Elizabeth."

Elizabeth held out her hands. "All I suggested was that he ask you outright how you felt about him."

Georgiana glared at her for a moment, and then it passed. "Come in and close the door," she said, losing steam.

Elizabeth closed the door and turned, waiting.

"The night I arrived," Georgiana said quietly, "Monty and I got drunk in the Regency bar and I ended up having a one-night stand with him. It wasn't even a one-night stand, it was more like—I don't know what it was like, but believe me, it was nothing anyone would feel good about afterward."

"He says he might be in love with you," Elizabeth told her.

Georgiana threw her hands up in disbelief. "He's in love with the idea of sleeping with me, Elizabeth, that's all. You must know that."

"I think he means well."

"Oh, come on," Georgiana said.

"No, I mean it," she insisted. "I think he does care a lot about you, or at least he thinks he does. And for what it's worth, although his bravado and ego can be pretty god-awful, I know, he's not really—"

"Elizabeth," Georgiana said.

"—what he appears to be," Elizabeth continued.

"Elizabeth," Georgiana said again.

"He's a decent man, really, I do think so. I'm sorry, what were you saying?"

"I'm gay," Georgiana said quietly. "Is that reason enough for you to stop encouraging him?"

"Oh," Elizabeth said, looking at her slightly wide-eyed. "Yes, I suppose it is." There was a moment of silence. "I must confess, Georgiana, I'm rather shocked."

Georgiana gave her a tired smile. "Yes, well, we come in all kinds of packaging."

"Oh, no, that's not what I meant," Elizabeth said quickly. "I meant I'm shocked that *you*, of all people, could have so many problems with your love life."

Georgiana looked at her.

"I mean, if you're gay and having sex with Montgomery Grant Smith! I'm sorry if I'm being terribly out of line, but it does seem to indicate a bit of a problem, doesn't it? I mean, Montgomery!"

"Don't remind me." Georgiana half laughed and half sighed, dropping into a chair and covering her face with her hands. After a moment she looked up at Elizabeth. "Suffice it to say, I am a person who absolutely should not drink. But that isn't really much of an excuse."

"I think it's a pretty good one," Elizabeth said helpfully.

"No," Georgiana said, shaking her head. "Fact is, Monty's got a certain kind of sexual charm." She smiled. "Being with him was like being a teenager again. You know, sitting around for hours, turned on and trying to hide it, and then finally acting on it, except that I never did anything like that as a teenager—I was Miss Goody Two Shoes."

"Me, too," Elizabeth admitted. She sighed then, leaning back against the couch as if she were exhausted. "I've wanted to be gay in the worst way."

This time Georgiana burst out laughing. "What?"

Elizabeth was smiling. "Well, if I were, it would explain so much about the romantic problems I've had. This way I'm just a mess no matter which way you look at it."

"That's ridiculous," Georgiana said, trying to stifle another laugh. "You're the most together person I've met in quite some time."

"I only wish I was," Elizabeth said softly, thoughts drifting.

Georgiana watched her for a moment. "You've had a great love gone wrong, haven't you?"

Without looking at her, Elizabeth nodded.

"What happened to him?"

"He's in the living room."

"I apologize for prying, Elizabeth," Georgiana finally said when it was clear Elizabeth was not going to volunteer any more information. She stood up. "Do you suppose we could get anything to eat? I'm starving. Pasta, that's what I feel like. And a big salad. Do you suppose we could order in?"

"It was David," Elizabeth suddenly said. "This is the first time we've seen each other in three years. Neither one of us knew the other was coming here for the meeting."

"Oh," was all Georgiana could manage to say for a moment, thinking, *Good Lord, he really is in the living room. And David—poor Elizabeth!* "And now he's making overtures to you again?"

Elizabeth looked at her. "What do you think?"

Georgiana shrugged. "I don't know the whole story."

"But you know David," Elizabeth said, "you've worked with him. Tell me what your instincts are."

Georgiana bit her lower lip, thinking. "To be very, very careful until you fully understand the situation you may be getting back into."

"He still runs around with a lot of women, doesn't he?" she asked.

Georgiana shrugged. "I don't know about now." She met Elizabeth's eyes. "But while we shot our movie—yes, I knew of at least two."

Elizabeth nodded, and then smiled to herself, as if amused by some thought. "May I ask you something, Georgiana?"

"Anything."

There was a knock on the door. "Excuse me," the housekeeper said, popping her head around the door, "but Mr. Lafayette asked me to tell you that he is on his way back here with Mrs. Kleczak."

"Okay, good, thank you, Sasha," Elizabeth said, getting up. She turned to Georgiana. "Well, why don't we find some place to order in pasta and salad for everyone? That's what you said you'd like for lunch, isn't it?" She started for the door.

"You wanted to ask me something," Georgiana reminded her.

"Oh, that," Elizabeth said, reaching for the door. "It was nothing."

"No," Georgiana insisted, catching her arm, "what was it?"

Elizabeth looked at her. "I was going to ask if you would find me attractive if I were gay."

Georgiana's mouth fell open. "Are you joking?"

"No," Elizabeth said truthfully.

"Elizabeth, you're wildly attractive. A knockout, do you hear me? You may be a little too bright for most of the world, but you certainly have everything anybody could want."

"Really?" Elizabeth asked, not quite believing her.

"Really," Georgiana said. "You should never, *ever* judge your desirability based on someone else's neurotic insecurities."

"You mean David?"

"I mean, Elizabeth," Georgiana told her, "you're the catch of a lifetime."

Elizabeth looked at the actress for a long moment. And then she smiled and said, "Thank you."

After a moment, Georgiana said, "Is there something else? You seem like you want to say something else."

Elizabeth hesitated. And then she took a breath. "I don't want you to think all of our problems were David's fault. I—what I mean to say is, I have problems. I mean I did. I guess I do, still—" She sighed, letting her shoulders sag, discouraged.

Georgiana smiled and put a hand on her shoulder. "Elizabeth, no offense, but sometimes you sound as old as Methuselah."

"Yes, well, being a student of history can do that to you." Elizabeth sighed again, looking to the floor.

Georgiana laughed.

Elizabeth raised her head, half-startled.

"Lighten up, Elizabeth, will you?" Georgiana said, giving her shoulder a shake. "You mustn't always act like you're going bravely to the gallows."

"On some level, though, that's what I've always felt like."

"I don't think so," Georgiana said. "No, I don't think you could be doing all this for the Hillingses if you weren't someone with an underlying faith that things can and will get better—even for you." Elizabeth was looking at her with a kind of hope in her eyes now that couldn't help but touch Georgiana. "You're just still reeling from an unexpected collision with your past. And, if you're anything like me, the past, if it has anything even remotely connected to love in it, will make you feel worthless and depressed in no time."

Elizabeth's astonishment was obvious. "You?"

"Well, look at me, Elizabeth," Georgiana said, stepping back. "Besides the fact that America's sex symbol is a closet gay who just went to bed with Montgomery Grant Smith, tell me what's wrong with me."

"Why, nothing! You're talented and beautiful and successful and—"

"And so no one, but no one," Georgiana said, interrupting, "ever thinks anything can be wrong with me, or that anything they can do to me can ever really hurt me, because I have everything they think they want."

Elizabeth looked at her for a moment. "But nothing's ever really been done to me."

"And maybe that's it," Georgiana said. "Maybe that's what you've always expected of people in the past—nothing. Because that's what you've always gotten. And maybe that's why you get depressed and sound so old and weary, Miss Methuselah. Because you think it's you, and maybe it is, but only in the sense that people who can't give emotionally will always make a beeline toward people like you."

Elizabeth frowned. "But that's not true."

"I know it could have been true with David," Georgiana said. "I know him, Elizabeth. And I know other women who've been with him."

As if on cue, David's voice called down the hall, "Bets? Where are you guys? Josh and Patty are on their way up."

"We'll be there in a minute!" Elizabeth called back.

"The truth is," Georgiana said quietly, "I know how much Dorothy Hillings loves you. You've never been just a client to her. From the very beginning, when she pushed you to convert your thesis into that biography, you've been a daughter to her. And she thinks the world of you. And most of the rest of the world seems to think the world of you, too. So, Elizabeth, when I see you like this now, looking and sounding as though you're carrying the weight of the world on your shoulders, I think, Dear God, if Elizabeth Robinson can't be happy, what hope is there for me?"

Elizabeth was speechless.

~ *30* ~

"You're going to temp in the office of the agent who's selling your book?" Ted yelled at Patty when she returned from New York Wednesday night. "And act as a spy?"

"Just for a day or two, to see if I can find out anything."

"And what are you going to do later when you go to ICA as an author? Oh, look, it's the temp, Patty Jamison—now she's author Patty Kleczak."

"They won't know," Patty said, spreading the next layer of low-fat cheese for the lasagna she was making for dinner. "The agent I've been talking to is in Los Angeles and she's never seen me. Besides," she added, "I'll be in disguise."

"Cool, Mom," Mary Ellen said, looking up from her Spanish book. "I always said you belonged in the Gestapo."

"Patty," Ted said, "I don't know who the hell these people are in New York who are putting you up to this, but I can guarantee you, they don't have as much at risk as you do."

"For heaven's sake, Ted," she said, exasperated, wiping her hands on a dish towel and then starting on the next layer of pasta, "don't make such a big deal out of it. I go in, I type, I answer the phone for a few days. I might learn something, I might not. Regardless, they'll treat me like a migrant laborer, never even know my name, and I'll make a few dollars."

Somehow it didn't sound quite as simple as it had when Elizabeth Robinson had called to talk to her about it. She had been so excited to be asked to do something, she hadn't really thought it through. And—oh, boy—if Ted was upset about this, she'd better not show him the wig she had come home with. Darn, she had been kind of looking forward to wearing it tonight after the kids went to bed.

"Of course people will know it's not your natural hair color," the theatrical wig expert had explained to her earlier that day in New York. "The wig is quite blond and your eyebrows are dark."

"Which looks absolutely marvelous!" Georgiana Hamilton-Ayres had cried. "Harry, you're a genius!" She bent next to Patty and talked to her in the mirror. "I've got to leave for the airport now, and so I will leave you in Harry's expert hands. He'll show you how to put the wig on, and you can practice."

"Thank you so much," Patty had said in a daze.

What an afternoon! She had taken the train in to meet with the Hillingses' lawyer, Joshua Lafayette, to go over the things she was to look and listen for at ICA. Then he had taken her to the Hillingses' incredible apartment, where, after talking about the need for a disguise, Georgiana Hamilton-Ayres, the beautiful young actress, had taken her across town to the theater district to meet Harry, the man who did all of Georgiana's wigs for her movies.

And Patty had to admit, she did look sensational as a blonde. Something between Madonna and Ellen Barkin, but with brown eyes. And kids. Big kids. Oh, well.

"I'm absolutely against this," Ted was saying. "It's crazy."

Patty finished the lasagna and threw it into the microwave. It did not help her cause to be late with dinner.

"I understand you feel that this is *your* business, because it's your novel and your agent, but all of us are part of your life, too."

She looked at him. "It's my decision, Ted."

"Damn it, Patty." He took off his coach's jacket, rolled up his shirtsleeves, and began to wash his hands furiously at the kitchen sink.

Mary Ellen's head was swinging back and forth between them.

"We'll discuss it later," Patty said, starting in on the salad.

"There's nothing left to discuss, if I hear you right. You gave your word to those people." He dried his hands on a kitchen towel, kicked the screen door open, and walked into the backyard.

As she tore lettuce, Patty was aware of Mary Ellen's eyes on her. "Do your homework, Mary Ellen. If you have to go back to summer school again this year, I'll strangle you."

"If you get rich are you going to leave us?" her daughter asked.

Patty slapped the lettuce down on the cutting board and looked at her daughter. "Yes, that's right, Mary Ellen, just as soon as I have the money, I'm out of here."

"Cool," Mary Ellen said.

"Mary Ellen," her mother said sternly. "Whether you like it or not, you are stuck with me because I love you and everyone in this family—with all my heart!"

"But not enough to listen to Daddy," Mary Ellen noted, turning back to her book.

~ *31* ~

"These flowers came for you this morning, sir," the room service waiter reported, wheeling in Monty's breakfast. A basket of exotic spring flowers was sitting on the cart, swathed in clear plastic.

Monty signed for the breakfast and opened the card.

> Dear Montgomery,
> Please forgive me. I promise never to advise
> you in matters of the heart again. As you can
> tell, it is not my field of expertise.
>
> Fondly,
> Elizabeth

He looked at the flowers again and then picked up the phone and called the Hillingses'. Elizabeth answered with a cautious, "Hello?"

"*Monty,*" he said, "I will forgive you if you call me Monty! The way you say '*Montgomery*' always makes me feel like I'm in trouble at Sunday school or something."

She laughed. "I'm so relieved. And I really am so sorry, Monty, I didn't mean to—"

"It wasn't you," he sighed. "I was angry and I lost my temper."

They talked a little more, about what the day held for them both, and he agreed to come over to the apartment after his show to go over the latest on the Hillings & Hillings situation.

"Professor," he said just before getting off.

"Yes?" she said.

"I still think you should be careful of that Aussenhoff guy. There's something not on the up-and-up about him."

"Now it's your turn to send flowers," she said, hanging up.

The ICA offices took up three floors on West Fifty-seventh Street in a fairly nice office building. Patty was there for only ten minutes before being shown to an IBM computer and handed a pile of dictation tapes. "Whose dictation is this?" she asked the woman to whom she reported.

"What do you care?"

"It would help to know whose name should be on the letters."

"Oh," the woman said coldly, walking away. "Carol Garten."

You could tell a lot about people by the way they treated their temporary secretaries, which is to say, at least in Patty's experience, that the people most abused in an office tended to head straight for the temps so they could kick *them* around. So far, so good. ICA was not terribly different from the offices Patty had temped for in New Jersey. What had been a horrible recession for most of the Northeast had been a heyday for temps, who were used to replace full-time clerical workers so big corporations didn't have to pay employee benefits.

Patty looked at the desks to her left and right. Both secretaries were doing their best to ignore her. "Excuse me," she said to the one on her right. "Do you know how to spell Carol Garten's name?"

"It's got an *e*," the secretary told her.

"C-a-r-o-l-e?" Patty asked. "G-a-r-t-e-n?"

"Yeah," the secretary said, picking up her phone.

Okay, fine, Patty thought, putting on the Dictaphone earphones and pressing the foot pedal on the floor. On the tape was the voice of a woman who was evidently some kind of foreign markets agent. Patty dutifully set to work, typing letters and reports and demands to people all over the world, flipping through the massive Rolodex assigned to her to check addresses and the spelling of names. On the spur of the moment, she flipped to H and found Hillings & Hillings with the scribbled notation: Dorothy—literary; Henry—dramatic.

Patty reviewed the names Elizabeth and Josh had given her:

Marion Ballicutt, James Stanley Johnson, Creighton Berns. She was to pay attention to anything she saw or heard in connection with them.

One thing was for sure, though, no one talked much at ICA; at least the assistants and secretaries were a very closemouthed group. When she tried to ask questions, the office staff pretty well ignored her. Later in the morning, when Patty was put off yet again by someone who wouldn't answer her questions about who did what at ICA, the secretary next to her whispered, "Look, every actress and her aunt sneaks in here as a temp. If you want your big break, it's going to have to come from walking through the door as your talented self. Okay?"

"You think I'm an actress?" Patty asked her, amazed and very, very pleased.

The secretary rolled her eyes and swiveled her chair so her back was to Patty.

When lunchtime came, Patty went into the ladies' room and very nearly jumped out of her skin when she passed the mirror. She had completely forgotten about the blond wig. Realizing that two women were staring at her in the mirror (well, what would she do if someone walked into the ladies' room and screamed, "Oh!" and jumped a mile high when she saw herself in the mirror?), she smiled and explained that she thought she had lost her necklace, but there it was, hanging around her neck!

The women looked at each other and moved out of her way.

She was given an hour for lunch, so Patty headed downstairs to the lobby to look at the building directory. Marion Ballicutt and James Stanley Johnson were both on her floor, but where? She got a sandwich at the New York Deli and went back up to her floor, casually asking the receptionist where Marion Ballicutt's office was.

"Why?" a voice demanded.

She turned to find an older, very prim woman staring at her.

"I'm sorry," Patty said, "I'm just a temp and I've been given a list of memos to distribute and I was trying to save time. I have to send things to people here and in Los Angeles and I don't know who is where."

Good answer! she thought to herself.

"Mrs. Ballicutt's office is down at the end of this hall," the woman said, pointing to a corridor that was far from Patty's assigned desk. "She's head legal counsel for the New York office."

"I see," Patty said humbly, "thank you very much."

"I will be out for approximately thirty minutes, Sylvia," the woman said, ignoring Patty. "I forwarded the phones."

"Yes, Miss Andersen," the receptionist said.

The woman walked out to the elevators without further word.

"They're all bitchy at that end," the receptionist explained as soon as the woman was out of earshot.

Patty nodded. "And where is James Stanley Johnson's office?"

"He's down there, too, next to Mrs. Ballicutt."

"Oh, do they work together?" Patty asked.

"Who knows?" the receptionist said. "They're so secretive down there these days they've just been given their own Xerox machine." She made a face. "They've always had their own bathrooms. I guess they don't think we're fit to mix with, if you know what I mean."

Patty thanked her and turned right down the hallway, instead of left. The major passageway seemed to head right again and so she kept going, emerging onto a small reception area. There was no one at the desk, but there were three office doors enticingly close by. She peeked in the first, but it seemed to be some sort of conference room. Gaining courage, she looked in the second and was startled to find a man in horn-rimmed glasses looking up at her from where he was sitting on the floor, surrounded by folders and papers that fanned out in every direction.

"Oh, excuse me," she said. "I was looking for Mrs. Ballicutt's office."

"Next door," he said, flicking his head in the direction of the office she hadn't peeked in yet.

Patty started to leave, but came back. "I'm sorry to interrupt again, but I can't help asking, What are you doing? I thought when people got to be as successful as you are, they were allowed to sit in a chair."

The man smiled. "Looking for a needle in a haystack."

"Well, if you need any help, I wish you'd ask to have me transferred down here," Patty said. "I'm temping at the other end and it's a madhouse down there. I like doing research and I wouldn't mind sitting on the floor."

He laughed. "Well, it's not as pleasant down here as you think, but thanks for the offer."

"You're Mr. Johnson, aren't you?" Patty asked.

He looked up again, startled.

"You're a great favorite with one of the girls down the hall," Patty said quickly. "Although she'd probably die a thousand deaths if you knew."

"Well, the truth is, I'm a happily married man." He gestured to a picture of a woman and two young children that sat on a nearby console.

"That's probably why she likes you," Patty said. They laughed. "Well, I better let you go," she said, moving on.

"Bye-bye," he said.

Patty saw the photocopying machine stuck right in the middle of the hall in a clearly haphazard arrangement for what were otherwise immaculate offices. Next to it, a desk guarded the entrance to Marion Ballicutt's office.

"What *are* you doing?" asked a voice from behind which she recognized from before as the secretary's. Patty's heart skipped a beat. Damn, she wasn't supposed to be back yet. Patty turned around, acutely conscious of the soda and sandwich she was still holding.

"I was just talking to Mr. Johnson, Miss Andersen," Patty said. "I got mixed up and didn't know which way was out."

The secretary was frowning. "I think you better go back to where you belong, don't you?" She moved over to her desk, picked up the phone, and punched in a number. "I'm back, Sylvia, thank you for taking calls." She hung up and looked at Patty.

"I'm not an aspiring actress or anything," Patty assured her.

"Obviously," Miss Andersen told her.

Unlike actors who were tied to a television series, Georgiana could essentially live wherever she pleased. She had chosen Los Angeles in recent years, but instead of buying in Santa Monica or Malibu, near the ocean, she had opted to rent in Bel Air, if for no other reason than it was the closest thing to a hometown she had ever known. In fact, there were still places in Bel Air where Georgiana could wave to an old neighbor, still there after all these years.

In Scotland she was a famous actress today, but her local celebrity in Inverness—bequeathed to her at birth as the only child of Lord Hamilton-Ayres—produced a kind of awe and admiration that far exceeded anything she could earn on her own merits. While "the mother" had been written off decades ago as utterly common, the area proudly claimed the beautiful and talented young heiress to the old Hamilton-Ayres estate as their own. It was a rather extraordinary life, but then, what marriage between Hollywood aristocracy and royalty had ever produced children with anything less?

After the accident with the renegade pest-control truck, Georgiana had not the heart or desire to get back into a classic car of any make. Instead, her business manager had leased her a new silver Jaguar convertible that, she had been assured, had an airbag in the steering wheel *and* on the passenger's side. It was in the garage when she got home from New York.

Georgiana took it out for the first time Thursday afternoon, driving down Stone Canyon Road, twisting and turning through the lush green of Bel Air's Santa Monica Mountains, until she reached the intersection with Sunset Boulevard. When the light changed, she turned left and zipped along Sunset through Beverly Hills, turning right on Doheny, right again into the parking lot of the ICA building. She had been surprised and oddly flattered that a call to Creighton Berns's office yesterday afternoon had gotten her a two-thirty appointment with him today.

She was checked in through security and took the elevator to the top floor. When she got off, she noticed the offices had been completely redone. It was as if Ben Rothstein and his famous ICA art collection had never existed. There was nothing to remember him by. Everything was different.

"Ms. Hamilton-Ayres," a young man said to her, shaking her hand, "how wonderful you look! One would never know you'd been in such a terrible accident."

Inwardly she winced, wondering how she would have been received at ICA *had* they been able to tell how badly her face had been smashed up.

"I'm Mr. Berns's assistant, Joseph Colum," he explained. "Mr. Berns is wrapping up a meeting and then you're to go straight in." Georgiana smiled and looked around for a seat.

"I know you don't remember me," he added, "but I was one of the members of the Hasty Pudding Club that presented you with the award three years ago."

"Oh," she said, sitting down, "yes, I thought you looked familiar. I felt very honored by that award, thank you." He grinned. "From Harvard to Hollywood, is it?"

"Yes," he said. "May I get you some coffee or something?"

"Some water would be lovely, thank you," Georgiana said. She picked up today's issue of *Variety* and flipped through it. A young woman brought her a bottle of Evian and a glass. Georgiana drank the water while she browsed through a copy of *Women's Wear Daily*, checking her watch periodically.

Interesting. He was keeping her waiting.

Finally his office door opened and Georgiana had to cover her surprise when David Aussenhoff walked out. She was unsure how to play it, and so she waited for a hint from him.

"Ms. Hamilton-Ayres," David said, extending his hand, "how wonderful to see you—David Aussenhoff. I hope and pray this agent of yours will encourage you to work on one of my films again."

"Thank you, David," Georgiana said, shaking his hand. She looked at Creighton Berns.

"Hello, Georgiana," he said, taking her hand and giving her a kiss on the cheek.

"Congratulations, Creighton," she said.

They said good-bye to David, and Georgiana went into his office, where they exchanged a few pleasantries about how well she looked, how the insurance company had come through to fully compensate for the accident, about how desperate Metropolis Pictures must be to have lost Creighton, and how evidently wonderfully well he had done at ICA already.

"But that's not what you want to talk about, Georgiana," he said, sitting back in his chair.

"Quite right," she acknowledged. She paused a moment, changing to the script she had written for herself. "Creighton, I'm not sure you're aware of this, but when I was a child I lived with Dorothy and Henry Hillings for over two years. And they were wonderful to me."

"They also sold your children's book," Creighton said.

"Yes, that's right. And so perhaps you can understand how terribly upset I am about the way this merger with ICA has been mishandled. And knowing you, Creighton, having worked with you in Metropolis, I've had a very hard time believing that you have any real idea of what has been going on in New York."

"What, exactly, are you referring to?" he asked her.

"The sudden impounding of the Hillings & Hillings offices, for a start."

He nodded. "That was a mistake, but you're quite right, it was done without my knowledge."

"And then there was the stealing of files."

He shook his head. "There was no stealing of files. The media's got that all balled up."

Georgiana made a mental note to tell Alexandra that DBS News had gotten things all balled up.

"And now there is this lawsuit against Dorothy and Henry, at a time when Dorothy is very ill."

"The suit is pure formality, Georgiana," he said, "you must know that. Whenever there is trouble in a business merger, certain procedures must be followed if one party won't honor their end of the agreement."

"Are you saying that the Hillingses somehow violated their agreement?"

"Oh, yes," he said quickly. "They violated the agreement on a number of points. The problem was, someone at ICA New York got fed up with them and went ahead and impounded the offices. As charming as the Hillingses are, there is a reason why they have been so successful over the years."

"What do you mean?" she asked.

"Henry and Dorothy Hillings are very, very good at what they do, and this was not the first time they tried to angle themselves out of an agreement because they couldn't control the deal. As a matter of fact, they have a long record of reneging on agreements if, for example, they did not like a certain producer or director the studio wanted to use on a particular adaptation of a book. Why people have let them get away with it for so long, I'm not sure. It could be that Ben was far more sympathetic to the Hillingses than he should have been."

Georgiana looked at him for a long moment. What he said had the ring of truth to it. Of course the Hillingses always tried to represent the best interests of their clients, and if there were administrative or creative changes to a deal they had made for one of their clients, they would naturally try to object, or get some control over what was happening. Even try to get out of the deal, if necessary.

Or was this simply a glossy lie? The kind she knew Creighton and any of the many successful executives-of-the-moment around town were capable of telling.

But maybe Creighton really hadn't known. He did say impounding the offices had been a mistake.

"So what are you going to do?" she asked.

"About what?"

"About the Hillingses," she said. "Don't you think you should sit down with them and sort things out?"

"Sort what out?"

"Well, the situation with the offices, for one."

"There's nothing to sort out, Georgiana. They belong to us and they've started a crazy campaign against us which has no foundation whatsoever." He paused. "And, true to form, they're using good people like you to do their dirty work for them."

"Creighton, let me get this straight," Georgiana said. "You're telling me that you've done nothing wrong—that all of this is simply a ploy on the part of the Hillingses to get out of their agreement with ICA."

He nodded. "I hate to be the one to tell you this, but they want to sell Hillings & Hillings to Ben Rothstein. They're old friends, and Ben could do a lot with the agency. Certainly he could foul up a lot of projects we have on the boards right now."

She didn't say anything.

"I suggest you talk to the Hillingses about all this."

"They're in seclusion now; Mrs. Hillings is still recovering from the heart attack she suffered when she discovered their offices padlocked," Georgiana said.

"Well, of course they would be unreachable at a time like this," Creighton said, in a way that seemed to confirm his point: the Hillingses were trying to get out of the deal so they could do one with Ben Rothstein, and were using their clients as a front to do it.

Georgiana felt vaguely ill. "Well, thank you for your time, Creighton," she said, getting up.

"Georgiana, you're very important to us," he said, coming around the desk. "When you need me, I'm here."

"Thank you, Creighton. I understand everything you've said, but I also want you to understand how important the Hillingses are to me and to my family. I want you to understand how badly I will take it if I find out that what you have told me is not true."

His eyes narrowed slightly, but he smiled as he took Georgiana's arm and walked her to the office door. "What I have told you is the truth, and I certainly would not like to see any bad blood spilled between us, Georgiana."

She felt a chill. There was a threat in what he had just said. She could feel it.

Elizabeth was on the telephone with Claire Spender Holland when the flowers arrived at the Hillingses' apartment. Sasha brought them in, explaining they were addressed to her. Elizabeth opened the card.

> My dear Professor,
> I didn't meant to hurt your feelings, but
> methinks the snake is out from
> underneath his rocketh. Please beware,
> fair maiden. I am a man. I know
> about these things.
>   Your friend and admirer,
>   Monty

Between Monty and Georgiana, Elizabeth thought, poor David was not exactly getting rave reviews. Why then, she wondered, did she not feel scared of him anymore? And yet still attracted?

*   *   *

After she was dismissed from ICA for the day, Patty hopped a Fifth Avenue downtown bus, jumped out at Twentieth Street, and walked east to Gramercy Park. It was such a shock, being in New York—with all the people, all the bustle, all the noise—that she could not make even this trek without consulting her pocket map nine times to reassure herself she was not lost. When she saw Gramercy Park and the Hillingses' building soaring up behind it, she felt a surge of relief, quickly replaced by a sense of freedom and adventure she had not felt in years.

Upstairs in the apartment she met with Elizabeth and Monty in the study. She started in on her day, focusing on the offices at the far end of the floor, her meeting with James Stanley Johnson, Marion Ballicutt's new photocopying machine, and so on.

Monty nodded as Elizabeth took notes.

"What about the papers he had on the floor?" Elizabeth asked. "Were they in a box or any kind of container?"

"Well, there were a ton of folders," Patty said.

"Were the labels handwritten or typed?" Monty asked.

She thought a moment and shook her head. "I'm sorry, I didn't see. But they were old, I could see that—a lot of paper was yellow with age."

Elizabeth and Monty looked at each other. "Could be," she said.

"There was a box, now that I think of it," Patty said. "But it wasn't a file box. I think it was a vodka carton."

Elizabeth had reached for the phone and was dialing. After a moment, Henry Hillings picked up in Water Mill.

"It's Elizabeth. May I ask you a question?"

"If you can assure me the yard will be done on time," Henry answered.

"You're not alone," she said.

"That's right."

"One quick question. Did you ever keep files in liquor-store cartons?"

"Is this a joke?"

"That's what I thought," Elizabeth said. "Thank you, good-bye."

Sasha was knocking on the door. "Mr. Smith?" she said, poking her head in the door. "Ms. Hamilton-Ayres is on the household line. She says it is very important."

"Coming," he said, jumping up and following her.

"Well," Elizabeth sighed, "I guess the papers James Stanley Johnson was going through could have been from another haystack, not the Hillings & Hillings one."

"But they could have been selected files that had already been pulled at Hillings & Hillings," Patty said. "Maybe they brought boxes with them."

"I wish we knew," Elizabeth said, nervously twiddling her pen.

"I'll try to get into his office again tomorrow," Patty promised.

"Please be careful," Elizabeth said.

"Oh, I will be," she assured her. "I know how to get in there now—at least long enough to glance at the labels on the files. And if I can't get in tomorrow, I'll try on Monday. They already said they need me next week."

"I don't know, Patty," Elizabeth sighed. "Having you there makes me such a nervous wreck, I can't tell you. And what about your family? Your husband can't be thrilled."

"My family doesn't love the idea and they'll be unhappy that I'm working in the city again next week," Patty said, "but, quite frankly, Elizabeth, I'm enjoying every minute of this. It's been years since I've been out of Stanton, much less running around New York with such a glamorous crowd."

Elizabeth smiled. "You're the glamorous one. I must say, you do look sensational as a blonde."

"Thanks," she said, touching the wig, which was so comfortable she kept forgetting she had it on. She looked at her watch. "It's getting late, though, I better call my husband."

"You know, Patty," Elizabeth said, "if you'd like, you're welcome to stay here tonight. There's another guest room. With the commute and everything I think maybe you should think about it. I'm sure I've got some clothes you can wear to work that'll fit you. And tomorrow's Friday, so you can go home for the weekend."

Patty's heart leapt. What fun it would be to stay! "Let me call Ted," she said, reaching for the telephone, dreading what his reaction would be but desperately wanting to make the call. She felt a sense of urgency about her own life right now that she hadn't ever felt. It wouldn't kill her family to fend for themselves for one night, would it?

While Patty was having a quiet argument with her husband over the telephone, Monty came into the study looking dark as a storm cloud. "You cannot believe what that sleazebag out there is saying," he said to Elizabeth.

"Who?"

"Creighton Berns, that's who." He sat down and repeated what Georgiana had reported to him.

"No, Ted!" Patty was whispering loudly into the phone. "What you could say is you understand how important this is to me, and offer to drive in some clothes!" Pause. "And just how many thousands of miles do you think I've driven over the last eighteen years, morning, noon, and night, bringing you lost equipment, playbooks, and missing players? Thousands, Ted! Thousands!"

Monty and Elizabeth looked at each other, trying not to listen.

Elizabeth cleared her throat and spoke a little louder. "There is a very good possibility that a lot of people will believe ICA's lies. Everyone knows how close Ben and the Hillingses are."

"Ben's in Bora Bora," Monty said.

"That's what I mean. Nobody can talk to him, so anyone can say what they like, and ICA won't talk to the Hillingses except through lawsuits—" She shook her head. "Something very weird is going on, Monty."

"We'll get to the bottom of it, I promise you."

"I hope so," she sighed. She glanced at Patty, who had turned her back to them to continue her argument. "Patty's going to try to get back in James Stanley Johnson's office tomorrow and see if she can get a look at one or two names on the files."

"What then?"

"Then we'll run the names by Henry and see if they mean anything to him. If we know what kinds of files they pulled, it could give us a clue about what they're after."

Monty nodded.

Patty hung up the phone but did not turn around.

Elizabeth turned. "Do you have to go back to New Jersey tonight?"

"No," Patty said. "I'm staying here tonight—if the offer still stands."

"Wonderful!" Elizabeth said. "I'm so glad, Patty. It gets lonely here at night."

"Yes, I'm very happy about it, too," Patty said, sniffing and turning around to smile. She was wiping tears from her eyes.

"I have an important announcement to make," Monty said, standing up. "I am taking you ladies out to dinner."

"Oh, no," Patty said, "you shouldn't—"

"If I want to take two gorgeous women to dinner, my dear Mrs. Kleczak," Monty said, "then who are you to deny me the pleasure?"

Patty sniffed again, and laughed.

Elizabeth stood up. "You're really buying?"

"This is correct, dear Professor," he said with a bow.

"Patty, come on," Elizabeth said, taking her arm and pulling her across the room, "let us wash our faces and brush our hair before he changes his mind."

Monty could hear them laughing in the hall. The sound made him smile. Amazing how quickly the moods could turn around in this house.

Three

~ *32* ~

They had bought the house on Cobb Road in Water Mill years ago, when the roof had been threatening to fall in and the front porch had been listing severely to the right. The floors and walls inside had fitted together like something out of a fun house, and the back staircase had required more additional wood for support work than there was original wood. On the north side of the house there had been two house jacks in use, keeping the building akeel, as it were, in the sea of unmowed grass. And yet, the Hillingses had been mad about it.

It was, after all, a giant Victorian farmhouse, with weathered cedar shingles; intricate wood moldings, borders, and shutters; and a deep shady porch wrapping around the front. Inside there was a huge kitchen, a parlor, a dining room, and a living room with a fireplace and real windowseats; and upstairs there were five bedrooms and, granted, only one bathroom. But the bay was across the street, and the oceanfront was scarcely a quarter mile down the road.

The twins, Peter and Susan, had been old enough to fall in love with the house, too, and that first year had been a true family project. They lived with the constant mess inspired by the local handyman, and the entire family—in between the children's adventures at the beach, Dorothy on the tennis court, and Henry on the golf course—endeavored to assist in the revitalization of the house.

Summer turned to fall, winter, and spring, and the Hillingses dutifully trekked out there every weekend. Henry burned and stripped one hundred years of paint to restore and refinish the interior woodwork, and then he moved on to strip and sand and refinish the wood floors; Dorothy wallpapered like mad, directed where the new wainscoting was to go, and then, in the spring, abandoned the house for the gardens that lay unturned for thirty years. The twins painted the porch and the trim on the outside of the house, sealed the cedar shingles with shellac. Between the two of them, they kept the lawn mowed and the hedges cut. Dorothy and Henry also took possession of the ancient barn, clearing it out so the family could use it as a two-car garage downstairs, but more importantly to them, the kids were able to clean out the second-floor rooms to create a place of their own. At the beginning of the family's third summer in Water Mill, the twins arrived home from their freshman year at college, to find that their "apartment" had been outfitted with a bathroom and running water!

In the beginning, the house had very nearly bankrupted the Hillingses of their savings, as old houses are wont to do, and while it broke their hearts, they had no choice but to rent it out the fifth summer so they could meet the expenses of the twins' senior year of college. It was the only year they had to do it; their children graduated, things picked up at the agency, and the house gradually evolved from being a very expensive haven to a most relaxing retreat, one which they could well afford.

Susan was married in the gardens behind the Water Mill house, and she and her husband had used the house as their own for years. When Susan had three children, it became particularly useful that it was so large. Peter, on the other hand, had moved out to the San Francisco area shortly after his marriage. He had two children now and as soon as the youngest turned four, all five of the Hillingses' grandchildren came to stay with their grandparents for two weeks in August.

What wild times those had been, Henry thought on Saturday afternoon, smiling to himself as he walked across the backyard. Especially that first summer: five children ranging in age from four to nine, two mother's helpers—who invariably got into more trouble than the children, at least at night, when they were apt to sneak to the beach to make out with boys, quickly getting in over their heads. Henry would have to go down and look for them in the dunes—an embarrassing business, tripping over blankets, peeking under upside-down lifeboats, and whispering to shadows beside bathhouses—and bring them home to Dorothy, who had to talk to them about the facts of life.

There were pictures all over the house from those years: Doe in clam-diggers, Henry in Bermudas, the children squinting with sunburned faces and gaps in their smiles where new teeth were coming in.

They had a great-grandchild now. Shocking, but true. Little Sally had gotten married too soon, both he and Doe thought, but it was her life. And now there was a sweet baby. What could they do, they had asked one another, except love and support the young couple as best they could?

But they were all so far away now! Susan's husband's agency had sent him to Hong Kong for three years. While one of their children was still with them, their eldest was working in a surf shop in Australia and Sally, the middle child, was living with her husband and baby in Portland. Peter, the Hillingses' son, was still working in San Francisco and living in Portola Valley; one of his children was at Stanford and the other was down at USC.

Both Peter and Susan had dropped everything and flown home to New York when they learned of their mother's heart attack, but when it became clear that Dorothy was going to be all right, they had returned to their own busy lives. But Henry wished it did not feel as though they were as far away as they were.

They were great children, the twins. Always had been. Smart, good-natured, popular enough to get into trouble occasionally, but well-grounded enough not to seek it out.

Doe missed them terribly, he knew.

At first he and Dorothy were disappointed that neither Susan nor Peter expressed much interest in the agency. But then it began to dawn on them that the poor kids had had so much of it as children—all day, all night, he and Doe talking about clients, deals, problems—that it was amazing they had not resented it more than they did.

Peter had worked at the agency for a year following his graduation from Yale. He had been bright and very fast to learn, but the Hillingses had quickly seen that their son lacked the personality to deal with writers. Peter thought everyone should stand on their own feet, emotionally and financially, which was a very fine thing if one were talking about stable and secure people, which, quite frankly, few of their clients were for any length of time. So while Peter could handle the business side adeptly, the clients were often thrown by his honesty; after listening to them for a while, he was apt to flat out say he thought they needed to grow up.

And so Peter went off to Wharton for the MBA he wanted, got a huge offer from a West Coast brokerage house, and became a Pacific Exchange millionaire in fairly good time. In 1986 he realized his dream and founded his own bank; today it was one of the few with an A rating in the entire state of California.

Henry heard a car on the gravel drive and walked around the side of the house to see who it was. A cream-colored Mercedes came to a stop and Millicent waved, getting out of the car.

"How good to see you," he said.

"Hello, Hill. I brought Doe some plants," Millicent said, gesturing to the roomy backseat which was covered with flats. "She told me she gets to start gardening soon, and I know that will prove to be very therapeutic for her."

"I hope you'll help her," Hill said, giving her a kiss on the cheek. "Between my knees and my back . . ." Ever since the morning of Dorothy's heart attack, both had been giving him trouble.

"Growing older is difficult for some, Hill, I know," Millicent said, implying that this was clearly something she did not know anything about.

They went inside and found Dorothy reading in the living room. It was a large room, with tall windows and padded window-seats which Dorothy loved to curl up on to read, but today she was on the couch, sunlight streaming in through the bay window behind her. "I'm reading the most wonderful novel," she told them, stretching like a satisfied cat. "Tom Leo and the two Georges sent it over."

The two Georges, as they were known, were co-owners of three bookstores, and Tom was the longtime manager of one, Book Hampton South, a pleasant, crowded store on Main Street in Southampton.

"Doesn't she look well?" Henry asked proudly as Millicent bent to kiss Dorothy.

"The country seems to be agreeing with you, I must say. If this change has been accomplished in only a few days, I can't wait to see you at the end of the summer."

Bernadette came in and asked if Mrs. Hillings would like her to make tea.

"Dearest Bernadette," Dorothy said, "you mustn't wait on us hand and foot." She looked at Millicent. "She has been extraordinarily kind in every way, and I'm quite worried that Henry and I will never get along without her in the future, so dependent have we become."

Bernadette smiled.

"*I* will make us tea," Dorothy announced happily, putting her book down.

There was a flurry of protests, but Dorothy won and the group moved into the kitchen to settle around the big round table. They had just started their tea when the phone rang. Henry got up to answer it.

"Hello, Henry, it's Elizabeth Robinson."

"Yes, how are you?" he said, careful to keep his face void of any real expression.

"I need to ask you a question."

"Fine," he said, turning his back to the breakfast table.

"Tell me what, if anything, these names mean to you: Galway-Stephens, Druttington, and Harriot Holt."

"I need to change phones," he said after a moment. "We have company." He made his excuses to the group and went upstairs to the study. "Okay, hang up!" he called.

In the kitchen, Bernadette hung up the receiver and sat back down at the table.

"He thinks I don't know what's going on," Dorothy said matter-of-factly to Millicent. "That phone call has something to do with the agency."

Millicent quickly changed the subject by mentioning that she had brought twelve flats of assorted summer flowers.

"Elizabeth?" Henry was saying upstairs. "Run that list by me again."

"Galway-Stephens, Druttington, and Harriot Holt."

"Those are overseas agencies and clients we represented years ago. Where did you get those names from?"

"Patty saw files with those labels on them yesterday in James Stanley Johnson's office at ICA."

There was a long silence.

"Henry?"

"Yes, Elizabeth, sorry, I'm thinking. So they did get some files out of the offices," he murmured. "Well, if that's what they're after, files like those, then they're out of luck."

"Why is that?" Elizabeth asked.

"Because what they have is a mere trifle," he said. "We have literally thousands of old files like those in storage."

"Hold on a moment, please, Henry."

He could hear Elizabeth repeating what he had just said to someone else.

"Henry," Elizabeth said. "Monty's here. He's getting on the extension."

There was a click. "Henry? Monty here. You've got files in storage they don't know about?"

"Thousands," he said. "The woman who organized them and shipped them out—Jean Halliday, who worked for us for almost thirty years—passed away about three years ago and her husband came to us with a notebook he'd found. In it was a record of all the old files and how to find them. Which was a darn good thing, I have to say, since we had forgotten all about them."

"Where's the notebook now?" Elizabeth asked.

"It's there in the study. In Doe's desk somewhere. Try the middle drawer."

"Henry, is this giving you any ideas about what they might be after?" Monty asked.

"Well," Henry sighed, "it does make me think we need to get a list of every property currently under development with ICA. I can't believe they'd be going to all this trouble unless there was quite a lot of money at stake."

"I found it!" Elizabeth said, excitement in her voice. "The files are in Queens at a place called U-File-With-Us."

"Listen, Henry," Monty said, "you're not going to like this, but you need to know that Creighton Berns is telling everyone that you and Dorothy are trying to back out of your merger agreement with ICA so you can sell the agency to Ben Rothstein."

"But that's not true!" Henry said, stunned. "I haven't even talked to Ben!"

"We know that," Monty said.

"But this is an outrage!" Henry yelled, hitting the table with his fist. "I have never backed out of an agreement in my life!"

"Is that Henry shouting?" Dorothy asked her companions down in the kitchen.

"I didn't hear anything," Millicent lied, asking for more tea and crunching noisily on a chocolate-covered biscuit.

"Would you like me to go upstairs and see if everything is all right?" Bernadette asked.

"Only if you do it discreetly, Bernadette," Dorothy said.

"He has twisted this situation beyond recognition and I not only resent it," Henry fumed, "but I will make him pay for every lie he tells!"

"What else can he say, though?" Monty said. "When you think about it, it's the only defense he has—to blame you while you're not able to defend yourself."

"What makes me so goddamn mad is that until I find out what he's after, a lot of people are going to believe his story. And it isn't true, I tell you! Although it's probably a good idea now. Goddamn it, it'll be over my dead body Creighton Berns gets my agency!"

"Uh-oh," Elizabeth said, "I was afraid of this. Had I known how upset—"

"Had you known nothing!" Henry came close to yelling, slamming his fist on the desk again. "You are to report everything to me, *everything*, do you hear? And I have half a mind to get on a plane to the West Coast and punch that son of a bitch in the mouth!"

Bernadette, standing in the hall, blinked several times. And then she went back downstairs to tell Mrs. Hillings what she had heard.

~ 33 ~

The new studio head of Metropolis Pictures quietly swore as he sliced the ball and it went sailing off into the rough.

"That's a tough one," Creighton Berns acknowledged.

It was Sunday afternoon and they were at the Los Angeles Country Club doing business.

The top financier behind Metropolis, who was in from Tokyo, teed up next. Creighton and the studio head exchanged discreet glances as the financier went through his meditation, or whatever the hell it was he did before hitting the ball—standing there, club in hand, rock still, closing his eyes (what was that sound coming from his throat?). The financier opened his eyes, looked fiercely at the ball, and then swung and hit it—damn near perfectly.

"Very nice, very nice," Creighton murmured, stepping up to the tee. He placed his ball, readied himself, concentrated, and swung, slicing the ball in the same direction as the studio head's.

"Too bad," the financier said, with a shallow bow.

Their fourth, an associate of the financier's, stepped up to drive his ball straight up the fairway.

"If anything should come to light," the studio head said to Creighton as soon as they were out of earshot, walking off to the rough together, "for God's sake act as though it's news to you, too."

"Of course," Creighton asked. "But I told you, I can fix it for you."

The studio head looked at him. "Are you all right?"

"Yeah, why?" Creighton asked.

"Got a cold? You look and sound horrible."

"No—well, yeah. Sinus, you know."

"Nobody does that stuff anymore, Creighton," the studio head said.

"Me neither, not anymore," Creighton said, wiping his nose with his handkerchief and jamming it back into his pocket. "How the hell did he get a membership here?" he asked, referring to their host from Tokyo. "Someday we're going to have to clear these guys out, you know? Can't even play golf in our own fucking country."

"We've got to keep them happy," the studio head reminded him. "We have to have the loan extension."

"I just wish it didn't mean screwing up my swing on purpose every time you want to talk to me out here," Creighton growled.

"Mr. Berns!" the caddie called from the golf cart. He was waving the telephone.

"Now what?" Creighton jogged back to the cart and took the portable phone. "Yeah?" His expression was impassive as he listened. "Are you sure?" Pause. "And they're still in New York?" Pause. "They're doing *what?* How the hell do they know?" He was squinting heavily now as if trying to visualize something. "I don't know anything about her, but him . . ." He frowned. "Okay, fine, bury 'em, I don't care," he said. Pause. "Yeah, Smith's big, but not bigger than me. Get the message across loud and clear—if he wants trouble he's got it, big-time." Pause. "Yeah. Robinson, too. Fuck up her series and let her know why."

By the time Creighton had disconnected the phone, the studio head had reached him. "What's the problem?"

"Huh? Nothing," he said, giving the phone back to the caddie. He turned and gave the studio head a slap on the arm. "I told you, you leave it to me. Everything's going to be fine."

"Sure as hell fucking better be," the studio head said.

~ *34* ~

On Monday morning, Patty Kleczak went into work at ICA early. It was a good thing because at ten minutes of nine Marion Ballicutt came tearing into the agents' end of the floor. Patty heard the lawyer bark into one of the offices, "I want whatever we have on Elizabeth Robinson and Montgomery Grant Smith on my desk within the hour."

The agent said something Patty couldn't hear. And then Ballicutt said, "Then get on the phone to PBS and find out! And if you can't get anywhere with them, call the BBC. I want that information—*with* the contracts—on my desk within the hour." She started to walk down the hall, stopped, and backtracked to the office. "And

I want an updated list of every radio station carrying the Montgomery Grant Smith Show." She turned on her heel and briskly walked back to her end of the floor.

"Melanie!" wailed the agent. The secretary next to Patty jumped and went scurrying into the office.

Patty dashed down to the building lobby and out to the street to find a pay phone. She dialed Joshua Lafayette's number and reported everything she had heard.

"Interesting requests to come from head legal counsel," Joshua commented. "Excellent work, Patty. Talk to you later."

The demonstration of Hillings & Hillings clients began at noon and created a tremendous traffic jam from one end of Fifty-seventh Street to the other. People in cars and people on foot rubbernecked to check out whatever it was that had captivated the interest of news cameras and such an enormous crowd near Fifth Avenue.

Gathered in front of the ICA building was a rather eccentric group of protesters:

ICA: INTERNATIONAL CRIME AGENTS, said the sign Dick Stone carried. The detective novel writer was dressed in a trench coat and wide-brimmed fedora, making him look rather like Humphrey Bogart.

GET SOME MANNERS ICA OR LEAVE THE TABLE! Becky Tomlinson's sign read. She wasn't able to march, so she was sitting in a folding chair with her sign propped up on a pole beside her. Wearing white gloves and a white hat, with a blue suit and matching pocketbook, she was smiling brightly, waving gaily to the crowd. Marta, her companion, was marching in the circle of protesters, carrying a sign that read, GO AWAY BERNS'S ICA!

THERE'S NOTHING ROMANTIC ABOUT BAD BUSINESS, Alice Mae Hollison's sign said. The lady herself was dressed in a very interesting flowing pink number, featuring feathers around the neck and little spangly things that caught the light. But it was the imitation diamond tiara on her head that really made the outfit. Miss Hollison informed the press that it had been presented to her at the very first romantic writer's convention in 1956.

BAD, ICA, BAD! read the little sandwich cards hanging on either side of tiny Pookiesnips, the little dog Clarky Birkstein was leading about on a leash. Pookiesnips was a crowd pleaser, winning hearts right and left.

TERMINATOR III—CREIGHTON BERNS, Warren Krebor's sign said. The old science-fiction writer was wearing all of the clothes and gadgets that had been licensed from his *Icono Trilogy.*

Sidney Meltner, dressed like Sherlock Holmes and carrying a magnifying glass, held a sign that read, NO MYSTERY WHO THE BAD GUY IS IN THIS CASE.

Lucy Boyle, still looking rather alarmingly like an old man, was marching about with great gusto in jeans and boots. The sign she carried said, BROADWAY BOOS ICA, and the tape recorder she was carrying was playing the original recording of Sondheim's "Every Day a Little Death," sung by Patricia Elliott.

Sissy Connors was marching about like a caricature housewife ready to clean—apron, bandanna over her hair, a mop and pail—and was carrying a sign that read, HELPFUL HINT #1: CLEAN UP YOUR ACT, ICA!

Anthony Marcell and John Gabriel Mendez carried no signs and were standing on either side of Claire Spender Holland. Claire was standing on a small carpeted box, addressing the crowd through a microphone. All three were dressed in elegantly somber black clothing, hoping to convey funerallike melancholy to the crowd.

"The agreement between the ICA Corporation and Hillings & Hillings spelled out in detail the terms of the transition," Claire's patrician voice rang out. "Suffice it to say, throwing out the chairman of ICA, Benjamin Rothstein, who had run the company for twenty-seven years, and then physically assaulting the Hillings & Hillings offices here in New York—padlocking doors, ransacking files, stealing confidential client information—was not part of that agreement."

"Where's Traubner the Trotskyite?" Monty asked Elizabeth as they stood in the crowd, watching. He had waffled all night between his desire to watch the demonstration and his duty to his radio show. To Elizabeth's surprise, the authors' protest had won out. His listeners would have to get along on a "Best of" show today.

"I don't know where he is," she said.

They listened to Claire for a while. She was great. She had an

Eleanor Roosevelt quality to her speech and deportment that made people take notice.

"Look," Elizabeth said, "there's the DBS News truck."

"CBS is over there," Monty said, pointing.

"Local or national?" she asked, craning her neck to see.

"I think both," Monty told her.

"I hope Henry can keep Dorothy from hearing about any of this," Elizabeth worried. "She'd be mortified to see how everyone's protecting her like she's a fragile old lady."

"Excuse me, Professor Robinson? Mr. Smith?" the DBS reporter introduced himself and asked if he could ask them a few questions on camera.

Monty and Elizabeth looked at each other. "Oh, hell, why not join the fray?" Monty said.

Sure, they told the reporter.

The floodlights went on, the crowd pressed in around them, and the reporter told his TV audience with whom he was about to speak. The other protesters looked a bit annoyed as the attention swung away from them and over to Monty and Elizabeth. "Kudos, Big Mont!" people called from the crowd, making Monty smile.

"Mr. Smith, are you accusing Creighton Berns of ICA of criminal intent?" the reporter asked.

That stopped Monty for a second, but he quickly recovered. "We are protesting the fact that under Mr. Berns's management of ICA, our agents, Dorothy and Henry Hillings, were economically, emotionally, and even physically damaged by ICA's reckless and inappropriate actions. What has happened to them is a crime," he added in a deep voice, "and we are demanding that ICA once more adhere to the transition plan as it was agreed upon."

"This transition that you say was agreed upon, was it in writing?"

"It was," Monty said, "but in letter form only, not as a part of the actual contract. Nonetheless, the agreement was binding. Suddenly the opportunistic new chairman, Creighton Berns, decides to play without rules—the very rules that you and I live our lives by. You and I wouldn't get away with this kind of behavior. Why should he?"

"Professor Robinson," the reporter said, turning to her, "we've been told that your affiliation with the BBC and PBS may be in jeopardy because of your involvement in this protest. Is that true?"

Elizabeth blinked. "I have no idea." She looked at Monty.

"Professor Robinson has always been primarily represented by Hillings & Hillings," Monty explained. "And that makes it very difficult for anyone to know what ICA is or is not doing to Professor Robinson's career. And may I add, if what you say is true and ICA is involved, they will find themselves with a whopping big lawsuit."

"The wire services are also reporting that you had a television pilot in the works which has been derailed. Is this true, Mr. Smith?" the reporter asked.

"Absolutely not," Monty said, smiling into the camera. "As over fifteen million radio listeners out there know, this is America, and America is the most wonderful country on earth. Not even Al Capone could get away with his crimes. I have every confidence American ideals will triumph in this situation, too."

"Are you comparing Creighton Berns to Al Capone, Mr. Smith?" the reporter asked.

Monty continued to smile into the camera. "I am merely remarking on the fact that in this country even the most powerful gangsters eventually fall. If you wish to somehow connect that statement with Creighton Berns and the people who have allowed him to take over ICA, I can't help that."

"Careful," Elizabeth murmured.

"They're going absolutely bonkers up here," Patty whispered to Josh from the ICA offices. "The phones are ringing off the hook, everybody's running around screaming at everybody else. Nobody's allowed in or out of the building."

"It is a new morning in America," Claire Spender Holland was saying. "And integrity and decency in business are the order of the day. Creighton Berns has the opportunity to mend a very bad situation, and we are asking him to please step forward and do so. Immediately."

The doors of the ICA building opened and security guards and policemen came out. Cameras went on. Behind the uniformed entourage were Marion Ballicutt and James Stanley Johnson. Marion asked for a microphone and had several thrust at her. Taking one, she looked into the cameras with a sad, compassionate face, and read, "ICA made a fair and substantial offer to acquire the Hillings & Hillings agency here in New York City, an offer which they accepted. Of the over four hundred clients who have been represented by Hillings & Hillings, I think it important to point out that these thirteen people you see here today are the only ones who are displeased. And may I add, with the greatest respect, that the majority of these writers have not produced any new work for many years."

"Yeah, right, Ballicutt!" Monty bellowed across the crowd. "I've got fifteen million listeners and a book that's been on the best-seller list for two years. Why am I here?"

She ignored him and continued to read her statement. "ICA entered the agreement in good faith but when Hillings & Hillings failed to meet the transition date, we were forced to make an attempt to obtain the client records from the firm so we could responsibly represent the many people who need us. Mr. Hillings is almost seventy-seven years old, and Mrs. Hillings is seventy and in ill health. In our judgment, it was in our clients' best interest to act responsibly and we did."

"Ms. Ballicutt?" a reporter from ABC said. "Do you mean to say that the clients protesting today are of no concern to you?"

"I am concerned that the truth be presented here today," she said coolly. "We have every reason to believe that the Hillingses are using these clients to divert attention from the fact that they have broken *their* agreement with ICA, so they can turn around and sell the company to their very old friend Ben Rothstein."

"And you deny any wrongdoing on the part of ICA?" the NBC reporter asked.

"I vehemently deny it," she said, "and in addition I am trying very hard to restrain myself from protesting—protesting against the shoddy representation Hillings & Hillings clients have been forced to endure for too many years, because two old people refused to retire years ago."

"How dare you!" Elizabeth exploded from the back of the crowd, pushing her way forward. "How dare you impugn the integrity and expertise of two individuals whose talent is of a magnitude that someone like you could never even grasp!"

The crowd and the cameras turned to her.

"Ladies and gentlemen," Elizabeth said, "the woman who has just spoken, Marion Ballicutt, was formerly with the law firm that jointly represented Hillings & Hillings and ICA on various media projects. You're listening to a common turncoat, the kind of despicable sycophant, bribed to jump ship and lead—"

"Professor Robinson is a well-known biographer," Marion Ballicutt said, laughing sarcastically. "You remember her—she's the one who's made her fortune depicting the tawdry sex lives of some of history's more despicable characters. A remarkable teacher, for all the wrong reasons!"

"You, madam," Monty shouted in his native Floridian accent, "are nothing but a common corporate ho-wah!"

The crowd gasped, the cameras swung.

"As you can see," Ballicutt said to the crowd, "for every hundred happy clients, we have one severely distressed—if not mentally ill—person who does not, cannot, see things the way normal people do. I have nothing more to say." She abruptly wheeled around and went back into the building.

Reporters were running for phones, photographers were chasing Ballicutt and Monty and Elizabeth. The other authors rather dejectedly put down their signs and stood there, looking at each other. Only Pookiesnips kept prancing about in circles, showing off his little sign.

"Good God," Henry murmured, standing behind Millicent in her beautiful study in Bridgehampton, eyes on the TV. The evening news was showing a clip of everyone at the demonstration screaming insults at each other. "They've made us out to be senile," he said in amazement.

"Well, you're *not* and everyone who knows you is aware of that."

"We certainly don't come off as very effective representation," Henry said.

"Well, you *are*," Millicent said firmly.

"I must say, Millie, I could use one of those," Henry said, sitting on the sofa next to her and nodding to the sherry decanter on the table in front of them.

"Of course." She quickly and adeptly poured two glasses. "That's why I brought this tray out before the broadcast. I thought we might need something."

"We need something all right," Henry sighed, throwing back his sherry in one swallow.

"Well, I do not understand this at all," Dorothy said, standing in the upstairs study of the Water Mill house with her hands on her hips. "The television was working perfectly fine a month ago—I remember watching Charlie Rose the last time we were here."

"I'm sorry, Mrs. Hillings," Bernadette said helplessly, fiddling with the set.

"You don't think we've suffered some sort of short circuit, do you?" Dorothy asked her. "The radio doesn't work either—oh, but the microwave wouldn't work then, would it?"

"I don't know, Mrs. Hillings," Bernadette said.

She sighed. "I wish Henry would come back with the newspaper." Suddenly she looked at Bernadette sharply. "This isn't an accident, is it?"

"I think you should rest now, Mrs. Hillings," Bernadette said, walking over. "Mr. Hillings said you might enjoy this." She handed her a handsomely bound copy of *Last Chronicle of Barset*, by Anthony Trollope.

"Ah, more Trollope, yes," Dorothy said, accepting it. "Did you know that during World War One the British government issued copies of his novels to soldiers in the trenches? They found that Trollope was the only writer who could take their minds off the horrors around them."

"No, Mrs. Hillings, I didn't," Bernadette said.

"That fact alone tells me the state of mind my poor husband is in," she sighed. She reached for the telephone. "No, my dear," she told Bernadette, when the aide started to protest, "not a word. I simply must find out what is going on." She started dialing. "Honestly, that poor man, to think he thought I wouldn't notice that the television and the radios have been dismantled." She smiled. "You'd think yanking the wires out of the back of my TV at the hospital would have been enough."

"Mrs. Hillings," Bernadette said seriously, "perhaps Mr. Hillings has good reason to want to protect you. Perhaps the stress on Mr. Hillings will only be increased if you are involved. Perhaps Mr. Hillings should be protected from any more stress."

"Oh all right!" Dorothy said, annoyed, putting the telephone down with a clang. "I'll wait a day or two." She pointed at the aide. "But that's it, I tell you. After that, all bets are off."

~ 35 ~

"Lady Georgiana!" Cachi, her housekeeper, called out the back door.

Georgiana had instructed her a hundred times not to call her that, but in private Cachi refused. She said Georgiana should be addressed with respect. Georgiana pointed out that not only was it an incorrect form of address, but it would mortify and disgrace her if anyone ever heard Cachi calling her that. Her father was only a viscount. He was Lord Hamilton-Ayres: she was The Honorable Georgiana Hamilton-Ayres. Cachi insisted that her employer was a great lady, but promised not to mortify and disgrace her in public.

"Lady Georgiana!" Cachi called again.

"Yes!" Georgiana answered, standing up. Although the house was a rental and she had the gardener do all of the heavy work, Georgiana could never resist doing some of the lighter gardening herself. It was a passion she had been born with, and one she shared with Mrs. Hillings. If there was one thing Georgiana had to thank her father for, it was the gardeners at Ayres House who increased her knowledge tenfold every time she visited. They teased her mercilessly, however. They said Miss Georgiana was nigh to cheating by living in California, since most anything grew there, unlike the sharp salty soil and air of Inverness.

"Mr. Berns's office is calling. They say it is urgent," Cachi said.

Georgiana sighed, took off her gardening gloves, and wiped the hair off her forehead with the back of her hand. She walked up to the terrace, tossed the gloves down, and picked up the portable phone. "Hello?" she said.

"Ms. Hamilton-Ayres?"

"Speaking."

"Please hold for Mr. Berns."

"Georgiana," he said, coming on. "I need a favor from you."

"What kind?"

"To appear at a press conference here today and issue a statement on the Hillings & Hillings fiasco," he said.

Georgiana looked at her watch. Yes, the time was about right. The demonstration must have gone very well in New York.

"What kind of statement?"

"I've already gone over it with Marty," he said. Marty was Georgiana's press agent. "Just a statement to the effect that there has been a misunderstanding. That you know the Hillingses personally, that you know some of their clients have taken action without their knowledge, and that you're represented by ICA and expect everything to be cleared up very quickly."

Pause. "You just told me on Thursday you thought the Hillingses were behind the protest, Creighton—that they were using their clients to back out of the deal."

"And I still believe that," he said. "But right now we need to calm the waters and if it means caving in to new talks, I might have to consider it. In the meantime, it's gotten out of hand in New York and the only way to stop it is for us to issue a statement out here."

Silence. Georgiana was thinking, looking out at the bushes. "Can I call you back?"

"Within five minutes?" he said.

"Within five minutes," she said.

She couldn't get hold of Elizabeth or Monty or Josh in New York, so she called Water Mill, but Henry wasn't there either. "Would you like to leave a message?" Bernadette asked.

"No, no, thank you," she said, hanging up. She started dialing. "Hi, it's Georgiana calling, is Alexandra there? It's rather important." She lowered the receiver. "Cachi!" she yelled.

"Yes?"

"Go in my office and get David Aussenhoff's phone number off the Rolodex and see if you can get him on the phone. Now. It's important. Aussenhoff—A-u-s-s-e-n-h-o-f-f."

"Georgiana?" Alexandra's voice said. "What's wrong?"

"I guess the author protest went well in New York," she said, "because Creighton Berns just asked me to come down to the ICA offices and issue a statement at a press conference with him."

"Careful, Georgiana, careful," Alexandra said. "And you're right, the protest did go well—so well that every film crew in town got Montgomery Grant Smith and Elizabeth Robinson screaming at the head of the ICA legal department."

"Really?" Georgiana said, starting to laugh.

"What does Berns want you to say in the statement?"

"That the Hillingses are personal friends of mine, that I know they personally have nothing to do with the protest, that the clients are acting on their own, and that ICA has assured me, as one of their clients, that everything will be straightened out very quickly." Pause. "What do you think?"

"I think you should realize that if you appear with Creighton Berns at a press conference, no matter what you say, the press is going to perceive you as a character witness for him."

"Oh, God," Georgiana said.

"On the other hand, Creighton Berns is a very powerful person right now, and I can't imagine that it will do you any good to refuse him."

"Why, what could he do?"

"Probably nothing—right now," Alexandra said. "But his type tends to have a long-festering memory."

"Yes, well, I do too," Georgiana said, wishing she felt a little more confident of her own power. Like any wise actress, she knew the power of mere actors in this town was fleeting at best—regardless of how many successful movies they'd been in.

"Can you issue a statement without appearing with Berns at the press conference?" Alexandra asked. "It'll make a difference—at least in how the press will interpret your affiliation."

"That's a thought," Georgiana said.

"Lady Georgiana!" Cachi called. "I have David Aussenhoff on the other line."

"*Lady* Georgiana?" Alexandra said. "Are you holding out on me?"

"Even the help's gone Hollywood," Georgiana said. "All that's missing are the trumpets. Anyway, I'd better go—thanks for the advice."

"Let me know."

"Will do." She punched to the other line. "David?"

"Hi."

"Thank heavens I got you. Listen, Creighton wants me to go down to ICA to issue a statement at a press conference with him."

"Me, too," David said.

"Really? What are you going to do?"

"I'm sitting here trying to figure that out."

"So your inclination is no," Georgiana said.

"My inclination is to continue working in this business, and, at the moment, the possibility seems highly unlikely if I tell him to go fuck himself."

Georgiana paused. "I've been advised to offer to make a statement, but not to actually appear at the press conference with Creighton. I've been warned that if I do, the media will perceive me as a character witness for him."

"So do you want to have character or a career, Georgiana?" David said wearily.

Georgiana frowned. "I have to say, I'm rather surprised at your attitude, David—knowing what you know, and knowing the Hillingses and what's been done to them."

"Yeah, well, I'm sure as hell not sure I want to blow up my whole life over this situation. Creighton's already threatened to put my movie into turnaround."

"Can he do that?" she asked him.

"Maybe I don't want to find out."

"Have you spoken to Elizabeth?"

"Oh, fuck, what is this?" he said, angry. "What do you want from me?"

"I don't want anything from you, David. Not a thing. Goodbye," she said, hanging up. She tossed the phone on a chair cushion and walked back to where she had been planting. She had to think, to hell with the five minutes Creighton had given her. She bent over and picked up a handful of earth in her bare hand, squeezing it, bringing the rich earth to her nose and inhaling deeply. Sometimes she desperately wished she were like everyone else.

She was long past the point where she felt any obligation to produce offspring for the financially disastrous Hamilton-Ayres estate. Her father's title would go to her male cousin, anyway, not to any child of hers. So instead she sent checks every month to three different banks in Scotland to help keep the estate afloat during her father's lifetime. Georgiana was also long past feeling that she had to be her mother's psychiatric nurse, running to her side after every suicide threat or hospitalization.

No, Georgiana's only obligation in life, as the Hillingses and her old therapist had told her over the years, was to grow up and build herself a life in which she could live comfortably and be herself.

She had always known the difference between right and wrong, and she had always known it was wrong for her to get married, but she had gone ahead and done it, early on, giving in to her insecurity over being singled out as yet another dysfunctional actress from a most famously dysfunctional family. Too, she had been anxious to rid herself of a possible sexual preference that some people would perceive as dysfunctional at best.

When Georgiana had told her father she had decided to marry an American, he had been very upset. But after she told him she had no intention of having children, at least not for a decade or more, her father had looked at her strangely and dropped all objections to the marriage. In fact, he came to heartily endorse it.

Attractive life that had been—after being married only a year and two months, she knew without a doubt that she had fallen head over heels in love with a woman in a way she never had with a man. She would always remember lying in bed with her husband and coming to the frightened realization that if she could have this woman, be with this woman, she would gladly give up sex with men forever.

Not a particularly productive realization for an ambitious actress who was evolving into an international sex symbol.

And so Georgiana had called Dorothy Hillings late one night, after several glasses of wine, to share her secret with the only person she felt she could tell.

"And so, I think I'm gay, what do you think about that?"

"I think all young girls should be gay," Dorothy had said, and laughed. "Particularly when there is so much unpleasantness in the world."

Clearly the older woman had missed her meaning.

"I think I'm in love with a woman, Dorothy."

"Yes, I know, darling, and I am very pleased for you. It's a very wonderful thing to be in love."

Georgiana had thought maybe she wasn't hearing correctly. "I just got married a year ago. Aren't you upset?"

"No, darling. I have seen far too many people force themselves into roles which only lead to a great deal of unhappiness for everyone."

"Mrs. H, do you think I like women because Mother is so messed up?"

"Well, I can't say that your father has ever been a terribly good role model either, quite frankly, so if your theory has any validity, your father would even things out, wouldn't you say?"

"An equal-opportunity mess," Georgiana said, smiling despite herself.

"I should think all this would be a rather valuable asset for a great actress. Now then, about the present situation, my dear, I strongly suggest that you call Alice."

Alice was the therapist Dorothy had first sent Georgiana to see when she had lived with them in New York.

"So you think my life is salvageable?" she had asked.

"I think your life is precious, and that you must treat it as such. Call Alice in the morning and call me after you do."

Funny what you remembered, Georgiana thought, taking a deep breath of the cool, fresh air. Funny how Elizabeth Robinson, in her own way, seemed to be emotionally banged up, too. Maybe that was Dorothy's hobby, taking in lost young women who happened to have everything and yet nothing.

Georgiana closed her eyes. Exhaled. Reopened her eyes. She lounged on the grass for a while, taking in the garden. Breathing. Waiting for the answer to come to her about what the right thing to do was.

Finally she got up, went into the house, called Creighton Berns,

and told him she didn't feel comfortable doing the press conference. If he would like, though, she would issue a separate statement
to the press.

Creighton said, "Okay, Georgiana, have it your way," and hung
up on her.

"Davey, what's the matter with you?" Susie asked, placing a
hand on his shoulder.

He was sitting at the kitchen table, staring out across the backyard, the telephone in front of him. He looked up at this beautiful
young actress who claimed to be in love with him. And maybe she
was. At the very least, she was probably in love with the idea of
living with a wealthy movie producer. The alternative for her was
not particularly cheerful: trying to keep the battered Ford Escort
running, slinging hash at some dreadful all-night place in Hollywood, another year of sharing a tiny apartment with three other
aspiring actresses, no contact with anyone in the business.

How old was Susie, anyway? Twenty-three? Eighteen years
younger than himself. Ten years younger than Elizabeth. And she
carried so much less baggage than Elizabeth! No years and years of
accumulated hurts and fears. It was simply easier to be with someone younger. They expected so much less. With Elizabeth the
demands had always been difficult and lasting: marriage, children,
forever. Who needed it?

What had attracted him to Elizabeth in the first place was no
mystery. Her very bone structure had turned him on. The way she
carried herself, the way she spoke, the way she looked, but most of
all, the way she reacted when he seduced her, breaking free of her
self-imposed prison. She was the kind of woman who lived so much
in her head, she had difficulty connecting to her body. When he
could get her to focus on her physical self, it was an event hard to
surpass. She was intense, passionate, euphoric.

Thrilling. God, how thrilling Elizabeth had become in bed.

But all that infernal intellectual chatter one had to put up with
in order to get her to bed.

Sometimes Elizabeth used to get so caught up in what she was
saying that David couldn't believe he was listening to a woman
living any earlier than, say, a hundred years ago. And sometimes,

when they were having dinner, he'd ask her if they couldn't talk about something that was happening now, in this century. His remarks would invariably trigger a passionate protest. If only David would listen and grasp the key to the era she was exploring, if only he could envision the times, the psychology of the people, if only David would let the past relive itself so he could fully understand!

It still gave him a headache just to think about it. He used to come in after working twelve hours straight, daydreaming on the way home about how much fun it was going to be to seduce the otherwise controlled and impeccable professor, how Elizabeth looked when he touched her breasts in a certain way, how undone she got, how crazy he got. Then he would find Elizabeth frantically running around the house organizing her notes for a lecture, going a hundred miles an hour, telling him about Captain Cooke or Irish illuminated manuscripts or the War of the Roses or some screwball thing. At times like that he could not shut her up. Or, if he did, she would be so stunned that she would shut down, silently pack up her notes, and take off in her car for parts unknown.

By the time she returned, of course, he almost always felt guilty. If you loved someone you did not try to change their essential nature. That's what he believed. But, to be truthful, he always knew that if he offended Elizabeth enough to make her disappear for a while, by the time she got back she would have worked that manic intellectual energy out of her system. She would return annoyed but docile, and in that mood she tended to want to snuggle, which in turn usually led to a terrific bout of lovemaking.

But the Elizabeth David had known and loved and lived with and nearly married had changed. Changed a lot. She didn't chatter anymore. Nor did she fidget, touching things as if tactile contact were the only thing rooting her to the present. She seemed so much older now, tired. Like she was retired.

No doubt about it, Elizabeth was definitely calmer now. But the sexual Elizabeth he had known seemed very distant. He had to wonder how hard it would be to awaken that in her again. Or if he could.

He loved her still. No doubt about that. And he still wanted her. Probably worse than ever. She was a class act, through and through—a woman who was extraordinarily attractive and a god-damn genius to boot. Her genes, in combination with David's, would produce kids that would blow all others off the map.

The idea of getting Elizabeth back both excited and scared David. He looked at Susie and felt guilty and sad. Someone was going to get hurt.

"What are you thinking about?" she asked.

"Berns wants me to appear at a press conference at ICA this afternoon," he said, avoiding her eyes.

"What for?"

"To vouch for the fact that he's trying to work out the situation with Hillings & Hillings, I guess."

"And is he?"

He looked at her. Her eyes were enormous, clear, beautiful. Trusting. So young. "I guess so, if he's having a press conference to say so."

"So what's the problem?" she asked him.

"The problem is," he sighed, taking her hand, "I get the distinct feeling that he's going to pull the plug on the movie if I don't do it—which makes me think there is a reason why I shouldn't do it."

"But isn't this what you wanted? Didn't you tell me the meeting in New York was to bring ICA to the negotiating table?"

He studied Susie's face. The movie would be a big break for her. For him it would be the next step, but for her, it was the opportunity of a lifetime.

If he was going to end up breaking her heart, she should at least get a shot at a starring role.

He called Creighton Berns and told him he'd be at the press conference.

~ *36* ~

The aftermath of the Fifty-seventh Street demonstration dogged Monty and Elizabeth into the evening. The media evidently no longer cared about what had drawn them to the protest in the first place. Now they only cared about the King of Right-wing

Laura Van Wormer

Radio and the Katharine Hepburn of Academe having a public screaming match with a vice-president of the most powerful talent agency in the world.

When the two finally got back to the Hillingses' apartment, the phones were ringing off the hook. They each received calls from their book publishers, who were actually rather enthusiastic about all the publicity their authors were getting, despite difficulties they might have with ICA down the road. The bad calls were more prevalent: the president of Monty's radio network voiced deep concern over his behavior; Monty's TV producer was expressing rage, grief, and promises of suicide, screaming that ICA was pulling the plug on the show; and the BBC wanted to know what the devil was happening over there in the States, because they were getting all kinds of pressure to dismiss Elizabeth from the series. There was even a message from Elizabeth's department chair at Balliol!

After Patty got off work, she came back to the apartment and snuck in through the service entrance to avoid the press people Elizabeth had warned her about. When she arrived upstairs, she found Monty bellowing over the phone at his lawyer, and Elizabeth pacing the living room, very near tears over the idea that even Oxford could be pressured to dismiss her.

Unfortunately, what Patty had to tell them only darkened their spirits further: ICA had already started gunning for them long before they knew about Monty and Elizabeth's participation in the demonstration.

"Which means?" Elizabeth said, looking to Monty.

"Which means this is war, goddamn it!" Monty thundered.

"No, Monty," Elizabeth said, "what I meant is, why didn't they go after us last week when we served the court order?"

"Hell if I know," Monty sighed, tired and discouraged.

"Maybe at first they thought the court order was an isolated incident," Elizabeth said. "Something you and I did on the spur of the moment."

"What difference would that make?" Patty asked her.

"Well, it would mean that the way they viewed us last week and the way they viewed us this morning are significantly different for some reason," Elizabeth said, feeling slightly ill.

The three looked at one another uncomfortably. Monty cleared his voice. "Clearly, then, someone must have told ICA that you and I are spearheading the opposition."

"But who would tell them about you?" Patty asked.

The phone rang and it was Josh, who wanted them to turn on CNN, quick. When they did, there was Creighton Berns standing at a podium loaded with microphones on the terrace of the ICA building in Los Angeles. He gave a short statement, saying there had been some confusion over the transition on the Hillings & Hillings acquisition, but that the authors formerly represented by that agency had acted on their own, distorting the real situation and creating a media circus. ICA would reevaluate the situation, Berns said, just as soon as the Hillingses—who were getting on in years and were not in very good health—emerged from their isolation. Berns then introduced three Hillings & Hillings clients and stepped aside.

Elizabeth gasped and Patty murmured, "What are they doing?" as David Aussenhoff and Jordan and Louise Wells filled the screen.

David introduced himself, explained his past affiliation with the Hillingses, his current affiliation with ICA, and told the press that he was confident a solution was being worked out that would be satisfactory to all.

"What solution?" Monty yelled. "ICA hasn't contacted Henry in over a month!"

"Be quiet," Elizabeth said.

David turned the microphone over to Louise, who stepped right up and said, "Jordan and I were in New York recently to check on this situation. Henry and Dorothy Hillings are good friends and we were very upset by what was going on. Now that we're back in Los Angeles, Mr. Berns has been kind enough to explain the situation to us and to promise that the merger will be restructured to everyone's satisfaction." She paused and then smiled. "So if you don't see our TV special 'Adam Falls' on the air later this year, you'll know that we've had a severe falling out with Mr. Berns over this matter."

"Good!" Monty said. "She's got Berns now. He can't touch them."

"Ms. Wells?" a reporter asked. "Are you saying that in exchange for appearing today at this press conference, ICA is packaging a television special for you?"

"Of course not," Louise said. "This special has been in the works for far longer than Mr. Berns has been CEO, and so, if something happens to it, you'll know that he didn't keep his word."

Creighton Berns was seen in the background with a smile frozen on his face, looking for the world as though he wished he had strangled Louise Wells instead of asking her to speak.

"Ooo, she's *good!*" Patty said enthusiastically. "Very smooth."

"Yeah," Monty said. "Unlike—" He stopped himself.

"No, David didn't come off very well," Elizabeth said quietly. "I'm afraid he's not very good at public speaking."

Patty and Monty looked at each other.

The in-house phone rang. It was the super calling to say that Ted Kleczak was downstairs at the delivery entrance and he was sending him up. Patty went to the front door to greet him, asking quickly if he could have said anything to the press that could blow her cover at ICA.

"What has gotten into you, Patty?" they heard her husband cry. "And what's that on your head, a wig? And what is all this makeup!" Patty evidently lost her temper, because she started shouting about being a live-in baby-sitter, housekeeper, and chauffeur, and then the phone started ringing again and Monty and Elizabeth were forced to turn their attention to other dramas.

David could hardly believe how badly he had come off at the press conference. He replayed the tape in his study and groaned aloud. He had agreed to go on, and he had been used beautifully as Berns's character witness. Had he been in his right mind? In contrast, Louise Wells had come off brilliantly, clearly on the side of the Hillingses, openly telling the world that if Berns took out his revenge on her, they would all know why.

He heard the battered Ford Escort pull into the driveway and he looked out the window.

"Davey, hi, I'm home!" Susie called, dropping grocery bags on the floor as she came in. After a few minutes her head appeared in the doorway.

"Hi," he said, frowning, hoping she would leave him alone.

Susie glanced at the TV set and video player, and came over to sit on the arm of his chair. "You shouldn't keep watching it, hon. It's over with. Forget about it."

"Forget about it," David repeated, thinking he'd be crying right now, if he were a woman.

"Isn't Creighton pleased?" she asked.

"Creighton's very pleased."

"Then what's wrong?"

He let out an anguished sigh. "I looked like one of his flunkies." He could almost hear her thoughts: Well, you do work for him, don't you, honey bunny? Yeah, but since when did a producer work for an agent? What the hell had happened over the last twenty years, anyway? He was the producer, he was the one who was supposed to have power. Instead, he was a well-paid forty-one-year-old whose only purpose in life was to make shit movies and disgrace himself in front of his friends.

In front of Elizabeth.

Oh, what did he care anymore? *Why* should he care?

Susie cleared her throat and David noticed her breasts. They were a nice distraction. There were many things he did with Susie he had not done with Elizabeth, but what was the point of being with Susie if he could not do what he wanted, when he wanted?

"Did you want to make love?" she asked him.

Susie was a very smart girl in many ways.

"Not really," he murmured, pressing his face into her chest.

"Did you want me to do you?" she whispered, rubbing his back.

"Not really," he murmured.

"What do you want, honey bunny?" she asked, pushing him back in his chair and taking off her tank top. She took his face in her hands and brought it up to her full, silky breasts. "I think I know what you want," she whispered.

It was not long before he had her spread-eagle across the desk.

"The point is," Georgiana said into her Bel Air telephone, "I refused to do the press conference and now my press agent tells me he can't work for me anymore."

"You think *you've* got problems," Monty said, "the TV show I've been working on for *two* years has gone to never-never land.

Goddamn that son of a bitch! When I get on the air tomorrow—"

"You'll not say a word until we find out what they're after," Elizabeth interrupted, taking the phone out of his hand. "Georgiana?"

"I was just telling Monty that my press agent told me he can't work for me anymore because Creighton's angry with me for not agreeing to appear at his press conference."

"So he asked you, too," Elizabeth murmured. "David did it and so did Jordan and Louise."

"I know," Georgiana said. "I'm afraid David and I had a bit of a row over whether or not he should sabotage his career for the Hillingses."

Elizabeth sighed. "I think we're all beginning to wonder about that. The BBC's being pressured to drop me from the series."

"Already?" Georgiana was amazed Creighton could move so fast.

"Yes," Elizabeth sighed, lowering her voice. "And Patty's in the guest room, sobbing her heart out because her husband came here and read her the riot act."

"Why?"

"Probably because she has three children at home, for starters," Elizabeth said.

"Yes, that would do it," Georgiana said. "But maybe that's why participating in this has become so important to her. You know, to have something of her own, a little adventure."

"Perhaps," Elizabeth said. "In the meantime, I'm afraid Monty and I are only helping to make things worse. Tonight when she insisted on finishing out the week at ICA, we didn't argue. We need her help. Meanwhile, tomorrow Monty and I start looking through all the Hillings & Hillings files that are in storage."

"I'll come back to New York to help, if you want. I'm not doing much of anything here."

"You don't have to, Georgiana," Elizabeth said. "If we need your help, we'll let you know."

"We need your help, Georgiana!" Monty shouted over Elizabeth's shoulder.

"Monty, stop it," she said, pushing him away.

"Seriously, Elizabeth, why don't I come back? There are some things I'd like to do in New York anyway."

"Are you sure that's a good idea?" Elizabeth asked.

"Oh, why not?" Georgiana said. "Creighton's already stolen my press agent, what else is he going to do?"

Elizabeth knocked on the guest room door and opened it when she heard Patty say to come in. The light from the hall fell across the gracious mahogany furniture. Patty sat up in bed. "I'm not asleep."

"I wanted to see how you are."

"I'm fine," she said, patting the bed. "Come, sit for a few minutes."

Elizabeth walked across the room and perched on the bed.

"I feel guilty as sin," Patty said, "and at the same time completely wonderful."

"Well, I feel guilty," Elizabeth said. "We shouldn't be asking you to do this."

"I volunteered and now it's more important than ever that I stay where I am," Patty said. "Besides, as awful as Ted was tonight, he did bring my suitcase, so at least I have clothes."

"How are your children?"

"The boys feel much like their father, though my daughter, it seems, is beginning to think I might be more than just a regrettable, nagging mom. She told Ted I was probably making up for having married so young." She smiled, shaking her head. "I was just lying here thinking she could be right."

Elizabeth smiled. "But they're getting along all right?"

"Oh, sure," Patty said. "They're wonderful kids, and Ted is a teacher and a coach—it's not as if he hasn't spent a major amount of time with teenagers and adolescents. And the kids are good about doing chores; even the boys can cook if a gun's put to their heads."

Elizabeth nodded. "Well, just remember, if you think it would be a help for us to arrange for someone to clean or cook—"

"Oh, God, no," Patty said. "If someone else were paying for it, Ted would go crazy."

"Okay, but you just let me know if there's anything I can do. All right?"

Patty nodded.

"Georgiana's coming back."

"Really?" Patty hugged her knees.

"On Wednesday. I suggested she stay here with us. She could use the Hillingses' room."

Patty threw her head back and laughed. "Oh, how my life has changed. Little League one day, houseguest with Georgiana Hamilton-Ayres the next!"

Elizabeth smiled. "Let's hope Monty will behave himself."

"Yes, I noticed that," Patty said. "What is it between those two?"

Elizabeth shrugged. "An error in judgment, I suppose."

"She didn't sleep with him, did she!"

Elizabeth lowered her eyes. She hadn't expected Patty to catch on so easily. "Look, I don't want to—"

"Oh!" Patty said, covering her mouth. "That's very funny!" Reading Elizabeth's expression she added, "It's not that I think Monty's unattractive. It's just that he's such an overgrown kid, you know? And Georgiana is so *deadly attractive.*"

"Interesting choice of words," Elizabeth said.

"How could he think a woman like that would be interested in him?" Patty mused.

Elizabeth looked at her. "You really don't like him, do you?"

"Oh, I do. It's just that he's such an awful braggart on the radio, he really drives me crazy. I always have to turn him off. But in person, I do like him, Elizabeth. Still, the thought of him trying to handle a woman like that . . ." Her voice trailed off.

"A woman like what?" Elizabeth asked.

"Let's just say I'm sure Georgiana's not exactly what his mother had in mind for him," Patty said, laughing again.

"So only a homely wretch could be interested in Monty, is that what you're saying?"

Patty looked at her for a moment. "No, Elizabeth," she said gently. "What I meant was, Georgiana doesn't seem intellectually or spiritually suited to him. As a matter of fact, it's a complete miss, and I guess I'm rather surprised he could think otherwise."

Elizabeth nodded, a thoughtful look on her face.

Patty touched her arm. "I haven't offended you, have I?"

"Me?" she asked, surprised. "Good heavens, no, I was thinking about Monty. I'm not sure I've ever met anyone so lonely, so cut off. And it's strange, isn't it? Since so many millions of people listen to him every day?"

"And what about you, Elizabeth?"

Elizabeth's eyebrows shot up. "Me?"

"And David," Patty said. "There's something between you, isn't there?"

Elizabeth hesitated and then nodded. "We used to live together. We were going to get married, once. But that was a while ago."

Patty looked shocked. "I had no idea."

"I had no idea he was coming to the meeting. He didn't know I'd be there either."

"It must have been quite a shock."

"You've got an early morning, you should get some sleep," Elizabeth said, standing.

"So do you," Patty pointed out.

"Monty and I are just going to go over some of the file notes and then we'll call it a day. I really appreciate what you're doing for us, Patty," she added as she opened the door.

"I'd like to think I'm doing it for myself, too. Good night."

"Good night," Elizabeth said, closing the door.

On the other side of the door, Elizabeth let out a long sigh. She wished she knew for sure how she felt about anything right now. Something was changing, that was for sure, but what, exactly, she didn't know.

~ 37 ~

He sneezed again.

"Monty, you've got to put one of these on," Elizabeth said, tossing him a disposable surgical mask like the one she was wearing. She was also wearing latex gloves. They were in a storage room of U-File-With-Us in Queens, searching through what seemed like endless stacks of cardboard boxes containing one dusty file after another.

"I wish to hell we knew what we were looking for," he muttered, reaching for the mask. After he broke the strap yanking it on, Elizabeth got up and went over to help him put on another.

"There," she said, "you look like a surgeon."

"I feel like a fool," he mumbled. "What, in God's name, are we looking for anyway?"

"We'll know it when we find it," she promised. "But in the meantime, pull anything that looks interesting." To her, this was like old home week, so accustomed was she to spending days on end in rooms just like this, operating on the faith that something of value was there. To her this felt extremely productive, but to poor Monty this was next to torture.

If the dust didn't get to the novice researcher, the hours of crouching and straining one's eyes did. And then, of course, there was the lack of a specific direction or precise goal. For people used to exact achievement, as Monty was, searching for "something" could quickly exhaust their patience.

"You're doing a great job," she told him. "Just hang in there— we'll find something."

She walked over to her area of boxes and squatted down again, sifting through the next one. Monty was watching her. "I brought you a radio for later."

"For what?" she said, distracted, looking through files.

"So you could listen to my show."

"Oh, thank you, that'll be nice."

"Nice," he muttered, watching her ignore him. He pulled the surgical mask down around his neck. "You're going to have to come on my show before this is over, you know. I haven't had a lefty on in years."

Her head snapped around. Now she was paying attention to him. "What makes you think I'm a lefty?"

"You're an academic. It goes without saying."

"You sound just like David," she muttered, standing up.

"Oh, great," Monty said.

"You're not all that different, you know. It's just that you make a living by espousing your views in an entertaining way."

"And so do you, Professor Robinson."

"Damn it, Montgomery!" she said, finally losing her patience. "How dare you say such a thing to me, having never set foot in my classroom! How dare you say that I teach my own personal political views! I am sick and tired of your pompous attitude, your sweeping generalizations, and while those might work on your radio show, I am *not* a member of your audience and I am *not* amused—I am a professional teacher, and I will not tolerate one more snide comment from you about something you know absolutely nothing about! Have I made myself clear?"

Monty felt as though a steamroller had just stopped a few inches from his face. "Looks that way," he said after a moment.

She stared at him. "Good. Because I've had it with you."

"Elizabeth," he said, sounding wounded, "I said you had made your point, all right?" He gave the box in front of him a shove. "Did it ever occur to you that I might say those things just to get a rise out of you? That you're not exactly a fountain of information about yourself? That you're not exactly easy to get to know?"

She looked at him.

"You practically refuse to talk about yourself and I'm curious," he said. "So I bait you and you talk. But I still don't know anything, except that you're in love with David Aussenhoff." When there was no answer he continued. "And what do you know about me? What have I told you?"

"You've been married and divorced once; no kids; you're from LaBelle, Florida; you never graduated from college; the Hillingses discovered you and got you a radio show; and you think you're in love with Georgiana—"

"Hey!" he said, making a cutting motion in the air. "You don't know that."

"Fine," Elizabeth said, walking away, "I don't know anything about you."

He watched her, disappointed she wouldn't talk anymore. "Not that I don't want to be in love," he added. "I think being in love is nice."

"Take it from me, it all depends on how it comes out," she said, sifting through another box. "Listen, Monty, we've got to get back to work."

"Yeah," he sighed, "okay."

"I'm going to start a pile over here for anything that looks like it could be something," Elizabeth said, squinting at a file and ignoring his forlorn look.

"Oh, wonderful," he grumbled, putting his surgical mask back on. "Anything-that-looks-like-it-could-be-something goes over there. Yeah, I got it."

"Like this," Elizabeth said, walking over to him. She knew that if she didn't get him excited about something fast, he would look at these files without seeing anything at all, his eyes glazing over and his mind wandering. Then she'd end up having to go through all the files he'd done all over again.

She squatted on the floor next to him. "This is an official transfer of an author's titles from another literary agency to Hillings & Hillings."

Monty frowned. "Shouldn't that kind of information be kept in the office?"

"It's probably on computer. As for this," she turned it over to look at it, "this is a carbon. The original document must either be in the office or with—" She stopped, noticing that Monty was staring at her in a peculiar way. "What is it?"

He yanked his surgical mask down, breaking the elastic again.

"I wish you would stop doing that," she said, taking it from him, "we only have about ten more."

He grabbed her arm. "Elizabeth."

"What?"

"I'll bet you anything Berns is looking for an original rights agreement to some literary property. If he just wanted general information, they could have gotten it off the computers."

"And the people he sent to search were a lawyer and an accountant," Elizabeth said, slowly standing up straight and pulling her mask down under her chin.

"Something to do with law and numbers," he said, getting excited. "I bet they're looking for the original of something so they can destroy it."

"Well, let's think," Elizabeth said calmly, starting to pace. "If that's true, what kind of documents do people try to destroy? Wills, certainly."

"Did Henry do wills?"

"I know he did a literary estate rider on my will saying where my papers go, who's the executor, that kind of thing."

"Did we see anything about wills in the record log?" he asked, looking around at the boxes and boxes of papers.

"No," she said. "But wills wouldn't be in storage, would they?"

"I don't know," Monty said, frowning. "So what else? What else do people destroy?"

"Deeds," Elizabeth said. "Property deeds."

"Property rights, in this case!" Monty said, hoisting himself up.

"That would make sense," Elizabeth said slowly. "This paper I was showing you is a transfer of representation of rights."

"Okay, but what kinds of rights?" Monty asked, looking down into his open box. "I don't know what any of these book projects are. I've never heard of them. We've got to talk to Henry. We can't figure this out ourselves."

"What we really need is Dorothy. She's the one who would know."

"So we'll start with Henry," Monty said, accidentally bumping up against her as he dusted off his chinos.

Their eyes met and they both froze there for a moment.

And then Monty murmured an apology and Elizabeth backed away a step, saying they needed to find a telephone.

"Georgiana," the smooth, pleasant voice said, "what luck to find you at home. It's Creighton."

"Creighton," Georgiana repeated, wishing she hadn't picked up the phone. She had actually stood there in the kitchen of her house in Bel Air thinking, *Don't answer it.*

"Georgiana, I've got to tell you how deeply hurt and disappointed I am in you. Last night, I was lying in bed, and my wife woke up and asked me what was wrong, why I wasn't asleep. Do you know what I told her, Georgiana?"

"No," Georgiana said, finishing pouring a cup of tea.

"I told her that you refused to do a favor for me. A favor that would have cost you nothing. And do you know what my wife said?"

"No," Georgiana said, reaching for the honey.

"She asked me why you didn't like me. Don't you like me, Georgiana? Aren't you my friend? I thought we were friends."

Creighton sounded as though he had gone off the deep end. "Well, Creighton," she said slowly, watching a thin stream of honey fall into her cup, "I didn't like your making my press agent resign."

"I didn't do it!" he practically shouted. "I would never do anything to hurt you, Georgiana! It's you who want to hurt me! I know it, don't lie to me!"

"Creighton," she said, a chill running down her spine. "I told you I was sorry I couldn't appear at your press conference, but my refusal to get involved with this controversy on a public level is hardly a hostile act toward ICA." She slowly stirred her tea.

"It's hostility toward me!" he cried. "I thought I could trust you! You're conspiring against me and I won't allow it!"

"Creighton, I think you're twisting things out of proportion," she said. "It's true that I've loved the Hillingses since I was a little girl, and that they took care of me—Creighton?"

He had hung up. Georgiana sighed, rubbed her eyes, took a sip of tea, and called him back. His secretary said he was unavailable. Could she take a message?

"You could tell me if he's all right," Georgiana said.

There was a moment of silence. "Yes, of course he is," the secretary said.

"I'm frightened for him," Georgiana said truthfully. "He sounds as though he might be having an adverse reaction to medication—or something."

"Mr. Berns has been working extremely long hours lately," the secretary finally said. "It may be he is severely overtired. I would not take it personally, Ms. Hamilton-Ayres."

Georgiana hung up, thinking, Fine, I won't, and called Elizabeth to tell her something was wrong with Creighton Berns, and she was getting the hell out of L.A. and coming to New York.

~ *38* ~

"No offense, boss," Monty's producer said during the break, "but the show really sucks. What's with you?"

"Tired," Monty sighed, throwing the headset down on the console and stretching, yawning.

"You haven't gone over any of the notes, any of the faxes, you're not even listening to half the callers," Mike continued.

"Any more Milky Ways?" Monty asked.

"And you're probably putting on five pounds a day with this junk. If we ever manage to salvage the TV show, what the hell are you going to look like?"

"Here's one," Monty sighed, pulling a candy bar out of the pocket of his jacket hanging on the back of the chair. He glanced at the clock and put his headphones back on.

"Try and pull yourself together, Monty," Mike said, "or at least explain to people what's going on. Everyone thinks you're losing your edge." He stormed out of the studio, closing the door behind him.

Mike had been with Monty since long before Monty became a household name. He was talented and ambitious, and he had been salivating at the thought of the TV program. The really big money was made in TV. And all he—and everyone connected to Monty professionally—knew was that the big guy's personal life was somehow threatening the success of the whole enterprise. And for what? A couple of old people who needed to retire?

In one regard Monty knew Mike was right. The show today was for shit. His listeners were annoyed with him for being exhausted, for having nothing left for them. The show was suffering; it lacked its usual punch.

Monty knew the schedule he had to keep to produce the show that had made him a star. First rule: no life outside of the show on weekdays. He was up at five and out for a walk, usually in the dark. He ate breakfast while devouring newspapers and magazines and faxes from around the country. He had no writers. It was all Monty's reactions to the news and opinions of the day and his "straightening out" his listeners as to the correct point of view. He went into the studio around ten and did the show at eleven, central time, opening with twenty minutes of commentary, followed by phone calls from around the country.

After the show, he went to lunch, went for another walk, and began the awesome task of reviewing the video bits his assistant producers had assembled of various news items of the day. At night, he watched the network news, CNN, DBS, C-Span, and whatever else was relevant. He owned three TVs and six VCRs and had to use them all to do his job properly.

He did not eat out on weeknights. He did not talk on the phone to people. He did not even open the mail. All of that was done on weekends, if a speaking engagement was not scheduled.

And Monty could feel how fast that routine—the routine that had made him a success—was falling apart after even the slightest deviation from his routine.

However, for the first time in a long time, he did not feel lonely and he was surprised to find how much that meant to him. He always experienced a flush of warmth and contentment when he arrived at the Hillingses' apartment, because there was always someone there to talk to, someone who asked him how he was, how his day had been; someone to eat with, to be with, and to meet other people with. Things were *happening* in his life; he was not just sitting around—alone—commenting on what was happening to other people and to the country at large.

But no one ever said success was achieved without sacrifice. And after this thing with the Hillingses was over, Monty would return to Chicago *and* to his routine, he would get his TV show back on track, and his life would once again belong to the career he had always longed for.

Only maybe it was no longer what he wanted.

Now that was a terrifying thought.

After talking to Henry briefly, Monty had gone off to do his show and Elizabeth had returned to the Queens storage locker to resume scouting the files. She was not a literary agent, but Elizabeth knew she had to train herself to think like one until she found out what she needed to know.

At two-forty, she finally took a break to stretch. She saw the radio Monty had left for her and turned it on to hear the last twenty minutes of the show.

"No, that's not the point," she heard Monty saying over the air, "the point is, the movement is trying to make everybody the same. And I don't know about you, but I don't want anyone pretending these loonies are like you and me. I don't want them out on the streets!"

"But don't you agree that mental illness can be treated, Big Mont?" the woman caller was saying. "That just because someone has been admitted to a hospital, it doesn't mean they can't get well?"

"Well, dear friend, if you would like to bet your life on that proposition," Monty said in a deep voice, "fine, but don't bet on it with mine. And I certainly don't want you spending my tax dollars to get them back on the streets so I have to deal with them as *dangerous* homeless people—the so-called normal ones are quite dangerous enough, thank you! I frankly think all these loonies can trace their problems to too much booze or drugs somewhere along the line."

Elizabeth sat down on a metal bench that was fastened to the concrete wall and closed her eyes. Monty and the caller ranted on at each other. When the show was over, the station went on to the news. When Elizabeth opened her eyes to turn the radio off, she had tears in them. She dried them and turned the radio off.

If mental illness was defined as not having the capacity to behave normally, as Montgomery Grant Smith seemed to think, then Elizabeth had been mentally ill all her life. There had not been any alcohol or drugs in her family, at least not that she knew of, but she had never been normal, not even as a kid. She had always preferred living in her head instead of in the world; she loved to read and make up stories and dream, and was usually so distracted in general that the other kids made fun of her.

God had watched over her, though. He had made her good-looking enough so that no one had ever really picked on her in an unkindly way. The worst the kids ever did was scream, "Wake Up, Brain Drain!" after a soccer ball had clonked her on the head or something.

In adolescence, Elizabeth had understood romance, but not sex. What the boys wanted to do was not the least bit exciting to her, but what her charismatic, gentle-spoken, handsome math teacher might like to do did excite her. Fortunately, young Mr. Dinardo had never dreamed of exploring such a thing. And so, through junior high and then at boarding school, Elizabeth seriously and publicly pursued a life that was primarily intellectual, and just as seriously but secretly pursued a love life in the form of sexual fantasies of Mr. Dinardo.

In college she had simply decided it was time to lose her virginity, but the experience had been rather awful. A repeated experiment with another boy the following year was no more enjoyable. Real sex, Elizabeth feared, was awkward, abrupt, and lonely. Her senior year she had a relationship with a young professor who taught her a bit more about sex, but he still did not arouse much passion in her. At Columbia, she met Greg, a successful magazine editor who actually had very little time for her. Though he was supportive and kind and smart and well-meaning, their sex life was perfunctory—at least for Elizabeth. Months turned into years and her dissertation became a book, and the book was published to acclaim and Elizabeth was suddenly a best-selling writer.

She had been invited to a cocktail party for one of the Hillingses' clients, a party Mrs. Hillings had encouraged her to attend. She always felt awkward and nervous at parties considered "hip," if for no other reason than she had been brought up to believe that people who wanted their names in the press were people best avoided in life. But Mrs. Hillings had explained how her—Elizabeth's—presence could help her client's book, and this was the kind of favor Elizabeth, as a fellow writer, should learn to extend.

And so Elizabeth had asked one of her trendier students to take her shopping for a cocktail dress and shoes, and she had done her best to arrive at the party looking worldly, wise, fashionable, and simply like someone who had enough going in her life that her favor was worth receiving. (This was infinitely preferable, she thought, to looking prematurely ancient and out of it.)

Within minutes a man named David had materialized at her side and was, clearly, determined to stay there. He was everything that would make her parents nervous. He had on a very expensive suit that would quickly date; he was wearing handmade Italian shoes; his great, dark hair was too stylishly cut to be the creation of a barber shop; and when he shook her hand, he would not let go for several seconds. His smile was perfect, and his charming, seemingly sincere words came far too easily. "When I read your book," he said, looking into her eyes, "I knew you were a woman I had to meet. Now I know I was right."

How was she supposed to have known it was a line? How was she supposed to have known that he was seeing four other women at the time? That to him she was an irresistible novelty, an extremely attractive but repressed academic whose sexuality, he sensed, was just screaming to be awakened?

What a fool she had been. But she had never had a passionate love affair before. At least not with someone real (i.e., Mr. Dinardo). Later, she realized there had been a benefit to being that way, for Elizabeth had never been less productive than she was after meeting David. Before that, her manic energy had always been directed toward her work; afterward she had a lover who was determined she direct it toward him.

They had gone to the Stanhope after the party for a long dinner. She had drunk wine and laughed and felt progressively more like someone else. David told her that he was far too ferocious to date her, that he was sure her boyfriend treated her with a great deal more care than he wanted to.

"What do you mean?" she had asked.

"I mean," he had murmured, his gorgeous, slightly pouting mouth seeming too long for hers, "I'm sure he doesn't want to do all the things with you that I want to do."

At that point Elizabeth had felt her insides turn to liquid heat and she had known she was going to go to bed with him, and the sooner the better. If she got to know him better, or if he lived in New York, she knew she wouldn't be able to do it. He had correctly sensed that she was coasting along in a comfortable life, dying for passion, but only from a safe distance.

He had a wonderful body. And great finesse. He got her through the door of his room at the St. Regis and onto the bed in a matter of seconds, deftly removing their clothes, piece by piece. He had known how to kiss her—again and again and again—and how to whisper the romantic things she had longed to hear for years. He felt and touched and tasted every part of her, allowing her to do nothing but enjoy it. He asked her to let him enjoy her, to let him make love to her, just this once, and by the time he was easing himself into her, tenderly, gently, she was half-mad with desire, desperately wanting him not to be so gentle. He started coaching her then, quietly, steadily, making her feel his every movement, making her appreciate her body and his body and the way their bodies worked together.

Elizabeth gasped and flexed—hard—and a moment later she knew she was having sex like she had never dreamed of.

So this is what it is all about, she had thought.

She virtually lost the next two years of her life. She became obsessed with his body, with the sex, with this incredible world of sensation, but also with David and trying to hold on to him, get rid of the other women, make him commit solely to her. That's when all the trouble began: she couldn't bear to see how other women looked at him wherever they went, how easily he could seduce women, how bored he could get if she didn't stay on top of her game.

And she had abandoned her career at Columbia to get him.

To *get* him. Get him and do what? Lock him up? What on earth had she thought she was going to do with him after she *had* him?

David had fallen in love with her; that she never doubted. But how well could a man love a woman when on some level he couldn't stand himself?

No, in the beginning, Elizabeth had no idea how terribly needy David was, and how tied into this was his obsession with sex, money, and cars.

Oh, they had been a pair all right. Elizabeth may not have learned a whole lot about healthy relationships in her life, but she did know that two needy people didn't add up to a whole one. She and David had found that out. And it had eventually nearly killed her.

Elizabeth gave Monty's radio a kick and it fell over on its side.

Certainly Monty could never understand her. Or evidently even like her. Not if he knew everything.

~ *39* ~

When Patty arrived at ICA Tuesday morning, a woman from personnel told her that she was going to be working out at the reception desk today. This made Patty a little nervous, because she didn't know whether the switch was accidental or related to something she had said or done.

"Is Sylvia ill?" she asked the woman from personnel as they walked down the hall.

"I don't know," she said coolly. She helped Patty get situated at the desk and pointed out the phone lines. Ah, the phones! She would answer the general numbers as well as specific office numbers if any of the secretaries put their phones on call forwarding. As soon as the personnel woman left, Patty searched the desk for a phone system manual, hoping to figure out how she could eavesdrop.

There wasn't one. She had known it was too much to hope for.

Being a receptionist, Patty found, was really a difficult experience. All kinds of press people were trying to get past her to follow up on the demonstration from the day before, and, while they may have managed to bypass security downstairs, it was Patty's job to smoke them out and call security if they wouldn't leave of their own volition. Most wouldn't, and while she waited for security to arrive, they tried to interview her about the Hillings & Hillings demonstration and what was going on within the company. Patty kept saying she didn't know, she was sorry, she was only a temp.

Mixed in with the press people were legitimate visitors and aspiring actors, wanting to drop off head shots and résumés. And then one guy came in who seemed clearly out of his mind, but Patty had a system to follow, and so she had to make sure that he was not, as he claimed, the missing Osmond brother before calling security.

Patty got more than a little nervous when one press person pulled out a hand-held video camera and started filming her response to the question, "Is it true that all hatches are battened down while ICA weathers this storm of controversy about Hillings & Hillings?"

"I'm sorry, no comment," she said, hoping her wig was straight and wishing like hell for a fake nose and mustache. How she was ever going to reappear at ICA as an author and not be recognized at this point was beyond her.

"Hello, Mr. Johnson," Patty said to James Stanley Johnson when he walked in.

He stared at her, obviously trying to remember where he knew her from.

"Sylvia's gone," he observed.

"I think she's sick," Patty said.

"She's not sick," Mr. Johnson told her.

"Oh, no?" she said.

He winced slightly and drew a finger across his throat.

"They killed her?" Patty asked him.

He laughed. "They gave her a little severance and a copy of *The Perfect Résumé.*"

It was amazing to Patty what this wig enabled her to do. Instead of being a tired housewife and mother of three, she was acting like an attractive flirt who could wheedle information even out of James Stanley Johnson.

At any rate, clearly yesterday poor Sylvia had been fired. Did it have anything to do with the demonstration, or was it coincidence? And how had James Stanley Johnson known the receptionist was fired?

"I'm the lost temp," Patty reminded him.

"Oh, right," he said. "Got a promotion, huh?"

"I'm still just temping."

"You can probably get this job, if you want," he said. "I'll recommend you."

He could be a nice man, she thought. Not unlike any one of the enthusiastic fathers who turned out for their son's baseball games. She wondered if the James Stanley Johnsons of this world went to Little League, and if their kids liked them. Did *they* sit their children down and explain right and wrong? Ethics? Morality? She would take Ted over any of these hotshot corporate guys.

Patty got to cover the legal counsel phones for twenty minutes during lunch. When Miss Andersen came through on her way out, Patty commented that she had not seen Ms. Ballicutt this morning, should she tell people who called that she was away? Miss Andersen stared at Patty a moment and then said, "You take a message. That's it. You do not say anything about anything. Do you understand?"

"Yes, I do," Patty said obediently.

The phones for the legal offices actually rang quite a lot in those twenty minutes. And although the names of the callers meant nothing to her, Patty carefully recorded them twice, once on the message pad for Miss Andersen, and once again on the pad in her lap.

She wished she could have answered the phones for longer, but Miss Andersen came back promptly, as promised, and switched the calls back to her.

Around three o'clock, Mary Ellen called. "Mom, I thought I better remind you that the varsity dinner's tonight. I know Dad wasn't going to say anything, but he's going ballistic around here and so—"

Oh, God! This was the varsity dinner for spring sports, where traditionally she played hostess. "Mary Ellen, thank you. As soon as I get off here, I'll take the train out."

"It's at seven," Mary Ellen said. "At school. Should I tell Dad you're coming?"

"Let it be a surprise."

Elizabeth and Monty arrived at the Hillingses' apartment within moments of each other. As they came in the front door, Patty was clattering down the hall in a sleek black dress and high heels.

"Wow, you look great," they chorused.

"I have to go home for my husband's annual varsity sports dinner," she said, stuffing a piece of paper into Elizabeth's hands. "Those are the phone numbers of the people who tried to call Marion Ballicutt and James Stanley Johnson during lunch today." She clattered down the hall. "Oh, God," she added, wobbling to a halt and turning around, "I don't have a handbag."

"I have a black one you can use. Come to my room," Elizabeth said.

"Oh, thanks," Patty said, clattering after her.

"You're missing an earring, Patty!" Monty called.

"What? Oh damn"—she stopped, feeling for it on her ear—"where the heck is it? And I've got to catch the 6:05 or—" She made a little cry and crashed to the floor. Monty and Elizabeth came running. "I tripped," she said. Monty helped her up and she looked down at the back of her dress and said, "Oh, God, I've run my stockings and torn the slit in the dress and I—"

And she burst into tears.

Elizabeth and Monty looked at each other.

"And now my makeup's ruined, and I'm going to miss the train—"

"I'll help you with dress and makeup," Elizabeth said quickly, "Monty will have a cab waiting downstairs."

"But I don't have the money for both a cab and the train!" Patty wailed, ashamed and embarrassed about it all.

"Can you get your car?" Elizabeth asked Monty.

"Right away," he said, moving down the hall.

"Come on, Patty," Elizabeth said, pulling her toward her room, "I've got a sewing kit, I've got extra panty hose, and I've got a bag you can borrow. We'll fix your makeup and have you on your way, pronto. Monty's going to get a car to drive you straight there."

Patty started to say something and then turned away.

"What? What is it?" Elizabeth said gently.

Patty shook her head, accepted a Kleenex, and pressed it to her face. "I don't belong here. Ted told me I wouldn't fit in and I don't. I try to pretend I do, but it's hopeless."

"Of course you do," Elizabeth said.

"No I don't!" Patty wailed. "I'm not like you people!" She cut herself off, clamping her mouth shut, tears burning down her face.

"Patty," Monty said from down the hall.

She looked at him, pressing the Kleenex against her mouth.

"The car doesn't cost me anything. It's part of my contract. I would like you to use it tonight to go to your dinner. Listen, Patty, I've been there—so don't worry, I wouldn't offer the car if I thought it would in any way compromise you. Financially or otherwise."

Patty dropped her hand from her mouth. "I—"

"No argument," Elizabeth murmured, touching her arm, "just get to your dinner."

Patty sniffed and said, "Thank you, Monty. Thank you."

The limousine pulled up in front of the Stanton High School at 7:15. The traffic had been awful and she was late, but Patty felt so much better (even more so after having some of the mineral water and crackers she found in the refrigerator of the limo). When she walked into the noisy, boisterous cafeteria, a series of hellos from students and parents followed her all the way up to the head table where Ted, whipping around after he heard someone say her name, was literally dumbstruck.

"Sorry I'm late," she said, kissing him on the cheek, "but traffic was bad." After beaming at her for a moment, Ted gave her a hug and asked everyone to take their seats. He was the master of ceremonies, and so there was the greeting to all the parents, the speech, the introductions, the giving out of varsity letters and awards, but, at least during the dinner, he had a few minutes to turn and say a few words to his wife before they switched seats for dessert.

"I couldn't believe it when I saw you," he murmured, squeezing her knee under the table. "I thought you had forgotten."

"I love you," she said, because she meant it but also to avoid telling him about Mary Ellen's call.

"I want to make love to you later," he murmured, looking into her eyes.

"Then I'll stay over," she said happily. "I'll send the car back to the city."

"Car?" he said. But he was interrupted when Jimmy came up.

"Mom, hi, it's great you could come," he said, giving her a kiss on the cheek.

"Oh, honey, I'm very proud of you," Patty said. "The only problem is, where are we going to find room for all these new trophies where we can see them?" They all laughed.

"Did Dad tell you I'm sleeping over at Chuck's tonight?" Jimmy asked her.

"Oh," Patty said, "no. But that's fine, honey, have a good time."

Oh, great, Patty thought, *Ted's already farming the kids out to other families.*

The banquet went on. Patty, watching her husband, wondered if she could go home and make love with Ted and then drive back to the city. She really should see Elizabeth before going into ICA tomorrow. On the other hand, Monty had forced a hundred dollars on her, saying she shouldn't have to pay for any travel expenses on her own. When she refused to take the money, he swore she could owe it to him until her book was sold. So she had plenty of cash for a train and a cab in the morning.

It was almost ten when the awards dinner finally ended. By then the Kleczaks' euphoric mood had turned to exhaustion. As they walked out the school principal gave a low whistle and said, "Who was here tonight? Whose parents use a limousine?"

Patty, her arm looped through her husband's, felt Ted stiffen.

"It's actually a friend's company car," Patty said. "I've been doing some work in the city, and he offered to let me use it to get to the dinner on time."

The principal made a crack along the lines that you can't keep the girl on the farm after she's sampled city life and that the coach better keep tabs on his lovely wife. He left, laughing at his own wittiness.

"Who is paying for this?" Ted demanded as soon as they were out of earshot of everyone else.

"It doesn't cost anything. It's Montgomery Grant Smith's car. He gets it as part of his contract."

"Somebody's paying for it," Ted insisted, "and I want to know who so we can pay them back."

The driver was standing outside the car, waiting for instructions.

"It doesn't cost Monty anything," Patty said.

"And why is *Monty* chauffeuring you around? What does *Monty* expect in return?"

"Ted! Nothing!" Patty stepped back, genuinely shocked.

"Yeah, right. Guy chauffeurs you around in a limousine and expects nothing in return. She's alone with him in the city, away from her kids and her dumb jock husband—"

"Ted, stop it! Do you want me to stay tonight or not? Because you're certainly doing your best to wreck my mood."

"Wreck your mood," he said. "You're wrecking our family, Patty! How the hell do you think I feel having you run around with some celebrity jerk who's got his limo at your disposal? Are you telling me he isn't expecting you back tonight? It's his car, isn't it?"

"What is it, exactly, you wish me to do?"

"That's your choice, Patty, isn't it?" Ted asked bitterly, walking away.

Patty dismissed the car and driver and rode home, in silence, in the station wagon with Ted. Mary Ellen and Kevin were already in bed, so she went in and kissed them and talked to each. Ted ignored her and got ready for bed, so Patty called Elizabeth to tell her she had sent the car back and would be taking the early train in the morning.

After she got off, Patty cleaned the downstairs of the house a little, went out to the all-night supermarket, and bought some groceries, put them away, and went up to bed. Ted was snoring. She climbed into bed, kissed his back, and lay there, unable to sleep right away. When the alarm went off at five o'clock, she found that Ted had already gone.

~ *40* ~

After Elizabeth and Monty got Patty off to New Jersey, they went into the kitchen to fix themselves some dinner. Sitting in the study later, balancing plates of chicken and vegetables and baked sweet potatoes, Elizabeth said she thought Monty had handled Patty with a great deal of sensitivity.

"Yeah, well, when she started crying and said she didn't belong, I knew exactly how she felt."

"And how is that?" Elizabeth asked, cutting her chicken.

He smiled. "Like a Cinderella zapped back to poverty right in the middle of the ball. You know—everything is going so wonderfully in a new phase of your life with new friends, and then reality hits and you feel like the failure you always thought you were, still stuck in the rut you should have known better than to try to climb out of." He was no longer smiling. "You wish you hadn't even tried—to do anything new, I mean. Because it only sets you up to feel all those old same feelings of failure again."

Elizabeth's fork was hanging in midair. She put it down. "When have you felt like that?"

He looked at her. "Who says I still don't?" And then he smiled. "Anyway, she's a great lady," he said, picking up his knife and fork and starting in on one of the two sweet potatoes on his plate.

"Monty?"

"Hmmm?" He had a mouth full of food.

"Why aren't you nice on the radio?"

He struggled to swallow. "But I am! I don't hang up on people. I don't swear. I let people have their say."

She was toying with her food. "But you're not really like the man on the radio show," she said. "I listened today."

"Oh, it was a lousy show. I'm sorry you did." He speared a slice of chicken.

"I didn't like what you said about mentally ill people," she said quietly.

"Yeah, well, people born to privilege rarely do, I find. Have you always been rich?"

Elizabeth looked at him. "I was never rich until the book royalties and the movie sale and everything. My father did very well, but he had two families to support. There were always things I wished I could do or wanted to buy and couldn't. I've always worked."

He continued to eat, but his eyes were on her.

"I tutored kids in reading when I was about ten."

"Ten?" he said.

She nodded. "I always did that—it was good money. And when I was sixteen, I got a job in a bookstore after school. That wasn't such a good job, because I spent everything I made on books, but I got a discount at least, and so for that reason I worked part-time in a bookstore all the way through graduate school."

"Did your parents pay for graduate school?"

"I received teaching fellowships," she said.

"But they were there if you needed them," Monty said.

"Yes," Elizabeth nodded, "that's quite true. But then *The Duchess of Desire* caught on and money hasn't been a problem since."

Monty scooped up a bite of sautéed spinach and looked at her. "Do you feel guilty about what you have?"

"No," she said, sipping her iced tea.

"Why not? You liberals are always screaming about how no one has anything, so I'm curious—why don't you feel obligated to give all your money to homeless people?"

"Why would you say something like that?" she said.

"I'm just asking you why you don't support your politics with your money," he said. "You and your kind never do."

"I wish you'd stop this, Monty," she said.

"Well, you are a Democrat, aren't you?"

"I am a former Republican, but I left the party, because people like you so hopelessly distorted its principles that I couldn't, in all good conscience, stay."

Monty threw his head back and roared.

"Every time I'm fool enough to think I genuinely like you,

Montgomery Grant Smith," Elizabeth said, standing up, "you go out of your way to make sure I don't." She walked out of the room, dinner plate in hand.

Monty sat there, frowning.

After Elizabeth had finished her dinner at the kitchen table, she came back to the study to apologize. "I'm tired and on edge, and I hope you know that I do like you, despite your utterly abominable politics." She gave him a slight smile.

"I'm not sure I didn't deserve it," Monty admitted. "When I get as exhausted as I am now, I instinctively go into a show-time mode. It comes from—well, you know, the show must go on, and so I fall back into my shtick." He groaned, put his plate down on the coffee table, and buried his face in his hands.

"What's the matter?" Elizabeth said, worried.

"It's happened, it's happened, it's finally happened," he moaned. "I'm hearing myself apologize for the way I am." He looked up. "Do you realize, Professor, that this could be the beginning of the worst demasculinization of power since the Fall of the Roman Empire?"

"That's what I like most about you," Elizabeth said, picking up his empty plate and carrying it out, "your sense of humility."

"Suz, we need to talk," David said, watching her back as she washed the dinner dishes.

"What about, hon?" she asked.

She was wearing stretch pants and a tank top that made her look sensational, and as if that weren't enough, she had made him his favorite meal of all time—roast chicken with stuffing, mashed potatoes with gravy, and string beans (as good if not better than his mother's). It was becoming increasingly difficult for David to ignore how kind and loving and adoring Susie was. He'd have to be dead not to respond to this young woman with his heart as well as his body. She had turned out to be a complete surprise.

"Sit, baby, I need to talk to you," he said.

Looking concerned, Susie wiped her hands on the dish towel, slung it through the handle of the refrigerator door, and came over to the table to sit down. He was looking at his hands. She reached over and took one. "What is it, honey?"

"Um, listen," he said, looking at her. She was probably the most beautiful woman he had ever been with. "Baby, look, our relationship seems to be getting to the point where I need to tell you something?"

She continued to look at him, eyes large, listening.

"First of all, let me say that I'm in total remission, so—"

"Oh, my God, Davey, you have cancer?" Susie said, grabbing his hand, her eyes welling up.

"No," he said quickly.

"Leukemia?" she asked.

"No—"

"It's not AIDS, is it?" She looked frightened.

"No, no, nothing like that," he quickly reassured her. "I, uh, I have herpes, although I haven't had an outbreak in a couple of years. But I wanted to tell you about it, so that you knew."

She looked puzzled. "Is that it?"

He nodded. "I wanted you to know because—well, you should know. Things are getting pretty serious, and if it ever comes back—"

"But, Davey, everybody has herpes."

He blinked.

"Honey, I've got it, too."

"What?" he said.

"I got it a couple of years ago from my boyfriend at Cal State. It's a real pain, but it's hardly anything to lose sleep over." She patted his hand. "And you were scared to tell me? That's so sweet."

"Why didn't *you* tell *me?*" he asked her.

"What?" she said absently.

"When were you going to tell me that you had it?"

"Oh, I don't know," she said, "I guess if I had an outbreak or something, but it's been years."

"But what if I got it from you before you told me?" he asked.

"And what if I got it from you before you told me? These things happen, Davey. It's no big deal. Forget about it."

"I can't believe we can't contact Ben Rothstein," Monty grumbled, sitting on the couch with his stocking feet up, thumbing through the papers on his lap.

"He'd call if he knew what was going on," Elizabeth told him, reading glasses perched on the end of her nose. "But you don't go to a place like Bora Bora unless you genuinely want to get away from it all. Only Henry knows how to reach him and he's not telling."

"His kids must know," Monty said.

"He had a son, but he died in a car accident years ago," Elizabeth said, turning another page. "Anyway, Josh says it's better that Ben isn't here." She glanced over at Monty. "The worst thing he could do right now is get involved and make it look as though ICA's right about Henry and Dorothy wanting to sell him the company."

"And that's exactly what Henry should do," Monty said.

"Back to your lists," she said. "We've *got* to figure out what it is Creighton Berns wants to get his hands on so badly."

They were quiet a while, each examining the records in front of them.

"What the hell are we looking for?" Monty said a moment later, dropping his papers in his lap.

"I swear to God, Montgomery Grant Smith, I am going to lock you up to get you off sugar. These mood changes are making me crazy!"

"No mood changes," Monty said.

"I can't keep feeding you candy bars to keep you stable!" she continued. "You're going to blow up or have a heart attack from sugar shock, I don't know which."

"Sugar has nothing to do with anything."

"Right, and you've got the temperament and physique to prove it." She winced. "Sorry, that was out of line. It's just hard for me to see the way you live and pretend I don't know what it's doing to you."

"Thank you, Professor. Your concern is touching."

"I'm sure it is," she said, trying to ignore him as he unwrapped a chocolate-covered peppermint cream and popped it in his mouth.

The phone rang and Elizabeth snapped it up. From the way she immediately lowered her voice, murmuring, "We're just going through file records, trying to get better acquainted with what is in storage," Monty knew she was talking to David and he jumped up, waving frantically.

She covered the phone. "What?"

"Don't tell Aussenhoff about the files in storage," he whispered.

Elizabeth glared at him, but she complied, changing the subject. Monty knew Elizabeth wanted him to leave so she could talk in private, but he refused to budge. It bothered him that Elizabeth had volunteered the information about what they were doing at the Hillingses this evening. God only knew what else she might tell him.

Monty was convinced Aussenhoff was not to be trusted.

He pretended to examine the records, trying hard to stifle a yawn. He was exhausted, and he needed to go back to the hotel, but he could not leave.

Fifteen minutes later, Elizabeth was still on the phone, her back to him, murmuring in a voice so low he couldn't make out a word.

"I don't know, Bets," David was saying on his end of the phone in Los Angeles, "I feel so rotten about the press conference. I wish I could just tell Berns to go fuck himself and not care if he pulls the plug on my movie, but I can't. I do care and I don't want to lose everything."

"Of course not, David," she said. "And you shouldn't torture yourself about it. There really isn't anything else you can do to help anyway."

"I could be there with you." His voice was sexy and low.

She couldn't say anything for a moment.

"You have your preproduction work to do," she finally managed.

"I don't care," he said, "I'm coming back as soon as I can. I want to see you."

"I want to see you, too," she sighed.

Elizabeth hung up the phone, paused a moment, and then turned around.

"So what was his excuse for going on TV? To secretly sabotage Creighton Berns by being his character witness?" Monty asked, instantly regretting his tone because he sounded exactly the way he felt—pissed, unsettled, and disgusted with Elizabeth for being susceptible to such a louse.

"No excuse," she said coldly. "It was a mistake. He's flying in later this week to help us."

That was it, Monty couldn't take it. "It doesn't bother you at all that he's coming here *after* helping Creighton Berns? He'll know everything we're doing and what time of day we're doing it!"

"Oh, Monty, don't be an ass," Elizabeth said.

"And don't you be a fool."

She glared at him. "I think we're both tired."

"Yeah, and I know tired of who," Monty said, getting up from the couch, throwing his papers down, and grabbing his shoes and jacket.

"Of whom," Elizabeth said, not bothering to see him out.

∼ *41* ∼

The phone rang just after midnight. Georgiana had been sound asleep, and it took her a moment to get her bearings.

"I'm sorry for calling so late."

"Alexandra?" Georgiana said, sitting up, holding her bedclothes around her. "What's wrong?"

"Nothing, really," Alexandra said quietly, "I'm fine." Then she laughed, a long, low laugh. "No, I'm not fine."

The comment shot straight through Georgiana. "What's the matter?"

"You're coming back to New York and I don't know what to do about you."

"You don't have to *do* anything, but we could see each other."

"I was thinking the same thing," Alexandra said. "Look, Georgiana, I have a small farm in New Jersey."

"I know, you told me," Georgiana said. How could she or anyone not know of Alexandra Waring's relationships with farms? The country's only solo nightly national news anchorwoman was born and raised on a farm in Kansas, and much of her ratings success, some Americans said, was because it had been so long since anyone had seen a "normal" person on TV.

A normal person, yes. Right.

Alexandra certainly had her work cut out for her if she ever wanted to live her own life, as opposed to acting out the one scripted for her. Like Georgiana's, hers had been a lonely, troubled childhood. For decades her father had been a powerful congressman, and he and Alexandra's mother had lived in Washington most of the time. They had insisted their daughter stay at the farm to be raised by her grandparents, which might have been okay if her grandfather had not been an alcoholic.

After college, Alexandra moved from San Francisco to New York to Washington, following increasingly important news jobs. Just as she was preparing to move back to New York to become the DBS anchor, she was shot and nearly killed on the steps of the Capitol by a deranged man. Later in the year, lightning struck twice and she was again the target of a gun-carrying lunatic. Alexandra landed in therapy, and that's when she finally began to examine the kind of life she led and why.

Georgiana knew there had been a longtime boyfriend and fiancé, but what had happened between them was a subject that was obviously still painful to Alexandra.

"The farm's not a big deal or anything," Alexandra was saying, "but it's mine and it means a great deal to me, and I wondered if you might want to come out next weekend. Didn't you tell me that you ride?"

"Yes," Georgiana said. "I love to ride."

"Then we can do that." She paused. "You'll have your own room and bathroom, of course, and everything will be pretty casual. What do you say?"

Alexandra's invitation touched Georgiana deeply. She knew it had taken a lot of courage for her to ask her, because she knew Alexandra was scared.

And Georgiana wondered if she should be, too.

~ *42* ~

"Are you still mad?" Monty asked over the telephone at seven o'clock the next morning.

"Not enough to walk away without seeing this thing finished," Elizabeth told him, pouring milk into a steaming cup of coffee.

"That's pretty mad," Monty said. "Look, Elizabeth, I can't help it if I'm a man."

She had to laugh. "What on earth does that have to do with anything? Are you suggesting all men think and behave like you?"

"No, that's not what I meant." He was entangling himself already.

"Then tell me what you did mean."

"I meant that it's difficult for a man like me to see a woman like you be drawn to David Aussenhoff. I'm sorry, but that's the truth."

"And what, may I ask, does my personal life have to do with you?"

"It has to do with what an amazing woman I think you are," Monty said.

"You're in love with Georgiana, remember?"

"Yeah, well, we're all entitled to a few meaningless daydreams in life."

"What are you eating?"

"Jelly doughnut," he said, with his mouth full.

"Oh, Monty," she sighed.

"I know it's got sugar in it," he said, "but it tastes good. Without two or three doughnuts and a lot of coffee, there's no way in hell I'm going to be able to get through this day. I'm bushed."

"Same," she said. "But we have to get going."

"Does that mean I'm invited back to the salt mines with you?"

"Yes," she said. "But I'll understand if you can't make it. After all, you've got your show to do."

"I'll pick you up in an hour," he said.

Elizabeth and Monty were silent for a while as they drove out to Queens, each thinking their own thoughts, sipping coffee, looking out the windows of the limousine, when Elizabeth suddenly cried, "What fools we are!"

"Huh? What?" Montgomery said, startled, reaching into the bar for a napkin to catch the coffee he spilled.

"The names and numbers Patty gave us yesterday," Elizabeth said, handing her coffee to him and ripping open her briefcase. "Does that car phone work?"

"Yeah," he said, putting the cup on the bar and opening the phone box.

"Okay, let's go," she said, pulling Patty's list out, "let's start calling these numbers and find out who these people are."

There were six numbers. Elizabeth called the first one, a New York number. Scott Bornan was a lawyer representing an opera star.

Monty made the next call to Mathew at an L.A. number. "Nobody'll be in yet in Los Angeles, but what the hey." Monty listened, frowned, hung up, and stared at Elizabeth. Then he murmured, "Let me try that again." This time he held the phone out to her. After several rings, a voice-mail system picked up, and a man's slightly affected voice said, "You have reached the office of Mr. Creighton Berns. Leave a message at the sound of the tone. Thank you."

They stared at each other a moment.

"We've got to call Patty," Elizabeth said.

Out at the front desk at ICA, Patty was sweating bullets. Elizabeth had told her that "Mathew" was either a code name for Creighton Berns or *something else*. "You must keep your eyes and ears open for it." Easy for her to say! What was she supposed to do?

When lunchtime came and Miss Andersen went out, Patty thought, *To hell with it, let's go for it*, and she abandoned her post, forwarding her calls to God only knew where. She hurried back to the legal offices, as if on a hasty errand. None of the assistants was there, nor was James Stanley Johnson in his office. His door was open, though, and on the couch was the box of files he had been going through the week before. If he hadn't found what he was looking for in there, then the chances were good she never would either.

Did she dare risk examining his desk?

Just do it, she told herself.

She closed the door and quickly scouted his desk. Papers, papers, papers. She touched one, thought she heard something, jumped, froze—silence—and then resumed looking around again. Mathew, Mathew, anything that looked like anything, and then she saw a piece of legal pad with 4/7 MATHEW penciled on the corner. There were a series of words and notes, but she didn't take time to figure it out. She simply took the paper, slipped it into her blazer pocket, and ran for the door. She peeked outside. No one.

"May I help you with something?" a woman's voice asked.

Patty nearly screamed. She turned around. Marion Ballicutt was standing by Miss Andersen's desk, holding some papers in her hand.

"No, ma'am," Patty said. "I'm supposed to be covering the phones at the front desk, but there seems to be something wrong with the call forwarding on Mr. Johnson's phone. I think it's fixed now." She offered a nervous laugh, edging away. "His calls have been going into the twilight zone, and we're trying to get it working again."

"I should hope so," Marion said, turning abruptly and walking away.

When Patty got her lunch break, an hour later, she raced out of the building, jumped into a cab, and headed for Penn Plaza. She was signed in by security, sent up in an elevator, and then escorted through a labyrinth of hallways that ended in a huge open room full of people sitting at desks. Farther along was an engineering studio, where Montgomery Grant Smith sat behind a large plate-glass window with headphones on, talking into a microphone.

"The great and the mighty will be back after these messages," he promised, signing off. He waved at Patty and stood up.

"You can go in," the engineer said.

"I think this is it," she said, breathless, pulling out the yellow piece of paper.

He scanned it and looked up at the clock. "Elizabeth will be here in about twenty minutes. I'll give it to her and we'll discuss it tonight at the apartment? You're going to be there?"

"Yes," Patty said, "but I've got to get back to the office now."

As she turned to go, he stopped her. "You did beautifully," he told her, impulsively giving her a big bear hug that momentarily picked her up off the ground. "When your book gets published, I'm giving you a whole hour on my show. And that's a solemn promise."

"A whole hour on romantic suspense?" She laughed, very pleased.

"Why the hell not? I'm Montgomery Grant Smith and I can do what I want!"

Laura Van Wormer

"And we're frankly hoping that Montgomery Grant Smith wants to go back on the air now," his producer said over the intercom, "because you have five seconds."

Dorothy enjoyed her daily walks to the beach and back. She was getting brown from being outdoors, and she had regained much of her strength, though she still slept what seemed to her to be incredibly long hours. But she was certain she was on the mend. As she turned into their drive, arms swinging, legs beneath her skirt working easily, she felt confident she would be able to make the most of the time that was left to her.

She had been sent a warning and she would remember to watch what she ate, exercise regularly, and get her rest. It was a fine and easy thing to follow instructions out here in the country, but back in New York... Well, the time may have come for her to face the fact that New York City was not particularly conducive to a less stressful existence. Her doctor had suggested a mild aerobics class, but she couldn't imagine herself in a leotard, leaping about with all those young people.

She laughed to herself, walking around the corner of the house.

Bernadette and Henry were sitting on the back deck, and Henry looked as though he had been caught whispering about her behind her back. She didn't know what was going on in New York and Los Angeles at this point, but she figured the time had probably arrived when she would be finding out.

"Hello, darling," she said to her husband. "What's the matter? Millicent hasn't made us another loaf of that ghastly 'health' bread, has she?"

"No," Henry said.

"I can't imagine why it's always so heavy," Dorothy said, slowly climbing the stairs to the deck. "Anyway, dear, the beach is just marvelous," she added, sitting down. "If you go fishing tomorrow morning, I'd like to come with you."

"I'm sorry, what?"

"Henry, what *is* the matter?" Dorothy said, watching his expression.

He looked pained. And then he sighed. "Doe, darling, I've been discussing the situation with Bernadette, here, and I wonder if you might be up for a conference call Friday morning."

"Saints be praised," Dorothy said to the sky. "Don't tell me he's finally letting me out of isolation!"

"It's not that I've—"

"Been keeping me a prisoner in my own home?" she finished for him. "Yes, darling, you have, but I know why and I am very grateful to you for seeing that I've had such a good rest." She looked at Bernadette. "You have told him the truth, haven't you? How really well I am?"

"I told Mr. Hillings that we need to be careful that you don't overdo it," Bernadette said carefully. "But I said I thought a conference call would be all right."

Dorothy looked at Henry. "You need me to help sort out the agency business, don't you?"

"Yes, I do. Rather, Elizabeth needs your excellent memory."

"Elizabeth?" she said.

"Yes, Elizabeth has been absolutely marvelous," Henry told her. "She's piecing together information for us in the most extraordinary way—I think it must have to do with her skills as a researcher. And Montgomery—"

"Montgomery!" Dorothy chuckled, shaking her head, trying to pretend his involvement was news to her. "This is rather amazing."

"And Georgiana's coming back to New York again to help," Henry said.

"*Georgiana?*" she asked. Now she really was surprised. "Darling, we don't even represent her!"

"She's been helping nonetheless," Henry said.

"Who?" Bernadette asked.

"Georgiana Hamilton-Ayres," Henry said. "The actress."

Bernadette's eyes grew quite large.

"And, according to Elizabeth," Henry said, "David Aussenhoff is flying back to New York today to help out as well."

"What is the conference call about?" Dorothy asked.

"Elizabeth and Monty seemed to think you hold the answers to a number of questions that can make sense out of this whole ICA mess."

"Quite likely they're right," she said.

Henry looked so relieved to hear this that Dorothy realized at once how much he must have been keeping from her all these weeks.

Oh, golly, how she loved this dear man!

~ 43 ~

Creighton Berns was talking with one of ICA's biggest film directors when his secretary buzzed him. "Yes, Mary?" he asked.

"Your old friend is on the phone," she told him.

"Would you excuse me for just a moment?" Creighton asked, snapping up the phone.

He listened. "Yes," he said. "Really." Eyes narrowing. "You must be mistaken." A nod. "All right, thank you. *Anything* that comes your way, I want to hear about." And he hung up.

Fifteen minutes later he had steered the director out of his office and down to the film department for a meeting with a producer.

When he was alone, Creighton summoned his assistant, Joseph Colum, signaling for him to close the door. Creighton sat back in his chair, knitted his hands together over his stomach, and said, "I want the numbers on Georgiana Hamilton-Ayres."

His assistant blanched slightly. "I know them, Mr. Berns. We made one point seven million in commission on her last year, and about fifteen times that from packaging her vehicles."

"Then I suppose we better count on a dip in Ms. Hamilton-Ayres's earnings for us this year," Creighton said. "Because I know for a fact she's no friend of mine."

~ 44 ~

By six o'clock Thursday evening, the Hillingses' apartment was filled with people and noise. Monty had come from the studio after his show; David and Georgiana had arrived from JFK not fifteen minutes apart; Patty dragged in from ICA at five forty-five; and Elizabeth, radiant and exultant, was walking around the apartment waving a copy of the Mathew memo from ICA, sure now they were on the right track.

By six-thirty everybody was in the kitchen, drinking and snacking, tempted by the delicious smells of a roast and the sweet potato soufflé Monty was cooking for dinner ("You people eat meat, don't you? How about you two from the Left Coast?"). They stood there talking, edging around the oven and stove, as hungry people are so apt to do.

They were also getting used to being together again after so much talking over the phone. David was never more than a foot from Elizabeth, not talking to her in particular but seeming to need to be in her orbit. When they got a moment alone David murmured, "I'm staying around the corner. I was hoping maybe later you and I could spend some time together."

She smiled, thinking how well he was aging, how handsome he was, and thinking back—just for a moment—to what it had been like to make love with him, and what it might be like now.

"I'd love to," she answered, leaning forward and kissing him on the cheek, only to find Monty's face looming over David's shoulder.

"I have to talk to you," he said. Elizabeth made a face of helplessness to David and allowed Monty to pull her through the swinging door into the dining room. As soon as the door swung closed, Monty whirled around. "This is a lousy idea, Elizabeth! And I resent having to do all this work, only to risk everything by telling questionable people about it."

"There are no questionable people here," she said.

"I stand corrected—questionable *person*. Georgiana didn't help Creighton Berns," he whispered hoarsely. "Patty didn't help him—I didn't, you didn't, but somebody did, and you can't tell me he's not here to spy for him!"

"You're acting like an idiot, Monty. Besides," she added, feeling particularly vengeful at this moment, "I'll be able to vouch for David because I intend for him to stay right here with me—all night—and tomorrow when we talk to Dorothy."

Monty glared at her. "You stupid, stupid woman. Fine! Go on, blow the whole thing sky-high because you need to feel like you can get him back. But remember," he said, pointing his finger at her, "I warned you!"

"Fortunately, Montgomery, I'm learning how to ignore you."
She marched back into the kitchen, announcing that she wanted to
bring everybody up to date on what they had learned in the past few
days.

Monty, his face scarlet, stood just inside the kitchen door, glaring at her.

"What Henry thinks Patty found at ICA are notes about some
kind of movie ICA is packaging."

"What movie?" David asked.

"We don't know yet," Elizabeth answered. "All we have to work
with is the name Mathew."

"Mathew Soaring," David said immediately. "The Fenton
movie."

Elizabeth stared at him. "What?"

"The Keeter-Fenton movie at Metropolis," David said.
"Mathew Soaring is the name of the lead, the kid who saves the
universe or something."

Now Monty and Elizabeth looked at each other.

"That's the big sci-fi film, isn't it?" Georgiana asked. "There've
been rumors about it for ages."

"Yeah, that's it," David said, nodding. "It's supposed to be the
next *ET.* The licensing deals have been in the trades for months, so
everyone keeps wondering why the movie hasn't been released.
Metropolis says they're just waiting for timing reasons." And then
he proceeded to tell them how the movie had been in the works for
five years and how the budget had ballooned to over one hundred
million dollars, which would be okay if it lived up to its press as the
blockbuster of the decade. "But few studios can afford to hold that
kind of film in the can for long," he said.

There was a moment of silence when he finished.

"Didn't I give you the number of a Mathew who called the ICA
legal department?" Patty asked.

"Yes, and the number Mathew left connected us with Creighton
Berns's office at ICA," Elizabeth said.

There was a moment of silence as people took this in.

"Tomorrow morning," Elizabeth continued, "we'll talk to Dorothy and try to figure out what the connection might be between
this movie and Hillings & Hillings."

"Let me get on the phone," David said, "and see what I can find out about the movie. I'll use the one in the study, all right?"

"Good," Elizabeth said, "go."

As David left the room, Monty walked up behind her. "Go with him!" he whispered. "He's probably calling Berns right now! Watch him every second!"

"Oh, Monty!" she said.

"I'm not kidding. I want you by his side!"

And so Elizabeth went in to sit with David as he started making calls to the West Coast about the sci-fi/fantasy movie. He took extensive notes. When he thought he had enough to closely describe the film to Dorothy, they rejoined the others. Patty and Georgiana were setting the table and Monty was putting plates in the upper oven to warm them. David briefed Monty on what he had found out, and Monty, not without a few sidelong glances at Elizabeth, seemed placated for the moment.

They lit candles in the dining room, and everyone took a seat as Monty began carving the roast at the head of the table. Elizabeth, who was sitting next to him, served vegetables and soufflé and the whole affair took on the atmosphere of an enjoyable family Sunday dinner.

They discussed what David's contacts had told him about the movie—the film had gone into preproduction under Creighton Berns before he left Metropolis for ICA; the release had been delayed for months; there were rumors of some sort of legal problem on it; the studio had taken out extensive loans to cover the delays—and they became convinced it had something to do with driving Creighton Berns to such strange behavior. The question was, did it have any connection to the Hillings & Hillings situation or not.

The dinner conversation sharply veered after Elizabeth asked David what effect, if any, he thought having a Democratic president was having on the movie business. Somehow this veered into homosexuals in the military, and Montgomery immediately rolled into one of his radio routines. For the next ten minutes everyone else was torturously reminded why politics was an inappropriate subject at the dinner table. "And last, but not least," Monty thundered as a conclusion, "the Bible says that a man who lies with another man like he would lie with a woman should be put to death."

"Leviticus," Elizabeth said. "Where it also says, 'For every one that curseth his father or his mother shall be surely put to death.' "

"So which do you prefer, Monty," Georgiana said, "death by fire or hanging?"

No one was eating at this point. Everyone's face was flushed.

"Look, Monty," Elizabeth said, "let's just conclude this discussion with the fact that we live in a democracy and the majority of Americans are in favor of gays being a regular part of our armed forces."

"Oh, polls!" Monty cried. "The little lady wants to talk about polls!"

"I find it so interesting," David said, "that America's so-called most popular radio talk-show host thinks the same way the Nazis did."

"Oh, boy, here we go!" Monty said, throwing his hands up. "The old Nazi defamation trick."

"It's no trick," David said. "Like you, the Nazis were willing to do anything to preserve a system that insured their superiority."

"We're talking about gays in the military," Monty said.

"I'm talking about the only other military organization that banned homosexuals," David continued. "And the Nazis didn't just take gays off to the extermination camps, as you might recall. Or perhaps gays are the only group that fat-ass southern crackers like you like to discriminate against?"

"Maybe people like you cause people to discriminate in the first place," Monty said.

David was out of his chair in a moment and on top of Monty. The two men fell backward with a crash and Monty, grabbing at the table on his way down, pulled the tablecloth and about a third of the dinner with him. Georgiana and Elizabeth sat there in shock, but Patty was on her feet in a moment, standing over them, pulling them apart and scolding them as if they were her children.

"Get off him, David," she commanded in a voice none of them had ever heard her use.

Sheepishly, David rolled off of Monty and stood up, food falling to the carpet.

Monty, lying on his back, with a plate mashed to his chest,

struggled to get up. "That's what I get for engaging in a discussion with an adolescent with a chip on his shoulder."

"Fuck you!" David yelled, as he stormed out of the room. In a moment, they heard the front door slam.

After another moment, Elizabeth started to laugh.

"I guess it is a little funny, isn't it?" Monty said, getting up and peeling his plate off his chest.

"Everything but the way you think," Georgiana said sharply. All eyes went to her.

"Mental illness," Georgiana said. "Is that really what you think homosexuality is, Monty?"

He nodded. "Yes."

"Then I second David's sentiments," she said, pushing back her chair and walking out.

The remaining three were silent. The candles were still burning, though skewed halfway across the table. Elizabeth finally reached for her glass of wine. "Here's to you, Patty, the only other person who has sense enough not to take Monty's vaudeville politics seriously."

"Hear, hear," Patty said. They clinked glasses and drank, as Monty righted his chair and sat back down at the table.

"You do look pretty silly, I must say," Elizabeth said.

"I meant what I said," he growled, scraping food off his coat with a knife.

"Yes, I know," Elizabeth said patronizingly, "and we all know you wouldn't let a homosexual within a hundred miles of you."

He snapped his head in her direction. "What's that supposed to mean?"

Elizabeth shrugged, smiling into her glass and taking a sip of wine.

~ *45* ~

David had stormed out of the apartment after dinner and Georgiana had retired to the Hillingses' bedroom suite, refusing to have further contact with Monty. As for the talk-show host, he quietly cleaned up the mess in the dining room while Elizabeth and Patty washed dishes in the kitchen. The women were done long before Monty, who, last Elizabeth saw, was on his hands and knees doing something to the rug with a cleaner and rubber gloves.

Montgomery Grant Smith may be a lot of things, but a man who didn't know how to cook and clean he was not.

Elizabeth went back to check on Georgiana. The Hillingses' suite consisted of a bedroom, dressing room, and bath. Georgiana was in a robe, sitting at the dressing room table applying cream to her face.

"I just wanted to make sure you were all right," Elizabeth said.

"Oh, I'm fine. Sorry not to have helped with the cleanup, but I think I need to steer clear of our great American phenomenon of the airwaves. Honestly, have you ever?" She looked at herself in the mirror and frowned. "When you make a mistake, Georgiana, by golly you make the very worst one you can find." She looked at Elizabeth's reflection. "What's the matter?"

"Oh, nothing," Elizabeth said, pulling her hair up off her neck.

"Have I offended you?" Georgiana asked.

"Me? Why, no."

"I hope not," Georgiana said. She turned around. "It doesn't bother you, does it?"

"What?"

"My being here—that discussion, my sexuality and everything."

"Good heavens, no," Elizabeth said.

"Because if it does, you just say the word and I'll move to a hotel."

"Georgiana!" Elizabeth said, putting a hand on her shoulder. "I am so sorry—my mind was somewhere else and you leapt to the wrong conclusion. I was disturbed by something else—someone else—and I assure you, it is *not* you. As a matter of fact, I wanted to tell you how glad I am you're here, and to say that Patty's in absolute seventh heaven."

"I like her." Georgiana smiled. "I can't even imagine what it would be like to grow up with a mother like her."

"I know," Elizabeth sighed, letting her hand fall from Georgiana's shoulder. Georgiana looked up at her and Elizabeth paused and said, "I'm upset about Monty."

"Good Lord, why bother?" Georgiana asked, beginning to wipe the cold cream off with a tissue.

"Because I like him," Elizabeth said frankly. "And it makes me upset to think I *could* like him—and yet I do. He's been great during this whole thing."

Georgiana gestured to the chair. When Elizabeth sat down, she said, "Let me tell you something about Montgomery Grant Smith. I'm hardly an expert—thank God—but I do think I have a pretty good fix on where he is."

"And where is that?" Elizabeth said.

"I think he was the fat kid in the class, if you know what I mean."

Elizabeth nodded. "He's the first one to admit it."

"And I think he developed a mouth to protect himself because of it. So I don't know about you, but I have always had a soft spot for the kid everybody picked on, no matter how old. In fact, I'm not sure I would have, well, made that mistake with Monty had he been any different."

She thought a moment before continuing. "There was something going on between us that night, something that had to do with my knowing that even if I were straight, I would not have been seen talking to a man like that, and yet I was talking to him and I was enjoying myself. No matter how much of a loser he was as a kid, there is something else in him—and that is the potential to be great."

Elizabeth was looking at her strangely. "What are you saying?"

"I'm saying that I see something great in Montgomery Grant Smith, and I know that is what attracted me to him."

"Are you joking?" Elizabeth asked, after trying to comprehend what Georgiana was saying.

"No, I'm not joking. The question is, will he ever break out of his cocoon and take some risks—personally, emotionally, you know what I mean. Grow up and be a full-fledged adult."

"He made a play for you," Elizabeth pointed out.

"Which, if you think about it, is the safest thing he could have possibly done: chase after the only woman he knows for sure has no interest in him."

Elizabeth didn't say anything. She sat there, legs crossed, hands folded on her knee, thinking.

"He's extraordinarily naive, you know," Georgiana said. "He's like an adolescent."

"I don't think he had an adolescence. Or a childhood. His father died when he was young."

There was a knock on the bedroom door.

"Come in," Georgiana called.

Patty popped her head in. "I'm sorry to interrupt, but David Aussenhoff's on the phone and he'd like to talk to you, Elizabeth."

"Okay, thanks," she said, getting up.

"Patty, come in, I want to talk to you," Georgiana said, standing up. She waved her into the dressing room and sat her down in front of the mirror. "How's the wig working?"

"Great," Patty said. "It's so comfortable, I forget I have it on."

"Well," Georgiana said, going to the closet, "when I was home, I saw one of my wigs from a movie and I thought, We should try that one on Patty, too. I think she's really meant to be a blonde."

"As dark as I am?" Patty asked the mirror, looking at her chestnut brown hair and deep brown eyes.

Georgiana had opened a small case and was lifting out a platinum blond wig.

"Oh, God, now I'll really look like Madonna," Patty said. "It'll look so fake."

"With your coloring, it's not supposed to look real, but it should look stunning." She was working with Patty's hair, putting it up and pulling the hairpiece down. "Yes," Georgiana declared, "I *was* right, this is a wonderful color for you. Look. You're absolutely to die for—your husband's going to go crazy, I assure you."

Georgiana was right, she did look fabulous! Ten years younger. Her bone structure was more pronounced, her eyes were wonderfully large, lustrous.

"I wanted you to try this on because I'm seeing my New York hair colorist while I'm here."

Patty's expression changed to fear.

"And Franco will do your hair for free the first time. He'll do that for a friend of mine. One of the privileges of being a walking advertisement for him," she added. "And if you decide you don't like it, you can put a dark rinse through it until it grows out again. There's only one drawback: once you go blond, it's going to take upkeep, which means going to a colorist and doing a rinse at home in between professional touch-ups."

The bedside phone was ringing. Georgiana went over to answer it while Patty sat in front of the mirror, smiling, wondering if she would ever dare color her hair.

Georgiana picked up the Hillingses' personal line.

"Hello, Georgiana?"

"Alexandra?" Georgiana said. "I thought you'd still be at the studio."

"I am, but I'm afraid I have some bad news."

"Are you all right?" Georgiana said, gripping the telephone.

"It's not about me, it's about you. Do you know what the A wire is in a newsroom?"

"No."

"It's the nickname for the unofficial news, the gossip coming in from other newsrooms around the country. There's a rumor on the A wire tonight that you're about to be outed."

Georgiana went numb.

"It looks as though it's coming out of Los Angeles. Nothing firm yet, we're checking. The report is that somebody is hawking an ex-lover of yours to the tabloids, print, and TV. The story is she'll swear you're gay. That's all we know, but I'm afraid it doesn't look good."

Georgiana sank to the edge of the bed.

"I'm sorry about tonight, David." Elizabeth was talking on the telephone in the study, twisting the cord around her arm and then unwinding it.

"Tomorrow night?" he said.

"Tomorrow night," she agreed. "And I'll see you in the morning. Sleep well."

"I love you," he said.

"I love you, too," she said, and hung up. She turned around and found Monty standing in the doorway.

"I'm going back to my hotel now," he said. "I think the rug's going to be all right. I'll get somebody to come over tomorrow and look at it."

Elizabeth nodded, folding her arms over her chest.

Monty sighed and took a step forward.

"I'm sorry, Elizabeth, I was way out of line. I was angry." He locked eyes with Elizabeth. "That guy really gets to me for some reason. I'm sorry. I'll apologize to him tomorrow morning. I'll apologize to everyone." He paused for a moment. "You hate me, don't you?"

Elizabeth shook her head. "Of course not."

"I don't know what's happening to me," he said. "I feel like I'm about to have a nervous breakdown."

She didn't say anything.

"I'll see you in the morning." He turned to go and she let him.

After hanging up with Elizabeth, David picked up the phone again and dialed California. "Suz?"

"Davey, thank God! I've been waiting for you to call. I couldn't stand it! I don't even know what's wrong between us. Why did you leave the way you did this morning? You were so cold and awful and I love you! You know that, don't you? That I love you?"

"I know," he said, lying back on the king-size bed, his arm beneath his head.

"Davey, what is it?" she said, nearing tears. "I've packed all my stuff and I'm ready to move back to my apartment. I can't stay here when you're like this—hating me."

"I don't hate you," David said. "I was just upset."

"But what did I do?"

"Look, Suz, I called to apologize for my behavior. It's not you, it's me. I don't want you to move back to your apartment. I want you to stay."

There was a long silence. He could imagine her clutching the telephone, tears streaming down her cheeks. She cried easily when her feelings were hurt.

"When I get home," he continued, "we have to sit down and have a long talk—about our pasts. It was the herpes thing that upset me. I think it just hit me how little we actually know about each other—and yet we're supposed to be getting serious."

"I am serious," she sniffed.

"Yes, I know. But we need to talk about some things."

"Okay," she said. "Okay. How is it going there?"

"Very well. It looks like I've already been able to help out the Hillingses some."

"Oh, good, I'm so glad, honey," she said. "You've been so unhappy about it all. And Creighton Berns won't find out, right?"

"We sure as hell better hope he doesn't," David sighed.

"Elizabeth?" Patty said softly, touching Elizabeth's shoulder.

Elizabeth's head jerked up. She had dozed off in one of the chairs in the study. Shaking her fatigue off, she looked at her watch and then at Patty.

"Something's wrong with Georgiana," Patty whispered. "She got a phone call and she got very upset and asked me to leave. She's in there crying, I can hear her through the door. I thought maybe you might be able find out what's wrong."

Elizabeth was on her feet in a second.

~ 46 ~

"Hello, I'm Elizabeth Robinson," she told Alexandra Waring, who was standing at the front door of the Hillingses' apartment a little after one-thirty in the morning.

The anchorwoman looked tired and worried, but nonetheless she smiled as she said hello and shook Elizabeth's hand.

Elizabeth led her into the study and closed the door behind them. "She's more angry than anything else, right now."

"Well, she's scared," Alexandra sighed. "Can you blame her?"

"It's Creighton Berns, isn't it? Behind this outing thing?"

Alexandra nodded. "From what all my sources can tell me, it looks like it."

There was an awkward pause. "She gave me your number only because I insisted."

Alexandra waited, her expression unreadable.

"She was very upset—I couldn't calm her down," Elizabeth continued. "But she said it wasn't her career she was upset about, it was losing . . . well, she said now she could never—" Elizabeth stopped and started again. "You see, she thought she might have finally found someone she really—"

The anchorwoman's slight flinch made Elizabeth stop. She was making a mess of this!

Elizabeth threw up her hands. "Look, Alexandra, I care a lot about Georgiana and what happens to her. Just tell me, did I do the right thing by calling you?"

"Yes," Alexandra told her.

"Come in." Georgiana was lying across the bed with her Filofax and a tear-stained pad on which she had made notes of what she needed to do, phone calls she needed to make.

"Hi," Alexandra said softly, closing the door behind her.

"Oh, dear God," Georgiana said, "you're the last person who should be here." And then she began to cry, hiding her face in a pillow.

Then she thought she heard the door being locked, and she raised her head to look. Alexandra was standing by the door, still dressed in her clothes from the newscast.

Georgiana sat up straighter.

Alexandra slipped off her suit jacket and tossed it over the back of a chair. Then she kicked off her shoes.

"What are you doing?" Georgiana whispered.

"Getting comfortable," Alexandra answered, hiking up her skirt and pushing her panty hose down and over her feet.

Georgiana gave a nervous laugh and wiped tears away with the back of her hand; she watched as Alexandra took off her bracelet, her necklace, and her earrings, placing them carefully on a small side table.

Alexandra smiled at her, but Georgiana could see that her hands were shaking as she undid the buttons on her blouse.

"You shouldn't do this," Georgiana said.

"I have to do this," Alexandra said, slipping off her blouse. Just as Georgiana had imagined, she was lovely—strong, slender arms, a flat tummy, breasts firmly harnessed in a pretty white lace brassiere. "I cannot let Creighton Berns win," Alexandra said, looking at her. "I will not let him take you away from me."

She unhooked her skirt, stepped out of it, and tossed it on the chair. She had great legs. As she climbed onto the bed, Georgiana was amazed at how timid she felt. Alexandra touched the side of her face softly, and then leaned forward and gently kissed her.

Georgiana was completely flummoxed now. "I—I don't understand."

Alexandra bent to kiss her neck as she pushed the Filofax away.

"Alexandra," Georgiana tried again.

"What?" Alexandra whispered, looking into her eyes.

"What are we doing?" Georgiana's hand slipped along the edge of the white lace bra.

"Kissing," she said, her full, soft lips pressing against Georgiana's. "Kissing," she repeated, nuzzling the side of Georgiana's face, her ear, her neck, coming back up to her mouth. Georgiana felt herself surrender, but then she began to worry that Alexandra would come to her senses and leave.

But Alexandra only continued to kiss her steadily, gently, as if she were trying not to frighten Georgiana. Frighten *her*, she who had done everything—or so she had thought.

Alexandra's mouth had a sense of urgency about it now, and Georgiana was acutely aware of the hand slipping from her shoulder and down into the folds of her robe, lying flat for a moment on her collarbone, as if to make sure it was really Georgiana there underneath it, in fact, and then Alexandra cupped her hand over one warm, soft breast.

Georgiana's reaction was an involuntary groan, and then blissfully she fell into the movement of her touch.

After a while, Georgiana kissed her face and whispered, "I love being touched by you," and Alexandra did something to her nipple.

With another groan, her face fell forward into Alexandra's neck. "I think you might have done this before," she whispered, smiling, but then abruptly sucked in her breath as Alexandra did something to her breast again.

"It's never felt this way before," Alexandra murmured, kissing Georgiana deeply, pulling her tight against her.

Their kisses were getting incredibly long.

"This has to come off," Georgiana managed to say, reaching to unhook Alexandra's bra. "Oh, yes," she murmured, feeling her— and feeling her respond, "you are a gorgeous creature." She took

Alexandra's breast in her mouth and thrilled as her body went very hard again, her sighs and muscle twinges telling Georgiana everything she needed to know.

No doubt about it, Alexandra Waring was a woman who loved making love with a woman.

Alexandra was looking at her through half-closed eyes. She pulled Georgiana's robe open and her eyes traveled down and stayed there. She swallowed. She gently let a hand follow the curve of Georgiana's friend's hip, and then brought her eyes back up. "I'll never be able to climb out of this, you know," she said, breath unsteady.

"Good God, I hope not," Georgiana said. "Because I'm in love with you."

Alexandra pulled her close, their breasts softly colliding.

Everything inside of Georgiana started to rock then, and before long they were all over each other, and Alexandra was pushing her down on the pillows, sliding a smooth thigh up between Georgiana's legs, and Georgiana knew she was going to come soon, but she did not want to.

At least not yet.

There was ever so much to do first.

Four

~ 47 ~

When the alarm went off at seven Friday morning, Elizabeth could barely drag herself out of bed. She threw on her robe and stumbled to the kitchen, where she found that Patty had not only started making coffee, but was on the phone ordering in croissants and muffins.

"I think I'm getting into the swing of this New York living," she said with a laugh. She was dressed for work, and Elizabeth noticed once again how wonderful she looked as a blonde.

Elizabeth went back to her room, halfheartedly tried to do some exercises, but quickly gave up in favor of a shower. When she returned to the kitchen, she found that David had arrived.

"Mornin', Bets," he said.

Elizabeth gave him a kiss on the cheek, noticed immediately that his eyes would not meet hers, and wondered what was going on with him.

The doorman rang to announce that Monty was on his way up. "He's promised to behave," Elizabeth assured David.

"Where are we going to do the conference call?" he asked, accepting coffee from Patty. "Thanks, this smells great."

"In the study, I guess, there's a speaker phone," Elizabeth said.

Patty let Monty in, and when she led him back to the kitchen, he stopped in the doorway, looking baffled.

"What's the matter?" Elizabeth asked him.

"What's Alexandra Waring doing here?" he asked, pointing his thumb back at the hall.

"Alexander Waring?" David said.

"I just passed her in the foyer," Monty said.

"She stopped by this morning to give Georgiana some advice," Elizabeth said matter-of-factly. She noticed that Patty was trying not to look at her. Patty knew full well when Alexandra Waring had arrived.

"What kind of advice?" Monty said.

"On how to handle Creighton, I think," Elizabeth said. "Now where could those muffins be? I'm starving," she said, changing the subject. "Why haven't they arrived yet?"

Georgiana appeared in the study promptly at eight, looking, Elizabeth thought, wonderfully flushed and happy and healthy for someone whose career was about to be undermined by her own agent. "Good morning, everyone," she said, smiling, "are we all set?"

"I'm calling now," Elizabeth said, picking up the phone. "Oh, by the way, everybody, now that we're all here, Monty has something he wants to say."

Monty looked a bit startled as he stood beside Elizabeth's chair, but he cleared his throat. "I want to apologize. To you, David, and to you, Georgiana," he said, looking at her, "and to you, too, Patty. I was out of line last night."

Nobody said anything.

"And, I have to admit," Monty said, "I said some things I don't necessarily believe, but I said them anyway to rile you folks up."

"Well, for God's sake, don't anyone ask him which things he meant and which he didn't, or he'll start in all over again," Georgiana said, and everyone laughed, breaking the tension.

When they connected with the Hillingses in Water Mill, who were on a speakerphone in the upstairs study, everyone shouted greetings and get well wishes to Dorothy. Then Elizabeth quickly led the conversation around to the topic they were so anxious to find out about.

"Dorothy," Elizabeth said, "David is going to tell you a story, and we want you to tell us if it sounds at all familiar to you."

"All right."

David proceeded, referring to his notes. "It takes place in the year 3000 and it's about a teenager named Mathew Soaring. Earth is living under the threat of invasion by the Wolfen planet, which claims earth is rightfully theirs. The Planetary Council meets and decides the Wolfen have no business taking over Earth. When the Wolfen actually invade anyway, all the other planets are afraid to interfere. Encouraged, the Wolfen go after other planets. Mathew, head of the Space Force, goes through the universe, creating trouble for the Wolfen. When the Wolfen are forced to spread their forces all over the universe to deal with the uprisings Mathew has started, he leads the Planetary Council forces to victory, first taking back Earth and then, one by one, each of the other planets. At the end, instead of destroying the Wolfen planet, the Council replaces their leaders with teachers who show them how to live peacefully. And the universe is saved."

It was so quiet they could hear the ticking of the clock.

"Doesn't ring a bell, huh?" Monty finally said.

"Well, of course it does, Montgomery dear," Dorothy Hillings said, "it's a metaphoric tale of World War Two."

"Oh!" Elizabeth cried. "Of course it is! No wonder it sounded so familiar. And Earth is Poland?"

"Figuratively speaking," Dorothy said. "But this is also, I believe, a version of a children's book, published around 1941—not very widely, of course, not with the war. In fact, if I recall correctly, it was originally printed by hand on brown paper."

"Published where, Doe?" they heard Henry ask.

"England," Mrs. Hillings replied. "It was called *Mathew and the Allied Planets*," she said. "Do you remember? By Stephen Collins? It was a large, hand-printed paperback. They hoped to publish it in the United States, but it never worked out."

"Why don't I remember this?" Henry said.

"I'm not sure we ever laid eyes on it until 1956 or so, when Helen Hollard passed away."

"Who's that?" Monty asked, trying to follow this.

"Helen was the last partner of Hollard & Borrs," Dorothy explained, "one of the first literary agencies in England. We purchased their list in 1956, when the firm was being dissolved. Henry, darling, don't feel badly—there were so many titles, quite frankly, I don't think you ever even saw this one. I remember it because it was such a labor of love, trying to publish a children's book in the middle of the war—and because the author, Stephen Collins, was a pilot with the RAF, and was shot down over Germany and taken to a concentration camp. He survived to see liberation, but died a few years later from complications connected with his incarceration—tuberculosis, I think it was. It was all very sad, you see, because he had written the book for his little boy—named, in fact, Mathew, I think—who never really got a chance to know his father."

"When did you say Collins died?" Henry asked her.

"I'm not absolutely sure," she said, "I'd have to look in the files."

"The files!" Monty cried.

"Files in storage?" Elizabeth asked.

"When, Doe, when did he die?" Henry said urgently, ignoring the New York crew.

"My guess would be 1947 or 1948."

"Doe," Henry said quickly, "this is very important—you say the book was never published in the United States?"

"They filed for copyright, I know, but we never—" Dorothy said. There was a pause and then a sharp intake of breath. "Oh, my word, Henry! You don't think all this started with—that they're trying to—? Oh, they wouldn't dare!"

"David," Henry barked, "what did you say the budget was on that movie?"

"It was eighty million and escalated to over a hundred twenty," David said.

"And it's Metropolis Pictures, isn't it?" Mrs. Hillings said, adding, in a deeply sarcastic voice, "as if I have to ask."

"Yes, it is," David said.

Silence.

"Well, Doe," they heard Henry sigh, "there it is."

"Yes," she said. "Really quite extraordinary. And what an arrogant, stupid, blundering idiot that young man has been to let it escalate to this. He is truly a fool."

Everyone at the Gramercy Park apartment was looking at everyone else, utterly confused. "Henry, Dorothy," Elizabeth said, "I'm sorry, but you've lost us."

"And it's just as well, dear, until we know for sure," Dorothy said. "On top of everything else, we don't need a libel suit right now—not until we know for sure."

"Know *what* for sure?" Monty cried in frustration.

"You'll know very soon, I promise," Dorothy said.

"Elizabeth," Henry said, "I want you to go out to the warehouse and find the files labeled Hollard & Borrs and bring them back to the apartment immediately. Monty, I want you to go with her."

"But—" he started to say. "Okay," he said instead.

"David," Henry said.

"Yes, sir?"

"I don't care what you have to do, but we must have a copy of the script to that movie."

"Okay," David said. "I'll try."

"You'll *get* it," Henry told him, "you have to. And I want it today."

Immediately after hanging up, Henry got Josh Lafayette on the phone and talked to him at length. When he was through, he hung up and walked back to their bedroom, where he found Dorothy packing her bags.

"I don't give a damn about your silly doctors," Dorothy told him. "We are going back to the city and straightening this out."

"No, Doe, you can't," he said, grabbing the sweater out of her hand and throwing it on the bed next to the suitcase.

"Mrs. Hillings, really," Bernadette said, "I don't think you should go."

"Oh, pooh, Bernadette, what do you know?" Dorothy said, irritated. "You've got your whole life ahead of you!"

"Now, Doe," Henry said.

"Henry, I could strangle you!" she told her husband, putting her hand on her hip. "You've got Georgiana mixed up with this—and with someone like Creighton Berns, you know damn well what that could mean!"

"Doe—"

"And it's absolutely beyond my comprehension how you could allow them to drag Patty Kleczak into this! The poor lamb never did a thing except slave to write her book while trying to raise a family, and now you've got her spying at the very agency that's supposed to be selling her book! Honestly!"

"I had nothing to do with it," he cried.

"And to tell David to get that script. You *know* what will happen to him if Creighton Berns gets wind of it."

"I know," he said. He leaned over and picked up Doe's sweater and folded it. "And you're right." He put it in the suitcase.

"We're going?" she asked him.

"We're going," he told her, turning. "Bernadette, please help Mrs. Hillings pack while I arrange for a car."

~ 48 ~

Creighton Berns's new conference room at ICA was already infamous around town, inasmuch as people were fairly sure it was the first one to be constructed of four walls of bulletproof glass. His staff referred to it as the "square fishbowl," but Creighton liked to explain to visitors, "We have nothing to hide at ICA."

Creighton didn't mention his private conference room on the tenth floor, which he preferred to use because he almost always did want to hide who came to his meetings.

In any event, Creighton was holding a meeting in "the fishbowl" with one of ICA's directors and the possible producers of the movie ICA wished to package. During the director's impassioned recitation of his vision, Creighton's assistant suddenly appeared behind the director, on the other side of the glass wall, making urgent hand signals at Creighton.

When the director stopped speaking, Creighton murmured his apologies and went to the door.

"Your old friend is on the phone," Joseph whispered.

"Find out what's up," Creighton told him. "I can't leave right now. Come back if it's urgent."

In less than a minute, a wild-eyed Joseph appeared on the other side of the glass. One look at his face prompted Creighton to excuse himself and leave.

Joseph whispered something to him and Creighton strode down the hall to his office. He slammed the door, went over to his desk, and pressed an automatic dial number on his phone. "Where the hell is she?" he said. "Then go fucking get her—I want her on this phone within sixty seconds." He slammed the receiver down. He stood there, body taut, waiting. In less than half a minute, his private line rang and he snapped the phone up.

"Don't 'Hi, how are you?' me, you stupid cunt," he said. "Do you know what's going on in your goddamn fucking office? Do you? NO? Well then let me tell you, Marion—*you've got one of the Hillingses' goddamn fucking clients working there!*"

At Creighton Berns's hideaway house up the hill from Hamburger Hamlet, the houseboy was receiving instructions over the telephone in the kitchen. When he hung up the phone, he walked through the house to the guest room and knocked on the door. "Miss Pratt?" he said.

"Just a sec!" came the answer. In a full minute, the door opened to reveal a very attractive dark-haired woman of about forty. The hyper gleam of her eyes belied the otherwise exhausted-looking consonance of her face. "Yes?" she said.

"Excuse me," the houseboy said, eyes flicking quickly from the telltale smudge of white powder under her nose, "but Mr. Berns called. He wants to forewarn you that he may need you to attend a meeting this evening."

"Did he say where the meeting's going to be?" the woman asked.

"No, ma'am," the houseboy said, "only that it would be with a journalist and that he wanted you to wear the outfit he picked out. Mr. Colum, his assistant, will be contacting you later."

"Okay, thanks," the woman said, and she shut the door. A moment later it opened again. "Hey," she said, "you wouldn't have any sinus stuff around here, would you?"

"Oh, yes, ma'am, we certainly would," he said.

∼ *49* ∼

Monty called the studio and told Mike he couldn't make it in today; he should run one of the "Best-of" shows again.

"What the hell is going on?" his producer screamed. "We're

stuck here in New York, you've canceled all your speaking engagements, and this is the second time in a week you haven't shown up for your friggin' show, Monty!"

"I've got family trouble," Monty said, and hung up. Then he and Elizabeth and David jumped into the limo and headed for the Queens warehouse. David made phone calls to the West Coast on the way, trying to find someone who would sneak him a copy of the *Race in Space* script. He found a likely source, promised all kinds of favors in return, and could do nothing more than wait for a call back from his contact. When they arrived at U-File-With-Us, Monty told the driver to come in and get them if anyone called on the car phone.

Elizabeth unlocked the door to the storage room, turned on the lights, outlined three areas of search, one for each, and forced the men to don surgical masks before diving into their assigned boxes. They had been searching for almost an hour and a half before Monty cried, "Bingo!" and dragged a box down from a shelf. Elizabeth and David dashed over to help him, and they found three more Holland & Borrs boxes. Inside one they found an ancient, crumbling copy of the children's book *Mathew and the Allied Planets*. They looked at one another and seemed to collectively hold their breaths as they opened the book. They gingerly turned the brittle pages and David skimmed them. "Sounds like it, sounds like it," he said, excited.

They carried the file boxes out to the car, stored them in the trunk, and piled back into the limo. David called his source again. Somebody on the other end said the man was expected back momentarily. Five minutes into the drive back to Manhattan, the phone rang and David snapped it up, listening. He covered the phone and said, "I need a fax number."

"I have a fax machine in here," Monty said, opening a cabinet.

Within two minutes, pages of the script for *Race in Space* were coming through.

"Georgiana," the voice said over the phone, "what luck to find you on the other end. Imagine that. I call Dorothy and Henry Hillings and I get you. Surprise, surprise."

"Creighton," Georgiana said, struggling to keep her voice calm.

They had all gone barreling off this morning, leaving her to man the phones.

"Actually," he said, "I'm not surprised at all. I *knew* you were there."

"Oh really," she said. "And how could that be?"

"A little birdie," he said, laughing—then stopping abruptly. "Listen, Georgiana, I'm calling because I've been hearing rumors about your private life, and I thought I better call and discuss them with you myself."

"What could you possibly mean?" she said in her coldest voice.

"Do you know a Madeline Pratt?" he asked.

She had been right. It was Madeline. He had found Madeline.

"She worked on one of my films," Georgiana said. "Why?"

"Word has it she's preparing to 'out' you in the press. That's what they call it, isn't it, Georgiana? When you expose homosexuals?"

"Yes, I believe so, Creighton."

"They say this woman can prove that you're gay."

"Who is 'they'?"

"The tabloids are looking for a deal," he continued, ignoring her question. "If I throw them something else, they'll kill the story. The question is, why should I bother?"

"I think this is called blackmail, Creighton."

"I think the situation is called hopeless, Georgiana."

She was silent.

"This Madeline isn't a very appealing character to be associated with, Georgiana. She looks like a drug addict."

"I'll put a good word in with her for you, Creighton, if you want," Georgiana said.

It was his turn to be quiet.

"Out with it, Creighton, what do you want from me?"

"I want you to stop this assault on me and ICA," he said.

"I can't and I won't," she told him.

"Then it's your funeral, dyke," he said, hanging up.

Patty glanced up from the invitations she was addressing for an ICA cocktail reception, and was startled by the sight of the personnel director getting off the elevator with a woman and a police officer.

"Miss Jamison," the personnel director said, coming in through the glass doors. "This woman will be replacing you at the desk. Would you come with us, please?"

"Where to?" Patty said, her heart thundering in her chest.

"Just bring your things and come with us, please," she said.

No one would meet her eye and so, trying to control her trembling hands, she picked up her things and followed them out through the glass doors to the elevators. The personnel director pressed the button for the elevator, and the police officer turned to Patty. "Mrs. Kleczak," he said, "I'm afraid you're under arrest for criminal trespass."

Patty could only stare at him.

"You have the right to remain silent," he began, reading Patty her rights.

"As per your instructions, Mr. Hillings," the manager of the Sherry-Netherland Hotel said, "Mr. Lafayette and two gentlemen and a lady are waiting upstairs in your suite."

"We need an additional room," Henry said, "a single, please, for my wife's nurse."

" 'My wife's nurse,' honestly!" Dorothy huffed. Over Henry's shoulder she added to the manager, "Sir, you would be doing me the greatest service if you would ignore his wildly inaccurate phraseology and simply give Bernadette a room."

On the way up in the elevator, Dorothy looked at her watch. "Four-thirty," she said. "Shall we call the apartment and tell them we're here?"

"Let's wait until after we hear what they have to say upstairs, Doe."

"I suppose you're right," she said.

"Who?" Bernadette asked them.

"Some people we're seeing," Dorothy told her.

"What people? Now, Mrs. Hillings," she said, looking serious, "I don't think it's advisable that you entertain after this highly stressful day."

Dorothy smiled. "I won't be, dear, Henry will. I'll be having a lie-down in the next room."

After a moment, Bernadette said, sounding dubious about this enterprise, "What kind of people?"

But neither Henry nor Dorothy answered. When they reached their floor, they merely directed the bellman to see Bernadette to her room while they went on to their suite. Henry inserted the magnetic key and pulled it out; the green light went on and he opened the door. Dorothy walked in ahead of him.

"Doe," the tall and darkly tanned man said, standing up and walking toward her.

"Well if it isn't the man from Bora Bora," she said, receiving his embrace.

"Hill," he said to Henry over her shoulder.

"Ben, how are you?" Henry said, smiling.

The royal family of agents then joined the others in the suite and the meeting began.

~ *50* ~

"We found it, we found it!" Elizabeth cried, putting one of the file boxes down in the Hillingses' study with a thump. It was filthy and so was she, but she couldn't have cared less.

"The Hillingses are coming back to the city today," Georgiana said, stepping from behind the desk.

"Fabulous! Monty, did you hear that?" Elizabeth asked, as he came in the door, carrying two file boxes.

"Yeah, that's great," he said, heaving the boxes onto a large cherry wood table and wiping his brow. He, too, was a mess.

"They're going to stay at a hotel, though," Georgiana added, sounding a bit distracted, "so Dorothy can have quiet. I must say, I feel bad about being in their room."

"David's downstairs receiving the script for *Race in Space* right now on the limo fax machine!" Elizabeth told her, excited. And then she stopped, noticing Georgiana's expression. "What's the matter?"

"Well," Georgiana began, "we have a couple of problems."

David came bouncing through the front door of the apartment yelling, "I've got it!"

"In the study!" Elizabeth called.

"Look, here it is!" David said, dashing in with the fax copy of the script.

"Give it to me," Monty said, reaching for the stack.

"Easy, boy, easy," David said, pulling back.

"Sorry," Monty muttered, withdrawing his hand.

"Here," David said, handing the first half of the script to him.

"Your office has left about a hundred messages for you, David," Georgiana told him.

"I'll call them in a minute," he said, thumbing through the second half of the script.

"Georgiana," Elizabeth said, "you said we had problems before—what problems?"

"Well, for a start," Georgiana said, "Patty's been arrested."

"What?" they all said.

"Somehow ICA found out who she was and they brought a cop in to arrest her for criminal trespass."

"How the hell did they know she was there?" Monty said, looking over at David.

"No one knows," Georgiana reported. "But it's clear that someone tipped them off."

"Where is she now?" Elizabeth asked.

"Someone from Josh's office is bailing her out over at the Midtown North station house," Georgiana said. "And I'm afraid her husband's on his way in, and well, he's a bit crazed, to say the least. In the meantime, no one seems to know where Josh has disappeared to."

Monty was still looking at David. "How do *you* think ICA found out who Patty was?"

"How should I know?" he said, sitting down on the floor and starting to pull files out of one of the boxes.

"You," Monty said, pointing to Elizabeth, "with *me—come—*we need to talk." He walked out of the study and down the hall to the kitchen. He was just opening a new box of cookies when Elizabeth appeared. He slammed the cookie box on the counter. "It's all a coincidence, right? Is that what you're going to tell me?"

Before she could answer, Georgiana appeared in the doorway. "Excuse me, but there's something else you should know."

Monty and Elizabeth looked at her.

"Somehow Creighton knew I was here. And I don't mind telling you, having him call me here was rather unnerving. And I would appreciate knowing how he found out."

Monty glanced at Elizabeth. "My oh my, Professor, how these coincidences seem to multiply whenever you-know-who is around."

"That's ridiculous, Monty!" Elizabeth snapped.

"Creighton's trying to blackmail me," Georgiana added. "If I don't stop this—what did he call it? this assault on him and ICA immediately—there's going to be a not very nice story about my private life released to the press."

"What kind of story?" Monty said.

"I'd rather not discuss it," Georgiana said simply. She looked at Elizabeth.

"What did you say to him?" Elizabeth asked her.

"I told him no."

"And he said . . . ?"

"It was my funeral."

They were silent.

Monty reached for the box of cookies and ate one. Elizabeth was leaning back against the counter shaking her head and looking down at the floor. After a moment, she looked up. "I think what we have to do is get you on the phone with him, Georgiana. You tell him you are trying your best, and that at the very least, you're willing to get on a plane tonight and come back to L.A. to try and help him present his side of the situation to the press."

Both Georgiana and Monty stared at her.

"I'm absolutely serious," Elizabeth said. "You have to stall him."

"What the heck does he have on you?" Monty asked Georgiana, amazed.

"No way, Elizabeth," Georgiana said, shaking her head. "My God, do you think I want to live under the thumb of a guttersnipe like that? No way, I'm seeing this through."

"But Georgiana—" Elizabeth started.

"How dare he try to make me ashamed of who I am!" Georgiana cried, angry. "How dare he imply that something is wrong with me! No way, Elizabeth, I've had it with people like him. And if he wants to come after me, let him come after me. If worse comes to worse, I'll go back to Scotland and be a spokesperson for argyle socks and sweaters or something, I don't care—so long as I see this bloody blackguard hang from the highest tree!"

"Oh, David, finally!" his secretary cried when he called in. "All hell's breaking loose around here and I don't know what to say to the people who are calling."

"Why? What's going on?"

"The bank says the Calsos are pulling their financing from the film. So the bank says if they don't have a complete explanation within twenty-four hours, they're pulling their financing, too."

"What?" David said, feeling his stomach sink. The Calsos were the Italian group who had bankrolled his last two movies—and with significant financial success. "Explanation for what? I mean, what did the Calsos tell them?"

"That both stars are backing out of the picture," she said.

"That *what?*"

"And everybody in town seems to know about it," she continued, near tears. "And everybody's wigging out, calling here and screaming at me, saying that you've been run out of town!"

Stunned, David listened as his secretary continued her description of how his movie was unraveling. When she finished, he called Metropolis Pictures. Yes, he was told, at noon his film had officially gone into turnaround.

"You think Georgiana made it up?" Monty said in a harsh whisper to Elizabeth in the kitchen. "That Berns not only knew she was in New York, but that she was here, in this apartment, today? And who else could or would have tipped off ICA about Patty? You *know* it was him, Elizabeth! Who else could it have been? And he's probably taking us on the wildest goose chase imaginable with this cockamamie movie. He's probably rigged the whole thing with Berns to pull us off track."

"Oh, Monty, shut up!" Elizabeth whispered back. "You have no right to say these things!"

"Who then? How? Tell me that! Every time the guy is told something, the next day somebody around here gets it in the neck. My TV show, your BBC contract, Patty, Georgiana . . ."

"It could be anyone," Elizabeth said.

"Like who?" he demanded.

"Jordan or Louise," she said.

"No way, nobody's even talked to them for days," he said.

"It could be your chauffeur, for God's sake; you've got the biggest mouth in America. Or someone in Josh's office."

"Or someone in David's—" Monty started.

"It is not David, I'd bet my life on it!"

"Thanks for the vote of confidence, Bets," David said from the doorway.

"See? Now he's eavesdropping!" Monty said, as if they suddenly had all the evidence they needed to send David to prison.

"Monty, it's not me. I swear it," David said, coming into the kitchen.

"Who then?" Monty wanted to know.

"I don't know," David said, "but it's not me."

"Maybe it's somebody close to you on the Left Coast," Monty said. "Maybe it's that Miss Susie Q."

"Who?" Elizabeth said. She looked at David.

"Why don't you explain it to her?" Monty said. "Who Susie is and why she lives in your house and sleeps in your bed."

David glared at him. "What are you talking about?"

"I'm talking about the stacked blond chick who lives in your house, Aussenhoff, the one with no visible means of employment. Maybe she's living off you, but maybe she's making a living on the side, ya know? Spying for Berns?" He looked at Elizabeth. "I checked this guy out, Elizabeth, and I think he should at least have the courtesy to get rid of his live-in mistress before he starts romancing you again."

David lunged at him, but this time Monty was ready. He yanked David by the jacket and smashed him in the jaw with his fist, sending him reeling backward through the swinging door and crashing onto the dining room floor. Elizabeth screamed and Patty appeared from somewhere, yelling, and then David was back on his feet, lunging at Monty, when Ted Kleczak and Josh suddenly pulled the two of them apart. Panting, furious, both of them looked ready to kill the other.

"I must say, gentlemen," Dorothy Hillings said, coming into

the living room and unpinning her hat, "but this is a rather fine how-do-you-do."

~ 51 ~

A great deal of confusion followed the Hillingses' dramatic arrival at their home: Why were Monty and David fighting? Why did Elizabeth run to her room and slam the door? Why did Georgiana look white as a ghost and excuse herself to lie down? Why had Patty been arrested? And why was everybody so upset when it looked as though they were close to solving the mystery of Creighton Berns's behavior at ICA?

Monty finally got his act together—obviously no one else was going to—and took Josh and the Hillingses into the study to show them the movie script and the files.

"Bets, don't believe him," David begged, standing in the doorway of her room.

"About Creighton, I don't," Elizabeth said, standing by the window.

He looked at her for a long moment and then went and slid his arms around her waist. "About Susie," he said, looking into her eyes.

She waited.

"She's been living at my house temporarily."

"As?"

"A friend."

Elizabeth broke away from him. "I don't need Monty to tell me when you're lying. God!" she cried whirling around. "You'd think after all this time you'd at least try something new! What the hell do you think you've been *doing?* Why have you been saying all these things to me?"

"Because I mean them," he said. "I do love you." He dropped his head. "She was with me before this all started."

"And what were you going to do?" Elizabeth said. "Try out a relationship with me here while you had a West Coast backup living in your home? Or was I the backup, David? If things didn't work out with her, there'd always be me?"

He didn't say anything.

"Oh, God," Elizabeth sighed, throwing herself down on the edge of the bed. "Tell me she's at least thirty."

He shook his head.

"Tell me she's at least not another aspiring actress," she sighed.

He shoved his hands into his trouser pockets and began to pace.

"Tell me she has some savings," she sighed.

He said nothing.

"Oh, David," she groaned, "you could at least try to find some-one who's a grown-up—or at least someone who really cares about you."

"She does care about me," he said. "And, because of that, I've been reluctant to hurt her until I knew it could work between us."

She looked at him. "I do not understand you, David Aussenhoff. I used to think I did, but I'm beginning to think you're emotionally retarded."

"I think I have been," he said simply.

"Well," she sighed, shaking her head, "at least you haven't dragged a long-suffering wife and children through this. I suppose that's something."

"You sound relieved," David said, frowning.

She looked at him.

"I know you pretty well, too, you know," he said. "And I think you're relieved to have an excuse to stop us from trying again. I could tell there was something strange going on last night."

She started to protest and then she looked down at her hands. "You're right."

"You're different now, Bets, very different."

She looked at him. Tears were in her eyes now. "You bet I am. Grief does something to you. I'm over you, David. I'm not mourning anymore."

When they emerged from the guest room, they found the Hill-ingses preparing to return to their hotel. Georgiana was arguing that *she* should be staying in the hotel, not them!

"Quite frankly, Georgiana dear," Dorothy told her, "if I had to stay here much longer, I'm quite sure my blood pressure would go off the charts. This place is a madhouse."

"Seriously," Henry said, "it's much better for us to be at the hotel this weekend. And you kids *should* be here together."

"Kids," Georgiana repeated to herself, smiling.

"We'll be holding a meeting here on Sunday at noon," Henry said. "By then I think we'll have all the answers we need."

Elizabeth squinted, slightly suspicious. "What exactly is going on over at your hotel?"

"Nothing special," Dorothy said, eyes twinkling and clearly lying.

"Where's Patty?" Elizabeth said, suddenly looking around. "The Kleczaks didn't go home, did they?"

"They're having a bit of a discussion in the guest room," Dorothy said. "And may I suggest we leave them to it."

The Hillingses departed with David, Monty went off to the study, and Georgiana and Elizabeth retired to their rooms.

"That's not it, Patty," Ted said, sitting on the edge of the chair, leaning forward, looking as though he were about to mark out new football plays on the floor between them.

"You can deny it all you want, Ted Kleczak," she said, "but for eighteen years you've had me exactly where you want me, and you can't tell me you're not furious to know that I can have a life apart from you and make new friends who like *me*—just me! Without kids! Without a husband! Without neighborhood gossip. They just like *me!*"

"You're partly right," he admitted after a moment. "I am angry that you can have a life apart from me."

She looked up, surprised.

"And I'm scared, Patty," he murmured, looking at his hands. "You're changing so fast, and I don't know how you can see and do all this stuff and still stay happy being with me."

She was astonished.

"These people are rich and famous and really smart." He glanced up. "I've heard Montgomery Grant Smith on the radio. He slept at the White House once, you know, when President Bush was in office."

She smiled. "He's not really that smart, Ted. Bright and fast and clever, but not really so smart."

"That's not the point, Patty," he said. "The point is, I'm a gym teacher—"

"You're a high school coach and teacher making fifty-seven thousand dollars a year," she said. "We own a house, we have three gorgeous perfect children, and you're the sexiest man alive. What more could I want?" She pointed to the door. "These people don't have anything we have, Ted. Don't you understand that? While we were putting everything into building a marriage and a family, they were putting everything into their careers. So yes, they're rich, they're famous—but they don't have anything else. I'm not even forty yet, Ted—we're young! Our kids are almost ready to leave home for college. Without the money from the novel, we'd manage to get them through school, you know we would. But when they leave home, what happens to me? What role do I have? I *have* to have something, and my writing is it. It led me to all these people, Ted. Mrs. Hillings gave me the opportunity of a lifetime, and then I was offered the chance to help *her*—a woman who has spent her entire life doing for others. And so I jumped at it. The fact that it imperiled my writing career made it all that much more exciting."

"Imperiled," Ted repeated. "Patty, listen to you. You don't even talk the same anymore."

"Oh, that's just from hanging around Elizabeth. Honey, listen," she said, getting up and moving over to sit on his lap, "we're young. We can't stop changing now. We've got decades and decades to go, yet."

"But what am I supposed to do?" he asked her.

"Love and adore me," she giggled, kissing him. "But most of all, just be yourself."

"Well, that first part's not hard," he said into her neck. "I do love and adore you."

"And you still make me crazy after all these years," she answered.

"Like the song?" he asked.

"Like the sex," she whispered, sliding her hand down between his legs.

His head jerked up. *"Here?* With all those people walking around out there?"

"Absolutely," she whispered, kissing him.

Patty slid off his lap, took his face in her hands, and kissed him. "Just a word of warning: I'm going to lock the door, and then I'm coming back to get you."

"Patty, this is crazy!" her husband whispered hoarsely. That was a good sign, the hoarse voice. For a man who spent most of his time bellowing across gymnasiums and playing fields, when he was aroused, Ted's voice began to fail him. The more excited he got, the worse it got, and the more excited she got.

She locked the door and turned around and smiled. He stood up. She walked over to him, reached up to kiss him, and then backed off slightly. And then she sank to her knees. "Let's see what we have in here," she whispered, unfastening his belt, unclasping his pants, and then tugging his zipper down.

Even after all this time, whenever she found her husband this excited, something major inside of her gave way.

There was more conversation in the hallway outside their door.

"Patty, for God's sake!" Ted whispered. "I can hear everybody—" He sucked in his breath and threw back his head, helplessly touching Patty's hair as she went ahead and did what she wanted to anyway.

Patty felt him tense up and not dare to move, desperately wanting to tell her they shouldn't be doing this with all those people outside, but desperate for her not to stop doing what she was doing.

His breath caught and he jerked slightly, holding her head more tightly.

It had taken a few years to learn how to do this. He couldn't help himself after a certain point.

"No, I'm going to go to my room," they heard Georgiana say right outside the door.

The Kleczaks froze, and Patty couldn't help but visualize the scene Georgiana would find in here: Ted standing in the middle of the room, tie and jacket still on, pants pulled down to his ankles, his wife on her knees in front of him.

"Come on," Ted said hoarsely, helping her up and pulling her to the bed. But instead of going on the bed, he pulled her down on the floor on the other side of it, and in a minute he was pulling her clothes off and was on top of her, thrusting himself into her, Patty already starting to arch toward him, aching, wanting, moving to the verge. And Ted went all out, hitting utterly home, and she couldn't help but cry out, clutching him, coming in waves, groaning in his ear, and with a little cry, he shuddered up against her, saying through clenched teeth, "Yes, yes, baby," and then he collapsed.

They lay there, holding on to one another, catching their breath. Patty wrapped her legs around him and squeezed, holding him, reveling in him. In them.

Things came and went in their marriage, but the passion always returned. The love never left either—it was just sometimes difficult to get in touch with it.

This wasn't one of those times, obviously.

Patty flexed her thighs, delighting again in the feel of him. Being glued to him.

Him. Her guy. Ted. The best damn lover in the world.

～ *52* ～

Friday night dragged on. Georgiana lay in bed watching TV and feeling anxious, alone, and scared. A little after ten the phone rang and she snatched it up. "Hello?"

"Hi," Alexandra said.

She smiled. "Hi. Your newscast was great. I just watched it."

"How are you?"

"I've been better, but the Hillingses were here tonight. They think they'll have all this cleared up by Sunday."

"Listen, Georgiana," Alexandra began.

Uh-oh, Georgiana thought, here it comes. The backing off, the "I made a mistake, I shouldn't have done what I did last night, we pushed ahead too soon, I'm sorry, but I'm not ready for this, Georgiana—"

"I was wondering if you would come and stay with me at my apartment."

In the silence that followed, Alexandra nervously cleared her throat. "Georgiana?"

Laura Van Wormer

"Yes," she said, "yes, of course I want to come." She crying. And smiling.

"You've got the number," Georgiana said to Elizabeth an hour later. Her bags had already been taken down to the lobby.

"Yes," Elizabeth said, smiling, holding open the door.

"Okay," Georgiana said, "then I guess I best be on my way."

Elizabeth gave her a hug. "Good luck," she murmured. "Although I don't think you'll need it."

"Thanks," the actress murmured, walking across to the elevator.

Elizabeth closed the front door, sighed, and leaned back against it.

Great. Just like old times. David had some young blond creature waiting for him at home, Georgiana was running off to what sounded like the love of her life, and Patty was snuggled away with her husband in the guest room, having only emerged once all night when pizza and beers was delivered. (The friction burn on Patty's cheeks told Elizabeth everything she needed to know about what they were doing in there.) And here she was, feeling as though something momentous was happening in her life, but not sure at all what it was.

Besides knowing that she was finally free of David.

Yes. She knew that for sure.

The only trouble was coming to terms with what she thought she might be feeling for someone else.

Oh, well, Elizabeth thought, sighing as she started turning out the apartment lights. Thank heavens Sasha was coming in the morning with a cleaning lady; the apartment needed a thorough cleaning with all the traffic lately. Still, she couldn't resist straightening a few cushions in the living room; afterward she turned off the lights in there, went through the swinging door to the kitchen—and was nearly scared out of her wits.

"Hiya," Monty said, in between spoonfuls of cantaloupe.

"What are you doing here?" she asked him, hand over her heart.

"I fell asleep in the living room. I just woke up."

"Oh," she said, dropping her hand. She walked over to the bread drawer and opened it. Inside were those ghastly sweet cookies

280 ~

Monty liked, Yes-Yeses. She pulled them out, got the skim milk, a glass, a napkin, and sat down at the table opposite Monty.

"You never eat that junk," he said.

"Tonight I do," she told him, opening the box.

He watched her for a while, spoon still in hand. Then he cleared his throat and resumed eating his melon. "I've given that stuff up," he said.

Elizabeth laughed, spraying crumbs out of her mouth before she could cover it with a napkin.

"Oh, to hell with you, Elizabeth," he said, putting his spoon down on the plate with a clang. "I hate you thin people. You don't have to do anything special to look the way you do."

"Don't be an ass," she said, "of course I do. I watch what I eat, I swim every other day and try to stay away from sugar."

"Tell me about it," he grumbled. "But without sugar, I'm afraid my whole radio empire's going straight to hell."

They continued eating for a while.

"Georgiana's gone to stay with a friend," Elizabeth said.

"What friend?" he asked, sounding suspicious, but not particularly jealous.

"I don't know," Elizabeth lied.

"Did Patty go back to New Jersey?"

"No," she reported. "The lovebirds are in the guest room." Monty looked at her.

"She emerged once to get a pizza delivery," she said, smiling. "Definitely lovebirds."

"Good for them," he said, meaning it.

"Anyway," Elizabeth said, standing up and clearing her things from the table, "if you help me change the sheets, you're welcome to stay over in the Hillingses' room."

He looked surprised. "I am pretty beat."

"I know," she said, closing the refrigerator door. "And to be honest, it would make me feel better to know that someone else was sleeping here tonight."

He got up to carry his plate to the sink. "Someone else sleeping *alone*, you mean."

She nodded. "Something like that."

"Glad to know I'm not the only one who feels that way."

They looked at each other for a moment.

"I'd love to stay," he said.

∼ *53* ∼

Georgiana was sitting on the windowsill in Alexandra's bedroom on Saturday morning, her back to the view of Central Park.

"I'm sorry I can't go with you," Alexandra said softly.

"It would be a mistake," Georgiana sighed, standing up. "I just don't understand why Elizabeth is coming with me."

"Neither of us want you to be alone, darling," Alexandra said, coming over to her.

"Where did you find these people again?" Georgiana asked, referring to the public relations team Alexandra had arranged for her to meet that morning.

"Between palimony suits and Larry Kramer making it his business to out famous people regardless of the consequences, a whole industry has sprung up," Alexandra said. "I've kept track of it." She smiled. "I guess in case I ever met you." She kissed Georgiana lightly on the mouth.

Georgiana sighed. "This woman Creighton's gotten ahold of is a major coke head and, I hear, desperate for money." She closed her eyes, as if the person she was thinking of could simply vanish from the face of the earth by her doing so.

"Is there anything else the press can use on you?" Alexandra asked. "For instance, were there drugs involved in your relationship with this woman?"

Georgiana stiffened and her eyes flew open. "With *my* mother's history? Do you think I would do drugs or intentionally get involved with anyone who did? My God, Alexandra, I can't even get near a *possible* alcoholic without wanting to run. Why do you think I've been mostly alone for so long? Because nobody wanted to go out with me?"

Alexandra was smiling. "No, silly," she said, brushing a strand of hair off Georgiana's face. "Listen, I don't think in this day and age that you'll have to defend yourself for once having a love affair with a woman. What this team is going to want to know is the likelihood of other women making the same kind of claim."

"Just how promiscuous have I been?" Georgiana said.

Alexandra nodded.

"Well, there were several men in my past, but no married ones, thank heavens. And, well, let's see, my first woman lover is happily married now, so she won't say anything. Later I was in a relationship with a woman for almost two years, but today she's more famous than I am, so that's okay—" She broke off, noticing Alexandra's openly curious expression.

"I'll tell you eventually, but it's not only my story to tell—do you understand?"

"Of course," Alexandra said.

"Anyway," Georgiana continued, "this woman Creighton's found was an ICA client once, a screenwriter. I got involved with her on location about two years ago. I thought she was terrific, but not right for me. She reminded me a little too much of my mother, and I think that's when I began to suspect something might be wrong. And so I quickly broke it off."

"And how did she react?"

"Not well," Georgiana admitted. "As a matter of fact, the night after I told her, she came banging on my hotel room door at two in the morning, loaded, and then she apparently moved on to coke in a big way, and now she's a mess. And broke. And desperate. Perfect for Creighton."

"And who has there been since her?" Alexandra asked.

"No one," Georgiana said. "She frightened me so much I thought it would be better if I were simply alone. It didn't stop at the hotel room that night—I heard from Madeline in Los Angeles, all kinds of crazy stuff. For a while I thought I was going to have to get a court order."

Alexandra was nodding.

"Listen, Alexandra," Georgiana said after a moment, "there's something I've got to tell you. I'm ashamed of it, but I've got to tell you." Pause. "Remember the night you flew off to Iraq? The night I came to New York?"

Alexandra nodded.

Georgiana closed her eyes, wincing. "I got drunk with Montgomery Grant Smith and had sex with him." Georgiana opened one eye.

Alexandra's mouth had fallen open.

"It was all of five minutes," she added, still wincing. "We used a condom."

After a moment Alexandra closed her mouth, swallowed, and said, "What does this mean?"

"It means I'm not going to drink anymore!"

Alexandra slowly lowered her head, shaking it. "Oh, Georgiana," she murmured. But when she raised her head, Georgiana could see she was fighting a smile. "Oh, Georgiana, how could you?" And then she burst out laughing.

"Oh, Ted, why haven't we done this before?" Patty sighed, lying in her husband's arms.

"Duck out on our responsibilities and tell the kids to go to hell?" he said.

She propped herself up on one elbow to look at him. Boy, he was gorgeous, this husband of hers. How had she ever been able to hold on to him? And he hadn't a clue how wonderful he was.

He smiled, absently sliding his hand up to caress one of her breasts. "You are so beautiful," he said.

"I haven't even worn the wig for you yet," she said.

He smiled. "I don't know about that, honey."

"That's what you can call me—Honey. Honey Kleczak." She laughed.

"Seriously though, Patty," he said, still stroking her breast, "I'm not sure we should leave the kids again today and tonight."

"Sweetie, I told you, Jill will stay overnight."

"And what are we going to do?" he asked.

"Whatever you want to do," she said, kissing him again.

What Montgomery Grant Smith had said about the leaked information was going round and round in David's head. Who was Creighton Berns talking to, anyway? Monty had made that crack about Susie making a living on the side. . . .

No, it was ridiculous. Susie wouldn't do anything like that.

Not even for an acting career?

But she loved him!

Maybe she's a far better actress than you think. It wouldn't be the first time you were taken in.

But she doesn't know anyone connected to Creighton!

She would be easy to get to. If Montgomery Grant Smith knew she lived in his house, certainly Creighton would know how and where to find her.

David left his hotel room and went out for a walk.

For the first time, Georgiana felt the full ramifications of what Creighton Berns was trying to do to her. When she and Elizabeth walked into Jessica Wright's apartment to meet the "damage control" team, Georgiana took one look at their faces and knew how bad the next few weeks could be.

Right away—as if to get the painful part over—Georgiana was handed page proofs of the piece scheduled to run on the front page of the *Inquiring Eye* and on the cover of a gay magazine. Georgiana glanced at the proofs—there was a picture of herself and Madeline on location in Arizona, and something about "lesbian lover" in the headline. She handed it back.

"No," the man said firmly. "I'm sorry, Ms. Hamilton-Ayres, but you must read it carefully, word by word, from beginning to end, so we may begin."

Begin what? Georgiana wondered. To lie and evade and deny, or, worse yet, to somehow be made to feel that what was happening between her and Alexandra was something to be ashamed of?

"Are you all right?" Elizabeth murmured.

"I'm fine," Georgiana said vaguely.

It was a very funny meeting in a way, because, as Georgiana realized after a while, the PR group thought Elizabeth was her lover. Jessica picked up on it, too, and found it amusing, particularly since Elizabeth didn't get it and kept saying things like, "Why wouldn't it be a good idea for me to be at the press conference with her? Are academics not considered credible people?"

"Ms. Hamilton-Ayres," the man said after a thorough discussion of the pending problems, "it's up to you. How do you want to handle this?"

"Like a grown-up," she said, feeling herself quake inside.

The plans were drawn. First stage, if the story about her affair with Madeline Pratt were released, Georgiana would do an hour on "The Jessica Wright Show" to set the record straight: She would say that the woman in question was known to have a drug problem; that the woman in question was being paid to release this information; and that, yes, Georgiana had slept briefly with this woman while on location as an experiment—one from which she had quickly withdrawn.

"We'll have the drug problem confirmed by Monday," the man told Georgiana.

"Confirmed?"

"She can sue you for libel if it isn't true," he explained.

"How do you find out?"

"Don't worry," he told her, "the important thing is to discredit her immediately. Then, at worst, you'll simply be another modern-day woman who tried an unsuccessful experiment."

An unsuccessful experiment. What a god-awful way to put what was suddenly such a precious part of her life.

The rest of the plan was hammered out:

Stage two: Georgiana was to acquire a serious boyfriend (they could help her find someone, if need be. There were several celebrity male clients who were in need of such a relationship as well), and a PR blitz about the romance would ensue.

Stage three: Would she be willing to marry? Better yet, have a child? It had worked very well for several high-profile careers they could think of—but not name.

Georgiana could only stare at them in disbelief, and when she realized they were perfectly serious, she said, "Absolutely not."

Okay. Backpedal. Stage three reenvisioned. Would she at least be willing to let them start rumors that she was pregnant?

"Absolutely not," Georgiana told them.

"Don't be angry, Ms. Hamilton-Ayres," the man said, "our job is to tell you honestly what your options are."

"I am not angry," Georgiana said, back ramrod straight. "I am merely telling you it is honestly out of the question."

Summary: they would stick with "The Jessica Wright Show" and the PR romance blitz, and if the threat to her career had not died out after that, Georgiana promised she would reconsider the options.

"Come on! You said we could do anything I wanted!" Ted cried, half pulling Patty into the lodge at Wollman Rink in Central Park.

"I am the mother of three small children," Patty pleaded to the man renting Rollerblades.

"They were 'responsible young adults' an hour ago," Ted said. "Size seven and half for the lady here, and eleven for me. Make sure to give us knee and elbow pads, and a couple of those helmets."

Within ten minutes Patty was clinging to the fence of the pedestrian walkway above the rink. "Come on, Patty," Ted said, prying her loose. "If you can go up against ICA, honey, you can Rollerblade." And he was right—she could! Well, after a fashion, anyway. As the mother of teenage children Patty had lost all ability not to imagine what a spill on the pavement would be like. She had witnessed too many skinned knees and chins, to say nothing of horrible-looking scrapes and gravel that had to be plucked out with tweezers.

But Ted was right there beside her as they skated and cruised the paved pathways, through fields and forests, up and down meadows. It was beautiful.

They stopped near the lake and ate ice cream. And held hands. And lay back in the grass to marvel at the shapes of the huge white clouds, and afterward, they skated on to watch some softball games.

"David, what are you talking about?" Susie demanded. "I don't know anybody at ICA!"

"But have you said anything to any of your friends about what's been going on?" he said, switching the telephone to the other hand.

"No!" she said. "You told me not to!"

"Are you sure?" he said.

"I'm sure about one thing," she said, "and that is, you're being a total asshole and I don't like it!" And she hung up on him.

By the time Georgiana got back to Alexandra's apartment on Saturday evening, the damage control team's suggestions had depressed and slightly sickened her. Alexandra's antidote was to put Georgiana on the Nordic Track for a half hour, then into a hot bath. She then wrapped her in a fluffy terry cloth robe; sat her down on the settee with an afghan; fed her salad, homemade vegetable soup, and hot crusty bread; and snuggled with her while watching a video.

It was bliss.

It was heaven.

It did the trick.

And though she was exhausted, Georgiana found herself making love with Alexandra again that night, as though nothing in the world could be wrong. And that's how it felt.

"What are you doing?" he asked in his deep, pleasant voice.

"I'm just lying here with George Eliot," Elizabeth said over the phone.

"*Oh*," David said, after a pause, "George Eliot."

"Yes," Elizabeth said, and laughed, "who did you think I meant? Anyway, it's a *Middlemarch* kind of night, and for lack of a specific directive, I've taken to my bed, determined to rest for at least twelve hours."

"That's good. Are you okay?"

"Yes," she told him. "And you?"

"I don't know anymore, Bets."

"You want another?" Ted asked when the waitress came around.

"I shouldn't really," Patty said, having already had two glasses of wine.

"Oh, go ahead," Ted said. "She'll have another," he told the waitress.

"I'm so glad you went to all this trouble to conduct your business during my act," the comedienne said from the stage.

"You want anything else, honey?" Ted asked. "Some nachos or something?"

"Hey!" the comedienne yelled. "You! I'm talking to you!"

"Ted!" Patty whispered. "She's talking to you!"

Ted turned around to look at the stage. Not only was the comedienne talking to him, but the fiery redhead was making her way down the stairs into the audience.

"Oh, no," Ted muttered, embarrassed.

"So is that what you do? Say to the babe, 'Hey, let's go to the Comic Strip so we can wreck Kimberley Travis' act?' I mean, whaddaya here for, honey," she said, standing over Ted now, "the food?" To the audience: "Everybody knows the Comic Strip for its *food*—right?"

Everybody was laughing. Ted was beet red.

They were in the Upper East Side comedy club Ted had seen on TV and had always wanted to visit. It was crowded, casual, and the drinks and laughter and music were plentiful. They had been having a ball—until now.

"So you just can't be from New York City," the comedienne said. "I mean, really, look at him, everybody—this poor schmuck thinks this is a place to eat. Some people go to the Four Seasons or Le Cirque or the Rainbow Room—but him? Naw, it's the Comic Strip for us, babe, this is the high life! Gourmet microwave pizza!"

Moments later the comedienne dragged Ted up to the stage and forced him to participate in her act. The audience was howling and the more embarrassed Ted got, the greater the response. But it *was* very funny, and Patty was laughing her head off. And Ted, now that he was over his initial terror, was having the time of his life.

There was a soft knock on Monty's door. "Who is it?" he asked.

"Elizabeth."

"Come in!" he called, straightening the covers. He was in bed in his pajamas watching TV.

"Hi," she said, poking her head in. "I'm sorry to disturb you, but I wondered if you would be interested in going to church with me in the morning? There's an eight o'clock service around the corner."

"What denomination are you?"

"Presbyterian," she said.

"Close enough. I'd be honored to accompany you to church tomorrow."

She smiled. And then she frowned, looking over at the TV set. "What on earth are you watching?"

"You've never seen this?" he asked, sitting up higher against the pillows. "It's 'Mystery Science Theater 3000.' But for those in the know," he added in his radio voice, "MST 3K."

On the television it appeared as though they were sitting behind some sort of puppets in a movie theater, watching a film on a big movie screen ahead of them. While the movie unfolded before them, the silhouettes of the puppets moved as they made wisecracks about it.

"You don't get it, do you?" Monty asked her.

"I'm afraid I don't," she admitted.

"Do you want to watch for a while?" he asked, feeling a tiny bit ludicrous.

"Sure," she said, pulling a wing chair near the bed and sitting on it. "So what's the movie?"

"Well, the movie is always one of the worst ever made," he said. "Tonight it's *Billy the Kid versus Dracula*, starring John Carradine as a vampire in the Wild Wild West."

"Monty," she said, watching him watch the TV.

"What?"

"You love this, don't you?"

He felt his face getting warm. "Yeah, I do," he said, looking back to the TV. "It reminds me of when I was a kid and my brother and I used to do the same thing—sit around making jokes while watching terrible movies."

She smiled. "Brings up good memories, then?"

"The best," he admitted. "We were kids then." He looked at her. "Do you know what I mean? We were really young and just . . . kids."

"I know what you mean," she told him.

"You watch much TV?"

"Almost none," she admitted.

"Good," he said, "then maybe watching this will create future good memories for you." Pause. "For you and me both."

They both smiled, and then they watched the movie.

～ 54 ～

"Now, then," Dorothy said, sitting in a Queen Anne chair at the head of the living room on Sunday, "are we all here?"

"First, may I ask who these gentlemen are," Monty said suspiciously, pointing to the two middle-aged men sitting on either side of Josh Lafayette. The group was spread out around the room with Henry and Dorothy near the door; Georgiana, Elizabeth, and Patty on the sofa; Ted perched on the arm of the sofa, one hand resting on his wife's shoulder; and Monty sitting in a wing chair near the window. Lining the other side of the room in chairs brought in from the dining room were David, Josh, and the strangers.

"Josh, would you please do the honors?" Dorothy said.

"This is Agent Maldwin Healy," Josh said, gesturing to the taller of the two. "Federal Bureau of Investigation. And this is Herbert Klein, special assistant to the attorney general of New York."

Elizabeth leaned forward to whisper, "I think you can trust them, Monty," and everybody laughed. She turned to Dorothy. "There's one more thing I think people should know before we start."

"And what is that, dear?" Mrs. Hillings asked her.

"David's movie was put in turnaround yesterday after Creighton Berns found out he was helping us. He pulled the stars and encouraged the backers to drop their financing—which they have."

They were quiet for a moment. Then Monty burst out, "How do we know this isn't a cover?"

Everyone looked at him.

"And why would you say that, Monty?" Dorothy asked.

"Because somehow Berns has been kept posted on what we're doing and who's involved. The leaks always happen when he's been around."

Dorothy looked around the group. "Is this true?"

Elizabeth sighed and explained that Creighton Berns had known early on about Monty and Elizabeth's involvement, that he had known Patty was working undercover at ICA, and that Georgiana had been threatened for her participation, among other things.

Dorothy leaned over to whisper something to her husband, who nodded, thought for a moment, and waved Josh over to whisper something to him. A horrified look came over the young attorney's face. "You're probably right," they heard him say.

Henry got up and left the room.

"Well, leaving that issue aside for the moment," Dorothy said, waving her hand as though to clear the air.

"Just like that?" Monty said. "We're going to go on with him still sitting here?"

"Trust me, Montgomery," she said to him, "the problem is being taken care of."

He narrowed his eyes. "Not to be rude, Dorothy, but how would you know?"

"I know because if anyone had told me about this before, I could have told you who the mole had to be then!" she said, annoyed. And then she sighed slightly, smiled, and said, "I apologize, everyone, but knowing all that I know now . . ." She shook her head. "I feel that I have not only been terribly violated, but that my personal life has been invaded as well. I'm anxious to set things right."

"You'll have your chance, Mrs. Hillings," the FBI agent assured her.

She smiled again. "Yes, indeed, I think I shall." She cleared her throat. "All right then, let us continue with the matters at hand. Needless to say, everything said in this room is to be kept in complete confidence until you are informed otherwise."

"I don't know," Monty said, shaking his head, "if there's something important to reveal, I don't think you should be telling all these people."

Dorothy looked at him. "First, we need the help of all these people. Second, I'd trust any one of you with my life. Third, while I am eternally grateful to you, Montgomery Grant Smith, if you interrupt me one more time I'm going to keep you after school."

Everyone laughed.

"Now then," Dorothy said, "the first thing you should know is that judging from the story bible and script that David obtained for us—at considerable cost to his career—it seems clear that the Metropolis movie in question, *Race in Space*, has indeed been substantially lifted from the children's story *Mathew and the Allied Planets*, written by Stephen Collins and published in England in 1941."

Henry came back into the living room and gave Dorothy a nod. She turned to the group and continued.

"It is our belief that Metropolis Pictures was for some time unaware that the movie extravaganza they had in production was based on the work of a writer other than the one listed on the title page of the movie script. As to whether the author of the screenplay realized where he had gotten the story and many word-for-word lines of dialogue, we can only note that his father was in England during the war, and, given the age of the writer of the movie, it is perfectly likely that a copy of *Mathew* had been brought home to him as a gift."

"How the hell can you know that?" Monty said.

"We have many new friends who are very well connected," Mrs. Hillings said graciously, nodding to FBI Agent Healy, who smiled.

"And so," Henry said, picking up the story, "what we have is a situation where a studio has a one-hundred-twenty-million-dollar movie to release, for which, they suddenly discover, the dramatic rights were never cleared."

"Hohohohoho," Monty said in his deep and nefarious radio laugh.

"So that's it," Georgiana said softly.

"Golly," Elizabeth said, on an intake of breath.

"Talk about trouble," Patty said.

"But upon researching the problem," Dorothy continued, "the studio, we believe, discovered that the author had died in 1947, and that the estate—the people who had inherited the rights to the book from Stephen Collins—had changed hands several times since then, to the point where it was doubtful they would even know they had inherited the rights to the book, much less the remaining copyright time on it. After all, there had only been perhaps a thousand copies of the work to begin with, since it had been out-of-print for over forty years, and the agent representing that one book of Mr. Collins's had gone out of business in 1956." Pause. "That was the good news for the studio."

She paused again for effect. "The bad news was that when

Hollard & Borrs was dissolved in 1956, Hillings & Hillings in the United States took over the representation of their backlist properties."

The room was dead silent until, as if coming out of a dream, Elizabeth said, "So you represent the literary estate of Stephen Collins."

Dorothy nodded. "Technically, yes."

Monty was confused. "So . . . ?"

"So," Henry said, "Metropolis immediately went to the person who had initiated the movie in the first place—"

"Creighton Berns," Georgiana guessed.

"Right," Henry said. "So Metropolis went to Creighton and asked him to negotiate terms with the Collins estate, not only because Creighton had just moved to ICA, but because the agency's ties to Hillings & Hillings were well-known."

After a moment, Ted Kleczak said, "And so did he try to negotiate terms?"

Henry and Dorothy both shook their heads. "No," Dorothy said, "that's just the point. Unfortunately for Metropolis, Creighton knew that ICA was buying Hillings & Hillings, and so he decided he didn't need to negotiate with anybody, he'd simply destroy the paper trail to the book when they took over the agency."

"At the same time," Henry said, "young Creighton was preparing his little coup with the board of directors at ICA, which, from what we understand, was a rather expensive proposition. So Creighton evidently told Metropolis to keep their mouths shut, he had cleared the rights for their blockbuster movie, but not only had he not cleared the rights, he had pocketed the money Metropolis thought it was paying to the estate to hush things up and smooth things over."

"Oh, man! Oh, man!" Monty was saying, bouncing in his seat.

"But how did he think he would get away with it?" Elizabeth said.

"Well, first things first," Dorothy explained. "As soon as he got rid of Ben, he decided to shut down Hillings & Hillings and find and destroy all the paperwork that existed on *Mathew and the Allied Planets*. That alone would buy him years of time."

"But wait," Monty said, "sooner or later—"

"Sooner or later the copyright was going to expire in England," Dorothy continued, "or so Creighton thought. And he knew that as soon as that copyright expired, the story would move into the public domain and Metropolis would be in the clear."

"The copyright laws in England are different than they are here in the United States," Henry said. "In England, the copyright expires fifty years after the death of the author. In this case, it would expire on December thirty-first, 1997."

"But that's over three years from now," Elizabeth said.

"Exactly," Henry said. "That's why it was so important for Creighton to destroy those files and buy time. Metropolis was desperate to release the movie, and he promised them they could release it this fall. But there was something Creighton did not know."

He kept them in deliberate suspense.

"Don't be cruel, dear," Dorothy said. She reached down beside her chair and came up with a copy of *Mathew and the Allied Planets*. She opened to a page and held the book up for all to see.

"What?" Elizabeth said, leaning forward, straining to see.

Mrs. Hillings tapped her finger on the page. "Here."

Elizabeth leaned closer and read, "First published March 1941. Second edition September 1941. Copyright, 1941, by Stephen Collins. Copyright, 1941, in the United States of America, by Stephen Collins."

"You see," Henry said, "what Creighton Berns did not know was that the second edition was filed for copyright protection in the United States shortly after the book was first published in England. Although it never did get distributed here, it is nonetheless protected by United States copyright law."

"So whoever lifted the story must have had the first edition of the book," Elizabeth said. "If they had seen the second edition, with this copyright page, they wouldn't have dared to steal it."

"And if Creighton had succeeded in getting our old files on the book," Dorothy continued, "he also would have seen that, as a matter of routine, we had the Collins heirs renew the copyright here in 1969."

"And if he had known that," Henry said, "then Marion Ballicutt could have told him that the 1978 Copyright Act had automatically extended all second terms of copyright protection to forty-seven years, which means, my friends, that all rights to *Mathew and the Allied Planets* are fully protected by law until the year 2016."

Everyone's eyes had been moving back and forth between the Hillingses as if they were at a tennis match. Now, out of habit, their eyes went back to Mrs. Hillings.

"Such a minor matter is dutiful paperwork," she said, "and yet such a major downfall it shall be." She smiled. "As I always say, one's whole life can change in any given moment, and I believe the life of Mr. Creighton Berns is certainly about to." Pause. "I will see him punished if it's the last thing I do."

There was a moment of silence as her words sank in.

"The next thing we need to find out is how much the executives at Metropolis Pictures knew," Henry said. "But regardless of how much they knew, they're still up to their necks now in a conspiracy to—" He looked at the FBI agent. "How did you phrase it?"

"To willfully violate the copyright law," the agent said, "and conspire to defraud the public."

"Defraud the public how?" Elizabeth asked.

"Well, see, it gets complicated," Henry said.

"And expensive," Dorothy added, eyes twinkling.

"Metropolis has licensed merchandising rights to this movie to several companies who have spent millions to design and manufacture toys, T-shirts, stationery, costumes, records, puzzles, tie-in storybooks, and on and on. These companies can't market any of this stuff until the movie is released," Henry said.

"And with the movie having been delayed and delayed, this massive inventory is collecting dust in more than a few warehouses," David said.

"So how is that defrauding the public?" Monty asked.

"Well, Metropolis doesn't own the rights to the story or, therefore, the movie. The licensees have filed for—and obtained—trademarks on merchandise derived from a story Metropolis doesn't have the right to license," Josh informed them. "So what you have, in effect, is a massive conspiracy of fraudulent copyright and trademark claims, with the willful intent to defraud the public."

"Jeee-sussss," Monty said, looking at Elizabeth.

"And," Henry added, "every company with a product licensed

from this movie is subject to legal action from the author's estate. The only way those companies will be able to clear themselves is to turn around and sue the institution that contractually guaranteed them the rights, Metropolis Studios."

"But what I don't understand, Dorothy," Elizabeth said, "is why Berns went after you so publicly, so antagonistically."

"He went after the office because he was after the files," she said. "But when I had the heart attack, and he couldn't find the files, he evidently saw an opportunity to depict Henry and myself as borderline senile—just in case we ever did see the resemblance between the Metropolis movie after it came out and *Mathew and the Allied Planets.*"

"Son of a bitch!" Ted Kleczak said, squeezing his wife's shoulder.

"And now, my friends," Henry said, "we wish to finish this affair, and that is why we asked you here today."

"If you'll excuse me, Henry," Dorothy said, rising from her chair. "I'm going to take care of that other matter now. Why don't you and Agent Healy proceed?"

Dorothy Hillings walked out of the living room and down the hall. Outside her bedroom she paused a moment, thinking. Then she opened the door and went in. Sasha and Bernadette were changing the sheets on the bed. "Thank you, Sasha," Dorothy said. "I wish to speak to Bernadette alone now, please. You can finish up later."

"Yes, Mrs. Hillings," Sasha said, leaving the room and closing the door behind her.

Bernadette looked a little confused. "We were getting your room ready for you," she explained.

"Actually, Bernadette, my husband asked Sasha to keep an eye on you. Sit down."

Looking startled, Bernadette perched on the edge of the bed. Dorothy walked over and crossed her arms over her chest, making her charm bracelet tinkle. "I suspect you know what it is I wish to speak to you about."

The aide looked worried now. "That you're feeling better?" she asked hopefully.

"No, Bernadette," Dorothy said. She just stood there, waiting.

"I don't understand," Bernadette said after several moments.

"Oh, but you *do*. Though I don't think you realized how many lives you would affect and how many people you would hurt. Certainly you didn't know that you could go to prison."

All the color drained out of the aide's face.

"Yes, Bernadette," Mrs. Hillings said. "I know it had to be you."

The aide buried her face in her hands and started to cry. "I'm sorry. I needed the money for the children."

"What children? You don't have any children, Bernadette, and I command you to stop this charade once and for all right this moment! Now tell me, how did he get to you?"

The aide straightened up, sniffing, eyes miserable. "My sister is the Bernes' nanny. He called me and said you would need someone to help out at home. He wanted me to take care of you—and let him know everything that was going on at your house. And then *you* hired me."

"Yes, that's true, we did," Dorothy said, sighing and putting her hand on her hip. "But it was not as if my husband and I didn't have a few things on our minds, Bernadette—like whether or not I was going to live." She shook her head. "Listen to me, Bernadette, there is only one way to save yourself, and that is to do exactly as we tell you from here on in. Do you understand?"

Bernadette nodded solemnly. "I'll do whatever you say, Mrs. Hillings. I swear I will. But please don't let him do anything to my sister."

~ 55 ~

The Kleczak children were beside themselves with questions Monday morning at breakfast. Where had their parents been? Why had they stayed in New York? Was it true that Mom had been arrested? Were they getting a divorce?

"A divorce!" Ted said, coming into the kitchen as he finished knotting his tie. "Mary Ellen, what the heck are you talking about?"

"Just wondered," she mumbled into the cereal she wouldn't eat.

"I knew you wouldn't get divorced," Kevin reassured his mom.

"Listen you guys," Patty began.

"Dad," Tim said, "did you get those cleats for me?"

"To tell you the truth, Tim," he said, going to the counter and pouring himself a cup of coffee, "I completely forgot. I'm sorry." He turned to Patty, sipping from his cup. "I told him I'd go to Paragon while I was in the city."

"I don't think we like what the city does to you guys," Mary Ellen said.

"And what, pray tell, does that mean?" Patty asked her.

"Well, for starters, you go there and completely forget about us," Mary Ellen said. "And we're your children."

"Children, you mean, as in 'ball and chain'?" Patty teased.

"Well, *you* had us," Mary Ellen pointed out. "It's not like we were given a choice."

Patty looked at Ted. "Why exactly did we abandon our poor helpless children this weekend?"

"Because they're not poor or helpless; they are perfectly capable of looking after themselves for a weekend while we try to remember that we have lives, too," Ted said, pulling out his chair and sitting down at the table. "Besides, there was an adult here with you."

"This is how divorces always start on the soaps," Mary Ellen told her brothers, "the parents go off to 'find' themselves."

"Oh, shut the hell up, Mary Ellen," Kevin said, pouring another glass of milk.

"Kevin!" Patty said.

"While you've been off finding yourself, he's turned into a hood," Mary Ellen dutifully reported.

"Cut it out, Mary Ellen!" Tim told his sister. He turned to his parents. "I'm just glad you're home. I've had enough of her."

"And who fed you all last week?" Mary Ellen wanted to know. "Ha!" she said, slapping the table. "That's gratitude for you."

"Now you know how it feels," Patty murmured over her cup of coffee.

"Your mother has to go back into the city this morning," Ted said, reaching for a banana from the fruit bowl and starting to peel it.

"But I'll be back before you get home from school," she said, reaching over to tousle Kevin's hair, "so you won't turn into a hood." She looked at her daughter. "Mary Ellen, darling, do you love me?"

Mary Ellen rolled her eyes. "Mary Ellen, *darling*—geez, you're gonna make us crazy, Mom. You're talking like one of the characters in your novel. So are you going to sell your book now or what? You said we could all go away somewhere really cool when you did."

"Mary Ellen," Patty said. "I'm serious. Do you love me?"

Mary Ellen screwed up her face. "Yes, *Mmmooommm.*"

"Then would you mind showing it once in a while?" Patty said, her voice starting to break.

Everyone looked at Patty. She sniffed sharply, blinking back tears. "Sorry," she said, getting up. "I'm just a little tired, I guess." And she walked out of the kitchen.

The kids all looked to their father.

"Dad," Kevin said, "what's happened to Mom? She's different."

"She's just going through changes," Ted said, swallowing a bite of banana. "Just like you guys are. Every day you change a little bit and your mother's just catching up, that's all."

"I thought adults weren't supposed to change," Kevin said. "That's why they're adults."

"Ah, but there you're wrong," Ted told his son.

"*You* told us that!" Mary Ellen said. "You said you grow up and you settle down and you don't change much after that."

He smiled. "I was wrong, Mary Ellen. You grow up and you settle down and hopefully you change a lot, always. So you're never bored with life and never take it or the one you've settled down with for granted."

Mary Ellen looked at Tim. "Now *he's* getting weird." She got up and carried her dishes to the sink, something, her father noticed, she had never done before without being reminded.

The group was assembled in the Hillingses' living room on Monday by ten o'clock, each looking a bit wary of the number of official-looking strangers in the apartment. Agent Healy of the FBI then divided up the group: Elizabeth and Monty were assigned to the study with a man and a woman; David and Georgiana were sent to the dining room with Healy and another man; and Patty Kleczak was assigned to the kitchen with another man and woman.

*   *   *

"Storage room eighteen is here," the man said to Elizabeth and Monty, pointing to it on the floor plan of the maze of rooms that made up U-File-With-Us in Queens.

"Yes," Elizabeth said, "you go in this way, through this door—"

"And this blueprint is correct?" the black woman said. "This is the only means of access?"

"Yes," Monty said. "Right, Elizabeth?"

"Yes, but this part is wrong," she said, pointing to the plan. "There are floor-to-ceiling shelves on this side of the room. They go along this way—not that way." She closed her eyes, trying to visualize. "Yes," she confirmed, "they're here, so you have to move around to the right."

"Use this, Professor Robinson," the man said, handing her a pencil.

Elizabeth leaned over and started to draw.

Monty stood there, looking not at the floor plan, but at Elizabeth, as if trying to memorize her face.

The man checked his watch and said to the woman, "I think the bureau can have that call placed now."

Monty looked at him. "How long have you been with the FBI?"

"He's with NYPD, Mr. Smith," the black woman said, "I'm with the FBI." She held out her hand, "Andraya Lafayette."

Elizabeth glanced up at her. "You're not related to—"

Agent Lafayette smiled. "Josh is my brother."

"No, that's where they have a big Xerox machine," Patty said, bending over a floor plan on the kitchen table with an FBI agent and a New York City policewoman. "There might have been a water cooler there before, but it's not there now." She pointed with the pencil. "This is still Marion Ballicutt's office, but this"—she drew in a faint line—"has been divided into a space for Miss Andersen. James Stanley Johnson's office is over here. They both have the file cabinets in their offices—here and here. The ones I would go for would be in the lower bottom file cabinet of her desk. The one with the lock."

"Is there a paper shredder on the premises?" the policewoman asked.

"I didn't see one," Patty said. "But I did notice a garbage disposal in the kitchenette."

In the dining room, Georgiana was frowning, shielding her eyes with her hand. Then she dropped it, opened her eyes, and stared at the floor plan again. "This is all different now," she said, pointing to the reception area of ICA in Beverly Hills. "But I'm almost positive the dimensions of the outer room—here—and Creighton's office are still pretty much the way they are shown here." She looked at the police officer.

"Mr. Aussenhoff?" agent Healy said. "Please come take a look at this."

David turned from the window and came over.

"Yeah, this is the old floor plan," he said after a moment.

"How do you think it goes now?" the policeman asked him.

"This outer reception area is different. But Georgiana's right, I think, Creighton's office and that little waiting room are still the same." He picked up the pencil. "The entranceway now goes like this." He started to draw. "Does that look right to you, Georgiana?"

"Yes," she said, watching. "There's a door there, isn't there?"

He stared at the plans and then shook his head. "I honestly don't know."

"Okay, Mr. Aussenhoff," the FBI agent said, unfolding another blueprint and spreading it out over the first. "Now, Ms. Hamilton-Ayres, Mr. Aussenhoff, I want you to look at this carefully."

"This is Metropolis Pictures," David said, recognizing the studio's trademark five-sided building and a number of smaller ones on the studio lot.

"But it's very different now," Georgiana said. "Isn't there a huge parking garage by the entrance?"

"Yeah," David said.

"Well, this is not a good sign," the agent sighed, "if we can't even get an accurate floor plan from the fire department out there."

"Let me think a minute," David said, looking at the plans. "This whole area over here is Bestar Studios, the TV people. They're just renting on the lot, so there's nothing there you want, I don't think."

"This is the movie area," Georgiana said. "The soundstages. Scenery. Dressing rooms."

"But where is the administration building?" Healy asked.

"Here," they said in unison, pointing to the five-sided building.

"But that's not where the big brass is anymore," Georgiana added. "They're over here in this little building."

"Mr. Aussenhoff, do you agree?" the agent asked.

"Yeah," David said slowly, "she's right. But what I'm trying to remember is—Georgiana, isn't there something here now? Where this parking lot is?"

"You're right. They ripped out these old offices and the lots here, and the new commissary's in here."

The agent looked at him. "This is very important," he said. "The parking lot is where?"

"Here." Georgiana pointed.

"And then you walk around this way," David said, "to get to the president's office." He picked up the pencil and started to draw.

"Okay, this is good," Agent Healy said. "We know what we're looking for now."

It was a very simple glassed-in office downtown. Bernadette, formerly employed by the Hillingses, sat across the desk from a man in a tweed coat. He pushed the phone across the desk to her. "Ready?"

She looked at the notes in her hand and nodded. She picked up the phone and dialed. She stood up then, moving about as if she were in a hurry.

"I have an urgent message for Mathew—take this down," she whispered. "Tell him everything is at U-File-With-Us, 2345 Manhasset Boulevard, Queens, New York, storage room eighteen." She repeated the information one more time. "That's right. Tell him everything he wants is there." She hung up.

"Well, my friends," Dorothy Hillings said to the group as Henry saw the agents and police officers out, "we simply cannot thank you enough. Will you stay for lunch? We thought we'd order in something special."

"Sorry, Dorothy, but I'll have to take a rain check," Monty said, going over to give her a kiss and a hug. "I'm on the air in thirty minutes."

"Oh, of course, Monty, dear, run along. But I expect to see you again before you leave town."

Leave town. The phrase seemed to cast a pall over everyone in the room.

"I won't be here when you get back," Patty said, walking over to Monty. She held out her hand, but changed her mind and threw her arms around him.

"I'll see you when your book comes out," he promised. "Remember, the whole show's yours—I'm a man of my word."

"I won't be here either," David told him. "I'm going back to L.A. in a couple of hours."

The two men looked at each other. Monty nodded, held out a hand, and they shook.

"I'm staying on for a few days, so no good-byes yet," Georgiana said, smiling, when he turned to her.

Monty nodded. He looked at Elizabeth. "I'll talk to you later?"

"Yes, I'll look forward to it."

He headed for the front door after giving Dorothy a kiss.

In a few minutes David, Elizabeth, and Patty went down together to the lobby. The doorman flagged a cab for Patty, and she went off to Penn Station to catch her train to New Jersey. David retrieved his luggage from the doorman's storage area and he and Elizabeth stood in the vestibule, underneath the Tiffany glass dome, while the doorman looked for another cab.

"Are we sure we don't have a—that we can't—?" David asked her.

She nodded, swallowing, holding her arms tightly across her chest. "Not you and me. It couldn't work."

"Elizabeth," he said.

She looked at him and saw the sadness in his eyes. She reached up, took his face in her hands, and kissed his lips softly. And then she smiled and walked back into the building, waving good-bye over her shoulder.

~ 56 ~

Their little luncheon—Dorothy and Henry and Elizabeth and Georgiana—was quiet and subdued. Everyone was distracted by his or her own thoughts.

Elizabeth did not even know what she thought about anything connected with her life anymore. She was coming and going and meeting herself in every doorway. A few weeks ago she had been living in England and now she wished she never had to go back. A few weeks ago her emotional life had consisted of her students and Elizabeth Farren, a countess who had been dead for almost two hundred years, and now her life was intimately involved with what seemed like two hundred people simultaneously.

"Excuse me, Miss Elizabeth?" Sasha said to her in the middle of their meal. "Mr. Smith's producer wishes to speak to you immediately."

Elizabeth excused herself and went to the telephone. Mike said to turn on Monty's show immediately, there was news breaking that Monty said Elizabeth needed to be aware of. Fast.

Monty had dashed to the studio straight from the Hillingses'. The show was well under way when a caller said, "I don't know what's the world coming to, Big Mont, if a beautiful girl like Georgiana Hamilton-Ayres turns out to be a lesbian."

"What?" Monty said, instinctively reaching for the off button he swore he would never use on a caller. "What are you talking about?"

"Georgiana Hamilton-Ayres is a lesbian," the caller repeated.

"I'm sorry, but you've got it wrong, my friend," Monty said. "So wrong, you cannot imagine."

"I didn't get it wrong, Big Mont," the caller said, "I got it straight from the news rack at the 7-Eleven on my way to work this morning. Everybody at the coffee area was talking about it."

That's when Monty's producer had come into the studio waving the new edition of the *Inquiring Eye*. "Let me see that," Monty's audience heard him say, crumpling the tabloid as he grabbed it.

Laura Van Wormer

"Georgiana Hamilton-Ayres's Lesbian Lover! Actress Loved Her and Left Her!"

"Ladies and gentlemen," Montgomery said, ignoring the pit in his stomach. "I, Montgomery Grant Smith, your fearless leader in all things correct, must, once again, rely on my own extraordinary life to set the record straight. There is no way—let me repeat, no way—Georgiana Hamilton-Ayres is gay. I know because I am dating her."

People started shouting in the control room.

"They don't believe me," he told his audience. "You should see them in the control room here, they're all making faces at me, shouting at me that I can't say that I'm dating the beautiful actress, Georgiana Hamilton-Ayres. Well, I am. Ask her. And now, dear fans, you know why I am in New York."

That's when he scribbled a note to Mike, telling him to call Elizabeth.

"She may get out of it, but it's gonna be close," the head of the public relations team told Jessica Wright over the phone at DBS. "I don't know how the hell you managed it, Jess, but Montgomery Grant Smith is just about the only person who could pull this off."

"Pull what off?" the TV talk-show hostess asked him.

"His defense of Georgiana," he said.

"What are you talking about?" Jessica said.

"On the radio—on his show. He's on the air right now saying there's no way in hell Georgiana can be gay because he's *dating* her. I thought you'd arranged it."

"*What!*" Jessica pushed her intercom. "Find Alexandra and tell her to turn on Montgomery Grant Smith's show, pronto. It's urgent."

"Why the disbelief?" Monty demanded of his audience. "Why doesn't anyone believe that Georgiana Hamilton-Ayres would go out with me?"

"Maybe because she's a classic Hollywood liberal, Monty," a sympathetic caller suggested.

"She's hardly a classic Hollywood liberal, my friend," Monty said in a high-handed voice. "She's a genuine British peer, that's what she is—her father is a viscount."

"Her mother's from Brooklyn!" the next caller cried. "How could she be a genuine peer if her mother's from Brooklyn?"

"Ah! And therein lies the beauty of her story, my friends," Monty said without missing a beat. "Her father is British nobility, but she prefers not to make use of her title: the Honorable—and I underscore the *honorable*—the Honorable Georgiana Hamilton-Ayres. And she prefers to work and live and pay taxes in America. If we had more immigrants like Georgiana, I'd say let them all come!"

Monty laughed. Now it was getting fun. The network was flooded with calls from all over the country. The pit in his stomach had eased. It was going to be okay, he thought. Regardless of what Georgiana had done or had not done, by the end of the day she would at least have fifteen million conservatives out there who would swear she was the target of a smear campaign simply because she was going out with Montgomery Grant Smith.

"Monty wants you to come to the studio," Elizabeth said breathlessly, holding the portable phone in her hand. "Can you handle going on the air with him?"

"Oh God!" Georgiana said, holding her face in her hands.

"Tell Monty she will be right over," Dorothy said.

Georgiana sat bolt upright. "But—"

"Elizabeth will go with you and you will go on the air and you will face this like the wonderful, talented, and courageous young woman you are!" Dorothy told her. "Besides, dear, Monty will help you. I know he will."

"All right," Georgiana said, jumping up.

The calls did not stop. AT&T said a circuit had blown with the overload on the 800 number. Evidently many of Big Mont's listeners had something to say about his dating a beautiful movie star who was being so brutally victimized by a smear campaign in that rag the *Inquiring Eye*.

"It's those feminist storm troopers, Big Mont, I tell ya!" a caller was saying.

The studio door opened and Georgiana was led inside.

"They can't stand the idea of her going out with you, so they say she's a queer like them!" the caller continued.

"Oh, God," Georgiana said, turning right around to go back out.

Elizabeth blocked her way.

"As emotionally dysfunctional as I tend to think most feminists are," Monty said into the microphone, "I don't think their sexuality is the problem, my friend. The problem is that they—and all these special-interest groups—want my job and my money without having to work for them the way I have to! And the Democrats buy it every time!" He shoved an ad cartridge into the console. "Okay, folks, we'll be back after this message with Georgiana Hamilton-Ayres. That's right, that's what I said—Georgiana Hamilton-Ayres will be here in the studio when we come back."

The on-air light went off and Monty slid off his headphones and stood up. "You okay?" he asked Georgiana.

"I think so," she said weakly.

"Sit there," he instructed. "Mike, get her a headset. Elizabeth, sit on the other side of her." Everybody started moving. "Erica," Monty said to Mike's assistant, "get Georgiana a cup of very strong tea loaded with milk and sugar."

"But—" Georgiana said.

"Do as Big Mont says," Monty told her. "And when it comes, I want you to drink it straight down. It'll help."

"Okay, can you hear all right?" Mike asked her.

Georgiana nodded, adjusting the headset.

"This is the volume control," Mike said, showing her the knob. "And make sure to speak into the microphone."

"She's only done a million interviews, Mike," Monty said. "Georgiana," he continued, sitting down, "you just follow my lead and we'll get through this."

She nodded.

Monty looked at Elizabeth and winked. "Piece of cake. It'll be fun. Relax, everybody." And then he leaned forward to switch on the intercom to the engineering room. "Cram any more people in there, guys, and you're going to knock the wall down." To Georgiana, "You've got a lot of fans rooting for you." He looked up at the clock.

"In ten, Monty," the engineer said.

He watched the clock, lips pursed. The light came on.

"And, as promised, folks, she's divine and gorgeous, the Honorable Georgiana Hamilton-Ayres is here in the studio," Monty said. "You should see the guys swooning in the control room. Hello, Georgiana." His audience heard the sound of a kiss. "Sit down over there, love."

Georgiana smiled nervously. She glanced behind her and saw that studio employees were packed into the engineering room, pressing against the glass.

"Well now, you've had quite a day," Monty said to her. "I warned you when we first met that anything was likely to happen if you hung out with me, that certain people wouldn't be able to stand it."

"Yes, well, Monty," Georgiana said nervously, "you were right."

Lowering his voice to a very serious tone, he said, "Quite frankly, Georgiana, no one believes that you'd go out with me."

"Well, they're wrong." Pause. Then a very deep, sexy laugh. "Aren't they, Monty?"

He made a groan of utter surrender and then whispered into the microphone, "Does this sound like a lesbian to you folks?"

"And I think there are several things that need to be laid out on the table," she added. "No pun intended, *Big Mont*."

People were screaming in the control room.

"Pandemonium, folks," Monty said calmly, "has just broken out in the control room."

"Monty," Georgiana said, "the first thing I think your audience should be made aware of is that you're one of the sexiest men alive. When Montgomery Grant Smith lets himself go," she murmured in an aside to the microphone, "believe me, there is no greater turn-on."

The crowd in the control howled and hooted and banged on the glass.

"The pandemonium has turned into riot," Monty said into the microphone. "And I am but merely sitting here, modestly blushing."

"Monty?" Georgiana said in her bedroom voice.

"Yes, Georgiana?" he murmured.

"I also want your listeners to know that, yes, it's true, I have been to bed with a woman. I don't want to lie to them about that."

Monty made a face as if to say: Watch it! Watch it! Don't do yourself in!

"And so I want to ask you, Montgomery Grant Smith," she continued, still in that bedroom voice, "if, in your opinion, that has made me a better or worse lover?"

The control room exploded again. After a few moments, the noise settled down and there was a moment of radio silence.

"It has made you the most exciting woman I have ever met, I swear to God."

This time the door to the studio opened, and all across America they could hear the hoots and whistles and screams and banging of the crowd in the control room.

Elizabeth was quietly laughing in her corner.

The interview went on for the next forty-five minutes. They fielded calls, went over their mutual sexual attraction, and Monty explained that their relationship was being forced into hiatus since they lived and worked in separate cities. Monty also made sure his listeners understood that Georgiana's bisexuality was something that made her even more attractive to him.

The screener wisely followed the producer's instructions and did not put through any of the outraged thousands of Monty's regular listeners who were flabbergasted by this entire thing.

When the show was over, Georgiana threw herself at Monty, kissed him deeply, and then went out to sign autographs for network employees. An hour later she was taken downstairs to Monty's limo and whisked off to parts unknown.

Exhausted, Monty and Elizabeth went upstairs to his temporary New York office. She sat back in a chair and closed her eyes, listening as Monty fielded a few outside calls from the press. Then he told his assistant to hold all calls, closed the door, and threw himself down on the couch. After a long sigh, he looked up to the ceiling and said, "You could have told me."

"It was not for me to tell," Elizabeth said, turning her chair around to look at him.

They sat there in silence. Monty with his eyes closed, arm over his face, Elizabeth watching him. The long striped sleeves of his shirt were rolled up, his tie was loose, he had a large ring of perspiration under his arm.

"It was wonderful, what you did," Elizabeth finally said. "Although the part about the feminists was rather dumb—" She stopped and smiled. "Oh, what the hell. You were great. I only regret we can't rewire your brain."

He chuckled. And then, from under his arm, "You know, Georgiana and I really did—I mean, we really—well . . ."

"Went to bed?" Elizabeth said casually.

"Yes," he said, bringing his arm down off his face to look at her. "Does that shock you?"

"No," she said. "Georgiana's right, you are a very attractive man—when you let yourself be vulnerable."

He blinked. "What?"

"I said you're a very attractive man."

"I need to lose weight," he said.

She shrugged. "If you want to, you'll lose it."

He winced a little and held the expression, looking at her through one eye. "You're not a lesbian too, are you?"

She smiled. "No, but it's not as if I haven't wished I were on occasion."

"You're in academe," he said, "you'd make a great lesbo."

"You are either the most obnoxious idiot, or the biggest genius, in the history of radio."

He laughed.

"Georgiana told me about you two—what happened," Elizabeth said. "That's when I knew I liked you, when I realized that it had been nothing to her but much more to you."

He was immediately embarrassed. "Nothing to her," he repeated, groaning and putting his hand over his face again. After a moment, he said, "So what did Aussenhoff ever do that was so special? Why are you so hung up on him?"

"But I'm not," she said. "I haven't been for a long time. I just needed to be reminded."

Monty lowered his arm and turned his head to look at her again. Now she was looking down at her lap, head hanging. It was not a pose familiar to her. He sat up suddenly and placed his feet on the floor. "I want to say something to you, Elizabeth, but I have to warn you, it makes no sense."

"Then maybe you'd better not say it," she murmured.

"I don't know how we can manage it," he said, "but I want to keep seeing you."

She didn't say anything.

"Elizabeth?" he said quietly.

She had one elbow propped up on the chair arm now, and was holding her face in her hand. "Do you remember what you talked about on your show the day you brought me the radio in Queens?" she asked him.

He tried to think. "No."

"You talked about people who try to commit suicide and about people in 'nut houses,' as you called them." Elizabeth raised her head. "Monty," she said, "I'm one of those people you talked about, who you said should be allowed to do everyone a favor and get rid of themselves so they won't be a burden on society anymore."

Monty sat there, not understanding.

Elizabeth stood up. "You have any Kleenex in this place?"

"Paper towels in the desk, middle drawer," Monty said. "I don't have a handkerchief, sorry."

Elizabeth went around the desk, found a paper towel, wiped her eyes, blew her nose, and walked over to the window. Hand resting on the pane, she said, "So what do you think about that, Monty?"

"I think," he said, standing up and walking over to her, "that Aussenhoff should be killed for what he did to you."

"But he didn't do it, that's just the point," she said, looking out the window. "I was heading toward a breakdown for years, only I had no idea." She turned to look at him. "There was never any reason for me to think I might be mentally ill. There's no mental illness in my family; there's no alcoholism, no drug addiction, no abuse, nothing. For absolutely no reason I was near the deep end— and it started when I was a child." She paused. "I was ill, Monty. I was one of those people you were talking about on the radio. Only I had money to pay for some very expensive care and other people don't. What I'm saying is, I heard you say that you should be spared crazy people like me. And I think you believe that."

"But you're not crazy, Elizabeth."

"Not anymore, no." She sniffed, looking down for a moment. "But I think you must be crazy to have some of these views you have. They're so defensive, so self-occupied; when I hear your show I feel like I'm hearing the whole country sliding into mental illness." She looked up. "I believe in kindness, Monty. I believe in helping people learn how to better themselves, to learn, to grow. And so I don't understand how someone like me can ever be acceptable to someone like you, and I certainly cannot pretend to understand my feelings about you—except to confess that I have been mentally ill and maybe my feelings for you demonstrate that I might still be." The last was said with a tearful little smile.

He came over and wrapped his arms around her. "Tell me," he whispered.

And so, standing there, in his arms, Elizabeth did. About her increasing insomnia over the years, the panic attacks that started after she moved in with David, the tranquilizers, which seemed to do the trick. At first. About running to England after David left her and how she was taking too many of those triangular little pills so that nothing was fully registering, nothing was getting resolved. And about the night she had been interviewing at Oxford, and she had gone to dinner by herself and had drunk wine by herself, which she knew she shouldn't do on those pills but did anyway. On the way home she wanted to buy some vodka and kill herself with the booze and pills, but she didn't because she could hear her mother saying, "Who would possibly do such a thing?"

Instead, Elizabeth went down into the underground to wait for a train. When she saw the headlights, she stepped off the platform, but she felt hands grab her and pull her back, and she had cried, "No, please, no, I want to die, I want to die!"

The police had taken her to a hospital. She awakened the next day in a psychiatric ward, and she had been frightened and scared. She told the doctors everything they wanted to know. She just wanted out of there, but they had kept her in that hospital with wire over the windows and the woman who told her the trolls would come at night and cut her heart out if she wasn't careful, and Elizabeth was sitting there in that awful green room with all the crazy women who were chain-smoking, not moving, not talking, trying not to look at the woman eating ice out of a bowl with a spoon, slurping, making dreadful sounds, when Dorothy Hillings walked in. Although Elizabeth had told them everything at the hospital, she had not told them she had a family because she was too ashamed and it seemed so unfair for such a strong family like hers to have to know "the brilliant one" was merely a sick and weak and crazy woman who was no good at life. So she had given them Dorothy's name as her next of kin and here she was.

Mrs. Hillings covered her alarm by saying in the most soothing way to Elizabeth, "What we must do, my darling, is get you somewhere safe and warm and restful. Then you will have a chance to sort all this out. Oh, dear, how did this happen, how did these bruises get on your wrists? There, there, don't cry, darling, but if you need to, then yes, cry as hard as you want and I'll hold you. We'll sort this out, I promise you, my dear." And Mrs. Hillings had sorted it out, and Elizabeth had gone to the Knight Institute in Kent, a lovely place full of caring people. When Elizabeth got the bills she could see why—"My God, what crazy people have to pay, Monty, to get someone to help them, you have no idea!" She stayed there for two months and worked very hard with her doctor to figure out what had gone wrong, where she had derailed. Now she was on an antidepressant, one of those drugs Monty made so many jokes about on the air, but it really had helped, she did not sink into that awful abyss the same way anymore, didn't feel compelled to hide for days and weeks and even months in her own head. She was sure Monty couldn't know what it was like to be ill, and to think there was no reason to be ill but to know that you were. To know that you were growing sicker each day, even though you were working like a maniac to cling to something.

"In the hospital I prayed they would tell me I was schizophrenic, but I wasn't. I wasn't even manic-depressive. I was only—I don't know what I was—I was a *teacher*, for God's sake. So now, you see, everything you thought about me has been confirmed, hasn't it? The one academic who wanted to be the exception to your case against them turns out to be mentally ill. Isn't that right, Monty? Isn't it?"

Elizabeth was sobbing into his shoulder and he was holding her tight and it was a while before she could hear what he had been saying in her ear, over and over and over again, like a mantra.

"Elizabeth, I love you. Elizabeth, I love you. Elizabeth, I love you."

~ 57 ~

The hand on Georgiana's arm startled her awake. "What are you doing here?" Georgiana said, looking at the clock. It was a little after 6 P.M.

"Harold's going to anchor tonight," Alexandra said softly. She was sitting on the edge of the twin bed, her expression one of concern.

Georgiana propped herself up on her elbows. "I must have fallen asleep," she said, looking down at her clothes.

"Why are you in here? In the guest room?" Alexandra asked, stroking her hair.

Georgiana looked at her. "I don't know. I guess I thought it was where I should be—if I should be in your apartment at all."

"You should be in our room," Alexandra told her.

Georgiana closed her eyes and reached for her. "I'm so scared something might happen to you," she whispered, clinging to her.

"The best thing that's ever happened to me is you," Alexandra murmured. "And I will not let you go."

Dorothy Hillings was smiling as she opened the door of the apartment, but she took one look at Elizabeth and the smile vanished. "Darling, what's wrong?"

"I'm fine," Elizabeth said. "I'm just tired. I need to lie down." She met the older woman's eyes. "I'm fine, really. I swear."

Dorothy nodded. "I'll peek in later and see how you are."

Elizabeth went down the hall to her room, leaving Dorothy standing there with Monty.

"She told me everything," Monty said in a low voice. "About what happened in London, the hospital and everything."

Mrs. Hillings nodded. "It was a very difficult time," she said carefully. She looked Monty straight in the eye. "She would have died rather than tell anyone she needed help. What do you think about that, Monty?"

"I think it's wrong that she was made to feel that way," he said softly.

"Do you really?"

He nodded. "I do."

She smiled. "Come in, dear, I think you and I need to have a chat."

"Everybody ready?" Patty yelled down the stairs.

"Yes!" Ted and Tim and Kevin and Mary Ellen yelled.

"Okay, close your eyes," Patty said, peering down into the living room. Her family had their eyes shut. On this score—playing games with established rules—they always did very well.

She quickly moved down into the living room, expecting the worst but feeling excited anyway. She had on the platinum blond wig and a black cocktail dress she had bought in New York with her temp money. Her makeup was done the way Georgiana had showed her.

She took a breath, struck a pose in front of her family, and braced herself. "Okay, open your eyes."

Ted reacted first, his eyes nearly bugging out of his head. "Patty," he gasped.

"Oh my God, Mom!" Tim said, with panic in his voice.

"Mom?" Kevin said, looking utterly lost and confused as to who this was.

Only Mary Ellen did not say anything, but simply stood there, looking at her mother.

"Honey, when you told me about the wig," Ted said, "I thought you'd look cheap or something. But this . . ."

"I don't like it," Tim said. "You look like the women in the magazine ads."

"I do?" Patty said, feeling wonderful.

"I don't like it either," Kevin said, disturbed.

"Why not, baby? It's still me," Patty said, walking over to touch him.

"It's not easy suddenly having a sex symbol for a mother," Ted observed.

"Oh, gross!" Mary Ellen said.

Patty turned. "That bad, huh?"

"Not you, Mom, you look great," Mary Ellen said. "It's Dad's icky pop-psych diagnosis."

"And what do you know about pop-psych diagnoses?" Ted asked his daughter, sneaking a pinch on Patty's bottom and making her jump.

"She watches 'Oprah' and 'Donahue,' " Tim said. He looked at his mother. "I'm sorry about what I said. You do look nice. It's just such a change."

"Well, I like it!" Mary Ellen announced, coming forward to get a closer look at her mother. "Turn around, Mom." Patty complied. "Yep," Mary Ellen said, "it's definitely a go, Mom. You and me? We're finally going to look like we're related."

There were no cars in the driveway when the cab dropped him off, and David thought no one was home. But when he unlocked the front door, the alarm didn't go off, and so he called, "Susie?"

"I'm here!" she called from upstairs.

He put his bag down and sifted through the mail that was stacked in the front hall. Susie came down in black spandex pants and a pink leotard top. "Hi," he said.

"You're home," she said, tentatively.

They kissed and hugged; then she slid away.

"Still angry?" he asked.

"Look, I didn't want you to get upset, but I really need to step back and see where this relationship is going—if anywhere."

He was confused. He held his hands out, questioning.

"I've moved back to my apartment," she said.

The anger surged through him and he blurted out, "Well of course, the movie's off, so why do you need me now?"

She stared at him for a long moment. "You've got a mind like a city dump."

He took a breath, the anger receding.

"I've been thinking, David, and I don't like what's going on. One day you're warm, the next cold. You're here and there and then you disappear, taking phone calls in the study, not calling from New York. And then you make that crack about the movie just now.

Well," she sighed, shaking her head, "to hell with you, if that's why you think I've been here. I've gotten a job on my own anyway."

"What job?"

"Listen to the way you say that. You sound so contemptuous, as if anything I could get on my own couldn't be worth having."

"Susie, that's not true."

"I'm so tired of feeling like nothing!" she said, bursting into tears and running out of the house.

~ 58 ~

On Tuesday afternoon, after his show was over, Monty walked across town to the Hillingses'. When he reached the square he spotted Elizabeth and Dorothy sitting on a bench in the park. Elizabeth was talking, making all kinds of dramatic gestures, and Dorothy was listening.

Monty turned around and quickly walked back to Park Avenue. He found a police car and waved it down. "Kudos, Big Mont," the policeman said, rolling down his window.

"Hi, fellas, good to see you. Listen, I need some information. If someone tried to kill themselves—like right here—and you stopped them, what would you do with them?"

"Take 'em to Bellevue," the officer replied. "They'd put them on the flight deck."

"Flight deck?"

"Psychiatric ward," the other officer said, leaning across the seat to see Monty better.

"If it was a homeless person?" Monty said.

"If it was anybody," the first policeman said. "If someone tries to kill themselves, by law they're supposed to stay under observation for three days."

Monty thanked them and flagged a cab and asked to be taken to Bellevue. The driver knew where it was without asking. Monty leaned forward. "You ever take anybody there?"

"Half of New York goes there," the driver told him, "and the other half belongs there."

Montgomery walked into the emergency room of the hospital,

feeling a bit spooked by the people in the waiting room. One guy was bleeding, holding wads of gauze on his face; a woman sat there struggling to control three small children; everybody else just looked awful. Monty walked up to the desk and waited for ten minutes before anyone was free to talk to him. In the meantime he watched a feverish-looking woman start gagging and throwing up. An orderly came out to get her and a maintenance person cleaned up the floor.

"Yes?" a hassled nurse asked. There were moans coming out of one of the rooms behind her.

"I'm Montgomery Grant Smith, the radio host?"

She nodded, unimpressed.

"I was wondering if you could tell me what would happen to a person if he or she tried unsuccessfully to kill themselves and was brought here."

"We would check them out first, and once we were satisfied that he or she was stabilized, we would admit them to psychiatric for observation."

"For how long?"

"Three days," she said.

"On the flight deck?"

She winced. "Psychiatric," she insisted.

"Could I see the ward?"

She frowned. "Why? Is a friend of yours up there?"

"He might be," Monty lied.

"What's his name?"

"Creighton Berns."

"Let me check," she said, picking up the phone. She asked for the correct spelling, spoke it into the phone, and shook her head. There was no one named Creighton Berns, but what did his friend look like? There were three patients in the ward with no identification.

"Um, well, he's Hispanic," Monty said.

"Creighton Berns?" the nurse asked.

"You know, darker complexion," he told her.

She looked at him as though he were crazy. "We have two black patients and one white patient who are unidentified."

"It may be him."

"Which?"

"The white one."

Now she was outright leery of him. "I think you ought to go to the administrative office in the front of the hospital and talk to them."

He did, only this time Montgomery said he had a black friend he thought might have been brought in last night for trying to kill himself.

"How?" the woman at the desk asked.

"I don't know. A friend just said he was taken to Bellevue."

"He may be able to identify bed six," the woman said to the security guard. "Take him up, please."

The "flight deck" was unlike anything Montgomery could have imagined. Two men in straitjackets were screaming; the others were either curled up or lying listlessly in their beds. The bed he was brought to contained a man in a hospital gown who was whimpering into his pillow. "Come on, fella," the security guard said gently, touching the man's arm. "We think this is a friend of yours."

The black man turned over and gave Montgomery a frightened look, pushed himself back up against the wall, clearly scared to death. "No, that's not him," Montgomery said quickly. "I'm sorry for disturbing you. I hope you get better real soon."

The black man screamed and Monty hurried out of the ward.

When he arrived at the Hillingses', Elizabeth immediately noticed how shaken he was. "What's wrong?" she said. "What's happened?"

"Nothing," he told her. "I just needed to see you." He took her in his arms, his throat closing up because he felt close to crying.

Early Wednesday morning all was quiet and still at U-File-With-Us in Queens. The security lights beamed down onto the dark lot surrounding the cement building.

Suddenly there was movement.

Two men dressed in dark clothes, each carrying something large, advanced through the shadows that surrounded the building. They put down their packages and one boosted the other up to a high office window. The tinkle of broken glass followed. They waited a minute, listening, and then proceeded. A hand unlocked the window and a figure slithered in. A few minutes later, a side door opened and the two men carried their loads inside.

They turned on a flashlight and looked at the floor plans in their hands, before moving down a hallway and stopping at a sign marked LOCKERS 10–42. They checked the numbers on the doors and stopped at eighteen. Ignoring the padlock, the two men started to work on the hinges with a crowbar. One hinge snapped and then, after quite a struggle, the other. The door was pried out and pulled sideways as their lights played over the shelves of boxes clearly marked HILL-INGS & HILLINGS.

"This is it," one man whispered, hoisting one of the heavy metal containers into the room. There was the sound of a cap being unscrewed just before the lights came on and members of the New York City Police Department and a fire marshal announced they were under arrest for breaking and entering with the intent to commit arson.

The suspects and eight gallons of gasoline were taken outside, where FBI Agent Andraya Lafayette and others were waiting.

~ *59* ~

On Thursday afternoon at one o'clock, Agent Healy told Bernadette to make the call.

She swallowed, dialed the number, and waited. "Mathew, please. It's urgent," she whispered. "Tell him I only have a few seconds." After a moment she said in a rushed whisper, "Listen, tomorrow morning the ICA offices in New York and Los Angeles are going to be searched, along with Metropolis Studios." There was a pause. "I don't know, the Hillingses are in there talking to the cops now." Pause. "Warrants and stuff. Something about files and some kids' movie." Pause. "Yeah, tomorrow morning, I'm positive. I don't know what time." Pause. "That's right, New York *and* Los Angeles. Hey, I gotta go!" And she hung up.

"Well done," an FBI agent said, taking off his headphones.

"Yes," Healy said, picking up another phone and dialing a number. "We just made the call," he said into the phone. "Give 'em twenty minutes and then go in. That should be just enough time for

Berns to alert everyone and send them running to what we want."

At 1:23 in the afternoon, James Stanley Johnson was returning to ICA with a special diet plate from a nearby delicatessen when he overheard a man in the reception area announce that he and the men with him were from the Federal Bureau of Investigation with a warrant to search the ICA offices of Marion Ballicutt and James Stanley Johnson. He calmly turned the corner away from the reception area and tore down the hall, nearly colliding with Miss Andersen, who had her arms full of files.

"Watch out!" she yelled, falling back a step and trying to keep the folders from slipping out from under her arms.

"Creighton called," Marion shouted to James. She was inside her office pulling files out of the cabinet. "We've got to get all the Mathew files out of here."

"The FBI's out front. It's too late!" James called.

"That's right," the agent said from behind him. "Kip, I think Miss Andersen needs some help with those files. Perhaps you should relieve her of them. Doris, why don't you help out that lady over there?"

"I want to see your warrant!" Marion Ballicutt demanded.

"Marion Ballicutt, I presume," he said, flashing his ID. "Maldwin Healy, Federal Bureau of Investigation." He snapped his ID case shut and withdrew some papers from his breast pocket as more agents came swarming in from behind him. "Not only do I have a search warrant for the premises, Ms. Ballicutt, but I believe I also have a warrant for your arrest."

Metropolis Studios had withstood many attempts to violate its security, partly because the famous actors who worked on films and television shows produced at its facilities tended to lure every nut case imaginable, but also because the studio had for years been linked to a money-laundering operation for a South American cocaine cartel. The FBI, DEA, and even the CIA, therefore, had been interested in the internal executive movements of the studio for quite some time.

So it was with the greatest of pleasure that the FBI dramatically descended upon the executive offices of Metropolis Pictures in no less than four helicopters. It was like a scene from one of the studio's own action movies, with agents charging all entrances and exits of the building, waving warrants, impounding the building, and relieving all workers of any papers on their person. Within fifteen minutes, Agent Healy in New York was notified that agents had obtained what they were after: a copy of the film *Race in Space*, and a file of handwritten notes between the president of Metropolis and the chairman of ICA, Creighton Berns.

Meanwhile, hovering over the administrative building of Metropolis Pictures was another helicopter, this one with the call letters of KPL-TV. It was the Los Angeles affiliate of DBS.

When the authorities smashed through the door to Creighton Berns's office at ICA, they found him in his private bathroom trying to stuff papers down the toilet. Unfortunately for him, even designer toilets back up when crammed with paper.

The authorities read him his rights, and perhaps because it was Hollywood, they put handcuffs on him before taking him outside past the cameras.

Ben Rothstein was standing outside with the press and waved a friendly bye-bye to Creighton as he was taken to a police car.

"It's all rather exciting, isn't it?" Dorothy said to Henry later that night, watching the events of the day play out on "The DBS Nightly News." They were in their nightclothes, propped up against the pillows in bed.

Henry remained silent, watching as the story unfolded on the screen.

"Josh did say they got everything they needed?" she asked.

"Yes," Henry said, eyes still on the screen.

"Then what's the matter?"

He didn't say anything.

"Henry, I'm speaking to you."

After a moment, he turned to look at her. "I overheard you on the phone today."

"Yes, well, darling, our clients have been without an agent for a month, someone has to get on the stick."

"But I don't want it to be us."

Dorothy looked at her husband for a long moment.

"I'm tired, Doe," he said. "I don't want to do it anymore. I'm too old."

"Nonsense," she said.

"But I am," he told her.

She picked up the remote control, pointed it at the TV, and clicked it off. She dropped her hand to her lap and the room fell silent.

They sat there like that for quite some time. Finally Dorothy said, "But I don't want us to be old, Henry."

Elizabeth, Monty, and Georgiana watched "The DBS Nightly News" broadcast from the control room of the West End Broadcasting Center with Jessica Wright by their side. In the middle of the broadcast they were joined by Cassy Cochran, the president of DBS.

"Word is," Cassy whispered to them, "the ICA board's so panicked they want to ask Ross Perot to be chairman."

They all laughed, feeling terrific. DBS News had broken the story earlier in the day, and although all of the networks were running with it now, DBS was still the only one with footage of the actual arrests. It was quite a coup. When Creighton Berns was shown being led out of the ICA building in handcuffs, the control room burst into cheers.

When the newscast was over, bottles of champagne and Perrier water were broken out in the newsroom. Today would bring DBS News Emmys; and tonight had brought them top ratings. When Alexandra Waring came in from the set, the group cheered again and the anchor merely grinned, curtsied, and gestured to Georgiana, Elizabeth, and Montgomery, saying, "Ladies and gentlemen, I give you the best damn stringers we've ever had!" The three received a near-riotous ovation.

A few minutes later Georgiana excused herself to use the ladies' room. When she came out, she found Cassy Cochran waiting for her in the hall. "Georgiana? May I speak with you for a moment?" she asked, leading Georgiana back into Alexandra's dressing room and closing the door. "Could we sit down for a moment?"

Georgiana felt vaguely alarmed as she slipped into a black-and-white Eames chair.

Cassy sat down opposite her, on the upholstered bench in front of Alexandra's dressing table. "You've had a rather rough week."

Georgiana nodded. "It's just starting, I'm afraid."

"Yes," Cassy agreed.

The tension in the air was unbearable. Finally Cassy said, "Alexandra and I are very close. And, technically, I am also her boss."

"Yes, I know," Georgiana said. Here it comes, she thought. "If you want to endanger your career, Georgiana, fine, but leave our star anchorwoman out of it."

"She's told me about the two of you," Cassy continued, turning, Georgiana thought, a little pink.

Georgiana didn't say anything.

"As the president of DBS, obviously I have to be concerned," Cassy said slowly. "It's my job. But personally, I couldn't be more thrilled for Alexandra. Or for you. I wanted to tell you that I think you may be the best thing that ever happened to her, and that I will be here to lend support—moral or otherwise—should either of you need it. It goes without saying the network stands behind Alexandra a hundred percent, no matter what she chooses to do."

Stunned, Georgiana could only sit there.

"Walk? In New York? What are you, crazy?" Monty asked when Elizabeth suggested they walk from West End to Central Park. She looked at him and he cringed. "Oh, God, I'm sorry—I didn't mean that!"

But Elizabeth only laughed and flagged a cab. "No, you're right, it would be crazy." She got in. "Let's go somewhere," she suggested.

"Where?" he asked, climbing in behind her.

"I don't know," she said. "Anywhere."

Monty thought a moment and then said, "Driver, take us to Brooklyn, the River Café."

"I've never been there," Elizabeth said.

The cab turned right on West End Avenue, heading south.

"I'll have to pay the moon to get a decent table," Monty explained. "But the food's great and it's really ro—" He stopped.

Elizabeth looked at him. "Romantic?" she finished for him.

He looked at her. "Does that bother you?"

"That you fall in love with every woman you meet in New York? Not really," she said, laughing.

"Hey, wait a minute! I just *thought* I *might* be in love with Georgiana. Besides, given the reality of her nature—say, what *is* the action between those two?"

"Which two?" Elizabeth asked.

"Georgiana and Jessica Wright. You don't suppose . . ."

"No," Elizabeth told him.

"You sure?"

"Very sure." They rode along in companionable silence. "Monty, I'm sorry, but I don't want to go to Brooklyn," she finally said.

"No? Where do you want to go?"

"I don't know," she sighed, looking out the window, "but somewhere."

"How about Chicago? Driver, we want to go to LaGuardia airport."

"LaGuardia!" the driver said.

"Yeah!"

The driver did a U-turn on Eleventh, came back up to Fifty-seventh, and turned right to go across town.

"But I don't want to go to Chicago tonight," Elizabeth said after a while. "I mean, do you? Really?"

"Well," Monty said, "where do you want to go?"

"If I knew, I would tell you," she said.

"Well somebody's gotta know!" the driver called back to them. "I can't be makin' like Nancy Kerrigan all night doin' figure eights out here!"

"Do you want me to take you back to the Hillingses'?" he asked.

"No," she said, looking straight ahead.

"Do you want to go somewhere with me?" he asked, placing his arm around her shoulder.

"Yes," she said, looking straight ahead.

Monty sighed, running his hand over his chin. "You're a real pain in the ass, Professor, do you know that? You know everything in the *Encyclopedia Britannica*, but do you know what you want? Nooooo."

She smiled, but she still looked straight ahead. "Yes, I do."

He threw his hands up. "So what do you want?"

"I want you," she said softly, looking straight ahead still, but settling in against his shoulder.

"Ask a smart question," he said, kissing her forehead, "get a smart answer. Driver, we're going to the Regency Hotel.

David finally found a parking spot down the block. He walked up Havenhurst Drive, trying to remember which of these West Hollywood complexes was Susie's. He finally found it—a split-level stucco affair. He walked up the stairs and let himself in through the iron gate. Some security. The complex wrapped around a swimming pool, where various people were lying in the sun, most of them drinking beer. David didn't see Susie and so he climbed the stairs to the second floor.

Her apartment door was open and music was coming out of it. When he stepped inside, it was obvious that a casual late-afternoon party was in progress.

Everybody looked at him for a moment and then turned back to their conversations. Finally one of the girls came over.

"Is Susie here?" he asked. "Susie Lanahan?"

She shook her head. "She moved out."

"Where to? I'm an old friend of hers and I want to say hello."

"Wait a second." She went off somewhere in the apartment and came back with a piece of paper, which she gave to him. It was an address in Santa Monica.

Santa Monica. Too far.

He decided to swing by the Sports Connection and take a look at the women working out. Maybe he could find a date there for tonight.

"I nearly died when Cassy started talking about us in your dressing room," Georgiana said, lying in bed. "I thought she was about to read me the riot act." She could feel the corner of Alexandra's face pull into a smile.

"I asked her for some time off," Alexandra said. "I had to tell her—I haven't volunteered for a vacation in five years, so she knew something was up."

Georgiana smiled.

"Where do you want to go?" Alexandra asked.

Laura Van Wormer

"I don't care."

"Mmm, well it would be nice to have some privacy."

Georgiana raised her head. "Fat chance, unless you're up for Antarctica."

Alexandra smiled, touching the side of Georgiana's face before kissing her softly. "You know, I'm very much in love with you."

"Thank heavens," Georgiana sighed.

"This is positively bizarre, Professor," Montgomery Grant Smith said, standing there in his boxer shorts and undershirt, feeling like a complete idiot.

"Well, you wanted to know what I was really like," Elizabeth said, dressed only in one of Monty's undershirts, sitting cross-legged on the big bed. "Talking is mandatory, even in bed." Her eyes were twinkling. "Well, *most* of the time."

He rolled his eyes, holding the pillow in front of him even tighter. He was dreadfully embarrassed. It was one thing to sleep with a woman, it was another to have her demand that they sit in his underwear and talk for a while. On the other hand, he knew Elizabeth was enjoying herself and felt completely comfortable. She had been talking on and on in a joyous way he was certain he had never heard before.

But did this mean she was *always* going to want to talk this way? Because if she was—

"I'm making you nervous, aren't I? I used to drive David crazy."

"Oh, Christ," Monty said, feeling a streak of jealousy, "we're not going to talk about *him*, are we?" The flash of anger got him to throw the pillow to the floor and crawl onto the bed.

"Heavens no, particularly since you're so much more attractive," she said.

By the time he was sitting cross-legged beside her, he was smiling. "You think so?"

"Honest to God, no comparison," she murmured. And she kissed him. Afterward, she sat back and smiled at him. "Nice mouth, Mr. Smith."

"Yes, well, that's what they tell me," he said in his radio voice.

"Oh, God!" Elizabeth suddenly cried to the ceiling. "Thank

you! For once in my life, I feel like I am exactly where I am supposed to be!"

"What?" Monty said.

She looked at him, smiling to beat the day. "I am crazy about you, do you know that?" she said, leaning forward to hug him.

Monty felt the pressure of her breasts against his chest and it was certainly not an unpleasant sensation. Nor was how Elizabeth's lips felt on his neck. And then there was the surprise of seeing the professor out of street clothes to begin with. Whether it was because she was in fact so utterly lovely, or because she was in fact so utterly Elizabeth, he wasn't sure, but he did know he was getting excited—big-time. But he was nervous, a little shy. When had he ever made love with a woman for the first time stone-cold sober?

"Are you all right?" she whispered in his ear.

"Best ever I've been," he whispered back, turning to give her neck a kiss. "To be honest, I was just wondering how I could hold back after even touching you once."

"But I don't want you to hold back," she murmured. "I want you to trust me as much as I trust you."

"That's good," he murmured back, sliding a hand over her breast.

Oh, yes, the professor was lovely. Big-time.

He was kissing her now and he felt something unhinge inside. It wasn't sexual; it was something else. His self-consciousness had lifted. He sat back slightly to look at Elizabeth and hold her face in his hands.

Her eyes were shining. She was happy, smiling. She was beautiful. And when her eyes narrowed, he knew she was as full of desire as he was.

"Do with me what you will," she said, smiling, as if she were reading his thoughts.

"And what about you?" he murmured, kissing her cheek.

"Don't you worry about me, Montgomery Grant Smith," Elizabeth said. "I know exactly what I want now, and I'll be sure to get it."

"Always the burning overachiever," Monty said, pushing her down on the bed.

Five

~ *60* ~

In the last week of July, Dorothy and Henry drove out to Long Island for a pleasant, quiet few days. The weekend included dinner with Millicent, who had been anxious to hear all the news. It was the first time they had seen her in nearly a month. When Dorothy came outside into the garden, Millicent took one look at the spring in her friend's step and the change in the color of her complexion and burst into tears. The two old friends flung their arms around each other. This pleased Henry enormously.

"If you think you've come all the way out here to Bridgehampton to have a lovely dinner under my grape arbor and you aren't going to tell me everything that's been going on," Millicent said to them, "then you've got another thing coming. All right, Dottie," she commanded, "spill it. What's happening?"

"I've never known you to have a radio out here," Dorothy said, noticing a portable sitting outside Millicent's gardening shed on a shelf.

"There's another radio inside, on the kitchen table," Henry said. "Could it be that our Millicent is suddenly listening to the radio these days?" He looked at his wife. "Now, whom do you suppose she could be listening to?"

"Oh, don't be daft!" Millicent said. "Now, Dottie, begin. I want to know everything."

"Well, as you know, Creighton Berns is gone from ICA," Dorothy began. "He was arrested—"

"But he's out now," Henry interrupted, "on five million dollars bail."

Millicent looked at him. "But you got him? I mean, you *really* got him?"

"We did." Henry beamed.

"And Ben's back at ICA," Dorothy said.

"Good. That's as it should be," Millicent said, nodding and smiling. "And now, what about the agency?"

"The merger will go through with ICA," Henry said, "but *without* Marion Ballicutt—who's out of jail on a million-dollar bail bond—and James Stanley Johnson and about half the board of directors. Our old staff has been rehired by ICA."

"And the offices?"

"We're going to let them go," Dorothy said.

Millicent opened her mouth to speak, thought better of it, and closed it.

The three sat there a moment, listening to evening songbirds.

"I'm going to sell Patty Kleczak's book," Dorothy finally said. "And that will be the end of our participation." She paused. "And we're putting the Gramercy Park apartment on the market."

Millicent looked at her.

"We want to go see Susan in Hong Kong while our health's still good," Henry said.

"We've been promising her for years," Dorothy added.

"And to visit with Peter in Portola Valley," Henry said.

"And really get to know our grandchildren," Dorothy said. "We can visit them and then, perhaps, they can come spend weeks in the summer with us."

Millicent was staring at them with what had grown to be a look of abject horror. "Well of all the nonsense!" she declared. "If you retire, then *I'll* have to retire, and I don't mind telling you, *I'm* not retiring!"

"You can't retire anyway," Dorothy said, "you're a writer."

"And you're my literary agent," Millicent said. "Now him?" she said, kicking her head in Henry's direction. "He's been old all his life—always has been and always will be. Let him go play golf with all the other cranky old lawyers in Southampton, but Dottie, my darling, you're younger than springtime and you have to have something to do besides smell the roses."

Henry looked at his wife. He sighed, shrugging. "I don't know, Doe. I know what I said, but Millicent's probably right."

"Well of course I'm right," Millicent told them impatiently. "When have I ever not been?"

After a delicious dinner at Millicent's, the Hillingses went home and climbed into bed. It had been a long, emotional evening, and they fell asleep quickly.

But then around two o'clock in the morning, Dorothy suddenly awakened and sat up, bedclothes falling to her waist.

"What is it?" Henry murmured. And then he jerked awake, alarmed, and sat up. "What's the matter? Don't you feel well?"

"I feel fine, darling," she said. "I don't know, I just awakened and thought, I love him so much."

"Who?" Henry asked, easing back into the pillows, immediately dopey with sleep now that he knew there was no emergency.

"You, darling," she told him. And then she snuggled in close to her husband and went back to sleep.

"Oh, God, Monty, I'm exhausted," Elizabeth said, collapsing on the antique oak bench in the Hillings & Hillings reception area.

"You're not the only one," he said, letting the broom fall and sitting down heavily beside her.

They had spent all day Saturday and Sunday supervising the cleaning of the Fifth Avenue offices. When Elizabeth had seen what the gang from ICA had done to them, she knew she had to get the offices in order so that Dorothy and Henry's last memories of them would be as they should be.

On Friday evening, however, Elizabeth had been so appalled by what they had found in the offices that she and Monty didn't wait for the cleaning people, but spent most of the night throwing out fast-food containers, shredded papers, and unidentifiable trash. They also tried to organize the piles of contracts and correspondence that were scattered, willy-nilly, across every inch of the handsomely appointed floor space.

Marion Ballicutt and James Stanley Johnson had left few stones unturned in their search. And when Monty insisted he would replace the eight or nine hundred books back on the shelves in the agency's library himself, Elizabeth knew why she had fallen in love with this man—this poor man who had flown in from Chicago, exhausted, to spend a quick, relaxing weekend with her in the Hillingses' apartment, and who, instead, within two hours had found himself being put to work in offices that looked like they'd been hit by a bomb.

But over the weekend the garbage had been taken out, the files were put back together, the furniture was put back where it belonged, pictures and plaques had been rehung, and the library looked as though it had never been touched.

Now she and Monty had finished and were sitting in the front waiting room. It was Sunday evening. He would have to fly back to Chicago in a couple of hours.

Elizabeth looked at him. Monty's khakis were streaked with ink and dirt and dust, and his blue-and-white striped Oxford shirt was not only filthy, but torn over one bicep. She smiled and reached over to rest her hand on his thigh. "You're wonderful, do you know that?"

He smiled. "Yes."

"Oh, you," she said, pushing him away.

"Me," he said, grabbing her arm and pulling her toward him, "wanttum professor. Or is that a politically incorrect dialect, too?" He stole a kiss, grinning like a delighted kid.

"Guess who's coming back to Chicago with you tonight?" she asked.

"But I thought—"

"I changed everything around," she said, smiling.

"You did?" It went straight to her heart, the expression his face took on when he seemed almost scared to believe she cared as much as she did.

"I can only stay a week, though," she said, smiling.

"I was kind of hoping you'd stay always," he said.

They were startled by the sound of a key in the door.

"Who the heck—?" Monty said.

The door opened and a figure appeared.

"Millicent!" Elizabeth said.

"Elizabeth," she said, smiling. And then to Monty she said, "You," not smiling.

"What are you doing here?" Elizabeth said, getting up. "I thought you said you'd never leave Bridgehampton again."

"Shhh," the older woman said, "my visit is not for public consumption." She put down the shopping bag she was carrying. "I thought I better see the state of the offices before Dottie came in tomorrow."

"We straightened out everything, from top to bottom," Monty told her. "The cleaners came and everything."

She squinted at his appearance. "Evidently they did not get to you." And then she openly frowned. "What are you doing here? You should be in Chicago."

"Why should I be in Chicago?" he asked her.

"To do your show," she said. "You were there on Friday."

"And how would you know that?" Monty asked her, suspicious.

She did not reply. She merely looked at Elizabeth. "Is it true? What they're saying? That the two of you are . . ."

Elizabeth hesitated and then nodded, smiling. "Yes."

"Ah, I see," Millicent said. And then she moved on to make a tour of the offices, while Elizabeth and Monty stayed there, looking at each other. In a few minutes Millicent was back. She went straight to Monty and took both of his hands in hers. "I forgive you," she said.

"Well, that's mighty big of you," Monty said.

"Monty!" Elizabeth said, but Millicent was laughing.

She clucked her tongue at Monty. "You have no idea how much love will change you, young man." Pause. "So I might as well begin to like you now." She waited a moment. "Now, don't you have something to say to me?"

"What? That I like you, too?" he asked her.

"No," Millicent said. "That you'd like very much for me to do your radio show."

~ *61* ~

When the merger of Hillings & Hillings with International Communications Artists was completed, the agency moved into the ICA building on West Fifty-seventh Street and Joshua Lafayette was named division president. A special assistant was also hired to do nothing but focus on the reselling of rights on backlist titles written by Dick Stone, Becky Tomlinson, Alice Mae Hollison, Clarky Birkstein, Warren Krebor, Sidney Meltner, Lucy Boyle, Sissy Connors, Anthony Marcell, Claire Spender Holland, John Gabriel Mendez, and Jorges and Luisa Mantos.

The old penthouse offices at 101 Fifth Avenue were taken over by two very successful and highly respected literary agencies the Hillingses admired: the Virginia Barber Agency and Loretta Barrett Books.

Dorothy and Henry Hillings moved out to their farmhouse in Water Mill, Long Island, and Dorothy opened an office in town and hired a secretary. She is still working as a senior consultant to the ICA Entertainment Group. Henry did officially retire and began work on a history of United States Army Intelligence in World War II.

The Hillingses recently returned from a trip to Hong Kong and California, where they visited their children.

Mrs. Valerie Collins Kirby—wife, mother of three, part-time schoolteacher of Newcastle, England—received a cash settlement of twelve million dollars from Metropolis Pictures for the right to base the motion picture *Race in Space* on her cousin's book, *Mathew and the Allied Planets*. Mrs. Kirby will also receive five percent of the movie's gross receipts, which, with the licensing fees, could add up to as much as another twenty million dollars, a large portion of which has already been earmarked for children's charity organizations around the world.

Creighton Berns was found guilty on twenty-three counts of domestic copyright-law violation, racketeering, conspiracy to defraud, and conspiracy to commit arson. He was fined one million dollars and sentenced to six months in a minimum-security prison and two hundred hours of community work in the Los Angeles Public Library system. One former member of the board of directors of ICA was found guilty on lesser charges, and his sentence was suspended with the payment of fines and the promise of one hundred hours of community-service work.

Two executives of Metropolis Pictures were indicted on conspiracy charges, as was Marion Ballicutt, who was disbarred following her conviction. Her sentence was suspended in lieu of fines and one hundred hours of clerical work in the public defender's office.

James Stanley Johnson also received a suspended sentence, and now works at a Wall Street consulting firm.

David Aussenhoff finished his movie about a serial killer, which is expected to do well at least in videocassette form. Susie Lanahan made a mouthwash commercial, bought a new car, and still refuses to take David's calls. David is currently dating a masseuse and an airline stewardess.

Millicent Parks is writing again and is being honored at the next American Booksellers Association convention. It will be the first she has attended in twenty years. The broadcast airwaves are still reverberating from her recent appearance on "The Montgomery Grant Smith Show."

Patty Kleczak's *Gone for Love* was sold in an auction for $291,000. ICA sold the television miniseries rights the following day. When interviewed by *Publishers Weekly*, Mrs. Kleczak admitted that the first thing she did after getting the news was go into New York and get her hair dyed blond. The second was book two weeks' vacation for her entire family at Club Med.

The stories concerning the sexuality of Georgiana Hamilton-Ayres served only to confirm her enormous appeal—sexual and otherwise—to the moviegoing public. Her latest film, people say, could win her an Oscar. When the Hillingses put their Gramercy Park apartment up for sale, Georgiana bought it, explaining to Barbara Walters in an interview that it was the nicest home she had ever lived in as a child, and so why not live in it as an adult?

Nobody seems to know exactly where the Honorable Georgiana Hamilton-Ayres disappears to on weekends, but some residents of rural northwestern New Jersey have seen her taking fences on a handsome chestnut mare, alongside an extremely well-liked celebrity farm owner who never seems to be identified.

Speaking of whom, while the ratings of "The DBS Nightly News" have remained steady, the press has noticed a slight decrease in the on-air time of the network's star, Alexandra Waring. When asked about it, the anchorwoman only smiled and said she had reached a place in her life where she realized that her whole life couldn't be work, that she needed a personal life, too.

Montgomery Grant Smith moved his ever-popular radio show

to network headquarters in New York City, a move which provoked many of his listeners to panic that something was happening to Big Mont, that the keen conservative edge of their fearless leader was undergoing some kind of insidious urban corrosion. Insidious corrosion or not, Monty's audience is still expanding, and his television show is back in the works. He has lost thirty pounds, simply, he says, by avoiding fatty foods and walking every day.

Elizabeth Robinson, Ph.D., moved back to New York City to resume teaching history at Columbia University. She currently lives in a lovely apartment on Riverside Drive, which she shares with a two-hundred-year-old countess named Elizabeth Farren, and a two-hundred-pound radio talk-show host, Montgomery Grant Smith, who is also soon to be her husband.

Acknowledgments

The path to completion and publication of *Any Given Moment* was perhaps even more complicated than the plot, and there are several people I must thank:

My parents, Marjorie (Law) and Benjamin Van Wormer, whose values and experiences in the Canadian Red Cross and the United States Army in World War II inspired this book;

Betty A. Prashker, Shaye Areheart, and F. Amoy Allen of Crown Publishers, for extraordinary editorial care and ingenuity;

Annabel Davis-Goff, Ann Douglas, and Dani Shapiro, three gifted writers who offered to read quickly and then responded brilliantly;

Carolyn Katz, James Spada, and Tom Zito, for their infinite wisdom and regenerative spirit;

Dianne Moggy, for coming so deftly out of the blue as the publishing angel she is;

Molly Timko, Richard Daugs and, finally, she-who-makes-it-all-work, my agent and friend, Loretta A. Barrett.

PS: And we all must thank Lona Walburn for the title.

About the Author

Laura Van Wormer grew up in Darien, Connecticut, and graduated from the S. I. Newhouse School of Public Communications at Syracuse University. She is the author of *Riverside Drive* and *West End* (in both of which the character Alexandra Waring also appears), and *Benedict Canyon*. Prior to becoming a novelist, she was an editor at a major book publishing house. She lives in Manhattan and the Hamptons of Long Island.